ALSO BY JULIA GREGSON

East of the Sun

Band of Angels

JASMINE NIGHTS

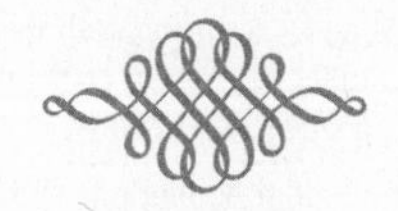

JULIA GREGSON

A TOUCHSTONE BOOK
PUBLISHED BY SIMON & SCHUSTER
NEW YORK LONDON TORONTO SYDNEY NEW DELHI

Touchstone
A Division of Simon & Schuster, Inc.
1230 Avenue of the Americas
New York, NY 10020

This book is a work of fiction. Names, characters, places, and incidents either are products of the author's imagination or are used fictitiously. Any resemblance to actual events or locales or persons, living or dead, is entirely coincidental.

First Touchstone hardcover edition June 2012

Designed by Akasha Archer

Manufactured in the United States of America

10 9 8 7 6 5 4 3 2 1

Library of Congress Cataloging-in-Publication Data

Gregson, Julia.
Jasmine nights / Julia Gregson.
p. cm.
"A Touchstone book."
1. Women singers—Fiction. 2. British—Middle East—Fiction. 3. World War, 1939–1945—Secret service—Great Britain—Fiction. 4. Espionage, British—Middle East—History—20th century—Fiction. 5. World War, 1939–1945—Theater and the war—Fiction. I. Title.
PR6107.R44494J37 2008
823'.92—dc23

2012009736

ISBN 978-1-4391-5558-5
ISBN 978-1-4391-5817-3 (ebook)

For Barry and Vicki

There are days we live
as if death were nowhere
in the background; from joy
to joy, from wing to wing,
from blossom to blossom to
impossible blossom, to sweet impossible blossom.

"From Blossoms" by Li-Young Lee

JASMINE NIGHTS

CHAPTER 1

Queen Victoria Hospital, East Grinstead, 1942

It was only a song. That was what he thought when she'd put her hat on and gone, leaving the faint smell of fresh apples behind. Nothing but a song; a pretty girl.

But the very least he could say about the best thing to have happened to him in a long time was that she'd stopped him having the dreams.

In the first, he was at the end of a parachute with about three and a half miles between the soles of his feet and the Suffolk countryside. He was screaming because he couldn't land. He was rushing through the air, a light, insubstantial thing, like thistledown or a dead moth. The bright green grass, so familiar and so dear, swooped toward him, only to jerk away again. Sometimes a woman stood and gaped at him, waving as he floated down, and then was gone on a gust of wind.

In the second dream, he was in his Spitfire again. Jacko's aircraft was alongside him. At first it felt good up there in the cold, clear sunlight, but then, in a moment of nauseous panic, it felt as if his eyelids had been sewn together, and he could not see.

He told no one. He was one of the lucky ones—about to go home after four months here. There were plenty worse off than him in this place of dark corridors and stifled screams. Every day he heard the rumble of ambulances with new burn victims, picked up from shattered aircraft up and down the east coast.

The ward, an overspill from the hospital, was housed in a long, narrow hut with twenty beds on either side of it, and in the middle a potbellied stove, a table, and a piano with two brass candlesticks arranged festively on top.

The ward smelled of soiled dressings, of bedpans, of dying and living flesh: old men's smells, although most of the fighter pilots in here were in their early twenties. Stourton, at the end of the ward, who had been flying Hurricanes from North Weald, had been a blind man for two weeks now. His girlfriend came in every day to teach him Braille. Squeak Townsend, the red-faced boy in the next bed with the hearty, unconvincing laugh, was a fighter pilot who'd broken his spine when his parachute had failed, and who'd confessed to Dom a few days ago that he was too nervous to ever want to fly again.

Dom knew he was lucky. He'd been flying a Spitfire at twenty thousand feet over a patchwork of fields when his cockpit was transformed into a blowtorch by the explosion of the petrol tank that sat in front of his instrument panel. His hands and face were burned—typical fighter-pilot injuries, the surgeon said—and in the excruciating moments between the flames and the ground, he'd opened the plane's canopy, fumbled for the bright green tag that opened his parachute, swooned through space for what felt like an eternity, and finally landed, babbling and screaming, on top of a farmer's haystack on the Suffolk coast.

Last week, Dr. Kilverton, the jaunty new plastic surgeon who now traveled from hospital to hospital, had come to the Queen Victoria and examined the burn on the right side of his face.

"Beautiful." Kilverton's bloodshot eye had peered through a microscope at the point where the new skin graft taken from Dom's buttock had been patchworked over his burns. "That'll take about six or seven weeks to heal; then you should be fully operational. Good skin," he added. "Mediterranean?"

"My mother," Dom explained through clenched teeth. Kilverton was peeling off old skin at the time, probing the graft. "French."

"Your father?"

Dom wanted him to shut up. It was easier to go inside the pain and not do the cocktail-party stuff.

"British."

"Where did you learn to fly? Tilt your head this way, please." The snub nose loomed toward him.

"Cambridge. The University Air Squadron."

"Ah, my father was there, too; sounded like jolly good fun."

"Yes."

Kilverton talked some more about corpuscles and muscle tone and youth still being on his side; he'd repeated how lucky Dom was. "Soon have your old face and your old smile back," as if a smile was a plastered-on thing.

While he was listening, Dom had that nightmare sensation again of floating above himself, of seeing kind faces below and not being able to reach them. Since the accident, a new person had taken up residence inside the old face, and the old smile. A put-together self who smoked and ate, who joked and was still capable of cynical wisecracks, but who felt essentially dead. Last week, encouraged by the doctors to take his first spin on his motorbike, he'd sat on a grass verge outside the Mucky Duck, on what was supposed to be a red-letter day, and looked at his hand around the beer glass as if it belonged to someone else.

During his first weeks in hospital, now a blur of drips and ambulance rides and acid baths, his sole aim in life had been to not let the side down by blubbing or screaming. Blind at first, he'd managed to quip, "Are you pretty?" to the nurse who'd sat with him in the ambulance that took him away from the smoldering haystack.

Later, in the wards, he made a bargain with himself: he would not deny the physical pain, which was constant, searing, and so bad at times it was almost funny, but emotionally he would own up to nothing. If anyone asked him how he was, he was fine.

It was only in the relative quiet of the night, in the lucid moments when he emerged from the morphine haze, that he thought about the nature of pain. What was it for? How was one to deal with it? Why had he been saved and the others were gone?

And only months later, when his hands had sufficiently healed, had he started to write in the diary his mother had sent him. Reams of stuff about Jacko and Cowbridge, both killed that day. A letter to Jacko's fiancée, Jill, not sent. Letters to his own parents, ditto, warning them that when he was better, he was determined to fly again.

And then the girl.

When she walked into the ward that night, what struck him most was how young she looked: young and spirited and hopeful. From his bed, he drank in every detail of her.

She was wearing a red polka-dot dress, nipped in at the waist, and a black hat with an absurd little veil that was too old for her and made her look a little like a four-year-old who had raided her mother's dressing-up box. She couldn't have been more than twenty-two.

He saw a roll of glossy dark hair under her hat. Generous lips, large brown eyes.

She stood next to the piano, close to the trolley that held dressings and rolled bandages. Half imp, half angel. She was smiling as if this was where she wanted to be. A real professional, he thought, trying to keep a cynical distance. A pro.

She explained in her lightly accented voice—Welsh? Italian? Hard to say—that her name was Saba Tarcan, and that she was a last-minute replacement for a torch singer called Janice Sophia. She hoped they wouldn't be disappointed, and then threw a bold look in Dom's direction—or so he imagined—as if to say *you won't be.*

A fat man in khaki uniform, her accompanist, sat down heavily at the piano, began to play. She listened, swaying slightly; a look of calm settled on her face as she sang about deep purple nights, and flickering stars, and a girl breathing a boy's name while she sighed.

He'd tried every trick in his book to keep her at arm's length, but the song came out of the darkness like a wild thing, and her voice was so husky, so sad, and it had been such a long time since he'd desired a woman, that the relief was overwhelming. *Through the mist of a memory you wander back to me.* So much to conceal now: his fear of being ugly, his shame that he was alive with the others gone. And then he'd felt a wild desire to laugh, for "Deep Purple" was perhaps not the most tactful of songs to sing: many of the men in the ward had purple faces, Gentian violet being the thing they painted over the burn victims after they'd been bathed in tannic acid.

Halfway through the song, she'd looked startled, as if realizing her mistake, but she'd kept on singing, and said nothing by way of apology at the end of it. He approved of that: the last thing any of them needed was sympathy and special songs.

When she'd finished, Dom saw that beads of perspiration had formed on her upper lip and rings of sweat around the arms of her dress. The ward was kept stiflingly hot.

When she sang "I'm in the Mood for Love," Curtis, ignorant bastard, called out: "Well, you know where to look, my lovely."

Dom frowned. *Saba Tarcan*: he said the name to himself.

"Two more songs," said Staff Nurse Morrison, tapping her watch. "And then it's night-night time."

And he was relieved—it was too much. Like eating a ten-course meal after starving for a year.

But Saba Tarcan paid no attention to the big fat nurse, and this he approved of, too. She took off her hat and laid it on the piano, as if to say *I shall stay until I've finished.* She pushed back a tendril of hair from her flushed cheek, talked briefly to the pianist, and took Dom to the edge of what was bearable, as she began to sing, "They Didn't Believe Me." The song Annabel had loved, singing it softly to him as they walked one night hand in hand beside the Cam, in the days when he felt he had everything: flying, Cambridge, her, other girls, too. As the tears dashed through the purple dye, he turned his head away, furious and ashamed.

Annabel was considered a catch: a tall, pale, ethereal girl with long, curly fair hair, a sweet smile, and clever parents: her father a High Court judge, her mother a don. She'd come to see him religiously at first, forehead gleaming in the stifling ward, reading to him with nervous glances around her at some of the other freaks.

"I can't do this, Dom, I'm not strong enough," she'd said after two weeks. "It's not you." She'd swallowed.

"I'm starting to dread it." She'd glanced at the boy in the bed beside him. The side of his face, grafted with his own skin to his chest, looked like a badly made elephant's trunk.

"So sorry," she'd whispered softly, shortly before she left. Her round blue eyes had filled with tears. "Can we stay friends?"

Not the first woman to have bolted out of this terrifying ward, not the last.

"Amazing how potent cheap music is": the kind of thing he might have said once to excuse the tears. His Noël Coward imitation had been rather admired at Cambridge. It wasn't even Annabel so much; it was everything lost, even the foolishly innocent things—perhaps particularly them.

His set, the self-proclaimed "it" boys of their year, had spent days spragged out on sofas, smoking and drinking cheap sherry, elaborately bored and showing off wildly about Charlie Parker, or Pound, or Eliot—anything that amused them. How young they seemed, even at this distance. The first heady days away from home, the steady stream of good-looking undergraduate girls smuggled into their rooms, and they'd had their pick. He'd tried to be fair to Annabel, telling her after her tearful confession that he perfectly understood, didn't blame her in the slightest, in truth he'd always had the guilty sense that his ardor did not equal hers, that she was not, as people said, "the one." There'd been so many other girls around, and Cambridge felt like a time when the sun would never stop shining.

Smetheren, whose famously untidy room was opposite his on the quad, had been killed two months ago. Clancy, one of his best friends, also a flying fanatic and among the cleverest men he'd ever met, shot down over France a month before his twenty-second birthday. And Jacko, of course. All changed within a year, and the boy he'd been could never have imagined himself like this: in bed at eight thirty in his pjs, desperately trying not to cry in front of a pretty girl. It was nothing but notes. He bit the inside of his lip to gain control: notes and a few minor chords, some well-chosen words. Only a song.

A clink of bottles, a rumble of wheels. The night medicines were coming around on a trolley. They were stoking up the boiler in the middle of the room, dimming the lights.

"Last one," she said.

She was wearing her ridiculous little veiled hat again. The pianist had put away his music, so she sang "Smoke Gets in Your Eyes" unaccompanied, her voice strong and clear, her expression intent and focused.

And then she'd walked around the beds to say good night.

Good night to Williams, who had both legs in traction, and to poor blind Billy at the end of the ward, and to Farthingale, who was off to theater tomorrow to have his eyelids sewn back on again. She didn't seem to mind them, or was that part of the training?

When she got to Dom, Curtis, the bloody idiot, called out: "Go on, love! Give him a night-night kiss." He'd turned his head away, but she'd leaned toward him, so close he could see the mound of her stomach under the red and white dress. He felt the tickle of her hair. She smelled young and fresh, like apples.

When she kissed his cheek, he'd said to protect himself, "You wouldn't kiss that if you knew where it came from," and she'd leaned down again and whispered in his ear, "How do you know that, you silly bugger?"

He'd stayed awake for the next hour thinking about her, his heart in a sort of delighted suspension. Before he went to sleep, he imagined her on the back of his motorbike. It was a summer's day. They were sitting on a grass verge outside a country inn. They were teasing each other, they were laughing. She was wearing a blue dress, and the sky was just a sky again, not something you fell from screaming.

CHAPTER 2

St. Briavels, Gloucestershire

My dear Saba Tarcan: his first attempt at a fan letter, written from the Rockfield Convalescent home in Wiltshire, was lobbed into the wastepaper basket. It was far too formal and avuncular for that mocking little face. Her address he'd cajoled from one of the nurses who organized the entertainments and who'd promised once the letter was written to forward it to "the relevant party."

Dear Saba, I would like to tell you how splendidly I thought you sang the other night when I heard you at Queen Victoria's. Oh, worse! That sounded like some port-winey old stage-door Johnny. Oh fuck it! Damn! He hurled it in the basket. He'd waited six weeks before writing to her, to make sure he was fit to be seen and thinking that once he was home again and not a patient, the old confidence would return and the letter would flow mellifluously from his pen, but if anything, he felt even more bewildered by what he was trying to say, which made him angry—a girl had never made him feel like that before. A poem ran through his mind—one he'd thought about in connection with her.

"Thank you, whatever comes."
And then she turned
And, as the ray of sun on hanging flowers
Fades when the wind hath lifted them aside,
Went swiftly from me.
Nay, whatever comes
One hour was sunlit and the most high gods
May not make boast of any better thing
Than to have watched that hour as it passed.

He'd copied it into his diary in hospital, certain he wouldn't send that either. Poetry made people suspicious when they didn't know you, and frankly, bollocks to the one-hour-being-lovely idea; he wanted to hear her sing again, nothing else.

"Coffee, Dom, darling?" His mother's voice wafted from the kitchen; she sounded more French when she was nervous.

"I'm in the sitting room." He glanced discreetly at his watch. Blast! He'd hoped to finish the letter first. "Come and have it with me," he said, trying with every ounce of his being not to sound like a person raging with frustration.

His mother was hovering. He'd felt her there all morning, trying to be unobtrusive. Thin as a wisp, elegant in her old tweed suit, in she bounded now with the tray, sat down on the edge of the piano stool, and poured the coffee. "Thank you, Misou," he said, using his childhood name for her.

He took her hand. "It's all right." He wished she would stop looking so worried. "Nothing hurts now. Look, hold it properly." A surge of anger as he felt her tentative squeeze.

She bobbed her head shyly, not sure what to say. She'd been so proud of him once. Now his injuries seemed to have brought with them a feeling of shared shame—there was too much to say and to conceal.

During his months in hospital, he'd fantasized about being exactly where he was today, on this sofa, in this house in St. Briavels, a tiny village on the borders of Wales and Gloucestershire. Sitting on the train that took him from Chepstow to Brockweir, he'd been determined to give his mother at least a few days of happiness to make up for the months of misery and worry she'd endured. No talk about flying again; no talk about friends, and maybe, in a couple of days' time over a glass of wine, an upbeat account of Annabel's departure.

A taxi had met him at the station. As they crossed a River Wye sparkling in the spring sunshine, a line of swans, stately and proud, were queening it across the water, and on the far side of the river a herd of Welsh ponies grazed, one with a sparrow sitting on its rump.

He asked the taxi driver to stop for a while. He said he wanted to look at the view, but in fact he was having difficulty breathing. The choking feeling, now familiar, came sudden as an animal leaping from the dark, and made his heart pound and the palms of his hands grow clammy. It would pass. He stubbed out his cigarette, and sat breathing as evenly as he could, trying to concentrate on only good things.

"Lovely," he said at last when it was over. "Beautiful sight."

"Perfect morning to come home, sir," said the driver, his eyes firmly ahead. "Ready to move off?"

"Yep. Ready."

As the car rose up the steep hill, he concentrated fiercely on the field of black Welsh cattle on his right, the scattered cottages bright with primroses and crocuses. He was going home.

A long rutted track led to the farm; from it he saw the Severn estuary gleaming like a conch shell in the distance, and when Woodless Farm came into view, his eyes filled with helpless tears. This was the charming whitewashed house his parents had moved to twenty-five years ago, when his father had first become a surgeon. Low-ceilinged, undistinguished, apart from large south-facing windows, it stood on its own in the middle of windswept fields. The small wood behind it was where he'd played cowboys and Indians with his sister Freya when he was a boy. They'd raced their ponies here, too, dashing along muddy tracks and over makeshift jumps. He'd been born behind the third window to the right upstairs.

The car crunched up the drive between the avenue of lime trees his mother, a passionate gardener, had planted in the days when she was a homesick girl missing her family in Provence. Sparkling with rain, glorious and green, unsullied by the dust of summer, they appeared like a vision. He'd grown to hate the severely clipped privet hedges surrounding the hospital lawns. Beyond the trees, new grass, new lambs in the field, a whole earth in its adolescence.

His mother ran down the drive when she heard the taxi. She stood under the lime trees and took his face in both her hands. "My darling Dom," she said. "As good as new."

As they walked back to the house arm in arm, dogs swirled around their legs and an old pony in the field craned nosily over the gate. She'd said, "How was it at Rockfield?" All she knew about it was that this was the place the burn boys were sent to, to shoehorn them back into "real life."

"Surprisingly jolly," he said. He told her about the lovely house near Cheltenham, loaned by some county lady, about the barrels of beer, the pretty nurses, the nonstop parties, the complaints from the neighbors, who said they'd expected convalescents, not hooligans. Hearing his mother's polite, anxious laugh, he'd fought the temptation to hang his head like a guilty boy; early that morning he'd been 10,000 feet above the Bristol Channel, zooming over the grazing sheep, the little patchwork fields, the schools, the church steeples, the whole sleeping world, and it had been bloody marvelous. Tiny Danielson, one of his last remaining friends from the squadron, had wangled a Tiger Moth kept in a hangar near Gloucester. Dom's hands had shaken as he'd buckled on the leather flying helmet for the first time in months, his heart thumping as he carefully taxied down the runway with its scattering of Nissen huts on either side, and then, as he'd lifted off into the clear blue yonder, he'd heard himself shout with joy.

Wonderful! Wonderful! Wonderful! He was flying again! He was flying again! In hospital, the idea that he might have to go back to a desk job had made him sweat with terror. He'd worried that he'd be nervous, that his hands wouldn't be strong enough now, but he'd had no trouble with the controls, and the little aircraft felt as whippy as a sailing craft under his fingers. The air was stingingly cold, there was a bit of cumulus cloud to the left, and he felt suddenly as if a jumble of mismatched pieces inside him had come together again.

Hearing his shout of pleasure, Tiny had echoed it, and a few minutes later clapped him on the shoulder.

"Down now, I think, old chap—we don't want to get court-martialed."

A noisy breakfast followed—toast, baked beans, and brick-colored tea—shared with Tiny and a pilot wearing a uniform so new it still had the creases in it. Nobody asked him any questions about the hospital; no one made a fuss—economy of emotion was the unspoken rule here. In the mess, there was even a "shooting a line" book that fined you for any morbid or self-congratulatory talk. And that was good, too. Four of his closest friends were dead now, five missing presumed dead, one captured behind enemy lines. He was five months shy of his twenty-third birthday.

"You'll notice a few changes." His mother, light-footed and giddy with happiness, had almost danced up the drive. "We've been planting carrots and onions where the roses were. You know, 'dig for victory' and all zat. Oh, there's so much to show you."

She took him straight up the stairs so he could put his suitcase in his old room. The bed looked inviting, with its fresh linen sheets and plumped pillows. A bunch of lavender lay on the bedside table. He gazed briefly at the schoolboy photographs of him that she'd framed. The scholarship boy at Winchester, flanneled and smirking on his first cricket team; and there a muddied oaf, legs planted, squinting at the camera, Jacko sitting beside him beaming. Jacko, who he'd persuaded to join up, who he'd teased for being nervous, who he'd last seen clawing at his mask in a cauldron of flame, screaming as the plane spiraled down like a pointless piece of paper and disappeared into the sea.

He must go up to London and talk to Jilly, Jacko's fiancée, about him soon. He dreaded it; he needed it.

His mother touched his arm.

"Come downstairs," she said quickly. "Plenty of time to unpack later."

A whiff of formaldehyde as they passed his father's study on the way down. On the leather desk, the same gruesome plastic model of a stomach and intestines that Dom had once terrified his sister with, by holding it up at her bedroom door, a green torch shining behind it; the same medical books arranged in alphabetical order.

"He'll be home after supper." His mother's smile wavered for a second. "He's been operating day and night."

"Things any better?" slipped out. He'd meant to ask it casually over a drink later.

"Not really," she said softly. "He's never home—he works harder now, if anything."

In the tiled hall, near the front door, he glanced at his face in the mirror. His dark hair had grown again; his face looked pretty much the same.

Lucky bastard.

Selfish bastard. He could at least have answered Jilly's letter.

Lucky first of all to have been wearing the protective gloves all of them were supposed to put on when they flew, and he so often hadn't, preferring the feel of the joystick in his fingers. Lucky to have been picked up quickly by an ambulance crew and not burned to a crisp strapped into his cockpit. Luckiest of all to have been treated by Kilverton. Kilverton, who looked, with his stumpy hands and squat body, like a butcher, was a plastic surgeon of genius.

He owed his life to this man. He'd gone to him with his face and hands black and smelling of cooked meat—what they now called airman's burns, because they were so common. The determined and unsentimental Kilverton, a visiting surgeon had placed him in a saline bath and later taken him into theater, where he'd meticulously jigsawed tiny strips of skin taken from Dom's buttock to the burns on the side of his face. All you could see was a row of pinpricks about an inch long and two inches above his left ear. His thick black hair had already covered them.

Last week Kilverton had called Dom into his chaotic consulting room and boasted freely about him to two awestruck young doctors.

"Look at this young man." He turned on the Anglepoise lamp on his desk so they could all get a better look at him. Dom felt the gentleness of those fat fingers, the confidence they gave you. One of the other chaps in the ward had said it was like getting "a pep pill up your arse."

"I defy you to even know he's been burned—no keloid scars, the skin tone around the eyes is good."

"So why was he so lucky?" one of the doctors asked, his own young skin green with fatigue under the lamp. Five new serious cases had come in the day before, a bomber crew who'd bought it off the French coast.

"A combination of factors." Kilverton's eyes swam over his half-glasses. "A Mediterranean skin helps—all that olive oil. His mother's French, his father's English."

Dom had smiled. "A perfect mongrel."

"The rest," Kilverton continued, "is pure chance. Some men just burn better than others."

Dom had gone cold at this.

Thompson had died in East Grinstead, after being treated with tannic acid, a form of treatment Kilverton had said was barbaric and had fought to ban. Collins, poor bastard, burned alive in his cockpit on his first training run. He was nineteen years old.

The same flames, the surgeon had continued in his flat, almost expressionless voice, the same exposure to skin- and tissue-destroying heat, and yet some men became monsters, although he did not use that word; he'd said "severely disabled" or some other slightly more tactful phrase. Having the right skin was, he said, a freak of nature, like being double-jointed or having a cast-iron stomach.

To illustrate his point, he'd lifted a pot of dusty geraniums from the windowsill.

"It's like taking cuttings from this: some thrive, some die, and the bugger of it is we don't yet know exactly why. As for you . . ." he looked directly at Dom again, "you can go home now. I'll see you in six weeks' time."

Dom had pretended to be both interested and grateful, and of course he was, but sometimes at night he sweated at the thought of this luckiness. Why had he lived and others died? Privately, it obsessed him.

"Can I fly again?" It was all he wanted now. "Can you sign me off?"

"I'll see you in six weeks." Kilverton switched off his light. He was shrugging on his ancient mackintosh, standing near the door waiting to leap into another emergency.

"I want to fly again." The obsession had grown and grown during the period of his convalescence.

"Look, lad." Kilverton had glared at him from the door. "Your father's a surgeon, isn't he? Why not give him and your poor bloody mother a break and let somebody else do the flying for a while? I'll see you in six weeks' time."

"My hands are strong. I'm fit. Four weeks."

"Bloody steamroller." Kilverton hadn't bothered to look up. "It'll be six months if you don't shut up."

His mother always did three things at once: right now she was in the kitchen up the flagstone hallway, making bread to go with a special lunch she'd prepared for him. Its warm, yeasty smell filled the room.

She was roasting lamb in the Aga. She had darted into the room to ask if he'd like a whiskey and soda before lunch, and now she was standing beside the gramophone wearing what he thought of as her musical face, as she lowered the needle.

Tender and evanescent as bubbles, the notes of Mozart's Piano Concerto No. 9 floated out and his throat contracted. Home again: music, roast lamb, the faint tang of mint from the kitchen, his mother humming and clattering pans. The cedar parquet floors smelling faintly of lavender where he and Freya had been occasionally allowed to ride their tricycles. The rug in front of the fireplace where they sat to dry their hair on Sunday nights.

He stretched his legs out and put his arms behind his head, and looked at the pictures his mother had hung above the fireplace. There was a reproduction of Van Gogh's *Starry Night,* a Gwen John self-portrait.

He stood up and stared at them, as if by examining the pictures he could see her more clearly. How cleverly she'd arranged them—not too rigidly formal, but with a plan that pleased the eye.

She did everything well: cooking, dressing, gardening, entertaining, and stitching. The sofa he sat on was covered, too covered for real comfort, in her tapestry cushions. He picked one up now, marveling at the thousands and thousands of tiny, painstaking stitches that had measured out her afternoons, pinning unicorns and stilled butterflies to her canvas.

While the Mozart swept majestically on, he heard the faint pin-pricks of a spring shower against the window. His mother had once dreamed of being a professional musician; as a child, Dom had loved lying in his bed with Liszt's Polonaises drifting up to his room like smoke, or the brisk rat-tat-tat of her little hands swashbuckling through her own rendition of the Ninth. But now her piano sat like some grand but disregarded relative in the corner of the room, almost entirely covered by family photographs. The gorgeous Steinway that had once been her life, that had almost bankrupted her father.

Dom's own father had put an end to it. Not intentionally, maybe. Two months after he'd married his clever young bride, he'd developed tinnitus and couldn't stand, so he said, any extra noises in his head. And then the children—Freya first, and two years later Dom—her husband's determined move up the career ladder, and lastly, in the cold winter of 1929, she'd developed chilblains and stopped for good. No more Saint-Saëns, or Scott Joplin to make guests laugh; no more duets even, for she had taught Dom as a little boy, and told him he would be very good if he stuck at it. What had once been a source of delight became a source of shame, a character flaw. Even as a child he was aware how it clouded her eyes when people turned to her and said: "Didn't you once play the piano rather well?"

Dom examined silver-framed Freya, on the front of the piano. Freya—of the laughing eyes and the same thick black hair—was in the WAAF now, in London, working at Fighter Command, loving her life "whizzing things around on maps," as she put it.

There he was, a ghost from another life, striking a jokey pose in a swimsuit on the beach at Salcombe. His cousins Jack and Peter, both in the army now, had their arms around him. They'd swum that night, and cooked sausages on the beach, and stayed out until the moon was a toenail in the sky. The beach was now littered with old bits of scrap metal, barbed wire, and sandbags, the rusted hulks of guns. In another photo, his mother's favorite, he sat on the wing of the little Tiger Moth he'd learned to fly in, self-conscious in his first pilot's uniform, almost too young to shave.

The year he and Jacko had started to fly had been full of thousands of excitements: first set of flying clothes; Threadnall, their first instructor, roaring abuse: "Don't pull back the control column like a barmaid pulling a pint, lad"; first solo flight; even the drama of writing your first will when you were twenty-one years old. There was nothing the earth could offer him as exciting as this.

That first flight was when he'd cut the apron strings, and all the other ropes of convention and duty that bound him here, and thought to himself, *Free at last*, shockingly and shamefully free as he soared above the earth, terrified and elated, over churches and towns, schools and fields. *Free at last!*

As the music dropped slowly like beads of light in the room, bringing him to the edge of tears, he thought about Saba Tarcan again: her daft little hat, the curve of her belly in the red satin dress, her husky voice.

He did not believe in love at first sight. Not ever, not now. At Cambridge, where he'd broken more than his fair share of hearts, and where, even at this distance, he now thought of himself as being a tiresome little shit, he'd had a whole spiel that he could produce about what a ridiculous concept it was. His reaction to Saba Tarcan felt more complex—he'd admired the way she'd carried herself in that noisy ward, neither apologizing, nor simpering, or asking for their approval. He remembered every detail: the fighter boys lying in a row, stripped of their toys and their dignity, some tricked up like elephants with their skin grafts, and the girl with only her songs, taking them beyond the world where you could define or set limits on things, or be in simple human terms a winner or a loser. What power that was.

"I've brought you some cheese straws." His mother appeared with a tray. "I saved up our cheese ration for them."

"Misou, sit." He patted the sofa beside him. "Let's have a drink."

She poured herself a small Dubonnet and soda, her lunchtime tipple, a beer for him.

"Well, how nice this is." She crossed her impeccable legs at the ankle. "Oh golly! Look at that." A small piece of thread that had come loose on one of her cushions. She snapped it off between her small teeth.

"Misou, stop fussing and drink up. I think you and I should get roaring drunk together one night."

She laughed politely; it would take her a while to thaw out. Him, too—he felt brittle, dreamlike again.

"Have another." She passed him the cheese straws. "But don't spoil your appetite. Sorry." The plate bumped his hand. "Did that hurt?"

"No." He took two cheese straws quickly. "Nothing hurts now. These are delicious."

She filled the small silence that followed by saying: "I've been meaning to ask you, do you have any pills you should be taking, any special med—"

"Mother," he said firmly. "I'm all right now. It wasn't an illness. I'm as fit as a fiddle—in fact, I'd like to go for a spin on Pa's motorbike after lunch."

"I don't think he'd mind—that sounds fun. He doesn't use it now." He felt her flinch, but he would have to start breaking her in gently. "It's in the stable. There should be enough petrol," she added bravely.

"For a short spin, anyway."

"So nothing hurts now?"

"No." It was no good, he simply couldn't talk about it with her—not now, maybe never—this wrecking ball in the middle of his life that had come within a hair's breadth of taking pretty much everything: his youth, his friends, his career, his face.

"Well, all I can say," she shot a darting look in his direction, "is that you look marvelous, darling."

Which didn't sit well with him either. His mother had always cared too much about how people looked. The reproach in her voice when she pointed out a nose that was too long or somebody who had a big stomach seemed to indicate that its owner was either careless or stupid, or both. Some of the boys in the ward had been so badly burned they were scarcely recognizable, but they were still human beings underneath it.

"Do I?" Impossible to keep the note of bitterness out of his voice. "Well, all's well that ends well."

And now he had hurt her and felt sorry. She'd moved to the other end of the sofa. He felt her bunched up and ready to fly.

"That music was wonderful," he said. "Thank you for putting it on. All we heard in hospital was a crackly wireless and a few concerts."

"Any good?"

"Not bad, one or two of them." *A singer?* He imagined her saying it, and then, with her sharp professional face on, *Was she any good?*

"I was thinking in hospital," he said, "that I'd like to play the piano again."

"Are you sure?" She looked at him suspiciously, as if he might be mocking her.

"Yes."

She took his hand in hers. "Do you remember last time?" She was looking pleased. "Such sweet little hands." She waggled her own elegant fingers in a flash of diamonds. "Like chipolatas. First Chopsticks," she mimed his agricultural delivery, "then Chopin. You know, you could have been very, very good," she said, "if you'd stuck at it."

"Yes, yes," he said. It was an old argument between them. "I did Walter Gieseking a great good turn when I gave up.

"And what about you nearly amputating these *sweet little hands*?" he teased. They'd had a corker of a row one day, when he'd been racing through "Für Elise" as loudly as he could, loving the racket he was making. She'd ticked him off for not playing with more light and shade, and he'd roared: "I'M A LOUD-PLAYING BOY AND I LIKE THINGS FAST." And she—oh, how quick and ferocious her temper was in those days—had brought the lid down so sharply she'd missed his fingers by a whisper and blackened the edge of the nail on his little finger.

She covered her face with her hands. "Why was I so angry?"

Because, he wanted to say, it mattered to you; because some things affected you beyond reason.

"I don't know," he said gently, seeing her furious face again, under the lamplight, stabbing at her tapestry.

"Listen, you loud-talking boy," she said. She stood up and walked toward the kitchen. "Lunch is ready. Let's eat."

"Yes, Mis, let's eat." It seemed the safest thing to do.

When they faced each other over the kitchen table, there didn't seem quite enough of them to fill the room, but at least she hadn't asked him yet about Annabel, a relief, for she would be upset—she'd approved of Annabel's clothes, her thinness, her clever parents—and then she'd be fiercely indignant at anyone foolish enough to reject her son. He'd rehearsed a lighthearted account of the episode, in truth, he was almost relieved now that Annabel had gone: one less person to worry about when he flew again.

Misou poured him a glass of wine and filled a plate with the roast lamb mixed in with delicious homegrown onions and carrots and herbs. He ate ravenously, aware of her watching him and relaxing in his pleasure.

Over coffee he said, "That was the best grub I've had for months, Ma, and by the way, I really would like to play the piano again."

And then she shocked him by saying: "You want to fly don't you? That's what you really want to do." She gave him a searching look; he could not tell whether she was pleading with him or simply asking for information.

He put his cup down. "Don't you think we should talk about this later?" he asked gently.

She got up suddenly and went to the sink.

"Yes," she said. "Later."

She ran the tap fiercely; he saw her drying-up cloth move toward her eyes. "Not now," she said several seconds later. "I don't think I could stand it."

CHAPTER 3

Pomeroy Street, Cardiff, 1942

Dom's letter to Saba had arrived in the morning post. Reading it brought a flush of color to her cheeks. She remembered that boy, but not clearly.

She'd been so wound up before the concert, terrified that she would fail, or be overwhelmed by the patients, and later so tremendously happy when it had gone well.

But it did mean something—quite a lot, actually—that he had found the evening special, too. She felt like dashing downstairs with the letter right away, forcing her family to read it—*See, what I do means something. Don't make me stop*—but since no one in the house was properly talking to her, she put it in the drawer beside her bedside table. There was too much going on in her head to answer it.

Her family were at war. Two weeks previously, a brown envelope had arrived for Saba with "On Her Majesty's Service" written on it, and all of them hated her as a result of it. Inside was a letter from ENSA, the Entertainments National Service Association. A man called John Merrett had asked her to attend an audition at the Drury Lane Theatre in London on 17 March at 11:30. She was to take her music and dancing shoes. Her expenses would be paid.

At that time she was living in the family's three-bedroomed terraced house on Pomeroy Street, down at the docks, between the canal and the river, a few streets away from Tiger Bay. It was here, in an upstairs room of this cramped and cozy house, that Saba had shot into the world twenty-three years ago. She was three weeks early, red-faced and bellowing. "Little old leather-lungs right from the beginning," her mother had once said proudly.

In peacetime she shared the house with her mother, Joyce; her little sister, Lou; and occasionally her father, Remzi, who was a ship's engineer and often away at sea. And of course there was good old Tansu, her Turkish grandma, who'd been living with them for the past twenty years.

Apart from Tan, asleep by the fire in the front room, she was alone in the house when the letter came. She tore the envelope open, read it in disbelief, and then got so excited she didn't know what to do with herself. She raced upstairs, crashed into her small bedroom, raised her arms in exultation, gave a silent scream, sat down in front of her kidney-shaped dressing table and saw her shocked white face gazing back at her from three mirrors.

Yah! Hallelujah! Saved! Mashallah! The wonderful thing had happened! She danced on her own on the bare floorboards, her body full of a savage joy. After months of performing in draughty factories and YMCAs for weary workers and troops, ENSA wanted her! In London! A place she'd never been before. Her first proper professional tour.

She couldn't wait to tell her mother, and paced all afternoon in an agony of suspense. Mum, who was working the day shift at Curran's factory, and who'd been at her to get a job there, too, usually got home about five thirty. When Saba heard the click of the front door, she bounded downstairs two at a time, flung her arms around her and blurted out the news.

Later, she realized that her timing was unusually off. Tea had to come before surprises. Her mother was highly strung, and, to say the least, unpredictable in her responses. Sometimes standing up for Saba, sometimes caving in, entirely depending on her husband's moods. . . . Or perhaps Saba should have told Tansu first. Tan, who had a theatrical flair for these moments, would have put it better.

Her mother looked tired and plain in the ugly dungarees and turban she now wore for work. She took the letter from Saba's hand and read it without a word, her mouth a sullen little slit. She stomped into the front room and took her shoes off, and snapped: "Why did you let the fire go out?" as if this was just an ordinary day.

The envelope was still in her hand as she looked straight at Saba and said, "This is the last bloody straw," almost as if she hated her.

"What?" Saba had shouted.

"And you're not bloody going."

Saba had rushed into the kitchen and then out the back door where they kept the kindling. When she returned, her mother was still sitting poleaxed by the unlit fire. Tansu sat opposite her, mumbling away at herself in Turkish the way she did when she was agitated or afraid.

"Give me that." Joyce snatched the paper and the kindling from Saba's hands. She scrumpled the paper, stabbed it with the poker they kept in a brass ship near the fire.

"You look tired, Mum." Saba, who'd put a few lumps of coal on top of the wood, was trying diplomacy. "I'll bring you in some tea, then you can read the letter again."

"I don't want to read the bloody letter again," her mother had shouted. "And you're not going anywhere until we've asked your father."

The flames roared as she put a match to the paper. Tansu, nervous and scampering, had gone to get the tea, while Joyce sat breathing heavily, bright spots of temper color on her cheeks.

Saba then made things worse by telling her mother that she thought it was a wonderful opportunity for her, and that even Mr. Chamberlain had said on the wireless that everyone should now do their bit for the war effort.

"I've done enough for the sodding war effort," Joyce shouted. "Your sister's gone and God knows when she'll be back. Your father's never here. I'm working all hours at Curran's. It's time you got a job there, too."

"I'm not talking about you, Mum!" Saba roared. "I'm talking about me. You were the one who told me to dream big bloody dreams."

"Oh for goodness' sake." Her mother snatched off her turban and lashed on her pinafore. "That was a joke. And anyway, Mr. Chamberlain didn't mean you singing songs and waving your legs in the air."

Saba stared at her mother in disbelief. Had she honestly and truly said that? The same Joyce who'd thundered roaring and laughing down the aisle with her at *Snow White* at the Gaiety when they'd asked for children on the stage. Who'd taken her to all those ballet lessons, squishing her plump feet into good toes, naughty toes. Who'd stayed up half the night, only three months ago, sewing the red dress for the hospital concert, and cried buckets when she'd heard her sing "All Through the Night" only the week before.

"It wasn't a joke, Mum," she shrieked, her dander well up now. "Or if it was, you might have bloody let me in on it." She was thinking of the harder stuff—the diets, the singing lessons, breaking two ribs when the trapeze they used for "Showtime" had snapped.

"Yes, it was. It was off a film, and we're not people in films."

And then Tansu, usually her one hundred percent friend and ally, had made that disapproving Turkish *tut tut tut* sound, the clicking of the tongue followed by a sharp intake of breath, that really got on Saba's nerves, and which loosely translated to *no, no, no, no.* Tansu said if she went to London, the bombs would fall on her head. Saba replied that bombs were falling on their bloody heads here. There had already been one in Pomeroy Street. Joyce said she would wash Saba's mouth out with soap if she swore at her gran again, then Joyce and Tansu stomped into the kitchen.

"Listen!" Saba followed them. "I could go anywhere: to Cairo, or India, or France or somewhere." As she said it, she saw herself silhouetted against a bright red sky, singing for the soldiers.

"Well, you can forget about that, too." Her mother slammed the potatoes into cold water and lit the gas, her hands fiery with chilblains. "Your father will go mad. And for once, I don't blame him."

Ah! So they had come to it at last: the real heart of the matter. Her father would go mad. Mum's emotional weathervane was always turned toward him and the storms that would come.

"I'm twenty-three years old." Saba and her mother faced each other, breathing heavily. "He can't tell me what to do anymore."

"Yes, he can," her mother yelled. "He's your flaming father."

She'd looked at her mother with contempt. "Do you ever have a single thought of your own, Mum?" That was cruel: she knew the consequences of her mother sticking up for herself.

Her mother's head shot up as if she'd been struck.

"You haven't got a clue, have you?" she said at last. "You're a stupid, selfish girl."

"Clue about what, Mum?" Some devil kept Saba going.

"What it's like for your father on the ships. It's carnage in the shipping lanes—half the time they go around with their knees bent, expecting another bomb to drop on their heads."

That brought them both to the edge of tears.

"I want to do something that makes sense to me. I don't want to just work in the factory. I can do something more."

"Uggh" was all her mother said.

That hurt, too, and made it worse—her mother, her great supporter, talking as if she couldn't stand her at a moment that should have been so fine. She ran down the dark corridor where photos of her father's severe-looking Turkish ancestors gazed down on one side, and her mother's glum lot from the Welsh valleys on the other. Slamming the door behind her, she ran into the backyard. She sat down in the outside privy, sobbing.

She was nearly twenty-four years old and completely stuck. The year the war had started was the year in which she had had a whole wonderful life worked out—her first tour with The Simba Sisters around the south coast; singing lessons with a professional in Swansea; freedom, the chance to have the life she'd trained for and dreamed of for so long. Nothing to look forward to now except a factory job, or, if she was lucky, the odd amateur concert or radio recording.

"Saba." A timid knock on the door. Tansu walked in wearing her floral pinafore and her Wellies, even though it wasn't raining. She had her watering can in her hand. "Saba," she gave a jagged sigh, "don't go ma house." *Don't go ma house* was Tansu-speak for "I love you, don't leave me."

"I don't understand, Tansu," she said. "You've come to the concerts. You've seen me. You've said I was born to do this. I thought we were all in this together."

Tansu pulled a dead leaf off the jasmine bush she'd planted in the backyard that had resolutely refused to thrive. "Too many people leave this house," she said. "Your sister has gone to the valley."

"She hasn't gone," Saba protested. Lou, at eight the baby of the family, had been sent away to a nice family in the Rhondda Valley to avoid the bombs. She came home with her little suitcase on the bus most weekends.

"Your father at sea."

"He wants to be there. It's his life."

"You no ma pinish." Another way of saying don't go.

"Tansu, I've dreamed about this for the whole of my life. I'll make money for us. I'll buy you a big house near Üsküdar." The place Tan always mentioned when she talked about Turkey.

"No." Tansu refused to meet her eye. She stood there, legs braced, eyes down, as old and unmovable as rock.

Saba looked over her head, at the darkening sky, the seagulls flying toward the docks. "Please help me, Tan," she said. They'd sung together once. Tan had taught her baby songs.

"I say nothing," said Tansu. "Talk to your father."

Saba's father, Remzi, was an engineer on the Fyffes' ships that had once carried bananas and coal and rice all around the world. Dark-haired and with a permanent five o'clock shadow, he was handsome and energetic. As a child, he seemed to her a godlike figure who ruled the waves. The names of the ships he sailed on—*Copacabana*, *Takoradi*, *Matadi*—intoxicated her like poetry or a drug. On his visits home, she'd ride high and proud on his shoulders down Pomeroy Street and into the Bay, listening to other local men stop and say hello to him or ask him respectfully whether he could put in a good word for them and get them work.

And the big joke, not so funny now, was that it was her father who had first discovered she could sing. They'd been at the Christmas party in St. William's church hall, and little old leather-lungs had stood on a chair and sung "D'Ya Ken John Peel" and brought the house down. His face had bloomed with love and pride, and he'd encouraged her to sing at family parties: Turkish songs, Arabic songs, the French songs he'd learned from sailors.

Her "Archontissa" performed with much wailing and fluttery arm movements, reduced strong Greeks to tears. He'd even taken her to talent contests—she remembered the choking sound he'd made when she won—and afterward they'd walk home together high as kites and stop at the Pleeze cafe on Angelina Street for ice cream.

But then, aged about thirteen, she'd started to grow breasts. Little buds, nothing really, but the first soft wolf whistles down at the YMCA had been her swansong as far as he was concerned. His eyes had glowered at her from the front row.

"Men are animals." He'd all but dragged her home down the street. "For some men, one woman is like another." His lips had twisted in disgust, as if she'd already fatally let him down. "They will lie down with whoever is around."

Horrified, embarrassed, she'd said nothing, not understanding that those whistles marked the beginning of her own dual life. When he was at sea, she did a few concerts—although there was hell to pay if he found out; apart from that, nothing but respectable events such as eisteddfods, and recitals down at the Methodist Hall, which frankly, as she often complained to Joyce, had become a deadly bore.

Her father had grown up on the outskirts of the village of Üvezli, not far from the Black Sea coast. She'd loved hearing him talk about it once. There were donkeys on the farm, plane trees, a pump, and chickens. On feast days, he told her, twenty people would sit down for lunch, and his mother would cook, roasted chickens and stuffed tomatoes and milk puddings with nuts in them. When he told her about these lovely things, his eyes filled with tears.

Once when she'd said, only half attending. "Don't you miss it, Baba?" he'd turned his hooded eyes on her and said savagely, "I think about my village every day. I remember every stone in our house, every tree in the orchard," and she'd felt a darkness fall around them, and that she must never ask him about this place again.

Nowadays, with the ships he worked on carrying nothing but coal for the war, and his little girl disturbingly grown, her father seemed in a permanent sulk, and Saba was fed up with it. He hated Joyce working full-time at Curran's, resented the fact that the three women seemed perfectly capable of running the house without him, and at home behaved like a permanent defensive guest. The way he sat brooding beside the fire in the front room reminded Saba of the new cock they had once introduced in the chicken house in the backyard, who'd sat frozen and alone on his perch amid a babble of companionable and clucking hens. She watched how Tan, who adored him, made hectic efforts to cheer him up. How she'd hover at mealtimes by his chair, ready to spring into the kitchen for any tasty morsel that took his fancy, and shake her head approvingly at almost everything he said, like a ventriloquist. She saw, too, how her mother, normally so confident and funny, changed into an entirely different person when he was home: the anxious, darting looks; the way her voice seemed to rise an octave; how she would often shoo Saba upstairs as if she was a nothing, to get his slippers or some book he wanted. It broke her heart to see Tan and Mum working so hard; why couldn't he try harder, too?

It was time to drop the bombshell. The ENSA letter had burned a hole in her pocket all week, and the pilot's letter had given her an extra boost of confidence. Her father's kitbag was in the front hall. He'd come home on Wednesday from Portsmouth, had a bath in the front room, and retired since then in virtual silence to his shed out the back, only appearing for meals.

Her mother, pale at the row that must come, begged Saba not to show him the ENSA letter until the day before he went to sea again. "He's already got the hump," she said. "Tell him now and he'll sulk for the whole ten days."

"Why do you let him, Mum?" Saba blazed. "It must be torture for you."

She'd lost patience with the lot of them, and decided in a few hours' time to step into the lion's den. Saturday night was the time when custom dictated that the family gathered around the little plush-covered table in the front room, got the best china out, and Joyce and Tan cooked favorite dishes. When Saba thought back to the best of these times, she remembered the fire crackling in the grate, glasses winking on the table, the little dishes Tan used to make: hummus and Caucasian chicken—cold shredded chicken with walnuts. Her father even danced sometimes, clicking his fingers and showing his excellent teeth.

Maybe Tan was trying to lighten the dreadful atmosphere in the house by reviving these happier times. For two days now she'd been in and out of the kitchen. She'd gone to Jamal's, the Arab greengrocer on Angelina Street, and wheedled cracked wheat and preserved lemons from the owner. She'd saved up her meat ration for two weeks to make the little meatballs that Remzi loved. As she cooked, the wailing sounds of Umm Kulthum, the famous Egyptian singer, burst from the gramophone and majestic sorrows swept through the house—like a funeral cortege drawn by big black horses. Remzi had collected her records during his Mediterranean tours.

While Tan was cooking, Saba rehearsed the best words to use.

It's a perfectly respectable organization, Baba; it's part of the army now. We'll be well protected . . .

There's even a uniform, it's not just a band of actors and singers . . .

They do so much good for the troops. It keeps everybody's spirits up . . .

It will give me a proper future in singing, I can learn from this . . .

She watched the clock all day, every bone in her body rigid with nervous tension. When six o'clock came, she took her place quietly at the table in the front room. A few moments later, her father walked in, erect, unsmiling. He'd changed into the long dressing gown he wore at home, which made him look, with his short, well-trimmed beard and his dark hooded eyes, like an Old Testament prophet. Peeping out from underneath it were the English gentleman's brogues he wore, which Joyce cleaned every morning before she went to the factory.

During supper they discussed only safe topics: the weather, dreadful; the war, showing no sign of getting better; Mrs. Orestes next door, everyone agreeing that sad as it was about her son Jim, killed in France a few months ago, it was time she pulled her socks up (Joyce said she hadn't been out of her dressing gown since, and still wouldn't answer the door, not even to take the cake she'd baked for her). When the plates had been emptied, her father thrilled them all by producing from the folds of his robe some toffees he'd bought in Amsterdam. Tan crept mouselike to the kitchen to get his glass of sage tea. When Joyce left, too, Saba took a deep breath and said to her father:

"Do you want me to give her a hand, or can we talk?"

"Sit down, Shooba," he said, using his pet name for her. He pointed to a footstool near his chair.

She sat, careful not to block the heat of the fire from his legs. She could hear her own heart thumping as she sipped her water and tried to look calm.

"I haven't spoken to you properly for a long time," he said in his deep voice.

True—she'd circled warily around him since he came home.

The sage tea arrived; Tan scuttled out again. He took a sip and she felt his hand rest softly on her head.

She handed him the letter. "I'd like you to read this."

"Is this for me?"

"Yes." Thinking *No, it's for me.*

A deep line developed between his eyebrows as he read it, and when he had finished, he snatched at the paper and read it again.

"I don't understand this." His expression darkened. "How do these people know about you?"

"I don't know." Her voice was wobbly. "They must have heard me somewhere."

Her father put his glass down. He shook his head in disgust. There was a long silence.

"You're lying to me," he said at last. "You've been out again, haven't you? You've been performing in public."

He made it sound as if she'd been in a strip show. She felt like a cowering dog at his feet, so she stood up.

"Only a couple of times," she said. "At a hospital, and a church."

He read the letter again, and then scratched his head furiously. Joyce, who must have been listening behind the door, appeared, a tea towel in her hand. She looked drawn.

"Have you seen this?" His voice a whip crack.

A look of complete panic crossed Joyce's face. They'd reached the end of something and it felt terrible.

"Yes."

"What did you tell her?"

"Nothing." It was rare to see her mother trembling, but she was. "They must have seen her at the Methodist Hall," she faltered.

"Yaa, eşek!" he yelled. The Turkish word for donkey. "Don't tell me lies."

The whoop of an air-raid siren stopped them all in their tracks for a moment, and then went away. They were used to false alarms in those days.

"You said she should have her voice trained," her mother ventured bravely. "She can't stay home forever."

"She's been ill," her father shouted. Saba had had tonsillitis six months ago.

"No, she's not flipping well ill, and if you were at home more, you'd know that!" her mother shrieked.

He threw his tea against the wall, the glass shattered and they all shrieked, thinking it was a bomb.

"Don't you talk back to me!" Her father on his feet, hand raised.

"I'm sorry. I'm sorry." Her mother's little spark of bravery went out; she was stammering again. She'd dropped her tea towel and was scrabbling under the table, picking up shards of glass with her bare hands, and when she crawled up from under the tablecloth, scarlet in the face, she turned the full force of her rage on Saba.

"You stupid girl," she said, her mouth all twisted with rage. "You have to do it your way, don't you?"

Later Saba heard them going at it hammer and tongs through the thin partition wall that separated her bedroom from theirs. His voice rising as he told Joyce it was her fault, that Saba was spoiled and stupid; his thump, her rabbitlike squeal and thin wail; his footsteps going downstairs. He slammed the front door so hard the whole house trembled.

The next day, Saba took her leather suitcase down from the top of the wardrobe and laid it on the bed. At the bottom of it she placed her red tap shoes, then her polka-dot dress, stockings, wash bag. She put the khaki-colored ENSA letter on top of the clothes, and was just folding the piece of paper with directions to the Drury Lane Theatre when she heard the sound of the front door click.

Apart from Tan, she was alone. Joyce was at the factory. She sat down on the floral eiderdown, every muscle straining as she listened to the squeak of his shoes on the stairs, the uneven sound of the cracked floorboard on the landing.

He came into her room carrying an instrument in his hand that they had often joked about when she was a child. It was a short whip with two leather lashes at the end of it. He'd told her once that his own father had thrashed him with it regularly. For her, it had only ever been a prop in a deliciously frightening childhood game they'd played together. Remzi, growling ferociously, would race around the backyard brandishing the thing, she squealing with delight as she got away.

But today he put the martinet down on the bed, on top of her sheet music. He looked at her with no expression in his eyes whatsoever.

"Daddy!" she said. "No! Please don't do this." As if she could save him from himself.

"I cannot let you go on disobeying me," he said at last. "Not in front of your mother, your grandmother. You bring shame on our house."

"Shame on our house! Shame on our house!" It was like someone in a pantomime. Someone with a Sinbad beard, a cutlass. But the time when she could have joked with him about that had gone. As she moved away from him, the ENSA letter fell on the floor. He swooped on it and held it in his hand.

"You're not going," he said. "Bad enough that your mother has to work in a factory now."

She looked at him and heard a kind of shrilling sound in her ears.

"I am going, Daddy," she said. "Because I'll never get another chance like this again."

His eyes went black; he shook his head.

"No."

If he hadn't torn up the letter then and there, everything might have stayed the same. But he tore it and scattered it like confetti over the floor, and then all hell let loose because that letter was living proof that something you wanted really badly to happen could happen.

And to be fair, she hit him first—a glancing blow on the arm—and then he rushed at her, groaning like an animal, smacking her hard around the head and shoulders with his fists. For a few breathless moments they roared and grunted, then Tansu rushed in shrieking like a banshee and throwing her apron over her head and shrieking, *"Durun! Yapmayin!"* Stop it, don't!

He left Saba sitting on the bed, trembling and bleeding from her nose. She felt horribly ashamed of both of them.

Her father had always been a strict, even a terrifying parent—your father runs a dictatorship not a democracy, her mother had told her once with a certain pride—but never, at least to her, a violent man.

She'd thought him too intelligent for that. But on this day, she felt as if she'd never known him, or perhaps only experienced him in bits and pieces, and that this bit of him was pure evil.

"If you go," his voice went all shuddery with rage, "I never want to see your face again."

"I feel the same," she said quietly, "so that's good."

She wanted to hit him again, to spit on him. It was only later that she collapsed in a flood of tears, but before she did, she wrote her first letter to Dominic Benson, an act of defiance that changed everything.

Dear Pilot Officer Benson,

I expect to be in London, at the Theatre Royal, Drury Lane, on 17 March for an audition at ENSA. Perhaps we could meet after that?

With best wishes,
Saba Tarcan

CHAPTER 4

Alone for the first time, and in London, when she swung her feet onto the cold floor and sat on the edge of her bed, her hands shook so much it was hard to do up her dress.

She'd been awake for most of the night in the nasty little bed and breakfast in Bow Street that ENSA had recommended. On top of the bedside table scarred with old cigarette burns there was a Gideon Bible and an empty water carafe with a dead fly in it. She'd lain with her eyes open under a slim green damp-smelling eiderdown listening for bombs and trying not to think about home, and Mum.

Her mother had taken an hour off work to walk her down to the railway station.

"When will you be back, then?" she'd asked, her face white as death under the green turban.

"I don't know, Mum—it depends. I may not get it."

"You'll get it," her mother said grimly. "So what shall I tell Lou?"

"Tell her what you like."

"It'll break her heart if you go."

"Mum, be fair—you started this, too." Well, it was true: all the lessons, the dreaming, the fish and chips at the Paleeze as a treat when she'd won the singing competitions, and seeing Joyce so magically transported.

Inside the train station, they'd looked at each other like shipwrecked strangers.

"Well, bye then, Mum," as the train drew in.

"Bye, love." But at the very last minute, Saba had buried her face in her mother's shoulder and they'd held each other's shuddering bodies.

"Don't hate me, Mum," she murmured.

"I don't hate you," Joyce said, her face working violently.

"Good luck," she said at last. The guards were slamming the doors.

When Saba stepped inside, her mother turned and walked away. Her thin back, the green turban, her jaunty attempt at a wave at the mouth of the station had broken Saba's heart. She was a monster after all.

There was a gas heater in the bed and breakfast. The landlady had explained how to turn on its brass spigot and where to apply the match, but Saba had avoided it, frightened it would explode. Instead she wrapped herself in the eiderdown and tried to concentrate on the audition. She was convinced at this low point that it would be a disaster, and regretted making the date to meet the pilot after it. He'd got her letter, and written back that, by coincidence, he would be up in London that week staying at his sister's house, not far from the Theatre Royal. Perhaps they could either meet for tea or maybe a drink at the Cavour Club. His telephone number was Tate 678.

At around three thirty, someone had pulled a lavatory chain in the corridor outside. Saba sat up in bed and decided to phone him in the morning and cancel the appointment. The audition was enough worry for one day, and he probably thought her cheap to have accepted in the first place.

Before dawn, the rumbling of bombers going over London woke her again. Forty thousand people had died here in the Blitz, or near enough; that was one of Mum's last cheery messages for her. Shivering in the inky black of her room, she put the bedside light on, moved the Bible out of the way, took her diary from her suitcase, and wrote LONDON on top of a new page.

I have either made the stupidest and worst decision of my life, or the best. Either way, I must write it down, I may need it (ha ha!) for my autobiography.

She gazed in disgust at the false bravado of the *ha, ha,* as if some other crass creature had written it.

Dear Baba, she wrote next. *Please try and forgive me for what . . .*

She crumpled it, dropped it in the wastepaper basket. It was his fault, too; she would not crawl and she would not be forgiven, she knew that now. It was the first plan she had ever made in her life without anyone's permission, and she must stick to it even if the whole bloody thing ended in disaster.

* * *

Her breakfast of toast and powdered eggs was a solitary affair, eaten in a freezing front parlor with the gas fire unlit and only her new landlady's collection of pink and white china dolls for company. After it, she walked the two streets to the Theatre Royal in Drury Lane, amazed at the crush of vans and shouting people.

In a telephone box on the corner of the street, she dropped coins into the slot, put the cloth bag that held her dress over one arm, and phoned Dominic Benson's number.

"Hello?" A woman's voice—charming, amused.

"Look, this is Saba Tarcan speaking. I have a message for Pilot Officer Benson. Can you give it to him?"

"Of course."

"I'm very sorry, we had a sort of arrangement to meet today, but I can't make it . . . I don't know where I'll be."

"Ah." The woman sounded disappointed.

"Can I ask who you are?"

"Yes, of course, it's Freya, his sister. I'll make sure he gets the message."

"Thank you." She was about to say she would phone later, but it was too late. The receiver clicked, the line went dead.

She stepped out into the street again, breathing rapidly. She was in such a state about the audition now, and the fact that she was in London by herself, it was all she could think about.

The first confusion was that the Theatre Royal, Drury Lane, was in fact on Catherine Street, so she got lost trying to find it. When she did see it, she was disappointed, what with the theater looking so drab and workmanlike in its wartime uniform. There were no thrilling posters advertising musical stars or famous actors hanging about, no twinkling lights or liveried doormen, no scented and glamorous ladies in furs outside—only a large painted officey-looking sign saying that this was the headquarters of the Entertainments National Service Association, and inside, what looked like a rabbit warren of hastily erected offices, out of which the Corinthian columns soared like the bones of a once beautiful woman.

She walked upstairs and into the foyer, where a harassed-looking

NCO sat at a desk with a clipboard and a list, and a pile of official-looking forms.

"I've come for the ENSA audition," she told him. She hadn't expected to feel so nervous on her own, but then Mum was usually with her.

"Overseas or domestic?"

"I don't know."

"Name?" He consulted his list.

"Saba Tarcan." She felt almost sick with nerves and regretted the powdered egg earlier.

"You're an hour early," he said, adding more kindly, "Sit over there, love, if you want to."

She sat on a spindly gilt chair, and gazed up at the gold ceiling, the one beautiful thing not covered by partitions and desks.

"Smashing, isn't it?" An old man in a green cardigan and with a mop and bucket had been watching her. His peaked cap looked like the remains of a doorman's uniform. "But nothing like it used to look."

His name was Bob, he said. He'd been a doorman at this theater for over ten years and loved the place. When a five-hundred-pound bomb had fallen through the roof during the Blitz the year before, he'd taken it hard.

"Wallop," he said. "Straight through the galleries and into the pit. The safety curtain looked like a crumpled hanky, the seats was sodden from the fire brigade. We've cleared it up a bit since then."

He asked her the name of the show she was auditioning for; she said she didn't have a clue—she'd just been told to come at eleven thirty.

If he had to take a guess, he told her out of the corner of his mouth, she'd be replacing a singer called Elsa Valentine, but it was a shambles here at the moment, particularly since the new call-up. In one company alone over in France, seventy-five percent of the performers, including the hind legs of a pantomime horse, were on the sick.

"So don't worry, love," he added. "They're really scraping the barrel now, they're that desperate."

"Well there's tactful," she said, and he winked at her.

"I'm joking, my darling," he said. "You're a little corker."

She hated it when she blushed, but right there and then she got what her little sister called one of her red-hot pokers—she felt it creeping up her chest and neck until her whole face was on fire.

Next, forms to fill in, stating her name and business, which she did with a shaking hand. An hour later, as she followed Bob up some marbled steps and down a dark corridor, he flung out snippets of history. This, love, was the boardroom, where Sheridan had written *The School for Scandal.* And there, he opened heavy oak doors and pointed toward the darkened stage, was where Nell Gwyn, "you know, the orange lady," had performed.

"Wardrobe"—he shouted toward a room full of whirling sewing machines, backcloths, wigs. "And here," he stopped and put his finger to his lips, "is where a body was found." He pointed into a dark room. "The most famous one," he added, his eyes very round. "A real body," he whispered, "under the stage here, and his ghost haunts us to—"

His hat hit the floor before he could finish the sentence.

"Bad boy!" A gorgeous blonde had appeared in a jangle of charm bracelets. She gave him a mock blow around the head, and kissed him on the cheek, and the air filled with the rich scent of roses and jasmine.

"Arleta Samson as I live and breathe." The doorman lit up. "No one told me you were coming."

"Audition. They should know how fabulous I am by now, but apparently not." She threw up her hands in surprise.

"Give me that, girl." Bob couldn't stop smiling as he took a pink leather vanity case from her hands. "So, where've you been, darling?"

"Palladium for two months, before that Brighton. And who is this poor girl you're trying to frighten to death?"

"Saba Tarcan." A further jingling of charms as she shook her hand. "I'm here for the audition, too."

"Well, I'm happy to meet you." Arleta's handshake was firm. "I'll take you to the dressing room."

And swept along in the wake of her rich perfume, the terrors of the night began to recede, because this was it! The famous theater, the ghost, the glamorous blond woman with her vamp walk and her swishing stockings, talking so casually about the Palladium as if everyone performed there, and soon, one way or the other, her future would be decided.

"Actually, Bob's right about the ghost," Arleta said as they walked down a long corridor. "Some young chap was murdered in, I dunno, when was it, love? Sixteen hundred and something. He was making whoopee with the director's wife. They found his body under the stage when they were doing the renovations, but his ghost only comes during the day, and only if the show is going to be a success, so we all like him." Her cynical rich laugh thrilled Saba. She estimated Arleta to be at least thirty.

"Have you seen him today?" she asked.

"Not yet, love," said Bob. "But we will."

The dressing room was part of a tangle of dim and dusty rooms behind the stage. When they got there, Arleta placed her vanity case in front of the mirror, switched on a circle of lights, and stared intently at her reflection, running a finger along her eyebrow.

"How many are they seeing today?"

"Seven or eight," said Bob.

"Are you quite sure, love?" Arleta sounded surprised. "The last time there were about a hundred. We waited all day."

Bob consulted a crumpled list. "Yep. Two gels, three acrobats, the dancer, and it just says comedian here, don't know his name. Cup of tea, my darlings? They've got a kettle up in Wardrobe."

"Little pet!" said Arleta. "You read my mind.

"I don't get it." She was still looking puzzled as the door shut behind Bob. "They usually send out a minimum of fifteen to a show. But never mind, hey." She sat down at a dressing table littered with dirty ashtrays and dried and decapitated roses from some ancient bouquet. "They do love their little secrets, and it means I can hog the mirror before the others come. D'you mind?"

"Help yourself." Saba hung her dress on a hook, wishing her mother were here to help with her makeup. In the old days Joyce would have been cracking jokes, smoking her Capstans; she'd loved all this before she'd seen how it would end.

"Right then." Arleta took a deep breath and gazed intently at herself. "Maximum dog today, I think," she said in a faraway voice. "I really, *really* want this."

She opened up the pink vanity case—its many terraced shelves bulged with lipsticks, pansticks, glass bottles full of face cream, cotton wool, a variety of brushes, a little twig for fluffing up her hair, rollers for heightening it. At the bottom of the case, a blond hairpiece lounged like a sleeping puppy.

She took out a stick of foundation and went into a light trance as she smoothed it over her high cheekbones with a little sponge. Apricot Surprise, she informed Saba, quite the best under lights. Next, a breath of Leichner's powdered rouge applied with a brush, a dab of highlighter under the eyebrows and on top of the cheekbones. Loose powder from a pink swansdown puff, and then "Phzz" as she spat into caked mascara and widened her eyes against the mirror, stroking the blackness onto each lash. She parted her lips into a mirthless smile and drew around them in pencil, and then a smear of lipstick, Max Factor's Tru Color. "Expensive," she told Saba in the same faraway voice, "but worth it." The generous hoop of red she left on a tissue looked like blood.

She pulled off her headband with a dramatic flourish, her hair falling in a mass of golden waves around her face. She began to hum as her fingers gently probed for tangles; a final haughty glance at herself in the mirror, and she caught the right side of her hair in her hands and fastened it with a gold barrette.

"Your hair is lovely." Saba was finding it hard not to stare. Arleta was easily the most glamorous woman she'd ever met, and there was nothing furtive about this performance.

"Oh, you wouldn't say that if you'd seen me last year!" Arleta bared her teeth to check for lipstick on them. "I was in a hairdressing salon in Valetta—that's in Malta—and this woman gave me a perm, and when I woke the next morning, half my hair's on the pillow beside me having a lovely little sleep. I nearly had a fit."

They were laughing when the door burst open. A fat old man in dinner suit, white gloves, and large patent pumps jumped into the room.

"Do I recognize that bell-like sound?" He raised his painted eyebrows.

"Oh my Lord!" Arleta stood up and gave the old man a huge hug. "Little thing! No one told me you'd be here.

"Now this," she told Saba, "is the famous Willie Wise. He was one of the Ugly Sisters in Brighton, and we've also been on the road together in Malta and North Africa, haven't we, my darling?

"And this gorgeous creature," Arleta added, "is Saba Tarcan. What are you, love? A soubrette?"

When Saba said she might be replacing a singer called Elsa Valentine, they both stared at her.

"Whoooooh!" said Arleta. "Well, you must be good. Did I hear a rumor that she had a breakdown in Tunis?"

Saba felt a wiggle of fear in her stomach. "Why?"

"Oh, I can't actually remember," said Arleta. "A lot do fall by the wayside. It's—"

"Now." Willie put his hand up to stop the flow. "Don't you dare put her off. I've been sent down here to tell you two to get your skates on and get down to the auditorium. You're on next."

As they walked down a dark corridor that tilted toward the stage, a beautifully dressed blond man with a significant walk pushed in front of them.

"Yes, sweetie-puss, I'm back," he said to the uniformed figure beside him. "I honestly feel like a mole here after all that light, but needs must." When his friend mumbled something sympathetic, the blond man pushed back his hair with a languid gesture. "Oh, she was an absolute horror," he said. "Complained about everything. Nothing like as talented as she thought she was."

Arleta dug Saba in the ribs and mimicked the man's swishy walk for a few strides. When he opened the door into the auditorium, her heart started thumping. Oh Jesus, Mary, and Joseph, this was it! The famous Theatre Royal stage; in a matter of minutes, triumph or humiliation to be decided. When her eyes had grown accustomed to the gloom, she saw that the stage, crudely boarded off for auditions, looked disappointingly small, far smaller than she'd imagined, and in a ghostly gloom without the front lights switched on. But never mind, she was here! Whatever comes, she told herself, I will remember this for the rest of my life. I'll have danced and sung on this stage, and that will mean something.

Her heart was thumping uncomfortably as she watched the blond man fold his coat fastidiously and put it on the seat behind him. He lit a cigarette and talked intensely to three uniformed men who sat in the stalls surrounded by rows and rows of empty seats, some of them still covered by dust sheets and bits of rubble from the bomb damage.

A pale girl in ballet shoes sat four rows behind them clutching a black bag on her lap. Beside her, silent and pensive-looking, the old comedian.

"Right now. Shall we crack on then?" A disembodied voice from the stalls. "We've got a lot to cover today. The old man, Willie, you first. Come on!"

A stenographer with a clipboard sat down quietly beside the three men. The music struck up, whistles and trumpets and silly trombones. A few seconds later, old Willie ran out, fleet-footed in his patent-leather pumps, shouting, "Well here we are then!"

Arleta clutched Saba's hand, digging her nails into the palm. "He needs this so badly," she whispered in the dark. "His wife died a few months ago. Married thirty-four years. Heartbroken."

Willie went down arthritically on one knee and sang "Old Man River" with silly wobbling lips. The silence from the auditorium was deafening—no laughter from the watching men, no applause. For his next trick he deadpanned what Arleta whispered was his specialty: a hopelessly garbled version of a nursery rhyme called "Little Red Hoodingride and the Forty Thieves."

Saba joined in with Arleta's rich laughter; Willie was really funny.

After his next joke, about utility knickers—"One Yank and they're off"—a shadowy figure stood up behind the orchestra pit and said:

"Mr. Wise, I take it you understand our blue-joke policy?"

"Sorry?" The old man walked toward the spotlight and stood there blinking nervously.

"If you get chosen, all scripts must be submitted to us for a signature. We're clear about the standards we want to live up to; we hope you are, too."

"All present and correct, sir." Willie stood in a blue haze, smiling glassily. "Appreciate the warning." He clicked his heels and saluted, and it was hard to tell in that unstable light whether he was mocking or simply scared.

The pale girl rose. She had long limbs, very thin eyebrows, and beautiful hands. She wafted toward the main spotlight and stood there smiling tensely.

"Janine De Vere. I'm from Sadler's Wells, you might remember." The posh voice bore faint traces of Manchester.

"What have you got for us, Miss De Vere?" from the dark.

"My wide-ranging repertoire includes tap and Greek dancing. Ah'm very versatile."

"Oh, get you," murmured Arleta.

"Well, perhaps a small sample. We don't have long."

Miss De Vere cleared her throat and faced the wings. She held a beseeching hand toward a woman in an army uniform and sensible shoes who put the needle down on the gramophone. Syrupy music rose and sobbed. Miss De Vere took a tweed coat off and in a sea-green tutu sprang into action with a series of leaps across the stage. With her long pale arms moving like seaweed as she twirled and jumped and with light patting sounds, she ran hither and yon with her hands shading her eyes as if she was desperately searching for someone. Her finale, a series of flawless cartwheels across the stage, covered her hands in dust. She sank into the splits and flung a triumphant look across the spotlights.

"Lovely. Thank you. Next." The same neutral voice from the stalls.

"Saba Tarcan. On stage, please. Hurry! Quick."

Dom, hidden in the upper circle of the theater, sat up straight when he heard this. He trained his eyes on her like a pistol. He'd gotten her message, and ignored it because he wanted to hear her sing again. It was a kind of dare—for himself, if nothing else—to prove he could have her if he wanted to.

He'd sneaked in after slipping half a crown to the friendly doorman, who'd shaken his hand and said, "We owe a lot to you boys in blue." He'd kept her original letter to him in his wallet: *I expect to be in*

London, at the Theatre Royal, Drury Lane, on 17 March for an audition at ENSA.

She walked down the aisle and onto the stage, childlike from the back in her red frock, he admired once again her fantastic posture, her refusal to scuttle. That kind of poise was a statement in itself. *Watch me,* it seemed to say, *I matter.*

He'd heard her laughing earlier—a full-throated laugh at the comedian. If she was feeling overawed by this, she certainly wasn't showing it.

She didn't see him at all. She stood in the weak spotlight, smiling at the dim figures in the stalls, thinking, *This is it, kid.* The accompanist took her music without smiling. She cleared her throat, and thought briefly about Caradoc Jones, her old music teacher from home. He'd given her lots of advice about opening her throat, and relaxing, and squeezing her bum on the high notes—"I'll train you so well," he'd told her, "you won't have to worry about your diaphragm or your breath or whether you'll be able to hold a high note, it will all be there." But what he'd talked about most, apart from developing technique, was being brave.

She'd gone to him first aged thirteen, pretty and shy, but keen on herself, too, having easily won two of the talent competitions organized by the Riverside Youth Club. She'd warbled her way through "O For the Wings of a Dove," thinking he'd be charmed as most people were.

And Caradoc, a famous opera singer before the booze got him, had not been in the slightest charmed. This fat, untidy man, with ash on his waistcoat, had listened for a bit and then asked:

"Do you know what all bad singers have in common?"

When she said no, he'd slammed down the piano lid and stood up.

"They do this . . ." He'd made a strangled sound like a drowning kitten. "I want you to do this . . ." He'd bared his ancient yellow teeth, his tongue had reared in his huge mouth, and he'd let out a roar so magnificent it had sprayed her and his checked waistcoat with spittle.

He'd glared at her ferociously. "For Christ's sake, girl, have the courage to make a great big bloody mistake," and she heard her mother gasp: *Swearing! Children!* "Nothing good will ever happen," he said, "unless you do."

Now the pianist rippled out the first soft chords to "God Bless the Child." She went deep inside herself, blocking out the pale and exhausted faces of the ENSA officials and the bored-looking stenographer, and she sang. For a brief second she took in the vastness of the space around her, the ceiling painted in white and gold, where the bomb hadn't got it, the rows and rows of empty seats, the magic and glory of this famous theater, and then she got lost in the song.

When it was over, she looked out into the auditorium. She saw no movement at all, except for Arleta, who stuck her thumbs up and clapped.

Dom sat and listened, too, confused and frightened. When he'd heard her first, or so he'd reasoned with himself many times, he'd been at the lowest ebb of his life, and she'd smelled so good, and seemed so young, and he was vulnerable.

But there she was again, with everything to lose—or so it felt to him—in the middle of the stage, making his heart race because she seemed so brave, so pure suddenly in the way she'd gathered herself up and flung herself metaphorically speaking into the void, where those bored-sounding fuckers in khaki sat with their clipboards and pencils.

And sitting on his own in the dark, he felt a tremendous emptiness. How foolishly schoolboyish of him to have written to her—she was everybody's and nobody's—but once again she'd called up a raw part of him, a part that normally he went to great lengths to try and hide. And although he'd always known he didn't love Annabel, or not enough, he was shaken still by the loss of her, the blow to his pride as much as anything, the sense of everything being so changeable.

"Anything else for us, Miss Tarcan?" one of the men asked. She did "Smoke Gets in Your Eyes," and hearing the stenographer give a little gasp, a sound she recognized, dared to hope that after all the many anxieties of the day, things were going well.

She sang her last song, "Mazi," on her own and when she finished, faced them close to tears. Tan had taught her that song; she'd sung it with her father in the chicken shed.

One of the nameless men who were watching her stood up. He took out a handkerchief and wiped his head. He looked at her aslant, as if she were a piece of furniture he would shortly measure.

The pianist smiled for the first time that day.

"Right-ho, a break for lunch now" was all he said. "We'll see the Banana Brothers at three and Arleta after them. We'll meet at four for our final decision."

"Flipping heck," Arleta joked to Saba. They had paused on the island between two rows of busy traffic; they were on their way to lunch. "Now I'm going to sound like something the cat's sicked up after you, so thank you very much. But actually"—she held out a protective arm as an army lorry passed—"I'm more in the novelty-dance line myself. I really just sing to fill in the gaps."

The lorry driver wolf-whistled; Arleta gave him a coy wave. "Naughty," she called out happily.

They ate lunch at Sid's, a workman's cafe with steamy windows, full of people in khaki. The set menu, a two-and-six special, featured strong tea in thick white china cups, a corned beef patty made with grayish potatoes, tinned peas, and a custard slice for pudding. While they were eating, the three Banana Brothers arrived. Lean, athletic men whose age Saba guessed to be around forty.

"Well, whoop de whoop," said Arleta, who seemed to know everyone. "Look who's here." She kissed each of them on both cheeks and did the introductions.

"This is Lev, and that's Alex." The two men folded into graceful bows. "This little titch," she pointed toward a younger man whose hair was dyed an improbable black, "is called Boguslaw." He closed his eyes dramatically and let his lips nuzzle their hands. "You won't remember that," she added. "You may call him Bog or Boggers, or Bog Brush."

She explained to Saba that they'd all worked together before, too, in pantomime in Bristol. "And they all behaved *appallingly.*" She narrowed her green eyes at them, like a lioness about to slap her cubs. The acrobats, squirming and smirking seemed to love it.

Close up, Bog was handsome, with a chiseled jaw and the kind of shine and muscle definition most usually seen on a thoroughbred horse. He sat down next to Saba, tucking his napkin in when the waitress came. He asked for a piece of fruit cake but refused the corned beef patty, because, he said, they were auditioning after lunch and he didn't like to do anything on a full tummy. He looked Saba straight in the eye as if he'd said something mightily suggestive.

Arleta was pouring tea for all of them from a stained enamel pot. "I hope we all make it, and I hope it's Malta," she added. "I had a lovely time there last time."

"Do you never know where you're going until they tell you?" Saba put down her knife. She was trying not to seem as shy as she felt.

"Never," Arleta said. "It's a complete lucky dip, that's what I like about it."

When the boys had gone, Arleta, pouring more tea, gossiped in a thrilling whisper about the acrobats. They were from Poland originally, she said, and were a first-class act. Lev and Bog were real brothers. They had lost almost their entire family during the war, and sometimes they drank and got angry about it, so it was better not to talk too much about families unless they brought it up. Bog, the younger one, was a womanizer and had got two girls, to her certain knowledge, in the pudding club. He had been excused call-up because of his hammer toes, although how you could be an acrobat with hammer toes was a complete mystery to her, but they wouldn't mention hammer toes either, unless it came up naturally, which it almost never did in conversation. Ha ha ha. Arleta, digging into her custard slice, was in high spirits. She told Saba she'd been very, very low indeed before the audition, but this was just what she needed. "It's the greatest fun on earth, ENSA," she said. "A real challenge."

"Are you nervous?" Saba said.

"Not really." Arleta winked. She took out her handkerchief and wiped the lipstick from her cup. "I more or less know I'm in," she said cockily.

"How?"

Arleta stuck her tongue into her cheek, closed her eyes and squinted at Saba.

"Let's just say I have friends in high places" was all she would say.

CHAPTER 5

After all the auditions had ended, Dom hung around outside the stage door for nearly two hours, waiting for her. The doorman, sitting in a glass box, read his *Sporting Life* from cover to cover. Dom watched prop baskets and racks of clothes come and go, listening with a certain exasperation to snatches of conversation: "I worked with Mabel years ago. She's a marvel, but puffed sleeves, imagine!" from a loud middle-aged woman with dyed hair, and "I'd try the wig department, if I were you" from a mincing little type in a checked overcoat.

And then, she emerged from behind him, so buoyantly that she could have been walking on air. There were bright spots of red on her cheeks; she was smiling to herself. It was starting to rain, and the street was full of dun- or dark-coated people putting up umbrellas.

She looked straight at him as she stepped onto the pavement.

"It's Dominic," he said. "I've been waiting for you."

"Waiting for me?" She looked confused and embarrassed, and then the penny dropped.

"Heavens," she said. "I'm not sure I would have recognized you out of your pajamas. You're as good as new."

The same thing his mother had said, and so untrue.

"Look, I'm sorry about today," she added, coloring. "It was all too much. It's my first time in London."

"And my first time for being jilted." He made it sound like a joke, but it was true. Almost.

"Well get you!" She was mocking him and smiling, too, reminding him again of their hospital kiss.

"Must you dash? Can't I buy you a drink? A nice cup of cocoa maybe?" Oh, the habits of facetiousness did die hard, even when your heart was going like a bloody tom-tom. It's only a dare, he told himself. Calm down.

While she considered this, he noticed the feverish look in her eyes, as though she was floating above the earth and not quite aware of her surroundings.

"Well, all right then," she said after a pause. "I'm absolutely starving. I was so nervous before." He touched her arm to warn her of a passing car that could have knocked her over, and she continued in the same dreamlike voice, "I can't believe it. Any of it. I honestly don't know what to *do* with myself."

They had to walk. It was rush hour now, the buses were crammed. He said he would take her to Cavour's in the Strand. When it started to rain harder, he took off his greatcoat and draped it around her shoulders.

Halfway up Regent Street she sat down on a bench like a vagabond and took her right shoe off. Her new shoes had given her a blister. Her hair was wet and plastered around her face, which was triangle-shaped and high-cheekboned, and she suddenly looked so vulnerable, cocooned in his greatcoat and with London rushing around her, and her little foot now curved for his inspection, that he wanted to take it in his hand and kiss it better. He touched her instep lightly; she did not move away.

"Nasty," he said. "Amputation? Ambulance? What do you think?"

She swung her handbag at his head.

"Idiot! Twit!" A tomboy moment that delighted him. He'd never liked ladylike girls with their pearls, and handbags on their laps, and talk of horses and Mummy and parties, but where did her high spirits come from? She was so very excited, and seemed to give off a kind of electricity.

"Honestly, what a day!" she said to him. "What a day," she repeated. "Such wonderful things!"

The waiter took their orders: half a bitter for him, a glass of lemonade for her, and whatever sandwiches the kitchen could rustle up. He asked for a seat as far away from the bar as possible so they could talk.

"Are you sure it shouldn't be champagne?" he said, making sure he sounded offhand.

"Well, maybe," she said quietly. "I got the job. I'm going to be measured for my uniform tomorrow."

She seemed to get an attack of nerves when she said that. She said she was going to be busy the whole of the next day, and that she was not actually normally in the habit of going out with strange men.

"I'm not a strange man. Don't forget," he teased her to hide his dismay, "we've kissed. Don't you remember? In hospital."

She looked sweet when she went red like that, but he saw her legs move away from him under the table and worried he might have pushed it too far.

"So whereabouts in Wales do you live?"

The blush had receded and the pale honey of her cheeks returned. "In Cardiff," she told him. "Pomeroy Street. Near the notorious Tiger Bay." She was teasing him now.

"And your parents? Are they singers?"

"No." She looked unhappy again. He thought that she had the most beautiful eyebrows he'd ever seen—dark wings over dark eyes.

"I'm not surprised you got the job," he said, hoping to cheer her up. "You were really quite good . . . that's what I came to tell you."

"Quite good." She shot him a look. "You silver-tongued lizard. Anyway, you don't know that: you didn't even hear me."

"I did. I bribed the doorman. I wanted to see you." He had nothing to lose now.

She narrowed her eyes and looked at him, mock-suspicious. "Why?"

"Because . . ." he took a sip of his drink, "because . . ." He closed his eyes, thinking *Hold it in, hold it in.* This was the last thing on earth that he wanted—to feel out of control again. "Because you're okay."

"Oh, very GI Joe," she said.

"Tell me more about the job," he asked. He wanted to hold her hand, for her to stay for a week or two so they could get to know each other better. "Do you know where you're going, or when?"

"No." She still had that coming-out-of-a-dream look, as if she couldn't quite believe what she was saying. "And even if I did, we're not allowed to say. All I know is I've got to have all the injections: you know, cholera, and yellow fever and typhoid."

She looked terrified when she said that. She was faking her air of calm. He recognized the signs all too well. His heart sank. So most likely the Middle East, where things were heating up, or India, or Burma, which was bloody miles away.

"Shame, I was hoping it would be down the end of the pier at Southend so we could do this again."

"Do what again?" All her dimples came out when she smiled at him like that.

"Well, talk, have a laugh."

"Well . . ." She gave him a quizzical look and took a sip of her lemonade. "It's not, so we can't—"

He cut her off quickly. "First time abroad?"

"Yes."

"Parents know yet?"

"No." She squeezed her eyes shut.

An uncle-ish part of him rose up when she said this. He wanted to scold her, to warn her of clear and present dangers ahead. Of men in remote places who would want to seduce her, of bad beds and frightening transport and bombs, and stinging insects.

"Will they mind?" He hoped they would.

"It's going to break their hearts," she said. She grimaced into her lemonade. "I thought I'd be able to go back and see them before we left—I promised my mum I would—and now it sounds like I won't, there's no time. That's horrible." She squeezed her eyes shut. "So let's talk about something else."

The bar was starting to fill up. The barman was reciting his cocktails—Singapore Sling, White Lady, Naval Grog—to a group of army officers. Dom was staring at her across the table, his brain trying to accommodate, to understand. It was all such unfamiliar territory.

"I know what that feels like," he said at last. "I'm flying again; my mother doesn't know yet. I'm going home next week to tell her."

"Why?" It was her turn to look shocked. "Don't they let you stop once you've been shot down?"

"I don't want to stop."

"Why not? Aren't you frightened now?"

"No." That could never be admitted, not even to himself. "I can't stop now. It feels like the thing I was born to do—if that doesn't sound fantastically corny."

She was staring at him properly now.

"No, not corny," she said. "Hard."

Her hands were resting on the table between them. A schoolgirl's hands, no rings, no nail varnish.

"Are you fit enough to go?"

"Yep." He didn't like talking about it, not with a girl, particularly. It made him feel breathless, hunted. "I'm fine now."

"How do they know?"

"Had the X-ray, been spun in a chair. Fit for active service."

She looked at him steadily. "I liked that poem you sent me," she said.

"Oh God, did I?" His turn to be embarrassed—he'd written it out, and when Misou came into the room, must have stuffed it into the envelope by mistake.

"Whatever comes, one hour was sunlit," she said dreamily. "Such a good thing to say. Sometimes one hour is enough."

"Pound actually rewrote the poem later—he said two weeks was better."

Her dimples appeared. "Dom—I'm going!" Playfully, as if they were children and the game was tag.

"I know, so am I. So let me walk you home," he said. "I could help you pack, or sew on your uniform pips or something. I'm good at sewing."

"No." She put her hands over her face.

"A cup of coffee, then." He had half a bottle of whiskey in his greatcoat, just in case.

"I can't." She touched his hand. "I'm definitely going to take that job. I decided as soon as they asked me. I can't let anything stop me now."

"I know." He did, too, understand. Unfortunately.

She laid the key to the B and B on the table. She'd produced it proudly for his inspection earlier, thought it was very trusting of her landlady considering this was London. He felt a pang looking at it. How easy it would have been to creep up the stairs together, and how blameless it would feel—all the old rules of courtship had been bent out of shape since the war began.

"Saba."

"Yes."

"When you're cleared for security, let me know where you are."

She was about to answer when the waiter interrupted. He'd returned to smile at them, to squint at the wings on Dom's uniform and ask what squadron he was with. The management would be honored to offer him and his good lady a cocktail on the house. They were brave men and they deserved it. Dom, going through the usual nonchalant disclaimers, felt shamingly pleased to be in the spotlight in front of her and also glad not to have to say more about the medical, which had for reasons not explicable made him feel angry and defensive, like a small boy required to drop his trousers.

They ordered Singapore Slings. She wrinkled her nose as she drank it, like a kitten dipping a paw into water. She wasn't half the sophisticate she pretended to be.

When her glass was half emptied, her lit-up look returned like a flash of lightning. He wondered if she was thinking about her job again; feeling at a sudden loss, he stood up, and on the pretext of hurrying the waiter along with their food, walked as casually as he could over to the bar.

He was standing there when a slight figure came out of the shadows, and stood in a puddle of light in front of him. It was Jilly, Jacko's fiancée. Later, it made perfect sense to him that she would come here to either torture or comfort herself, but on this night they gaped at each other like actors from different plays. She was wearing a blue dress, with the small RAF wings brooch Jacko had bought her pinned to the lapel. She was thinner.

He expected her to cut him, but instead she moved toward him and hugged him hard.

"Dom," she said at last. She was gripping his hand so hard it hurt. "Are you all right?"

"Not bad," he muttered back. "You?"

"Awful," she said. She put her arms around his neck again. "I tried to find you at the funeral."

"You did?" He'd avoided her all day, couldn't cope. "I had to go. I'm sorry I didn't speak to you then."

He'd been throwing up in the bushes in a muddy field behind the graveyard, sure she must blame him for everything. Who else had talked Jacko into flying at Cambridge, and later, teased him in the mess the week before he was shot down? Good joke, Dom—one of your better ones.

Jacko screaming behind the Perspex of his cockpit and in flames. The rictus of his almost smile before his aircraft went down.

"I missed you."

"You did. I—"

"But I can't talk now." When she grabbed both his forearms, he saw she was slightly tight, not that he blamed her. "I'm with someone."

A tall chap got up from the booth, she put her hand on Dom's face and said: "Wonderful to see you, Dom, you look as good as new. Sorry to hear about Annabel, by the way—you must come and have a drink with us soon." She was gabbling, her new man frowning, and protective, sliding an arm around her waist.

Dom stood there frozen for a while, and when he turned, Saba was gone. Jilly had kept her hand on his arm while they were talking. Saba must have seen it all. When he went back to their table, their half-drunk cocktails were still there, the waiter hovering unsure.

"Did you see the lady go?" Dom asked him.

"Yes, sir. She must have left this." The waiter dived underneath the table and came up with a blue coat over his arm. Dom took it and ran out into the street.

It was completely dark outside the restaurant now. The streets still wet. He ran almost all the way back down to the Theatre Royal, worried about her on her own, desperate to return the coat, to say goodbye properly. No sign of her. The crowds of London rushed by him, splashing him, no lights, no stars, the statue of Eros at Piccadilly all covered now to protect it from bombs.

When he reached the theater, the doorman he'd bribed earlier stood under a dripping tarpaulin.

"Evening, gov," he said. "Stinking day, innit? You can stop inside if you like."

"I need to find Saba Tarcan," he said. "She was at the audition earlier. I have her coat."

"I don't know her, sir. We have hundreds coming every day at the moment. Do you want to leave it here in case she comes back for it?"

"No, No. I have her home address." He'd suddenly remembered. "I'll post it."

No time left for him to try and find her; his leave was over the next day—he'd be training again for the next few weeks.

"Any idea where the company is going next?" he asked casually, fumbling for another half a crown.

"No idea whatsoever, sir." The doorman looked stolidly ahead at the crowds and the rain, at London preparing itself for another night of bombs. "But I suppose if I had to take a wild guess, I'd stick my pin in Africa."

CHAPTER 6

There was no time to go home and say good-bye. After the injections and three days of rehearsals, Saba was fitted for her ENSA uniform, which she thought was pretty hideous: khaki, rather like the ATS uniform, with a badge on its shoulder, three Aertex shirts to go with it, two terrible-looking brassieres and some huge khaki-colored knickers.

When she asked Arleta where she thought they were going, Arleta said Aertex shirts meant somewhere hot, but apart from that, not a clue: it could be an aerodrome, a desert camp, Malta, Cairo. "From now on, darling," she said, "consider yourself a little pawn in the big boys' war game—you won't know a thing until the last minute, and if you try and work it out, you'll go a little mad."

So more waiting, endless cups of tea, and then, on the Thursday of the following week, Saba, Arleta, and Janine were told to pack a light bag and to tell no one they were leaving. Their families would be informed when it was safe to do so.

They waited all afternoon and half the night for the ghostly looking blacked-out bus to pull up outside the Theatre Royal. Props and wig baskets were loaded, and when they hopped aboard, Saba was surprised to find the interior of the bus half empty. Sitting next to the driver were two ENSA staff. One was a bossy, relentlessly smiling man, all mustaches and a leather swagger stick, who said his name was Captain Crowley, and that he was responsible for their safety and welfare. Beside him was the other, a pale young soldier who was reading a map by torchlight.

The acrobats sat at the back; Willie, the comedian, next to Arleta; Janine pale as death at the front; and Saba in the middle of the bus, her feet, unfamiliar in their clumpy new shoes, resting on her kitbag. When the outskirts of London had given way to the blackness of countryside, Crowley handed them each a cardboard box with two stale cheese sandwiches in it, a tiny bar of chocolate, and a bottle of water. He warned them to make it last: it could be some time before they reached where they were going.

Their plane touched down at four in the morning on a narrow strip of tarmac on the edge of a desert, under a night sky dazzling with millions of the brightest stars she'd ever seen. "North Africa," Arleta whispered, shortly before they landed. "I've just heard."

It was heaven to feel fresh air again, even though it was surprisingly cold and stank of petrol fumes. They stood at the edge of the runway, the wind blowing small heaps of sand around their feet. A lorry arrived, seemingly from nowhere, with two British army officers inside it. They had guns tucked into their holsters. They shouted at some men wearing what looked like long nightshirts and stained woolen hats who swarmed onto the plane, deftly unloading the portable stage, a generator, and, to Willie's shouted instructions—"Ere, watch it! Mind that!"—his ukulele case.

They were held up for hours while the paperwork was sorted out, and it was already getting warm by the time they left in a cloud of dust. Saba, peering through the lorry's canvas flaps, felt a shiver of wonder move up her spine at the sight of the desert stretching out as far as the eye could see, now stained with the beginnings of a blood-red sunrise.

Arleta fell asleep, her head resting on her kitbag, her hair spilling onto Saba's knee.

"I'd get some shut-eye if I were you," she'd advised earlier. "If we're going south, it's miles and miles of bugger all—we could be driving for days."

But Saba was too excited. She'd been sick three times on the airplane, and felt, as it rose above the clouds and lurched and swooped, so bad not saying good-bye to Mum and Tan, it was like an empty ache inside her, an actual physical pain, as if she'd been kicked. But this! Well . . . already hope was starting to bloom inside her like the sunrise. This was living! What she'd come for. The greatest adventure of her life so far.

Their lorry accelerated through an abandoned airfield, lined with rolls of barbed wire and the rusted hulks of old aircraft, and once again she could see desert on either side of the long, straight road. The sand was crinkled and dark like the sea at dusk, and there, flat and parched as an overcooked omelet. A large sand dune, as big as the hills at home, and then a water hole winking like a ruby in the dawn light. The phenomenal space of it—such a relief after the cramped aircraft—dwarfed everything; it made their noisy lorry feel as temporary and insubstantial as a child's toy.

When she woke, they were passing through a small village with flat-roofed mud houses on either side of them. A man standing outside his hovel was feeding a donkey from a bundle of bright green leaves. A woman drawing water from a well stopped and shielded her eyes as they passed.

The sun was frazzling her eyes and sweat dripped down the inside of her blouse and stuck her back to the lorry seat, which was almost too hot to touch. Captain Crowley, now wearing khaki shorts that displayed long white legs, was making some sort of announcement. She heard his jaw grind. The matey version of Captain Crowley had gone; he was back in the army now. Janine, who sat on his right, listened as alert as the star pupil in a deportment class; opposite her, old Willie, cradling his head, an exhausted bulldog as he lifted his eyes.

"It needn't concern you where we are at the moment," Crowley barked. "All you need to know is that we expect to arrive in Cairo at roughly thirteen hundred hours. You three girls will be staying at the digs that are on Ibrahim Pasha Street behind our offices. You chaps," he said to the men, "have temporary digs at the YMCA."

The men were too tired and too hot to make jokes about leaving them. Willie in particular looked green with fatigue. Earlier, Arleta had confided in a perfumey whisper that he'd had heart troubles toward the end of his run in *Puss in Boots,* but he didn't want anyone to know about them. She said he was a tough old bird and that Dr. Footlights would see him through, or he'd snuff it on stage, which would probably be the best possible thing for him anyway.

"At around sixteen hundred hours," Crowley continued, "assuming we can organize the transport, we'll pick you up again, and you'll be taken to our H.Q. in the Kasr-el Nil Street. If we can't, get a gharry. At H.Q. you'll be briefed about security arrangements, rehearsals, and concerts. I'm afraid it's not going to be exactly a picnic from now on, but at least we won't be flying for a while." He gave Saba a hard look, as if to say: *Listen, girl with three sick bags, I hope you're up to this.*

Their driver shifted gears and slowed down; they'd reached a ramshackle collection of tents, a grim little town. Saba saw two British soldiers do a perfect double take as Arleta, freshly lipsticked and combed, gave them a regal wave. The men's thin faces swam into focus and disappeared into a dusty wake.

"Those poor sods look done in." Willie had joined them at the back of the lorry.

"I'm not surprised," Crowley said quietly. "It's been a long, hard slog, and there's worse to come."

They were covered in a fine white dust by the time they arrived in Cairo, and the light was so bright that Saba felt her eyeballs shrink back in their sockets.

Their digs were on the top floor of what had once been a hotel but was now converted into flats. It was a narrow, stained building with small rusted wrought-iron balconies that overlooked the street. "A bit of a dump," Janine was quick to remark, gazing up at it mistrustfully.

An old Egyptian man in a djellaba welcomed them inside with a broad smile. His name, he said in broken English, was Abel; if they wanted anything, he was their man. They followed his battered sandals and cracked heels up to the second floor, where he stopped outside a door labeled *Female Latrines.* Inside, he proudly showed them a dim little bathroom with an old-fashioned geyser and a cracked lavatory with a huge bottle of DiMP repellent resting on the lid.

On the next floor was their small two-bedroomed flat with cool tiled floors. The sitting room, furnished with dark old-fashioned furniture and faded lithographs of desert scenes, gave on to the small balcony, with intricately carved shutters on either side, that overlooked the street. A woman padded into the room with a glass bowl with three oranges and three bananas in it. Saba's mouth filled with saliva. She hadn't eaten a banana since the war began.

"Shukran," she said to the woman. "They look lovely." Adding in Arabic, "This is a very nice place."

"Blimey," said Arleta when the door had closed again. "Where did you learn to speak wog?"

Janine, who'd sat down, ankles crossed, on the edge of a cane sofa, looked equally startled, as if Saba had committed a serious faux pas.

"I grew up near Tiger Bay," Saba explained. "There were two Arab families living in our street and one of them was my friend, and by the way, it's not wog, it's Arabic."

"What was an Arab doing in your street?" Janine had a superior way of lowering her eyelids when she spoke.

"There were all sorts there." Saba resented her already. "Greek, Somali—our fathers went to sea together. Still do. My father's a ship's engineer."

Janine thought about this. "So he's an educated man?"

"Yes. He reads books and everything." Stuck-up idiot, Saba was thinking. She had half a mind to boast about how much her father knew about astrology, how many languages he spoke, how his own father had been the headmaster of a school, but decided against it. This was already the most words they'd ever said to each other.

"Well, gosh," Janine said softly, with a slight shake of her head. She rearranged her elegant limbs. "It takes all sorts." The slight northern nasal twang broke through her carefully pitched voice. They stared at each other for a while.

"So." Arleta leapt to her feet suddenly. "I am absolutely pooped. Which bed do you want, darlings? I can sleep anywhere, so you two can fight it out for the spare room."

"Well, in that case," Janine said, "would it be all right if I slept alone? The slightest thing wakes me up, and sometimes I like to read at night."

"Absolutely fine, darling," Arleta said and grinned.

Stopping only to pick up a banana, Janine left the room bouncing on the balls of her feet, like a principal ballerina leaving the stage after tumultuous applause.

"Oh for Christ's sake!" said Arleta, when the door had closed behind her. "What horse did she ride in on?"

"I think she was in the corps de ballet somewhere," Saba whispered back. "She's quite posh."

"Oh." Arleta went all bendy for a moment and fluttered her arms in a perfect arabesque. "Sorry I spoke.

"So"—she pointed toward a piece of faded chintz hanging from a pole—"which side of this beautiful wardrobe do you want?"

Saba didn't care. Her legs still felt fuzzy from the plane and her head was buzzing. While Arleta unpacked, she lay down fully dressed on the bed, and listened to the babble of sound in the street outside, the honk of traffic, the clip-clop of horses' feet.

When she woke up, Arleta was sitting on the bed opposite her. She was staring intensely at a photograph and then she put it away and wiped her eyes. It felt like a private moment so Saba pretended to be asleep, but through half-closed eyes she examined Arleta.

Her feet were bare, and she'd changed into a peach silk nightdress that emphasized her narrow waist, her perfect bottom shimmering in silk.

She unpacked a pair of pink feathered slippers, the two gym-mistressy shirts that were standard army issue, a delicate pair of silver sandals, a khaki hat, a vanity bag bulging with little bottles, a penknife, a blond wig, a gorgeously boned corset with satin drawstrings. This weird variety of things reminding Saba of a cardboard doll she'd had as a child that came with clothes to hook on for a marvelous variety of lives: glamour puss, vamp, ice skater, horsewoman.

And now . . . ah! Horrible! She was undoing a cloth bag and had taken a small animal out. She turned and laughed when she heard Saba gasp.

"Don't worry, pet, it's not alive." As she held a mink stole against her face, Saba caught a draft of some rich perfume. "But isn't it heaven? A present from an admirer, and absolutely useless here," she said, "but I couldn't bear to leave the poor thing behind." She spoke about it softly, sadly, as though it really was alive.

Saba wondered who had given it to her, and if he was the one who had made her cry; she didn't know her well enough to ask yet.

There was a faint tang of soap in the air when Saba went into the bathroom later in the afternoon. She took off all her clothes and washed herself from head to foot. She felt shockingly adrift and needed a job to do. Couldn't bear to think of home at all. Mum in the floral chair by the fire, how her face would look. Janine had been at the basin before her, laying out her flannel, her toothbrush, her jar of aspirins and her shampoo, so neatly she might have used a set square to do so. Saba changed into a clean uniform shirt, brushed her hair, and gazed at herself in amazement. Was this really her? On her own, in Cairo, and part of a professional company?

They were out in the street now, in the blinding light and an oven blast of heat. Arleta, like the old hand she was, flagged down a gharry and instructed the driver to take them to the ENSA offices.

Crowley had warned them earlier that every hour was rush hour in Cairo at the moment: in the last three months more than thirty thousand Allied troops had arrived from Canada, the United States, and Australia. When Lev, the acrobat, had asked why, Crowley had rolled his eyes and said, "Polish, do you spend your entire life hanging upside down on a flaming trapeze? There's a war on here; the Germans are coming." He'd given his hostile smile, and when he'd turned away, Lev had thrust his two fingers violently in the air at him and murmured, "Bastard." With an ugly look on his face.

Unreal city. Peeping from behind the stained curtains of the horse-drawn carriage clip-clopping through the streets, Saba almost forgot to breathe she was so excited. There were shops bursting with silks and clothes and shoes, dark passages like the mouths of tombs hung with handbags and pots, piles of mouthwatering oranges and peaches. On the narrow pavements, khaki-clad soldiers jostled for room alongside women holding children, a man on a donkey carried a huge candelabra on his back.

At the crossroads, a policeman stopped them as a red Studebaker car passed, narrowly avoiding a camel airily depositing a load of dung. When they slowed down outside a restaurant called Ali Baba's, Arleta informed them that this was where the troops drank. "Other ranks, you know," she said in a posh voice.

A couple of soldiers who seemed to have been drinking all afternoon appeared from the restaurant and did mock staggers at the sight of them. The little one whistled at them like a bird and waggled his hips.

"Oh honestly!" Janine shrank behind the soiled canvas of their gharry, her face almost comically prissy. "If it's going to be like this, I'd just as soon go home."

"Where are you going, darl?" the tall soldier asked Saba in an Aussie accent. He had a long scar on his face and a hungry expression.

"We're performing artistes." Arleta's hair was dazzling in the sunlight. "You'll have to come to our concerts to find out."

"Woo-hoo, get you." She'd made them laugh. "So where will you be?" the other one insisted. Both men were jogging alongside their gharry now, much to the amusement of the driver, who made a playful attempt to touch one with his whip.

"We haven't got a single clue yet," Arleta said. "Watch for the posters."

"I'll come, love," the taller man assured Arleta breathlessly, "but not him. He's as mean as shit." More gasps from Janine. "He's got snakes in his purse."

Their carriage shot off. Their delighted driver shouting, "Very naughty boys!"

"For goodness *sake*!" When Janine pulled her skirt down, Saba noticed that she bit her nails quite badly. "Why on earth encourage them?"

When they arrived at the offices and the driver discovered they had no money, his cheerful expression turned into an incredulous snarl. Rolling his eyes and clawing at his mouth, he made it plain that they had now ruined his life. His horse would never eat again; neither would his wife and four children.

"I'm so sorry," Saba explained in her pidgin Arabic. "No piastres, but if you wait, I will get."

An army officer, thin and red-headed, burst down the narrow stairs aplogizing profusely. He said his name was Captain Nigel Furness. His freckled hand pressed a bundle of notes into the waiting driver's palm.

"We were going to pick you up ourselves," he explained with a weary, insincere smile, "but we're desperately short of transport. Four groups of talent arrived all at once, so we're a bit of a shambles."

Willie and the acrobats waited for them in a cramped office on the first floor. Beside them, two uniformed typists clattered away at their typewriters surrounded by teetering piles of manila folders and baskets labeled *Props.* A large fan ground away in the corner.

Furness sat down underneath a wall chart with a large map of Africa on it studded with pins. The sight of that map made Saba feel almost weak with excitement. She was here! This was it! God knows where they'd be going from now on!

Arleta, who had a fabulous walk, stately and self-regarding and designed to show off her body, took her time entering the room.

"Any chance of a cup of tea or a biscuit?" she asked Furness as soon as they'd sat down. She smoothed her skirt over her knees and added huskily, "I'm starving, darling."

Saba heard one of the secretaries titter softly and Willie murmur, "Oh good girl."

"Less of the darling, thank you." Furness fought down a smirk, but his pale skin had flushed. "We're in the army now."

"Oh heavens! Sorry!" Arleta wiggled on her chair like a naughty schoolgirl and gave him her deadpan look. "I shan't be bad again." She gave Saba a slight wink; Furness turned his back on them and got busy with his wall map. In a muffled voice he asked one of the secretaries to bring them all tea.

Tea arrived in thick china cups stained with old brew-ups, and a plate of Garibaldi biscuits and they all fell on it. When Janine, sitting with her legs at an elegant slant, said only tea for her thank you, no sugar and no biscuit, they looked at her in amazement.

"You haven't eaten all day," said Arleta, forgetting the banana.

"I may have some little thing tonight," Janine said faintly. "I eat like a bird even at the best of times."

Furness, looking at Arleta over the rim of his cup, said, "You should go out and have dinner after this. Can't think on an empty stomach." He smiled, shy as a schoolboy.

When Arleta whispered, "You're an angel," and looked deeply into his eyes, one of the typists, a plain woman with hockey-player calves, rolled her eyes, but Saba was fascinated. Her own mother had once accused her of being a born flirt and she had found the remark confusing—it seemed to her that if you liked someone you let them know. It was not a thing you decided to do—well not always. But with Arleta it was like watching a flirting champion in action; there was a hot teasing energy about her performance that felt like a game, and she didn't give a damn who saw her.

Furness stood up quickly. "I think we'd better crack on." He moved purposefully toward his wall chart. "For obvious reasons," he picked up a pointed stick, "there's only so much we can or want to tell you about the current situation in Egypt and the Mediterranean, except to say in the most general terms that what happens here in the next few months could be, in strategic and political terms, absolutely vital to the outcome of this war."

He stuck a piece of blank paper on his wall chart.

"So, potted history," he continued. "In the last three months, Allied troops have been pouring into Cairo from Canada, the United States, and Australia. Why have they come? Well, now that France has fallen and large parts of the Mediterranean have been cut off, there aren't many places where our lot and the Commonwealth troops can engage the Germans."

He drew a vast spider with legs on his sheet of paper. "We're at the center of this." He pointed to the body of the creature he had drawn, then scrawled a rough approximation of Egypt, with Libya on one side and the Suez Canal on the other. "Our boys are here to protect these areas." He pointed toward Suez, and the oil fields in Iraq and Iran. "Down here," he indicated an empty space below his map, "we have thousands of men in the desert. Some of them have been here since 1940, and they've had a pretty tough time of it. The heat, as you'll find out, is merciless, food and ammunition often in short supply. They're desperately in need of some light relief."

Janine was chewing the inside of her lip; she was staring at the map. Arleta wound a strand of hair around her index finger.

"I'm telling you this," all vestiges of public-school bonhomie had gone as Furness let his gaze travel from one face to the next, "because some of the artistes who've been here recently have thought of Cairo as a kind of foxhole, or a rest cure. It's not, and it's important that you understand the gravity of the situation at this present point. As a matter of fact," he lowered his voice, "H.Q. were on the point of canceling this tour, and it's still entirely possible that you may have to be evacuated at a moment's notice. I say this not to frighten you—we'll do everything we can to keep you safe—but to warn you."

"Can't you even tell us where we're going?" Janine asked in a strained voice. "No one's said a thing yet."

"You'll be moving quite a bit in the next few weeks," Furness said. "You'll have to learn to be flexible about arrangements. At the moment," he sighed heavily and mopped his brow with a handkerchief, "I'm not sure whether you'll be in a Sunderland Flying Boat, a lorry or a hearse, and I'm not joking."

Arleta and Saba laughed anyway; Janine's left foot was tapping the floor, her eyes were closed as if she was praying.

"I traveled in a pig lorry in Malta," Arleta told them. "The smell—indescribable. I had to wash my hair for days afterward." She lifted it in her hands and let it fall in shining waves around her shoulders.

"So, splendid, splendid." Furness looked at her with relief. "You know the score." He glanced at his watch. "Some forms for you to fill in." He handed out seven buff-colored cards. "Don't bother with them now, do them over breakfast."

"What's an N-fifteen?" asked Janine.

"If you're captured," Furness said, "it's to let the enemy know that you're now members of the British Armed Forces. Let's hope you don't need it.

"Couple more things: food—don't eat from local stalls or drink water without boiling it. The rule with fresh food is: Can you boil it or peel it? If not, forget it. Locals: never walk around on your own here, not around the camps and never, never in the native areas. Some of their men have the wrong idea about our women." He cleared his throat. "They think you're, how shall I put this . . . ?"

"Pushovers," Arleta said helpfully. "A man once offered two thousand sheep for me in West Africa. I probably should have taken it."

"That sort of thing." Furness's thin skin had flushed faintly again. He ripped his spider diagram from the chart and seemed anxious to be rid of them.

"So, what about pay?" Arleta prompted. "Or did I miss that bit?"

"Ah. Sorry." Furness unlocked his desk and handed each one of them a small manila envelope. "Here's your first week's salary: ten pounds each in advance. From now on you'll be collecting it from NAAFI, the canteen and shop. But by the looks of you, you could do with a good meal today. Also, while you're on tour you have officer status and are entitled to use the mess."

On their way down the clattery stairs he told them they would start rehearsing the next day and do a couple of concerts before the end of the week. "We're hoping Max Bagley will get here tonight," he said. "He's your tour director." He hesitated for a moment. "As long as you do what he says, I don't think you'll have any problems with him. He's certainly experienced. That's all for now. Dismissed." Their brief conversation had ended.

CHAPTER 7

Dear Saba,

I am so sorry about the other night. It must have looked very strange to you, but that girl was not a girlfriend, but someone who has recently lost a chap I flew with, a friend. When you are cleared for security, let me know where you are.

He couldn't bring himself to go into more detail about Jacko; it felt cheap to use him as an excuse.

Jilly had kept her hand on his arm while they were talking. Saba had seen it all. When that other chap had left the table to claim her, Jilly had given Dom a guilty smile and he'd probably returned it. How strange that grief might look so like lust.

Dear Pilot Officer Benson,

I wonder if you can help me? I happened to open, in error, the letter you sent to my daughter. She's gone away to . . . (the censor had cut a large hole here) and we've not heard a word since. Have you? I wonder if, being in the services, you might find out more information for us. My husband and I are very worried about her.

Yours sincerely,
Joyce Tarcan

He was stationed at Brize Norton when he got the letter, training young pilots, champing at the bit because it was so much quieter now than during the Battle of Britain days, and when they weren't flying, the air in the mess was stale with boredom, endless games of cribbage, cigarette smoke. He'd gone as soon as he could get a day's leave, grateful for a semi-legitimate reason for doing so.

As the train entered the Severn Tunnel, Dom felt a denser darkness outside him. He heard the hissing of steam as the brakes were applied, and then the vague announcement from a sleepy guard that they might be here for quite a long time.

This was greeted by jeering and good-natured laughter from the other passengers in the stuffy carriage—delays were an inevitable part of life now. But Dom, sweating in his greatcoat, felt both feverish and furious with himself. Since the crash, he'd suffered from a form of claustrophobia, which he knew he had to fight if he was to fly in combat again. These attacks leapt out of the dark at him with no warning, the first sign a crushing in the throat, a sense that his whole body had been transformed into a violently overworking pump that would explode if he didn't breathe properly, or run somewhere. He was dismayed that even a train stuck in a tunnel could affect him this way.

He sat breathing heavily with his head down, sweating, terrified, and when the feeling passed, as it usually did, he asked himself what he was doing on this wild-goose chase anyhow. The girl had gone to North Africa, or so the doorman had hinted, she'd have no use for the blue overcoat that he'd placed in the luggage rack above his head. In the right-hand pocket of the coat, he'd found a delicate filigree gold charm shaped like the palm of a hand. He'd put it in the pocket of his greatcoat. It was new.

He touched the charm now. As a boy, he'd been obsessed by magic amulets, and he recognized this one as a Hamsa hand, which was supposed to ward off the evil eye, the envy of others, the kind of envy that could kill a person's dreams and wishes stone dead. The reason why peasant Egyptian mothers dirtied up the faces of their children, why English children were taught not to boast.

Cambridge and the RAF had trained the magic-thinking guff out of him, yet his fingers had clutched the gold charm during his fear attack as if the tiny hand would help him. And when his heartbeat had slowed to normal, and the prickling sweat on his body had dried, he mocked himself: Dom, the great cynic, was on a train going nowhere—oh, the potency, et cetera, of cheap music.

A pretty WAAF sat opposite him, stockinged legs gracefully aslant, clumpy shoes carefully arranged. She unwrapped a packet of sandwiches and asked if he would care for one. When he said no thank you, she ate hers daintily, and, after wiping her mouth with a handkerchief, asked what squadron he was flying with now.

When he said none as yet, she began a tentative conversation about some friend of hers in 55 Squadron who was flying night fighters over France. Her eyes were questing: Are you enjoying this? Am I going too far? She had a heart-shaped face and auburn hair. Good legs, too. On another day, in another mood, he might have answered her properly. They might have had a drink together later that night, exchanged telephone numbers, gone at some point to bed. That was the way of it now: you took comfort where you could, and she looked like a nice girl, a good sport. He sensed her smile fading as he glanced at his newspaper again.

Half asleep, he heard another soldier talking to her. The scrape of matches as they lit up fresh cigarettes. The pleasant burr of the man's Gloucestershire accent was telling the girl that this same train had been chased only a few weeks ago by a German fighter plane, and how the engine driver had put his foot down to ninety miles an hour. She replied, pleasantly, "Gosh, I hope that doesn't happen again today," with a mildly discouraging conversation-closed thread running through her voice. Who could ever fathom the randomness of human desire? Why him, now feigning sleep behind his newspaper; why not her?

He was thinking of Saba's eyes now, dark brown or mid-brown? They'd gazed at him like caged animals through the veil of that mad little hat; they'd glowed with life. And one of the songs she'd sung about God blessing the child who'd got its own was a plea for independence, for life, for dignity, but not, now he came to think of it, for a man.

She was pretty, no doubt about it, but he'd had plenty of time in hospital to mistrust mere attractiveness in another human being. He thought about the girls who'd run screaming from the ward when they'd seen the new faces of their former loves. Annabel had at least exited with some degree of decorum, assuring him over and over again it wasn't him, it was what she'd termed vaguely, her pale blue eyes flickering as they did when she was being sincere, "the whole situation." A thought that led him to Peter, a close friend from Cambridge, a man with a passion for girls, T. S. Eliot, and cars. It was Peter who had sat on a bridge near the Cam and read to him aloud from the *Four Quartets: Teach us to care and not to care* was the line Dom suddenly recalled.

A year before his aircraft had been shot down over France, Peter had bought himself a dazzlingly green Austin 10 for £8 from a local mechanic. He was amazed by his good luck and they'd extremely driven through the Oxfordshire countryside in it on one glorious day in summer. The car exploded after a week, and the last time Dom had seen Peter, he was sitting on the grass, its remnants spread around him.

"It's my fault," Peter said. "I was a fool. I was taken in by the color like a girl with beautiful eyes." After a short silence he'd added: "It's a hopeless fucking machine."

It was still dark in the tunnel. To give himself something to do, Dom read the mother's letter again by torchlight. When he'd first read it, he'd felt the sting of disappointment—so Saba had definitely and defiantly gone—and he'd been longing in his impatient way to put the thing to rest. But then he'd felt something like relief.

Because what did he know about the girl? Only that she sang, and that he admired her courage, and that for that one moment, when he had told her where his skin graft had come from, they'd both roared with laughter like young people again.

There were moments like that in life, he thought, that you couldn't really explain or understand but that had the perfect rightness of a billiard ball falling smoothly into a pocket, or of a mountain bend taken at high speed, but with a slowed-down perfection.

And the bird called, in response to the unheard music hidden in the shrubbery. Oh what a perfect bloody fool he had become. He blamed the war.

* * *

A light rain was falling over Cardiff Bay as he walked toward Pomeroy Street. It fell softly over a pearly sea where there was barely a line between water and sky, and blurred the edges of a row of houses above which the seagulls cried. It splattered on the tarpaulins protecting the vegetables outside a Middle Eastern grocer's shop on the edge of Loudon Square. This is where Saba lives, he thought.

He put up the collar of his greatcoat and checked his watch. He had a twenty-four-hour leave: three hours at the most between now and the return train.

A woman in a sari with a mackintosh over it smiled at him at the street corner. A boy went by on a bicycle: "Where's your plane, mista?" he said.

At the corner of the next street, a house sliced in half by a bomb stood shamefully exposed, like a girl with her knickers down, or a shabby stage set with its faded rose wallpaper, and green cooker, and sooty rafters. A poor house, in a struggling poor street.

Saba's streets. "The notorious Tiger Bay." She'd warned and teased him with it.

Because she had a natural dignity and the stateless confidence of an artiste, he had not given much thought to her background, and was struggling now to hold those two images of her together in his mind. Annabel's parents had owned a lovely old Tudor house in Wiltshire with a moat with swans and ducks floating on it, as well as an apartment at Lincoln's Inn. His own mother had thoroughly approved of them, their cleverness, their impeccable furniture, their season tickets to Glyndebourne. She'd probably planned his wedding in their garden. He hadn't had the heart to tell her yet.

The front door of the house in Pomeroy Street had a brass knocker shaped like a lion's head. He took a deep breath and banged it.

An old lady appeared wearing a black dress and Wellington boots. Her eyes gleamed from the gloom of the hall—dark and inquisitive.

All the way here, walking down the sooty streets that led to the bay and to Pomeroy Street, he'd had a conversation with himself that had ended in an agreement. He was here simply to return the blue coat; if her mother wanted help, he would do what he could in a dignified way and then beat a discreet and hasty retreat. There must be no whiff of the stage-door Johnny about him; it was a simple act of kindness.

But the old lady's face lit up immediately when she saw him; she put her hand on his sleeve and became immensely animated.

"Quick, Joyce!" she shouted over her shoulder, as if he was the prodigal son. "Come! Come quickly. The boy is here!"

A door at the end of the corridor burst open and a handsome woman, fortyish he guessed, came toward him. Her thick dark hair looked freshly waved and she was wearing lipstick. A woman who kept herself nicely, or who had dressed up especially for his visit.

She led him into the parlor on the right of the hall—a cozy room with a small fire burning in the grate. In the corner was a piano with a sheet of music on the stand. The old lady saw him glance at it and smiled encouragingly.

"I can play," she boasted. "Saba ma teach me. She like very much."

"Tansu," the younger woman said firmly, "go and take your boots off. I'll make Mr. Benson a cup of tea—or would you prefer coffee? We have both."

"Coffee, please," he said. "If you have enough," and then, embarrassed, "I mean, with rationing and everything."

"Turkish? English? My husband works on the ships, that's one thing we do have."

"Turkish, please." He'd never had it before, but why not? Everything was strange enough already.

"Oh, and I've called you Mister." She gazed at him warily. "And forgotten your rank."

"Pilot officer," he said. His rapid commission had never felt quite real to him anyway; it felt unearned, like being alive again.

He glanced quickly at the wall of books, and the gramophone, with a pile of records neatly stacked beside it. These were not what he thought of as normal working-class people.

Above the gramophone there was a framed photograph of a stout-looking woman in sunglasses standing proudly in front of the Sphinx.

"Umm Kulthum." The old lady had returned. She was wearing a

pair of floral carpet slippers, and looked at the photograph with a look of extreme adoration on her face. "Very, very good." She gestured toward the records and touched one or two gently. "Beautiful," she said softly.

While they waited for coffee, she brought him another photograph and put it down gently on his lap. It was Saba. She was standing in front of a band wearing a long dress of some satin shiny stuff; she had a flower in her hair and was smiling that reckless smile toward an audience of young men with short hair and boyish necks. Like sea anemones searching for light or food, they leaned toward her in the gloom of what looked like a large hangar. Knowing what terrible thoughts lurked inside them brought a moment of insecurity. This visit was ridiculous.

"Saba and the Spring Tones," the old lady was proudly explaining to him. She held up two fingers. "Second concert." And she mimed boisterous clapping. Her carpet slippers did a little shuffling dance.

"Tansu." Joyce came back with a tinkling tray. "Take the poor man's coat, let him have his cup of coffee. Please."

"Thinking of coats . . ." He handed her the bag at his feet. "Saba left hers—we were having a drink together."

"Ah, Lord." The mother put down the tray and snatched the coat out of the bag. "Goodness me, she's careless. Typical. Look . . . I don't want to be rude, but how long have you got?" She fixed her eyes on him. "I'm on shift work. I've got less than an hour."

"My train leaves at four," he said. "I'm flying tomorrow." He said this to comfort himself, not to boast.

"And do you fly Spitfires or Hurricanes?" The polite hostess again, pouring his coffee from a small brass pot.

"Harvards at the moment," he said. "I'm at a retraining unit. I actually met your daughter in hospital. I had a bit of a prang over France. I'm all right now."

"I can see that." She smiled for the first time.

"She came to sing for us."

"Yes, she did a bit of that before she left . . ." Her expression was thin-lipped and guarded again. She took a sip of her own coffee, and then put it down and sighed sharply.

The old lady had returned, this time with a bowl of chickpeas on a wooden plate.

"Please." She pointed toward them. "Eat. Come on."

"Thank you, Mrs. Tarcan."

"Tansu," she said firmly. She put her hand over her somewhat magnificent bosom. "My name is Tansu.

"Oh!" She'd seen the blue coat, and her gnarled fingers touched the cloth tenderly, as if it was a holy relic.

"Tell me more about where you met Saba," the mother said.

At the mention of her name, the grandmother let out a groan and fixed her anxious old eyes on Dom. Joyce fiddled with her cup; she hadn't taken a sip yet.

"I was in hospital. East Grinstead," he said. "She came to sing—she said she was a last-minute replacement."

He looked at Joyce, who was sitting on the edge of her chair. *Go, go, go, said the bird.*

"I thought she was wonderful." For a moment they looked straight at each other.

"Yes," said Joyce. She shook her head and gave a deep sigh. "And *selfish.*"

Her voice shuddered with suppressed fury.

"Selfish?"

"Yes." She swallowed hard and put her cup down. "We haven't had a night's sleep since she left."

"Where is she?"

"That's the point, we don't know."

The old lady had been following their conversation with her eyes. She let out an almost inaudible squeak, and covered her face with her apron.

"Tansu, would you get cake. Get *cake* from the kitchen."

When she was gone, Joyce said, "She doesn't understand everything, but I don't want her to hear this. She cries herself to sleep every night."

Dom saw she had blue circles under her eyes, the numb look of panic barely held in check.

"You have no idea where she is?"

"We had an aerogramme a week or so ago saying she was in Egypt.

In Cairo and would be leaving soon. We were not to worry. Since then . . . nothing."

He saw it took tremendous effort to control herself, and felt for the the first time in his life the desolation of those left behind. He hadn't allowed himself to think like this before—of his own mother, in her cold sitting room, stitching and waiting, or lying in the dark listening for the slow rumble overhead of a plane that might be his.

"A week isn't long," he reminded her gently. "The posts are terrible. Where is . . . is there . . . ?" He asked this delicately. You couldn't assume anything nowadays.

"Her father?"

"Yes."

She directed his gaze toward the mantelpiece. The man in the photograph had a strong-jawed, handsome face, piercing dark eyes, thick black hair—he didn't look English.

"His name is Remzi," she said. "He's an engineer with Fyffes. He hasn't spoken to me since this happened." She shuddered. "He blames me for everything."

The old lady had returned with the cake tin in one hand and a lute-like instrument in the other.

"This mine. Tambur." She held the thing up proudly.

"Ah, a household of musicians," he said politely.

"She doesn't play it; her husband did," the mother said. "But there's lots of music down here in the Bay—we actually had Hoagy Carmichael come here before the war broke out."

The old lady put the cake down on the table. She held out a new photograph.

"My son," she said. "I have four sons: three finish." Her face twisted. "He no here now. When he—"

"Tan, leave it to me," Joyce almost shouted. "Please!"

"When she go," the old lady ignored her, "when she go," she pointed toward Saba's photograph, "he . . ." She picked up an imaginary stick and mimed a beating, then she shook her head violently. "Very very bad," she said.

In the short silence that fell, Joyce fiddled with the coffee cups.

"It's true," she said at last. "He's not a violent man, but he was furious with her when he found out she'd been performing. ENSA was the last blimmin' straw. But what could she do?" she asked him, her eyes naked. "Singing's like breathing for her, she needed to do it, and all of us encouraged her at first—he was as proud as Punch himself. You've heard her."

"I understand," he said. "I really do."

The old woman's eyes fixed on them again, and then she leapt up and fumbled with the lid of the gramophone, as if she wanted to play them something.

"Not now, Tan," Joyce said. "I don't have time. I need to say this quickly.

"Look at me running on." She smiled suddenly, "I haven't a clue why you're here."

"Well, really to . . ." He looked at the blue coat, ashamed of the flimsy lie already.

"But can you help, now you know the situation?" Her eyes brightened at the thought of it.

"Maybe, I don't know. Is there anything else you're worried about?"

"Well . . . it sounds a bit silly, but my husband thinks there's something fishy going on."

"Why?"

"Well, normally, you have to be twenty-five to get into ENSA; she's twenty-three, she was gone in a flash; normally, he says, they'd leave a few months for the jabs against yellow fever, the forms, and the other stuff. Where was the rush?"

"Maybe they just needed entertainers there fast—I think something like three and a half thousand Allied troops have moved to North Africa to be with the Eighth Army." His mind was racing furiously. The desert war was where the action was now.

"I don't even understand what we're doing in Africa," she said mournfully. "It seems such a long way away."

"It is," he said gently. He briefly thought of explaining its strategic importance, but this was not the time for a history lesson, and half his mind anyway was thinking about 89 Squadron's wing in North Africa. He'd been there once on a training run, two weeks waiting in the desert, mostly drinking bad gin by a wadi waiting for a fight.

"It's not impossible," he said out loud. Flying through the vast emptiness of it, the huge blue skies, the closest he'd ever come to being a bird.

"Do you know anyone there?" she said.

"Not many—a few." It felt wrong to raise her hopes. "But to go back to what you were saying. Why does your husband think they want her there?"

"I don't know," she said, her expression closed. "You'd have to ask him. He could be exaggerating it all. He has terrible memories of Turkey and that part of the world. Lots of people disappeared from his village during the First World War. He was away at sea. He thinks his brothers were executed. Poor bugger." She sighed heavily. "No wonder he's frightened."

"Does Saba know this?"

"No. She's his little ray of sunshine—or was. He wanted to keep her like that."

"What was she like?" The question popped out. "As a child, I mean."

"Naughty, wonderful! My auntie once said, 'I've never known a child light up a room like she does.' Headstrong. We used to go up to the valleys to see my parents; they had this horse and cart, and she always wanted to take over the reins, even when she was four years old. 'Give them to me, Mam! I can do it! You're not the boss of this horse and cart.' When the horse ran away with us one day she loved it, said it was the best day of her life!"

She was a pretty woman when she laughed like that.

"She was mad keen on all kinds of singers: Billie Holiday, Dinah Shore, Helen Forrest. When we got her the record of 'Deep Purple,' she must have played the thing five million times, it drove us mad, and she'd be up there in her bedroom hour after hour, learning the phrasing.

"But careless." She glared at the coat again. "Half the time she's thinking of songs, so . . ." She looked up suddenly. "Look, will you help if you can?"

"I don't know. She's probably fine. The posts are famously slow there—you'll probably get a letter as soon as I leave."

"I'm torn," Joyce said. "She did sound happy, she's always happy when she's working, but she's much too gullible."

"If I should find myself there," he was thinking hard, "what should I say to her? I can't just turn up a perfect stranger, or almost, and order her home." The absurdity of this had suddenly struck him.

"No! No! No! Don't do that." Joyce's face had suddenly lit up, and she'd shed ten years. "It's a wonderful experience for her. Just go and see her. I don't know, tell her I do understand but . . . I just want to know she's safe, and maybe you'd be kind enough to give her this.

She reached underneath her chair and brought out a brown parcel.

"What is it?"

"It's a dress. I made it for her."

She glanced at the clock on the mantelpiece. It was four twenty.

"I've got to go," she said.

"Me too."

"If you like, we can walk down together."

"Last question." He felt he had to know. "Do you open all her letters? I mean, the ones other people send to her."

"Most of them." She looked at him defiantly. "I don't want her father to be any angrier than he is already, and nor would you if you knew him."

"And has anyone else written to her?"

"Only young men like yourself."

The stab of envy he felt was sharp and took him by surprise. He had no right to feel like that about her, but he did.

"You mean, men who've heard her sing?"

"Yes, and Paul, of course."

"Paul?"

"Her fiancé, for a second," Joyce said bitterly. "Fine young man, training to be a schoolteacher, lovely family. He would have married her like a shot. She left him shortly before she went to London, got out of the car one night and ran off in a paddy. I still don't really know what happened, but he's brokenhearted. People like her are a bit like electricity, but on a different wattage—they don't realize how badly they can hurt people."

A warning, this, or a threat? He couldn't be sure.

But later, as they walked together down Pomeroy Street, he found himself filled with a tremendous, impatient unexpected excitement.

He needed a new challenge—he wanted to fly and fight again for complicated reasons, not all of them to do with Jacko. Saba's presence would add to the adventure; provided he could approach it all in a lighthearted, cautious way, he was pretty sure he would not get his fingers burned.

CHAPTER 8

Cairo

The girls had started to breakfast in the courtyard restaurant of the Minerva, a small hotel around the corner from their flat. It was a pretty spot, with jasmine and bougainvillea scrambling up its walls, and a small fountain in the middle splashing water with a gentle, silky sighing sound that was hypnotic. A couple of weeks after they'd arrived, Saba was sitting there on her own when a lanky Englishman sauntered over.

He introduced himself with a charming smile. "My name's Dermot Cleeve. I do some of the Forces recordings for the BBC. I'm hoping to meet you all soon." As if to reassure her this wasn't a pickup.

He was young, good-looking, with his long aquiline nose and very intelligent blue eyes. She took off her sunglasses. They were the first pair she'd ever owned, and she was ridiculously pleased with them. She slid them into their pigskin sheath.

"The other girls have been held up," she said, in fact by a fierce squabble over the bathroom. She toyed with the idea of lighting up a cigarette, another new habit, but was worried it would make her cough.

"Would it be a frightful bore if I joined you for coffee?" Cleeve asked. "I'll shove off when the others come."

"Of course not," she answered. There was a small pause while he sat down and placed his panama hat carefully on the chair beside him.

Samir, her favorite waiter, bounced through the beaded curtain brandishing a silver platter above his head piled with fresh peaches, melons, and bananas. He'd been delighted to find that Saba was half-Turkish, and already made a fuss over her.

"Your usual breakfast, madame?" he said. Every morning so far they'd indulged in real coffee and real eggs and real butter and eaten the small *Musa cavendishii* bananas, which they declared the best and tastiest in the world.

"I'll wait for the others," she said, putting on her sunglasses and putting a cigarette in her holder. "I can't believe the food here," she told Cleeve. "It makes me feel such a heel after rationing."

"Oh, you mustn't feel like that." He clicked his lighter and held the flame toward her. "Enjoy it while you can; it'll be hard tack and bully beef once you get on the road. Do you know when you're leaving, by the way?"

"No, not yet."

"It won't be long," he said. When he stretched out his legs, the two small birds that had been tussling over a bread roll under the table flew away.

Samir fussed around them for a while, adjusting napkins and pouring coffee. When she asked him how he was that morning, he turned his radiant smile on her and said, *"Il-hamdu li-llah,"* and Cleeve smiled at her lazily, approving.

"What did he say?"

"*Il-hamdu li-llah* means God be thanked—it covers everything from 'fine' to 'I'm at death's door but mustn't grumble.'"

"And do you always speak to waiters in their own language?"

"No," she laughed. "Only a few words. My father taught me—he's actually Turkish." She stubbed out her cigarette: ugh! It would take a while to learn to like it.

Cleeve took two sugars and stirred them into his coffee.

"So you speak Turkish?" He pushed his floppy boy's hair out of the way and squinted at her through the sun, amused and curious.

"I can get by in it. We spoke it at home."

The two sparrows were back again, pecking furiously at the bread.

"Cheeky blighters," he grinned. "They must be the fattest birds in Cairo—they probably have to rent that pitch."

There was a small commotion at the door to the restaurant. Arleta had arrived, her uniform tightly belted, hair gleaming in the sunlight.

"Listen," he rose quickly, "I'm going to shove off and leave you to your friends. Bon appétit.

"Oh, I meant to ask you." He picked up his hat, and turned. "Where are you rehearsing?"

"At the old cinema in Mansour Street," she told him. "Today's our first proper rehearsal with Max Bagley."

"Nervous?" His smile was quizzical.

"A little."

"I might pop by later," he said. "I've known Bagley since Oxford. We've done a few programs together."

She hoped he'd add, "You must come and sing on one," but he didn't.

"Don't be frightened of Bagley, by the way" were his last words. "He has a terrifying reputation but he's actually a sheep in wolf's clothing, and very, very talented. You'll learn from him."

"Nice," Arleta said approvingly, watching Cleeve's elegant back disappear. "What did he want?"

"He said he runs the Forces broadcasts here." Saba said, "D'you know him?"

"No, they change their producers all the time, but a bit dishy, I thought."

"He was charming, too," said Saba. "Very friendly. I'll be twenty stone if I go on like this," she added, putting butter on her second hot roll. "These are the best breakfasts I've ever had."

"All right today?" Arleta took her hand and gazed at her kindly. When she'd caught Saba having a gasping, choking cry in the bathroom the night before, she'd put down her sponge bag and given her a huge hug.

"I'm fine," Saba said. "You know, it's just . . ." The homesickness had pounced on her like a wild animal; she hadn't expected it, still couldn't talk about it with complete confidence. That look on her mother's face as the train pulled out. Her last wave. She wished she hadn't made that mean remark before she left about Mam never standing up for herself. . . . Who would in her shoes? And now, what if a bomb dropped on her? On Tan, on all of them?

Arleta patted her hand. "It's like a kick in the guts sometimes—but you're doing fine, kiddo, and we'll be working soon."

"I'll be better then." Correct. Work was a powerful anesthetic as well as everything else, but she was starting to well up again, and was hoping Arleta would stop talking now and eat breakfast. Samir had just swooped with more coffee and a fresh basket of buttery croissants.

"Ladies, please—more, more, more," he said, anticipating their pleasure. "You are too . . ." He brought his hands in to show disapproval at their tiny waists, and turned his mouth down.

"They do so love pinger here," Arleta said when he'd gone.

"And a pinger is?"

"The kind of fat lady who goes *ping!* when you do this." Arleta poked her finger in Saba's side.

They were laughing when Janine arrived looking pale and almost transparently thin in this bright sunshine. As she sat down, a plane thundering overhead made their table shudder. She'd slept badly, thank you very much: too many flies, too much noise from the street. When Samir arrived with his fruit platter, she waved him away saying it would give her a gippy tummy—she'd have black tea and a piece of toast instead.

A mangy cat regarded her. It moved from its spot in the shade and rubbed its back against her legs.

"Don't touch it, don't talk to it." Janine's eyes were trained on her tea. "A friend of mine with Sadler's Wells had to have twenty-eight injections in her tummy after being bitten by a cat in West Africa. She's still not right. Shoo! Shoo! Away, you foul creature." She aimed an elegant kick at the cat. "Another friend, poor woman," she continued, wiping her mouth carefully with her napkin, "had got lost in a jeep in the Western Desert. A sand storm. She and the rest of the company had run out of water and had to drink their, you know, natural fluids, until they were rescued on the point of death."

"Were you always such a cockeyed optimist?" Arleta asked her when this was over, and Janine had called for more hot water and perhaps a slice of lemon.

"It won't be hot—the water," she said when Samir had gone. "They never get it right. I'm being a realist," she continued. "You heard what Captain Furness said, we shouldn't even be here, most of the companies have been evacuated. There's no point in being an ostrich."

And Saba felt momentarily out of focus. There was another world out there, as close as the dark kitchen behind the beaded curtain, a world that might hurt them.

A dog appeared from the shade of a jasmine bush. It flopped down under their table and looked at her with its pale amber eyes. When she absentmindedly patted its head, Janine almost shouted, "*Don't!* I said don't," and then apologized. "I'll be better when we start working," she said. "I'm more highly strung than I look, you know."

Arleta sagged and rolled her eyes behind Janine's back, but Saba, for the first time, felt sorry for her. Sometimes it seemed realistic to be scared.

Their rehearsal studio at Mansour Street smelled strongly of Turkish cigarettes and faintly of urine. Once a cinema, none of the overhead fans worked and the poorly converted stage was rickety and inclined to give them splinters in their feet, but they were, as Furness impatiently explained to them, lucky to have it—there was a desperate shortage of accommodation in Cairo that month, with more and more troops flooding in.

Max Bagley, their musical director, a small, plump, carelessly dressed man in a cravat, was standing at the door looking livid when they arrived. Behind him, the straggling notes of a trumpet warming up, a burst of violin music.

"You're late." He tapped the watch on his hairy wrist. "I said ten thirty, not ten forty-five. Do that again and I'll dock your wages. I've got a band here ready to go."

They'd been told via Arleta, who knew a friend who knew a friend, that before the war Bagley, a onetime organ scholar at Gonville and Caius, Cambridge, had been a rising star in London in the world of sophisticated revues and musical comedies. According to Arleta's friend, although he was a plain little man, half the women who worked with him ended up in love or in bed with him. Honest to the point of cruelty, his secret was to make you feel he had understood yours, and that he would do his level best to bring out the best in you, which, let's face it, not many men did, Arleta had concluded.

During their ticking-off, Janine flushed with rage. She traveled with two alarm clocks in case one malfunctioned and had wanted them to leave earlier, but Arleta had insisted there was masses of time, which there was until a car in front of them had broken down and the road ahead was blocked by shrieking men striking their foreheads.

When Arleta blustered, "Darling, we're absolutely *mortificato,* we—" Bagley snapped, "My name is Mr. Bagley; I'll let you know when I want you to call me darling."

"Oops," said Arleta softly to Saba as they walked into their dressing room, "crosspatch." But Saba admired the way she didn't make a big fuss about it, or look too mortified herself. Arleta, she was beginning to understand, had a core of pure steel.

It was bone-meltingly hot. Saba's fingers slipped as she fumbled with the hooks and eyes on her black skirt and wrestled on her leotard and tap shoes. She pulled her hair tightly behind her head and put on a slick of lipstick. Janine, panicked by being late, did something out of character and stood by the window bare-bottomed, saying "Don't look" as she wrestled her pink tights on.

"Absolutely nobody is looking at your bottom," Arleta said, running her tongue around scarlet lips.

"So, ready, girls?" she said when they were all dressed and standing by the door. "Into the mouth of the dragon."

They walked onto the stage where Bagley was talking to Willie and the Polish acrobats, also late, and a scruffy-looking six-piece band, The Joy Boys, who had been in Cairo for three months now. Willie was giving Arleta an elaborate eyes, mouth, and chest salaam when Bagley said, "That's enough of that, let's get cracking."

He stood in front of them, sweating and fierce, and told them to regard themselves, at least for the next few weeks, as artistic sticking plaster and not really a fully fledged touring company. There were too few of them for that, and as they probably already knew, there was a distinct possibility all of them would soon have to be evacuated from Cairo. He warned them that this work was cumulatively exhausting, and if they went over the top too soon they'd be in trouble. A previous performer, he said, had got her knickers in such a twist about all the traveling and performing that she'd burst into an unscripted tirade at the end of a concert in Aswan that had crescendoed in "This is all bollocks," before exiting stage left into the desert in full costume and makeup.

"Honestly," murmured Janine, who hated swearing.

"That was Elsa Valentine," Arleta whispered to Saba. "Your predecessor."

The show he'd been writing, Bagley continued, resting his leg athletically on a chair as he spoke, was provisionally called *On the Razzle*. The plan was that they would open it for one night at the Gezira Sporting Club in Cairo, and then take it out on the road to all the random desert spots and aircraft bases and hospitals that were on the itinerary, most of which they would never know the name of.

"How does that sound?" He suddenly smiled at all of them, an infectious boyish grin.

"Lovely, *Mr.* Bagley, sir," Arleta said.

Saba felt Janine shudder beside her, and although she couldn't stand the woman, she felt some sympathy for her. Sometimes Arleta could seem a little overconfident, and the truth was that she was scared, too.

From ten to one, they worked solidly on new routines, new songs, entrances and exits. First on came the acrobats, flinging themselves across the stage in soft thumps and complaining about the splinters.

Lev, the oldest, had the wiry body of a young boy, and Saba thought the saddest eyes she'd ever seen. He stopped suddenly at the end of a dazzling row of cartwheels and addressed Bagley over the footlights as if he'd only just thought of something.

"Are there any more solo acts coming? They said in London we are joining another company."

"Well, they may come and they may not" was all Max would say about this. "We may all be gone soon."

The faint whiff of that rumor again, that Rommel's troops were advancing, that soon Cairo would have the same blackout restrictions and air-raid drills as London.

"But no war talk during rehearsals," Bagley shouted to them. "If

I've only got you lot to work with, I've a mountain to climb." He raised his arms, the sharp smell of his sweat filling Saba's nostrils.

Now Arleta was under one weak spotlight, her khakis tightly belted, a jaunty naval cap on her head.

"Right, ducky, off you go," Max shouted.

She sang a mildly suggestive number called "Naval Boys," much saucy grinning, flapping hands, and then, "Let Yourself Go."

"That's all fine," Bagley said as he jumped athletically onto the stage, "but I'm thinking a kind of hornpipe flavor, a hip, hop, change, when you sing 'the sea.'" He held Arleta's arm and pushed her toward the flats. "Then a step ball change before you go *la la la.*" He sang the notes confidently. "Otherwise, all moving in the right direction."

Willie—his paunch already soaked with sweat, a handkerchief knotted over his bald pate—sang "*As soon as I touched me seaweed, I knew it was going to be wet*," and rattled off a few gags in his deadpan style. He put on a fez and did a belly dance, his hand pointing like a unicorn's horn from his head.

"I'm off now," he said at the end with a ghastly leer, "to pop me weasel."

Max said it would do for now, but when they got back from the tour they'd work up some new stuff together.

"Happy to oblige." Willie sat down on a chair on the stage and stared gloomily at his feet.

"And let's not make the jokes any bluer," Max added. "The snake-charmer one might have had its day."

"Blimey." Willie's voice was weak and fluttery. "I go much bluer than that."

"Well don't," warned Max. "There are spies in ENSA who swoon like a bunch of virgins at anything even vaguely smutty," he said. "We can't afford to offend them."

Willie had stopped listening.

"Are you all right, old man?"

"Never better," Willie wheezed. "How about you?" His breathing sounded labored, there was a heat rash all over his face.

Saba's turn now. As she jumped onto the stage, the door at the back of the theater opened in a flash of sunshine. The blond man who had talked to her at breakfast walked in, and took a seat by himself at the back. He gave her a pleasant smile when she glanced at him and put his palms up as if to say *ignore me*, which she did. She was concentrating now, one hundred percent, on trying to sing well and impress Max Bagley who stood next to her.

"So," Bagley said narrowing his eyes, "let me tell you what I want from you. Are you frightened of heights?"

"No." She stared back at him.

For the important opening number, he said, he wanted her and Arleta to appear down a golden rope in the middle of the stage. He sketched this out with his plump hands. Saba would sing a song he'd written called "The Sphinx Is a Minx," Arleta and Janine would cavort around her. The lyrics to this song would be presented by Arleta, dressed as Cleopatra, as hieroglyphics drawn on ancient tablets; that way the soldiers could sing along.

"But I'm searching for a big song to end the show with," he was staring at Saba and talking to himself. "What I really need to do today is test you."

"Test me?" She gave him a quizzical look.

"To know your vocal limits. Once you're out there singing two concerts, sometimes more, a day, it's going to really count."

She could hear Janine making agreeing noises in the wings. She took a deep breath and looked back.

"Don't you think you should listen to me before you test me?"

He pinched his nose between his fingers. "Fair comment. I don't *know* what I want from you yet. Look, you lot clear off now," he said to Arleta and Janine who were waiting.

"Can't we stay?" said Janine. "We all came in a taxi together."

"Don't care. Do what you like." His eyes were trained on Saba again. "It's just that this may take a while. There's something I need to know I can get from this young lady."

Saba felt her heart thump. The blond man at the back was sitting with his legs stretched out as if this was some kind of spectator sport.

The band was dismissed, apart from the pianist, Stanley Mare, an aggrieved-looking man with smoke-stained fingers, who lit another cigarette and left it smoldering in an ashtray on top of the piano.

"What do you want?" he asked.

"Not sure." Bagley retreated inside his own circle of smoke; he was thinking hard.

Saba was conscious of the rest of the cast staring at her from the wings, an unpleasant current of excitement in the room. She was under pressure and they were enjoying it.

"Let's start with 'Strange Fruit,'" Max said at last. "Do you know it?"

"Yes, I know it, and the other side, 'Fine and Mellow.'" She'd played the record obsessively when it first came out, made Tan laugh by using the bottom of a milk bottle as her microphone pretending to be Billie Holiday.

"OK. Then go," Max said softly. "Start her off in D, Stan."

Stanley rippled his hands softly over the opening bars. If he was confused at Bagley's choice of this dark song about lynchings and death, he didn't show it, nor did Saba, who closed her eyes, relieved he'd chosen something she knew and determined to give it her all.

She sang her heart out, and when she'd finished she heard a smattering of applause from the rest of the company.

"Well, that'll wipe the smile off their faces," Willie said loudly. "I thought we was supposed to be jolly."

Max said nothing. He'd put a pair of dark glasses on and it was hard to see what he was thinking.

"It's not going to be in the show." He'd heard what Willie said. "I'm listening for . . ." He sighed heavily. "Doesn't matter. Next song. How about 'Over the Rainbow,' but not like Judy does it."

"I don't do it like Judy does it, I do it like I do it!" He was beginning to get her goat.

She was halfway through it, enjoying her own voice soaring, sad and flung like bright streamers against the sky, when he held his hand up.

"Stop! Stop! Stop!"

He took his dark glasses off and looked at her very coldly.

"It's early days, but let me try and explain what it is that I think I'm not getting from you." He thought for a while.

"Are you familiar with that line of poetry—Coleridge, I think—that talks about how *I see, not feel* how beautiful the stars are. I want you to feel it more and sing it less. No need to be operatic."

"I *am* feeling it." She was stung to the quick by his words. She'd wanted to show everyone how good she was, not a public dressing-down.

"So, let me put it another way," he said in his soft, well-educated voice. "You're just a shade too chirpy for my taste." When Saba saw Janine close her eyes in agreement, she wanted to knock her sanctimonious block off. "Feel it to the maximum, and then pull it back a little."

She opened her mouth to start again, but he was looking at his watch.

"Damn, time's up—we'll have another run at it tomorrow."

As the band was packing up their instruments to go, he turned to her and said unsmiling, "Don't be discouraged; we'll find something for you to sing." Which made her feel even worse. "There are some songs," he said, "that have a natural flow more suitable for young girls. You'll see where the sentences are going," as if she was some kind of halfwit.

She gazed at him numb and miserable, wishing he would stop now. The blond man from the BBC had beaten a hasty retreat, too. He probably thought she was rotten as well. Awful, awful day.

As she left the theater, blinking in the sudden glare of the street outside, a lorry full of GIs slowed down. The wolf-whistling sounded like an aviary of mad birds.

"Well, they certainly appreciate you, and so did I," said a soft voice behind her. Dermot Cleeve skipped a couple of paces to keep up with her. "As a matter of fact," he added, "I thought you were rather good."

"Thank you," she said, believing him. If she had not known him better, she might have explained that she hadn't minded Bagley's criticisms—or not that much. She liked clever people. She enjoyed hard things. The most painful part had been their airing in front of the smug and unbearably delighted Janine.

"So, can I tempt you with an ice cream in Gropp's?" Cleeve asked. "It's not far from here."

She said no, she was too het up, and besides, she'd heard vague rumors of a dress-fitting appointment later that day.

"Well, at least take my card." He shook one out of an elegant little silver holder and put it in the palm of her hand. "I'll be seeing you," he sang softly, and then he tipped his hat, and to her relief disappeared into the crowd.

CHAPTER 9

That night, unable to sleep, and raw still from her strange and disappointing day, she wrote a letter to the one person who had once had the power to make everything feel better.

Dear Baba,

You may have heard this already from Mum, but I wanted to let you know that I have arrived in Cairo, and I am safe. Work is going not too badly. The other artistes in the company are very kind and we take good care of each other. We will be gone soon on tour, and I hope one day you might be proud of me. You can get a letter to me c/o the NAAFI. I hope you will write, but maybe you still find it hard to forgive me.

Love Saba

Next, after some debate with her internal censor, she wrote to Dom, a protectively jaunty letter saying sorry she'd run away so quickly that night, but she had work to do and could see he'd met up with a friend, as she had herself later that night. She, by the way, was in Cairo now and hoped he was safe and had got the posting he wanted.

Childish of her to add the imaginary friend, but she had been surprised and deflated by what happened. He'd seemed so intense before, so lively, so happy to be with her. It had felt like a night of celebration whose jarring ending had . . . well, it didn't matter now.

A carefully casual conversation with Arleta about it had been unsatisfactory. All those fighter-pilot boys were the same, she said, immature and stuck up—they thought they were God's gift to women.

* * *

Two weeks after she sent the letters, she stood at the NAAFI counter.

"Quite sure there's nothing for me?" she said to the soldier. He'd searched, twice, through the large blue canvas bag. "I've been here ages now."

"Quite sure, love." The soldier's weary face was sympathetic. "We've lost a few mail planes recently, and it's not called the Muddle East for nothing."

He handed Arleta three letters with SWALK and ITALY plastered all over them in a splashy purple writing. Janine had two aerogrammes, which she snatched and took off like a dog with a bone.

They moved to a table behind a tattered rattan sunscreen. A thermometer strapped to a dusty palm tree registered 105 degrees. Arleta, pouring lemonade and tearing open her first letter, read it with little squeaks and moans, occasionally patting Saba's hand saying she was not to worry, she was sure to get heaps on the next plane.

But Saba felt ludicrously upset. She was abandoned, simple as that. Dom hadn't replied and she felt a fool for writing at all.

No letter from Mum, or her father either. Saba felt the sweat pour down the front of her blouse. The rehearsals had helped the homesickness quite a bit, but thoughts of her family played beneath her present life like a tune with the volume turned down low but always there. What if they all hated her now? Maybe her father destroyed her letters. He'd said he didn't want to see her again. What if she could never go home?

Hearing her sigh, Arleta gave her hand a squelchy squeeze.

"Thinking too much." Arleta was frowning. "What are you thinking?"

"That I'll go mad if we don't get on the road soon," she replied without thinking. "I really will." Once they were out there, performing in hospitals, army camps, it would shock her out of this fear she carried around now like an extra skin, and why else would she be here unless she was the stupidest person in the world?

On their way back to their digs they bumped into Captain Furness walking in a self-important, head-down, arm-pumping sort of way toward the office, swagger stick under his arm.

"Splendid, splendid," he said when he saw them. "I've been looking for you lot." He burrowed around in his briefcase and said he had an invitation somewhere for them for an evening reception at Mena House Hotel on the following night. He added, "If it's not canceled, of course; at the moment, we're assessing the military situation day by day."

"Has it changed?" Janine asked.

"We'll brief you on that when necessary," he said. "All you need to think about at the moment is getting ready for the party tonight—this kind of socializing is jolly important out here."

"I'm starting to hate that patronizing little prat," Arleta said as she watched his stiff back disappear into the crowd. "Won't tell us when we're touring, won't tell us what's happening with the war, and now he behaves as if a party was a form of water torture. The Mena House is divine—wait till you see it. Maximum dog, I'm thinking."

Maximum dog in Arleta-speak meant posh frocks, full makeup, lashings of Shalimar, and her mannequin-on-castors walk.

"Don't worry, darling," she added. "We'll soon be suffering, enjoy it while you can."

The next day Max Bagley pushed a letter under their door telling them to report to the props and wardrobe department on Sharia Maarouf and borrow clothes for the evening reception. They were to look as glam as possible.

"This is a fabulous opportunity for us." Arleta snatched the note from Saba's hand. "Because I happen to know the man who decides on all the talent at the Mena. His name is Zafer Ozan, he's an absolutely sweetie, and very, very rich, and if he likes you, your future is pretty much assured."

"How do you know him?" Janine asked suspiciously.

"We had a steaming affair," said Arleta, who would stop at nothing in her game of shocking Janine. "He was heaven. We went to his tent in the desert. He smelled of sandalwood and was incredibly generous. He was the one who gave me a necklace," she added to Saba.

"Oh honestly." Janine closed her eyes. "She's joking, you know," she warned Saba. "She doesn't mean it."

* * *

Later that morning, a severely elegant woman called Madame Eloise met them at the door of the props department, a dim and shuttered building three blocks from the Nile.

Madame had once been a model for Lanvin, the famous Parisian designer. Her commanding height and the baked-in-the-oven perfection of her chignon was intimidating at first, but her smile was warm. She sped them through a room lined with racks of clothes and meticulously organized shelves covered in wigs and boxes. "Oh, this is fun," she said, "three gorgeous girls. I must put my thinking cap on."

At the end of the room she stood them next to a floor-length mirror, and went into a light trance.

"Dresses." She tapped her teeth with her finger and regarded them impersonally. The blackboard beside her was covered with mysterious messages: "Ten wigs, Tobruk, rolled scenery and portable generator Ismailia. Ten Tahitian skirts, base number 32. Five pink hats, 'On Your Toes.'"

And Saba, hearing the faint drone of an airplane moving overhead and seeing their three drab khaki reflections in the mirror merge and separate again, thought, this is a mad, mad world I'm in now. Three girls in hot pursuit of the perfect dress, at a time when Cairo, so the rumor mills went, was about to be bombed to smithereens or invaded by Rommel. Furness had promised them earlier they'd be gone soon from the city, with its neon lights and nightclubs and dress shops. Picked up from the fairy ring and dropped into the desert like brightly wrapped sweeties; the kind grown-ups hand out to frightened children to distract them from the dentist, or some other alarming operation. She stood in the clammy air and shivered.

"You." Madame was looking at Saba. Her manicured finger tapped her teeth. "Dark hair, olive skin," she muttered. "Got it!" She darted into the racks and produced a white garment bag. "Something quite fantastic. This dress was made originally from the most divine sari fabric. I copied an old Schiaparelli design and it's . . ." She stopped modestly. "Well, see for yourself."

She whisked out the dress.

"Ooh!" They gasped like children. The dress fluttered like a butterfly in the breeze from the fan, its bodice inlaid with filaments of silver so fine they looked like gossamer thread; its long silk skirt so delicate that it shivered in the wind, and then they stood wincing as the airplane noise outside rose to an intolerable level.

"Not fair, not fair at all." Arleta pretended to bat Saba about the head. "I want it, and I'm older than her."

"It's been on tour with *Scheherazade.*" Madame held it against Saba. "I made it out of a shawl that belonged to a maharajah's daughter; that's real silver in the bodice by the way. What is your waist size?"

"Twenty-four inches."

"Perfect, try it on. Wash your hands first, please." She indicated a bowl and a piece of soap in the corner of the room.

Saba slipped out of her dusty uniform. She peeled the shirt from her back. A sluggish breeze came from the window tinged with the smell of petrol.

"There." Madame squirted her quickly with a tasseled bottle of scent; the dress surged over her head. "Stand here." She was pulled in front of the mirror. "Hold in there." Madame lashed a delicate silver rope around her waist. "Hair down." She tucked Saba's hair behind her ears.

"Now look." She scrambled through a glass-fronted cupboard with many drawers in it, and came out with a tiny diamanté brooch, that she pinned onto the bodice of the dress. "No jewelry apart from that," she ordered. "The hair waved, the pin and the dress, *à suffit.*"

"Oh Lord." A band of gauzy sunlight fell diagonally across Saba and she stood in shock. The dress had changed her into a marvelous mythical creature and her eyes filled with tears because she'd just pictured her mother, who was poignantly susceptible to luxury, standing next to her gasping.

But then she remembered the slant-eyed, ciggie-smoking aspect of her mother, who might have ruined this outing altogether. They'd had a shocking bust-up once when Saba had refused to wear a hideous dress her mother had made on her sewing machine. Lots of swearing, lots of shouting, Saba storming off to bed, shaking the house with her slamming door, Mum shouting upstairs very sarky: "Oh little Miss Know-It-All upset, is she? Oh dear! Dear! Dear!"

The dawning sense that quite a few of Mum's creations hadn't quite hit the mark had crept up over the last few years. That polka-dot dress, for instance, though conceived with dash, did have quite an uneven hem, and hasty bits of bias binding over the neckline. Things changed whether you wanted them to or not. Just as Mum changed like a weathervane whenever her father was around.

"Can I really wear this?" she asked Madame Eloise.

"Of course. But if you spoil it, you pay for it." They were talking to each other's reflection, so it was hard to see if this was a joke or not. "How much do they pay you now?"

"Ten pounds a week." Saba still couldn't quite believe it. "Four pounds for the chorus. It's a fixed salary for all the artistes. And you?" she asked back. "Fair's fair."

"None of your beeswax." Madame made the gesture of a geisha hiding behind a fan. "Not enough money to stay here if the war gets too hot, which I hear . . . Oh, never mind." She pretended to smack her face. "Concentrate on important things. A dress for you now, Arleta."

Arleta, stripped to her peach underwear, was combing her hair luxuriously by the window, enjoying the play of sunlight on its gold and red tints. When Madame asked if she'd ever helped the color along, Arleta said Coty's Tahitian Sunset had been used once or twice, but mostly God did all. She flicked it dramatically over her shoulder.

Madame said they were a riot and turned confidential. She also ran a service, she said, that tailored men's uniforms, and the men were every bit as vain as women; the way they carried on about fitting a trouser, or the exact positioning of scrambled egg on the shoulder of a senior officer, was a caution. She offered them coffee and a piece of halva and warned them to watch out for the serving men here, who were sex-starved and like wild animals. The stories she'd heard she would not repeat. She promised that when they got back from their tour, she would take them to a bazaar shop that sold the finest silks in Cairo. She asked them whether they had boyfriends here.

"We've been told not to go into the native quarter," Janine interrupted her. She'd been sitting by the window, deep in thought, her hands folded in her lap.

"Oh pouf, boring!" said Madame. "Go. It's exciting. You're in much more danger near the British barracks, and besides, I like the Egyptians, they are so funny, and so intelligent—I mean, please! They built the pyramids, wonderful art, the first telescope, and we treat them like . . ." she turned her mouth down in comical disgust and waggled her hand, "wogs, gyppos! So stupid!"

"Hmm." Janine was not convinced.

"So you!" Madame looked at Arleta. "For you, something sensational." She returned with a dress coiled over her arm and covered in sequins the color of old gold.

"Oh *ding dong*!" said Arleta when it was on. She stared at herself in the mirror and shimmied her hips. She kissed Madame and said she felt like a mermaid in it, and who would have thought you'd have to go to Cairo to find a decent dress. "Would it be entirely impossible," she asked winningly, "for me to take it on tour when we leave? I'll look after it."

Saba knew this was not true. Arleta stepped out of her dresses at night and left them where they lay on the floor, much to Janine's disgust. Janine said it only took an extra five minutes to put things back on their hangers.

Janine got a pale green chiffon dress with silver shoes, and a rope of long, fake pearls, which Madame knotted dramatically at her waist.

"Voilà." She lined them all up side by side in the mirror. "Let me see you all together. Not there, there." She changed the angle of Saba's brooch. "Beautiful, beautiful girls," she purred. "One more thing." She darted toward a velvet pincushion and pulled out three hatpins. "In your handbags, just in case."

"In case of what?" Saba asked.

"Attack," said Madame. "I've told you already, the men are a long way from home, and some of them are very fresh. I don't think they mean to be," she said, hearing Janine's squeak. "It's just that out here, particularly in the desert, men get lonely—the kind of loneliness that nothing but a woman can drive away. Simple as that, and who can blame them.

"You're looking very shocked, dear." She gave Janine's arm a little pat. "But you're a dancer, you must know these things. There are certain professions that excite men more than others.

"Speaking of which," she said quietly to Saba as Janine disappeared behind the curtain, "your taxi is waiting outside. You're running late."

"Just for me?" she said, surprised.

"Just for you," she answered. "The message came from the ENSA headquarters, so it must be right—off you go."

CHAPTER 10

An unmarked taxi picked her up outside the props department and sped her across town toward the recording studio for the British Forces Overseas. But then to her confusion the car veered from the main road, Sharia Port Said, bumped down a nondescript street, and stopped outside a block of gray flats with washing hanging from their windows. When they arrived, the taxi driver handed her a typed note: *go up to the fourth floor; you'll be picked up in an hour.*

Inside the ancient clanking lift, she looked around nervously at the filthy glass light on the ceiling half full of dead flies and sand, and at her own wavery reflection in a wall mirror. This didn't look like a recording studio.

Dermot Cleeve was standing on the landing of the third floor. He pulled back the wire door.

"Lovely," he cupped her hand, "what a treat. It's very sweet of you to come." Today he was smartly dressed in a tropical suit and wearing a spotted bow tie. The fine blond hair that flopped over his eyes and his broad artless smile gave him the air of a bouncy schoolboy.

He led her into a small, dark flat that smelled faintly of fenugreek—a spice she recognized from Tan, who loved to cook with it, and whose dresses smelled of it.

"I hope you don't mind meeting here," he said, "rather than at the studio—it's easier to talk."

She felt herself relaxing as she sat down on the edge of a sofa scattered at one end with records and sheet music. The untidy room, with its shelves crammed with books and tapes, its bottles of Gordon's gin, its gramophone, felt homely and familiar if not exactly what she'd expected.

The small kitchen at the end of the room had no door; while he bustled around making tea on a gas ring, he chatted as if they were old friends, first about tea, which he said he drank too much of, but you could get some delicious blends out here if you knew where to look, and then about cooking. His *suffragi*, Badr, he said, did the cleaning and the errands, but got cross with him for wanting to do his own cooking; he hated people bowing and scraping to him and it was easier, to do for himself, particularly with the hours they worked.

With her tea he brought out a plate of delicious cakes—"You must try these," he said, "they're from Groppi's. The family is Swiss, and they make the most perfect macaroons and strudel I've ever tasted—absolutely divine."

She was crunching away at a chocolate-flavored macaroon when he said he thought Max Bagley had been far too harsh with her the other day. "I thought you were marvelous, and your 'Strange Fruit' raised the hairs on the back of my neck—as a matter of fact," he jumped up to look in the mirror, "one or two of them may still be up," which made her laugh, not that it took much today; she felt keyed up and strangely excitable.

"It's such a powerful thing to be able to sing well." He gazed at her with frank admiration. "And a wonderful thing to see how the faces of serving men change when they listen to a decent song. It seems to soothe them, makes them human again.

"You know one of the things the top brass don't get," he stirred some sugar into his tea and took a delicate sip, "is that men by and large fight for their sweethearts and for their mums, their children; none of that—excuse the French—balls about freedom and democracy. And men need reminding of that, and that's what you do, and it's much, much more important than most people will ever understand."

He was saying the perfect thing at the right time. The heat, the homesickness meant she'd had trouble sleeping for the last few nights, and in the darkest hours everything that had seemed so exciting about coming to North Africa had turned into everything that was shallow and dreadful about her. You're a wicked girl, the nighttime goblins had told her: black with sin and ambition and a terrible daughter to boot. Your poor mother is crying at home, your father hates you. No wonder you get no letters.

More tea was poured. She tried not to scoff the macaroons; she was starving suddenly. He'd gone on to talk in the same admiring way about the absolutely splendid extra work that some female singers had undertaken.

"I can't name names of course, but they have been an absolutely vital part of the war work. They have tremendous power, more than they realize, because they're obviously able to travel around freely without it seeming suspicious, and also, of course, to make people forget themselves. Do you understand what I'm getting at?" He watched her carefully and then, in a curiously personal gesture, brushed crumbs off her cuff.

She wasn't sure, and if she did, it seemed presumptuous, even fanciful, to say so.

"If anything did come up like this," his long fingers played with his pen, "would you be game?"

"Game?" In Wales it meant something not quite nice, as in *on the game*.

He corrected himself quickly. "Interested?"

"I might be, but I don't really know what you're asking me to do."

"Let me give you a small example," he said. "Tonight, at this party at the Mena House, you'll be part of the main group, but you could, if you agreed to it, do a little job for us."

"What sort of job?"

"An easy-peasy job," he said, "and you don't have to do it if you don't want to. You told me earlier that you speak some Turkish, and that was of interest because there is a man who will come to the party. His name is Zafer Ozan, and he is a Turk who also happens to be an influential figure in North Africa. Would you be prepared to sing him a song or two in Turkish?"

"Only that?"

"Only that." He grinned at her. "He loves European singers but he's a fierce patriot, too, so I think he'll love you, and of course if he does, it could lead to lots of work for you after the war."

"Gosh," she said, "that sounds quite exciting."

He uncapped his golden fountain pen, and made a few marks in a small notebook.

"But I don't understand, I thought I'd come here to do a wireless broadcast . . ." She glanced at a large tape machine on his sideboard.

"Oh definitely, I'm very keen for you to do that, too. I've just started a Forces Favorites hour, it's gone down a treat with the men—we play some songs, let them record their own messages home, it's very, very moving. It's just that this new thing has come up, and honestly, I cannot stress enough that if you don't want to do it, that's fine, too. I imagine though that you're someone who likes being busy," he added pleasantly.

"We're all keen to start work," she said, scooting up a bit on the sofa. "We should get our itinerary this week."

"I've seen it," he said evenly. "You're going to be flat out soon." And then, more quietly, "That's partly why I needed to see you now. Go on, have another." He pushed the last two cakes toward her.

"No thanks," she said. There was still a chance he might ask her to sing, and she couldn't do that stuffed with macaroons. "So you've seen our itinerary? I thought it was all very hush-hush."

"It is, although you've probably twigged already that nothing is very hush-hush out here—they say that gossip seems the only reliable source of news.

"Saba." When he looked at her, his pale blue eyes were tired; they had thin veins of blood running through them and close up he was older than she'd first thought. "I don't have much time," he glanced around the room, "and neither do you, so I'd better get on with it. As well as my broadcasting here, I do have a working relationship with another key part of the government that, from time to time, does more secret things. Do you know what I'm getting at?"

"I think so." She felt a slither of alarm inside her, and a vagrant excitement, as if she'd suddenly been inducted into a grown-up, serious world.

He rubbed his nose. The skin on it was very pale and she could see a tracery of burst capillaries.

"So tonight"—he got up and adjusted the curtains, sat down again—"this is a very small do, so don't look worried." He patted her knee in a friendly uncle sort of way. "It should be fun, and we have no interest in throwing you in at the deep end; if you like, it's a little test, to see how much you want to do with us—you'll be perfectly safe. In fact, I'll be there, but you won't talk to me.

"There will be the usual mix of people—the few Brits who are left, some businessmen, some army officers, and some important locals who we want to do business with. They often ask the girls to these shindigs to pretty things up—no one will think it the slightest bit odd that you're there and they'll want you to sing."

Cleeve was whispering now, the twinkly look in his eyes had disappeared and he was entirely focused and serious.

"This man, Ozan, is one of the richest men in the Middle East and, by the way, a very nice man, good fun. I don't know how much you understand about Turkish politics at the moment, but Istanbul is now strategically and politically one of the most important neutral cities in the world—both the Allies and the Axis forces are simply itching to get their hands on it, so any little crumb—"

"But—"

Cleeve clutched her hand quickly and let it go. "Let me finish, I know what you're going to say. 'Of what possible use can I be?' Here's the point. Ozan's passion and weakness is music. Before the war, he got all the great musicians to come here—Bessie Smith and Ella and Edith Piaf, and some wonderful singers from Greece you may not have heard of, and now the man's frustrated: there's an embargo on bringing foreign artists here unless of course they're with ENSA, or the Yanks. When he hears you, I guarantee he'll be interested, he's a great talent-spotter."

Saba licked her lips nervously. Oh how exciting it all sounded. And one in the eye to bloody old Bagley.

"After the war is over, he'll go back to doing what he enjoys doing most, organizing tours all over the Mediterranean. It's a very lucrative market, and he'd be a helpful person to be friends with."

"So?" she whispered.

"Well, they have a very good band at the Mena: an Egyptian band that knows how to play all the old standards. At some point in the evening, I'd like you to surprise him by singing one song in English, and another in Arabic or in Turkish, it doesn't matter which. Can you do that?"

"Yes, my gran and I were always singing them at home. But what then?"

"Nothing really, except if Mr. Ozan asks you to sing at his club, which is what we're hoping for, simply send me a postcard here that says *The show went well.* I'll know what you mean. Don't sign your name. Here's my address." He scribbled it on a piece of paper. "Look at it now and memorize it. Is that clear?" He smiled at her encouragingly. "Not too difficult, is it?"

"I thought you said you'd be there."

"I will, but I don't want you to talk to me." He threw back his floppy hair and twinkled at her again—the bad boy of the quad organizing a midnight feast.

She looked at the address, scrumpled up the piece of paper and handed it back to him again.

"Am I supposed to eat this or something?" she whispered.

He grinned at her. "Any more questions?"

"Does Arleta or Mr. Bagley, or Captain Furness, or anyone else in the company know anything about this?"

"Max Bagley knows as much as he needs to know," Cleeve said confusingly. "But nobody else, so never discuss it with anyone. Regarding the girls, casually drop it into a conversation that you might be doing a couple of songs for me on the Middle East Forces Program. It's transmitted over the Egyptian State Broadcasting. That leaves it open. Anything else?"

"Just one thing." She gave him a frank look. "When you say I'm to make friends with Mr. Ozan, you do mean just a friend?" Because if he honestly thought she'd go any further, he had another think coming.

"Oh, you should see your eyes flashing," he teased. "Your mother would be proud of you. *I'm not that sort of girl,*" he mocked in a high falsetto.

"I repeat," he said, "all you have to do is sing a few songs and keep your ears open, and you may get the chance to do something that will make you feel proud of yourself for the rest of your life . . . but if you want to go away and think about it . . ." He opened his arms to release her.

"No, no, no, I want to do it," she said. She had a fizzy, excited feeling in her veins. She'd already imagined telling her father about it one day, the softening of his craggy features, the look of pride in his eyes as she said: "You see, Baba, I wasn't just singing, I was helping the British government."

"Good." Cleeve's long fingers squeezed her hand. "You're on."

CHAPTER 11

No one seemed to notice she'd been out when she got home, mostly because Arleta and Janine had had an enormous row, and Arleta was full of it.

"In the taxi going home," she explained, "I said it was complete balls what Madame Eloise said about women here needing hatpins in their handbags to preserve their modesty—half the WAACS and WAAFS I've met here and in London simply hurl themselves at anything in trousers." And good for them, too, Arleta continued, in full cry: war meant freedom for women and men—freedom from lies and hypocrisy. Cairo for a young woman was like being a child in a sweet shop—so much choice, so many lonely men around the girls called them meal tickets.

"Then she said," 'Have you *quite* finished yet?'" Arleta, who did a brilliant Janine, closed her eyes and wobbled her head. " 'Because personally speaking, I don't want freedom from convention at all, and I feel sorry for girls who do—men know when they're handling soiled goods.'

"Soiled goods," Arleta snorted. "What a twit. She's upstairs now with the burned feathers and the smelling salts. Much too good for this world." She closed her mouth prissily.

Arleta asked Saba to take Janine's evening dress to her room—Arleta was going to have a bath and some shut-eye—she couldn't bear to look at the silly cow.

All these overwrought emotions gave Saba a sense of the fragility of the world they lived in. Bickering about frocks and men when outside the dusty window she could hear planes grumbling and tanks mingling with the sounds of a typical Cairo rush hour—the blasting of horns, the increasingly desperate shrieks from the man who sold fly whisks on the corner; the bubbling sound of passersby beneath their window speaking in a dozen or so different languages.

Janine was asleep when she walked in, as still as a wax doll. She'd put a green satin eye mask over her eyes and stuffed her ears with cotton wool. On her chest of drawers there was a photograph of her parents in Guildford—a tensely smiling couple—next to her Pond's cream and her bottle of gut reviver. Her leather-covered alarm clock said it was five fifteen, three hours to go before the party.

Saba looked down at her. Poor Janine. Nobody had taken to her. Willie had told her earlier that Janine was older than she looked, thirty he reckoned, and had never married. The narrowness of her training, her strange obsessive personality seemed to have made her better at dancing than life, but she wasn't such a bad stick really, just hard to warm to. Gossiping about her yesterday, Willie had hinted she might still be a virgin, an ENSA first, he'd added.

Arleta was asleep, too, when Saba went back to their room: strangely innocent-looking with her blond hair mussed and wafted by the fan, her soft lips parted, arms spread out as if she was saying yes to pretty much everything. It wasn't fair, thought Saba, looking down at her: Arleta was everything your mother had warned you never to be, the perfect mixture of damage and glamour, and men adored her for it. Women liked her, too. Arleta, for all her outrageousness, was kind—it was only narrow-minded people like Janine who got her goat. And yet, people were complicated, never exactly one thing or the other, because earlier, and for the first time, Saba had seen that look of hurt and slight competitiveness in Arleta's eyes when Saba had mentioned she might be doing a wireless broadcast for Cleeve. Most performers couldn't help themselves like this. It was the chimp-house thing: when one chimp was handed an extra bunch of bananas, everyone was thrown.

When Arleta woke up, she switched off the fan and got out of bed wearing nothing but silk pajama bottoms and a frothy bra—she'd thrown all her khaki underwear in the dustbin on their first night in Cairo, crooning, "Nice knowing you."

"Can I bag first bath?" Arleta said yawning. "I must wash my hair."

"Only a ten-turner," warned Saba.

The turns referred to the egg timer that Janine had brought on tour with her to stop people hogging the bath. They were absolutely essential, she'd said.

Inside the bathroom, there was a cracked bowl underneath the sink with Janine's leotards soaking in it and the bottle of shampoo that she marked with a pencil like an old brigadier hoarding sherry. Saba heard Arleta turn on the taps from which the rust-colored water trickled out at an agonizingly slow pace, and while she splashed and groaned, Saba moved restlessly around the room thinking about her strange conversation with Mr. Cleeve, a conversation that had thrilled and frightened her.

Her borrowed dress was hanging in front of the wardrobe like a new life waiting to begin; the shadows were lengthening in the street outside, and her stomach was in knots. For that moment everything in her existence felt unstable.

To calm herself she ran through possible songs she might sing for Mr. Ozan, moving her hips and humming the first bars of "Mazi," one of her father's favorites. It was ages since she'd sung a song in Turkish, and every time she sang it she felt a wave of sorrow and rage sweep over her. Not a word yet from her father, how mean of him, and what a loss for both of them who had once been so close. Singing the next verse for him straight from the heart, it seemed to her that the song had taken her over and was singing her—a strange effect she'd noticed before, particularly when she sang in Turkish. When it was over, she dashed her tears away. Damn you, Baba. You were the one who told me I could sing. Why should I stop?

When it was her turn to get in the bath, her mood flipped again and Dom stole into her mind. Seeing him with that other girl in Cavours had hurt her pride, but she still thought about him. She wanted him to be here tonight, to see her in this wonderful dress, take account of how much she had already changed and what a prize he had missed out on. Soaping her armpits, she ran a film of it in her mind. Dom on a terrace in a dinner jacket, rumpled hair, palm trees behind him, she walking toward him in the sunset, a woman now in her Schiaparelli dress, cigarettes and pearl holder, her smile slightly mysterious now because of the important war work.

"Saba!" Janine's tight voice through the keyhole. "Could you please stop making that horrible noise, and also, you've had at least twenty turns in the bath," followed by Arleta's bellow: "Come in, boat number four—taxi in half an hour."

Later, stepping into the street, even Janine was forced to admit it was the most perfect night for a party. The evening air was soft and warm, and as they drove past the bronze lions on the Khedive Ismail Bridge, the lights of the river barges made red and gold reflections on the surface of the Nile. In the distance against a lurid horizon, the sails of the feluccas fluttered like large moths.

A jeep crammed with hooting and whistling GIs drove by as they got into the taxi. They made obscene gestures at the girls. One man clawed at his mouth like a starving man.

"I absolutely hate that," said Janine, regal in pale green and clasping her evening bag tight. "It's so unnecessary."

Now they passed through Cairo streets loud with rackety music, past a stretch of water with what appeared to be a dead donkey floating on top of it. A crowd of men in white djellabas were holding lanterns over it, and ropes to get it out.

"Oh golly!" Janine held her nose and winced. "What a *dreadful* pong."

"Nah, lovely," Arleta joked. "It's Eau de Nile."

Saba laughed out loud. This morning she'd felt so distraught, so wrong about everything; tonight the randomness of driving through Cairo's corkscrewed-streets in a borrowed evening dress felt marvelous.

Clear of the city a brand-new life sped past her window—some large and luxurious houses surrounded by trees, an old man sitting by the road having a quiet smoke by a fire; a skinny horse waiting patiently to be unloaded, a group of street children jumping and laughing. Samir, whose wife cleaned their rooms in the mornings, had already told them how dreadful this year's crops had been, a disaster, great hardship for the villagers, and yet there was a feeling of almost enviable peace and ordinariness about these scenes. Of quiet worlds that would continue stubbornly despite the Desert War.

* * *

It took about forty minutes to get to Giza and the hotel. In a long drive lit with flaming torches Arleta turned and said with some ceremony:

"Girls, I want you to pay attention to me. Tonight is a blue-moon night—and you're to enjoy every minute of it."

Janine, who had complained of car sickness on the way out, looked puzzled, but Saba understood and approved. Blue-moon nights were Arleta-speak for the choicest gigs you could ever possibly get, the magical nights that might only happen once or twice in a lifetime. It was important to recognize them, bask in them, and use them as nourishment for when you were back in some crummy digs in an English seaside town doing pantomine.

When the car set them down in front of a glowing building, a uniformed porter wearing a huge ornamental sword stepped forward and helped them out.

In front of her, Saba saw were the three ancient pyramids of Giza, jutting out into a night sky that glittered with a thousand million stars. She was stunned by their beauty—in her mind pyramids belonged with unicorns and mermaids in some other mystical world; they were not the backdrops for a party.

Even Janine was impressed. "Golly," she said, her highest accolade. "This is actually quite pretty."

The hotel itself stood on the crest of a small hill against a cobalt-blue sky. Dozens of lanterns shifting in a slight breeze made the building seem to float against the sky like a skittish little pleasure craft, and lavish planting of jasmine bushes on the terraces made the air piercingly sweet.

"Ready, girls?" Arleta took both their arms. "Down we go."

Arleta had a fabulous red-carpet walk, both slouchy and stately, which she deployed to maximum effect on these occasions and which she and Saba sometimes practiced for fun in their PJs in their digs. You blanked your eyes, lengthened your neck, stuck your hips out, and swung your bottom negligently as if you didn't give much of a damn about anything.

They were having fun with it now as they walked down the short flight of steps that led to the party. A dramatic pause on the first terrace, then the band struck up a jazzy tune, and a group of young men in dinner jackets froze at the sight of them like Pompeii statues. Captain Furness, wearing a regimental bum-freezer dinner jacket that showed a large and surprisingly girlish bottom for a military man, stepped out of the crowd, eager to claim them.

"Before you get lost," he put a moist hand on Saba's arm, "there are quite a few people I'd like you to meet," and then, as if remembering Mr. Manners, "Girls, well done, you look jolly nice."

Down to the lower terrace where red-faced servants were adding sprigs of rosemary to an open fire on which two whole skinned lambs were roasting. On a long table beside the fire, a feast was laid out: wobbling terrines, jewel-colored salads, a large turkey, a mountain of salmon and prawns. Saba, who had hardly eaten since breakfast, felt her mouth fill with saliva, and then the usual pang of guilt. So much food here, and so little at home, it did feel wicked sometimes.

"Look, look, look!" Arleta's hair had turned to liquid gold in the firelight. She was as excited as a child. She led Saba down another flight of steps to where a swimming pool framed by masses of tiny candles shimmered and shifted like a vast sapphire.

Saba began to search the roaring faces for the famous Mr. Ozan. She'd imagined him to be old and fat and rich and Middle Eastern–looking, but saw no one who matched that description. The faces on the terrace were mainly pale and European.

"Girls, round me." Furness, who seemed slightly plastered, wanted to introduce them to everyone.

"Jolly nice to have some new blood," one of the English wives bellowed, an anxious red face gleaming in the lamplight. "Lots of us have gone, you see."

They were handed from group to group, smiled at, examined closely and asked more or less the same questions: Had they come by sea or air? Were they singers or dancers? Gosh, what fun, how marvelous! What discipline! So necessary, one added, to have treats for the men. Now, did they play any instruments? Yes, Arleta extemporized gaily, she played the xylophone; her friend Saba, she'd given her a pinch here, was a dab hand at the Welsh harp. Some admired their frocks and asked for news of home. A couple said they felt guilty about rationing, but what could one do, no point in starving oneself. Another said that when she'd stepped off the ship in Durban with her banker husband a year or so ago, she'd been bowled over by two things: the stunning brightness of the light, and the food, but now she absolutely longed for gray skies, for rain, for home. It frightened her being separated from her children. Particularly at a time like this.

"Now, now, now!" her husband interrupted. "You know the rules. No war talk on a night like this." He bared his teeth at the girls. "Enjoy it while the going's good, what?"

"You'll probably leave too soon," the woman muttered before she was led away. Most of the wives and families of military personnel had already gone to South Africa or Sudan, somewhere safer than here. Her sensible Home Counties face sweated in the flickering light. She pointed out the young, recently widowed wife of a naval officer who'd somehow slipped through the net and not been evacuated. Awfully brave. The woman was listening, polite and attentive, to an older man who was leaning toward her telling a story. She had a small glass of sherry in her hand.

The moon rose higher, lighting the tips of the pyramids, more stars came out, dazzling the dark velvet of the sky. The girls were handed around and around like delicacies, until eventually the faces on the terrace grew indistinct, and the older officers said, Gosh! Was that really the time? and pressed sticky hot hands into theirs and said how lovely it had been to meet them, and they would be sure to come and see them in concert. But still no sign of Mr. Ozan, and no sign of Mr. Cleeve either. Saba didn't know whether to be disappointed or relieved.

When the old people had gone, the young men loosened their bow ties and took off their dinner jackets. A band started to play some sleepy jazz on a small dance floor fringed with palm trees near the swimming pool.

But no Mr. Ozan. To fill in time, Saba danced with a gaunt young Scottish doctor, who apologized for stepping on her toes. He said he'd been out near Tripoli, operating for six days straight. "It's pretty hairy out there, sorry I'm such a lousy dancer." She was rescued by a group of rowdy Desert Air Force pilots who sank to their knees in front of her and declared undying love.

She was tempted to ask if they knew Dominic but felt she couldn't face being teased about him, or explain a relationship that basically didn't exist, and yet—what an idiot—she'd pictured him earlier on the terrace waiting for her, thinking how lovely she looked in her dress.

She was laughing in a hollow way at herself when suddenly she was aware of a dip in the laughter and the conversation; the band's tune abruptly ending. The partygoers were turned toward a portly man in a startling burgundy-colored dinner jacket, making his stately way down the steps. He was patting arms, he was smiling graciously, and now a small wave at the band that had struck up "For He's a Jolly Good Fellow." As he walked toward the dance floor, Arleta appeared at Saba's side, a gold mermaid in the moonlight.

"One second, darling." She smiled charmingly at the young doctor waiting for another dance. She drew Saba aside.

"Zafer Ozan," she whispered, her eyes mocking and mirthful, "the one I told you about. The stinking-rich one."

Ozan had spotted them; he was looking at them both from across the dance floor.

"Don't you think," Arleta blew him a kiss, "he's rather attractive?" She waved him over.

Saba stared at Ozan and looked away. She saw his teeth flash as he shook the hand of another guest. "Everyone loves him," Arleta said, her blond hair tickling Saba's ear. She was wiggling her fingers at him discreetly like a shy little girl.

"You're a shocking flirt," said Saba.

"I know," said Arleta happily. "And I can assure you he doesn't mind."

As he walked toward them, Arleta said quickly, "Darling, as a treat for him, I'm going to ask the band to play 'Night and Day.' Would you sing it? It's his signature tune."

"Why don't you sing it?" Saba was thoroughly confused now: Had Cleeve arranged for Arleta to sing, too, or was this pure coincidence?

"Come off it, darling. I'm the dancer; you're the one with the voice. Even bloody old Janine says that."

"She does?" Saba was amazed. "She never told me."

"Well of course she hasn't, silly—she's jelly bag. I am, too, but I'm better at hiding it." She play-pinched Saba on the arm. "Hop up now before he meets you."

Saba got onto the small stage. The little band with its piano and tenor saxophone and double bass apparently knew she was coming. They slipped into the music and when the pianist gave her a wink she joined them, nervous at first because of the strangeness of all this and then forgetting because in the end a song was a song and beyond things. She blotted them all out and closed her eyes and sang into the jasmine-scented night. Happiness flowed like golden honey through her veins. This was what she loved; what she was good at.

There was a roar of approval when the song was over. Ozan came to the edge of the stage, stood in front of her and just looked at her. His eyes dark, almost bruised-looking, the flames from the fire reflected in them.

"Do you know other songs?" he said. "Sing one for me, please?"

And knowing this might be her only chance, she launched into a Turkish song, "Fikrimin Ince Gülü," a song her father had once sung and translated for her. *You are always in my heart like a delicate rose; you are in my heart like a happy nightingale.* The audience looked puzzled, but she saw Mr. Ozan's eyes light up, and how the waiters bustling around him glanced at her in surprise. Next—oh how she was enjoying this suddenly, the night, the challenge of it—the band joined her in a verse of "Ozkorini," a famous Arabic song that Umm Kulthum, the greatest Arabic singer of all, sang. *Ozkorini*, her father had once explained, meant think of me. Remember me. The waiters surged toward the stage thrilled and clapping, as Saba sang an extract from a song they recognized.

Saba felt nervous at first stepping in the footsteps of this goddess, but she gave the sobbing lyrics their full worth, and when she'd finished, cries of "Allah!" and *"Ya Hayya!"* came out of the darkness, and her eyes filled with tears. For that moment her father, her hateful, lovable father, was powerfully with her, and yet he would have hated this.

Mr. Ozan said nothing; he looked at her and shook his head.

"It's too noisy to talk here," he said, gesturing toward the crowd. "Tomorrow," he shouted. "I'll see you tomorrow."

The band clapped as he walked away, as if he was the true star of the evening, and then, almost immediately, Captain Furness, who must have been lurking in the undergrowth, jumped onto the stage.

"That was interesting. I didn't expect that," he said into Saba's ear. Although his lips were smiling, his hand on her arm was tourniquet tight. He said he'd taken the liberty of ordering a taxi for them. He advised Arleta in his barking voice to put her shoes back on; there were scorpions that sometimes hid in the cracks of the pavements. Janine said that was quite right, a friend of hers had ended up in hospital with a very nasty bite. There was still no sign of Cleeve.

CHAPTER 12

By the time they got home, the stars were fading and the pale streaks of dawn could be seen over the Nile, an interlude of peace before the insane muddle of daylight in Cairo began.

"Isn't this so often the best time of a party?" Arleta stretched out her legs. "When you take the wampum off and put on your jammys, and stop showing off."

It was four in the morning, and the air was like warm milk. Janine, after doing her fifty splashes, went straight to bed; Arleta and Saba were sitting on their balcony in their pajamas under a cotton sheet.

Down in the alleyway, a donkey croaked; the man who sold fly whisks slept beside it on a raffia mat with a few rags over him.

When Arleta got up to make tea, Saba stayed where she was, her feet still throbbing from the dancing, the music pounding in her veins like a strong drug. She felt the relief a high diver might feel, or a mountain climber, when the scaring thing was done, but "Night and Day" had sounded good, and she hadn't made a complete fool of herself with "Ozkorini," even though she'd suddenly felt shockingly nervous before singing it.

"Bliss." Arleta put a cup of tea and a biscuit in Saba's hand. "Don't they call this *l'heure bleue*?" She'd tied her hair back in an old scarf and changed into a silk kimono. "The time when it's not quite light and not quite dark," she closed her eyes, "when most people die or fall in love.

"Well, you were a big success tonight," she said in the same sleepy voice. "The belle of the ball, or should I say the belly dancer of the balley. Mr. Ozan was very taken."

"Where did you meet him?" Saba said. The moment the question was out of her mouth, she felt awkward; she didn't want to start spying on Arleta, but she was curious.

Arleta yawned. "On my first tour with the Merrybelles; the rules were more relaxed so we were allowed to sing for a couple of nights at his nightclub in Alexandria, the Cheval D'Or. It was fun, and I thought he was very attractive and . . ." She lit a cigarette and flicked the match away. "As I said, we were lovers for a while, but not for long. He'd just got married, I think for the third time."

Her cigarette hadn't lit properly, she groped around for another light, and although Saba was shocked, she couldn't help thinking that Arleta was the least hypocritical woman she'd ever met. She liked sex, she liked men, none of that mealy-mouthed talk about being led on, or letting the stars get in her eyes, no talk of being duped or dumped or feeling guilty. What a revelation!

"I knew it wouldn't last," Arleta ruminated through a plume of smoke. "But it was great fun. I'd just come out of an affair with a real Frigidaire Englishman and it was just what I needed. Also, let's be frank: he's the biggest booker of talent in the Middle East and I want to go on working when the war's over. He's a good contact for you, Saba." Arleta had her professional voice on now. "He loves English girls and he was very taken with all that headless horror stuff you did." Her name for Eastern music.

"But tell me something, darling," Arleta leapt in quickly. "I've been meaning to ask you, have you ever been really in love?" She squeezed Saba's hand briefly. "Don't look so shocked—it's usually the first thing women want to know about each other."

"I'm not sure."

"If you're, um, *not sure*, you definitely haven't been."

"Ah, so, trick question."

"Oh get on with it!" Arleta's voice came like a lazy slap across the night. "Ugh! This tea is vile," she said. "That ghastly buffalo milk always tastes so funny. There's half a bottle of champers in the fridge, Willie put it there—it's a bit flat but better than tea. Come on, and don't be cross—I want to know everything about you. I bet you've had dozens of boyfriends." A barefoot Arleta padded back with two glasses and a bottle in her hand. "You're so pretty."

"I was engaged, but only for a bit," Saba explained. "And that was because my dad approved of him, and thought I should marry him.

His name was Paul Llewellyn. He was in the class above me at school. He was sweet and kind. He wrote poems for me, said we would marry one day. I don't know why I'm talking about him in the past tense. He's still alive, he's in the army, he wants to be a schoolteacher when the war's over. All his family are schoolteachers. He hated me being a singer." She dipped her head, remembering the terrible row. "He liked the eisteddfods and the singing competitions, but when he saw me performing in front of men, well, he went bloody mad. My father hates it, too."

She seemed to be blurting things out suddenly, perhaps the champagne or the late hour.

Arleta tutted and took another sip. "Not bad is it, there are still a few bubbles left—carry on."

"Well, I was doing this show in a factory near Bristol. My first big show really. Lots of men there, but perfectly respectable. I went on stage and sang 'Where or When' and a few of the men did, you know, the wolf whistles and whatever. But it was *so* exciting, Arleta, my first show, and a dressing room even—well, just a little bit curtained off. Paul wanted to come. He sent me flowers, he tried to be happy for me, he'd even hired a car, but when we were driving home, he went absolutely silent, and when I asked him what was the matter, he suddenly shouted," Saba put down her cup and did his voice, " '*You,* you're the matter. You made a real spectacle of yourself tonight.' He said he felt like a twerp sitting there on his own with nothing to do."

"Oh Lordy, what a fibber he sounds. The truth was, he couldn't bear it, nor could your father."

"Bear what?"

"You being the center of attention. Normal male behavior in my experience. So then what?"

"It's different with my father, Arl, it goes so deep with him it hurts, but anyway, this Paul, when he said that, I knew in a flash it wouldn't work. I can't stop doing this." The pain seemed fresh for a moment. "I know it's not what some men want, but I've got to do it. I told him to stop the car, and I got out." And she had. They'd been a mile or so from home, and she'd run back past the canal, down to the docks, sobbing her heart out. Her mother had been waiting at the lit door, dying to hear how it had all gone, and one of the worst things about it all was showing up like that all tear-stained and with the new dress Mum had spent hours on splattered with mud. It was like murdering two dreams at once. Her mother had listened, frozen-faced, then sent her to bed and she'd lain there awake most of the night, her heart filled with a feeling of dreary darkness, a foreboding she couldn't name.

"The next morning, I posted his engagement ring back. Paul said I was being dramatic, but I knew it couldn't work. My family haven't forgiven me either. He was suitable and he was—"

"Oh Christ!" Arleta interrupted with some violence. "*Suitable.*"

Saba could still see his face all twisted and wet. She'd felt so bad and so bloody determined at the same time, but she wanted to stop her story now.

"Are you a virgin?" There was nothing prurient about Arleta's question; it was a straightforward inquiry.

"No."

"I think it's very overrated," Arleta said, taking a swig of her champagne.

Saba silently agreed with her. She had lost her virginity in Paul's bedroom in Cardiff. His parents were away for the weekend visiting relatives in Tonypandy. He'd turned down the sheets of his narrow boyhood bed and kept his pajama bottoms on until the lights were out, and it had happened surrounded by his school pictures and hockey sticks, and afterward she'd felt calmer and freer. It was something she'd worried about a great deal, and now she didn't have to. In the middle of that night, safely back in her own bed, she'd woken feeling a little wicked (God knows what her father would have said) but mostly happy, as if a great weight had been lifted from her mind.

"Unless of course," Arleta stared thoughtfully into her glass, "you get PWL."

"PWL?"

"Pregnant without leave. It happened to a girl in the Merrybelles on my last tour, and she was sent back home immediately with no pay. The hypocrisy was appalling, the brass hats swooning away like virgins themselves when half the men here have the clap."

"What about you?" Saba said. "Are you in love?"

"Oh, plenty of time for that later." Arleta's voice was a little slurred.

"No, play fair." Saba took a sip of champagne. "Off you go."

"Well . . ." Arleta didn't seem to know where to begin. "The answer is no," she said after a pause, "but there is someone—a submariner, Bill, in the navy. I have no idea at all where he is now. He bought me this." She jangled her charm bracelet. "He's got no money.

"I'm in a bit of a bind about it actually." Arleta had gone unusually still. "We got carried away on my last night in England, because he was terribly frightened about going away and getting killed, and now he thinks we're going to get married. I've been a bit of a coward with this one. . . . He's very sweet, though," she added with a wan smile. "I'm not very good at breaking things off . . . hopeless actually."

"So, not the mink buyer?" The indiscreet question slipped out, but Arleta had surprised her. She'd imagined a string of rich admirers.

"No, no, no, no, no." Saba heard the clink of her glass and another sip. "Another admirer altogether—he's got pots of it. The thing about Bill is he made me laugh, or did, but so much has happened since then, I can hardly remember him." She stopped suddenly and laid her head on Saba's shoulder.

"Isn't that awful? Awful but true." She sighed. "I'd better show you the love of my life." She went into their bedroom, and came back with a small, creased plastic folder that she thrust into Saba's hand. Inside it was a polyphoto of a small boy with sleepy blue eyes and blond curls. He had Arleta's curved humorous mouth and was roaring with laughter. "His name is George, he's three, and as far as ENSA knows, he doesn't exist."

"Arlie!" Saba, shocked, took the photograph. "You must miss him horribly."

"I do, I do—can't bear to think about him actually." Arleta took the photo and gazed at him deeply. "He lives with my mum at the moment, in Kent. I'm saving all my money for him. Don't tell anyone, will you?

"Don't forget to have a baby, Sabs," she offered suddenly. "People are so busy telling you how much it hurts, and how hard and ghastly it is, that they forget to tell you how much fun it is, too. I have such a laugh with George—he's so noisy and cheeky and opinionated, he's got the dirtiest laugh. I'll tell you more about him later if you like." Her face was completely lit up. "Not that I want to bore you," she added hopefully.

"He's gorgeous, Arlie, and I want to hear all about him," said Saba. She surprised herself by adding. "You're lucky," and meaning it. Normally speaking, she found people being soppy about their children boring, all that talk about its little fingers and funny little ways, but in this impermanent world, having a baby seemed quite a wonderful thing, an act of bravery in itself.

"Yes, I am lucky," Arleta agreed. "As long as I can keep a roof over that little varmint's head, I'll feel proud of myself, and so far, I have . . . because what I . . ." Her voice was drifting, and trailing; sleep was creeping up on her at last. "What I . . . one day . . ." but she'd already gone to sleep.

Janine woke them at nine o'clock the next morning. She stood, feet in third position, the perfect arc of her eyebrows raised in the direction of their empty bottle, the overflowing ashtrays, their smudged mascara, and, worst sin of all, the fact that they'd slept in their makeup. She tapped her feet rhythmically until they opened their eyes.

"Sorry to be the bearer of bad tidings," she said, although a small twitch seemed to have developed in her lip, "but we're leaving for the desert tomorrow. Max Bagley came around earlier in an absolute fury because you were so late to bed. I hope I heard this wrong, but I think he said something about sending you both home. He'll be back in an hour."

CHAPTER 13

Ignore the stupid cow," Arleta said when Janine, having dropped her bombshell, waddled off in her feet-splayed ballet-dancer way. "There's one in every company—in the Merrybelles we called them the EMS: the Envy, Malice, and Spites—and it's written all over her. It's probably because she wasn't asked to do one of her special dances last night."

But Janine hadn't made the story up. At eleven thirty, a muffled male voice came through the door. "Are you decent, girls?"

"Oh damn it to buggeration." Arleta, who'd run out of Tahitian Sunset was standing in her silk kimono with half a bottle of peroxide on her head. "Wait! Wait! Wait!" she shouted as the knocking grew louder.

She wrapped her hair in a turban and opened the door.

"Mr. Bagley!" She switched her professional smile on. "What a lovely treat, but why so early?"

His linen suit was rumpled; he looked as if he hadn't slept.

"Cut the flannel, Arleta," he said, curtly. "I'm furious with both of you, but no time to talk now. All Cairo concerts canceled. I've been up most of the night making the new arrangements. We leave tomorrow."

"Oh for God's sake!" Arleta tugged at her turban. "Darling, do give me a second, I've absolutely got to wash this stuff off."

"I haven't got a second." Bagley's eyes were bulging, he was breathing like a train. "I must dash round and tell the others."

"Why are they moving us so fast?" Janine walked in, her face shining with cold cream.

"I think they think the Germans are coming. Yet again." Bagley smiled unpleasantly.

"Well, I've got my panic bag packed." She shot the girls a triumphant look. "You see, I knew this would happen."

Janine's panic bag, as she was fond of telling them, held her emergency tutus, her pajamas, her medical supplies, toothbrush, makeup, and gut reviver. Arleta had tried to pull her leg when she'd first heard about the gut reviver. "It's for tennis racquets, but it prolongs the life of my ballet shoes," Janine had told her without the trace of a smile.

"Yes, I think panic bags are a good idea," said Bagley quietly. "Leave anything inessential at the ENSA offices. With any luck we'll be back soon, or so they tell me."

"So you'll be traveling with us? Definitely?" Janine stared at him like a child about to be separated from its cuddly toy.

"Yep, I'll be there; Captain Furness will be pulling our strings from Cairo. Now, if you'll excuse me," he turned on his heel, "I've got a mass of things to do. Saba, put your shoes on and come with me. I need to have a word with you in private.

"She'll be back in about an hour and a half," he informed the others. "Pack up the flat while she's gone."

"What in hell were you up to last night?" Bagley exploded as soon as they were alone in the car together. He was driving erratically, one hand on the wheel, the other clenched. "Who asked *you* to get up and sing? Who asked you to sing in Arabic, for God's sake? For all I know, you could have been singing 'Eskimo Nell.' I really should send you home immediately, the *cheek* of you." When he turned and looked at her, his face was so contorted with rage she thought he might strike her.

Saba was thunderstruck. She'd assumed Cleeve would warn him, but now, what to say in her defense?

She heard herself mumble, "I'm sorry, it was only a bit of fun."

"A bit of fun." Bagley roared the engine and drove wildly for a while in and out of the traffic. "Do you have any idea, Saba, how stupid that sounds? This could not be a more sensitive time." He spat the words out one at a time.

"I know."

"No you don't. No," he gunned the engine again, "of course you don't. You don't think because your head is up your . . . because you have an ostrich mentality. You don't see that the brass hats think of us most of the time as a bloody nuisance because we can't follow orders, or that last night, after you'd had your *bit of fun*, I got hauled over the coals by Captain Furness."

"I'm sorry," she said. "I really am." Inwardly raging at the unfairness of this.

"The other thing is"—he pulled the car over to the side of the road, almost knocking over an old man selling watermelon juice; he turned off the ignition and jerked on the brake—"and perhaps more importantly, well at least to me, you *weren't very good*."

Ouch, that hurt.

"The band seemed to like it."

"Shut up," he shouted. "What the hell does it matter what the band likes? You probably thought you were marvelous, but you weren't. And that matters to me. My reputation is on the line."

She could hear herself breathing shallowly; he was attacking her, and not for the first time.

Two days before, they'd had, at his request, a private session together, ostensibly to choose new songs, and it had not gone well. She'd sung, "The Man That Got Away" for him without accompaniment, and halfway through, he'd held his hand up to stop her.

"No, no, no, no, that's hopeless," he'd said at last. "And I'm going to tell you exactly why—will you mind that?" He'd pulled her around so that she stood right in front of him.

"Of course not," she said, feeling completely exposed.

He'd lit a cigarette, removed a piece of tobacco from his tongue, and looked at her again.

"You're a good-looking girl," he said, exhaling smoke. "Men find you attractive. You could stand up there and wiggle your shoulders and flash your smile and sing in tune—and there is no question that because your natural voice is good, you will, for most known purposes, thrill them to bits. But the problem for me is I'm not getting *you*. Not yet."

"What do you mean, you're not getting me?" She wanted to smack him round the chops but was determined to remain calm. How dare he manhandle her like that?

"Don't get me wrong," his kindness almost more upsetting. "Your voice is warm in tone, and sometimes you're brave in your delivery—the image I get is of a child flinging herself off a rock into the sea—but at the moment, I only get that girl in flashes." He sighed, ignoring the tears that had started their maddening descent. "It's potent stuff when I get that: for example, yesterday, when you sang 'Deep Purple,' the hairs stood up on the back of my neck. But then you did 'St Louis Blues' like some weary old black lady that's got to pick a bale of cotton before she goes to bed, and that's when I feel I'm getting Saba doing a pretty good imitation of Bessie Smith; you used all her intonations and phrasings, and why not, she's brilliant. But that's lazy stuff, and at some point you have to ask yourself: Do I want to be a second-rate imitation of Bessie Smith, or Helen Forrest or whoever is your idol, or do I want to be me?"

Her anger died and she felt instantly shamed; what he said was partly true. She'd learned her jazz standards from the records of the people who sang them: she'd breathed when they breathed, asked her accompanists to play the tunes as close to their arrangements as possible. Was it laziness or insecurity that had made her swallow their magic whole? She'd never really questioned this before, nor for that matter had anybody else.

And the most painful part was that although she didn't like Bagley, she held him in high esteem—they all did. The cast had nicknamed him BG for Boy Genius, and she'd seen in rehearsal the lightning speed with which he transcribed music into different keys, or picked up a harmony and sang with you. How he could make up lyrics on the spot. When he'd talked about finding her special songs to sing her spirits had soared, thinking she could learn from him, but now she saw she had desperately disappointed him in every way.

It took her a while to realize that he had been driving her around in a circle for the purposes of this rocket. Outside on the streets, she saw more soldiers and airmen than she had before, and it seemed to her that the sky was darker than usual although she could not be sure.

"Please don't send me home," she said. "I couldn't bear it now, not without doing a proper concert." Going home now would feel like one of the biggest defeats of her life.

"I can't," he said grimly. "No replacement, but do that again and you'll be on that plane so fast you won't know what's hit you. Understand?"

He slipped his hand suddenly down her brassiere and squeezed her breast hard.

"*Understand?*"

"What are you doing?" She leapt away, her face scarlet.

"Nothing," he said coldly. "What did you think I was doing?"

"Something," she said, glaring at him. "Do that again, and I'll deck you one."

He dipped his head and gave her a blank look, as if she was speaking some obscure foreign language.

"Oh dearie me!" he muttered. "Don't we take ourself seriously."

"Not really," she spat out, "but I don't like that."

"Well, there is something else you might like to know," he continued smoothly, as if absolutely nothing had taken place. "A probably more important thing," he said with a sarcastic smile. "From now on, we'll be going to some very dangerous places. Last week one of the ENSA groups at a hospital camp near Alex was bombed very badly. A shocking do, blood and bodies everywhere. It hasn't been on the news yet, but you'll soon hear. So the party is well and truly over. Got that?"

"Got that. Why didn't you tell us?"

"I didn't want to frighten you. You can still go home if you want to."

"I can't," she said. "I don't want to."

"Well done," he said. He was gazing at her intently, and then lifting her hand from the car seat, he kissed it and gave her a very strange look indeed.

"I'm sorry," he said. "Are we friends again?"

She said an almost inaudible yes without meaning it, feeling compromised and miserable and disliking his rather patronizing smirk but not knowing what else to say. She was going to have to watch him now.

Next they drove to the ENSA offices at Sharia Kasr-el-Nil, Bagley told her to stay in the car while he dashed upstairs to talk to Furness about a portable stage.

A few moments later, an NCO clattered down the stairs with the car keys in his hand.

"Mr. Bagley says they've had a message from radio ops. I'm to take you over to Port Said Street."

Cleeve's address.

"Are you sure that's right?" She was terrified now of doing anything without Bagley's permission.

"It's written down here, miss." The NCO showed her the official form. "And then you're to go straight back to your quarters and pack—you're leaving Cairo at sixteen hundred hours tomorrow."

"Relax, Saba," Cleeve said, when she told him this. They were in a small, anonymous cafe two blocks from his apartment. It was empty apart from them. "I know your itinerary, and we have time for coffee, ice cream, and a chat. Cheer up, old bean," he handed her one of the cones, "it may never happen."

"It almost did," she said. "Max Bagley heard me singing last night at the Mena House. He's livid. I thought you said you were going to tell him. Listen, I didn't order this, I don't want it, you eat it."

He licked one of the glistening scoops.

"Yum, yum," he said. "You should try this mastika one—it has a kind of raisiny, liqueury flavor and is much better than the strawberry one. Quite sure I can't tempt you?"

When she didn't answer, he said, "Saba. Listen. Bagley will be dealt with, and you were marvelous last night—you did so well." He tapped his ice cream spoon against her arm. "Ozan's sure to book you."

She gave him a watery smile. "Really?"

"Really. I mean, my Arabic is not perfect, but you looked and sounded so right. The dress, too . . . absolute perfection."

"I like singing those songs," she told him humbly. "They remind me of home." Battered after her horrible morning with Bagley, she was soaking up his compliments like a thirsty plant.

"I didn't see you there," she said suddenly.

"I didn't want you to," he said quietly. "And I didn't expect Max to be there either, so sorry about that. Did you say anything to him?"

"You told me not to."

"Good," he said quietly. "Next time we ask you to do something, we'll clear it with him, but don't forget, as far as he's concerned, I'm only the broadcast man.

"You're very special, young lady," he added randomly.

She could see through the cafe window the NCO walking toward them.

"You'll be off to the Canal Zone soon, and then touring," Cleeve said quickly—he'd seen him, too. "But I have a small job for you before you go."

"How do you know where we're going? We haven't been told."

"I know." He licked a smear of ice cream from his lips; drained the rest of his coffee. "I'll be in contact again, maybe in a week."

"How?"

"I'll do a broadcast. Some of the troops in Ismailia have been badly neglected. It won't ruffle any feathers whatsoever."

The NCO got out of the car and folded his arms.

"He's waiting for me," Saba said.

"Before you go," he said softly, "one last question."

"What?"

"Do you have a boyfriend?"

"No."

"Good. Safer for everyone. If you get one, be careful what you write to him."

"I will." Her heart began to hammer in her chest, as if it knew something she didn't.

"And the best of British, out in the desert." Cleeve's hand was moist with sweat as he shook hers. "It will be an experience you will never forget."

Willie was practicing his fez routine in his room at the YMCA when he saw the first flutterings of charred black paper go past his window.

A drunken soldier had warned him, two nights before, in the Delta Bar, that the burning of official papers at the British embassy would be the first sign that the Germans were coming. And so, it had come. He felt both calm and brave as he took off his fez, sat on the bed and put his shoes on. His first thought was for Arleta—he'd loved her for so long, and now he must get his fat old carcass across town and rescue her and the other girls.

It was hard to find a taxi, so he shuffled and wheezed the three blocks toward the girls' digs. He toiled his way up the dark and narrow staircase, bent double near the bathroom on the first floor to get his breath back.

Janine opened the door.

"Are you gels all right?" he gasped. Three buttons of his pajama top had come undone, and the sweating mound of his stomach poked through.

"Fine," Janine regarded him with some distaste, "but desperately busy. We're all leaving tomorrow—Saba's on her way back now."

He sat down heavily in a wicker chair.

"I know," he said, "but take a look at this." He hauled himself out of the chair and opened their shutters. The air outside was smoky and full of charred bits of paper.

"Oh good God." Janine's shoulders had collapsed. "What on earth . . . ?" She started to cough delicately.

Arleta appeared from the bathroom, damp and delicious in a silk nightie.

"What's up?"

Willie led her by the hand to the window. The burned papers fluttered on down. Janine slammed the shutters. "Don't let them see any light," she said.

"What is it, pet?" When Arleta squeezed the old man's hand, his heart swelled with protective love for her.

"The situation is as follows." Fear made Willie maddeningly slow and inarticulate. "I was having this drink the other night with a squaddie I met . . . not the Grenadier but the other one . . . Do you know the place on . . . Oh damn, what is it? . . . Oh yes, Soliman Pasha Square. Anyway, I was having a beer with this fellow from . . . it was either the Royal Scots Guards or the—"

"Darling, could you put this in a slightly smaller nutshell?" Arleta asked tugging at her turban. "We don't need to know every little thing." When she stroked the back of his head he almost sank into her arms.

"Well," Willie's old eyes were milky and unfocused, "he said they was burning all the official papers at the embassy; that all the other civilians left town last week and that it's a bloody disgrace they've left us here. The three other groups have gone to Alexandria." The words at last came out in a spurt.

"Oh blast it to buggeration!" Arleta grabbed her turban and ran out of the room.

"She's taken it hard, love her," said Willie as the door slammed. "We can't just crack up at the first thing. Our job," a sterner version of himself emerged out of the mists, "is to keep calm and carry on."

"She's had trouble with her hair dye. The first lot didn't work," said Janine. Muffled shouts from the bathroom from Arleta.

"Oh God." Willie, who'd had a difficult wife, understood the significance of this. He hauled himself to his feet. "I'll leave you ladies to it then." He said he was going home to pack, had been told that they were to stay put until transport was organized. "I don't care what it is at the moment," he said with a wheezy laugh. "A sidecar across the desert would do me fine at the moment."

After he'd gone, Arleta appeared, her hair a pale green color.

"Well it's a disaster," she said. "I can't imagine what I was thinking about doing it twice."

"The Germans coming, maybe." Janine's voice was low and bitterly sarcastic. "I wonder if that felt *slightly* more important than your hair."

The shimmering silence in the room was like the still before an electrical storm, and then she added breezily, "Even if it does fall out, which of course, *dear,* I very much hope it doesn't."

Arleta had warned them in advance about her terrible temper. Janine's fake concern fell like a lit match on a well-laid fire.

"I'm sorry? What did you say?" Arleta's green eyes widened and narrowed. She appeared to be listening very intently.

"I said, I very much hope it doesn't fall out," quavered Janine.

Arleta stepped forward, and pointed her index finger squarely at Janine's forehead. "You," she said, "are a stupid, stupid cow, and I'm sick of your whining, and all that splashing in the bathroom, and your twirly bits," she spun around on the floor, "and I'm sick of the bloody Germans, too: they stopped me having a wonderful run in Southend in *Puss in Boots,* they completely buggered up my run with the Follies at the Palladium. They're taking me away from Cairo, and they're about to make me blasted well bald."

"I had a career, too," Janine screeched. "I was learning ballet from the age of three, I practically bankrupted my family, I was about to join Sadler's Wells, and anyway, don't exaggerate, stupid woman yourself!" Her face was contorted with malice. "It's only gone a bit green."

When Saba burst into the room, their lips were furled, their color high, and Arleta was screaming. It was almost funny, except the palm of Arleta's hand was open and she was balancing herself on the balls of her feet as if about to give Janine a perfectly timed forehand drive to the head.

Saba stepped between them.

"Hey! Hey, hey, hey! Stop! Stop, stop! Calm down. Your hair is fine, stop it!"

"Don't you dare say stop it." Janine's pale face was a map of bulging veins. "The city is on fire, the Germans are coming."

"The city isn't on fire," said Saba. "I've just driven through it, and I didn't see any Germans. I'm sure it's all right." When she went to the window and opened the shutters, it was a bit of a shock to see the sky full of floating gray paper, the light beyond it coppery and shimmering.

They heard the boom, boom, boom of shoes on the stairs, stiffened in terror as the doorknob turned and sagged with relief as the door burst open. It was Bagley. He was agitated and had a piece of burned paper stuck to his forehead.

"Panic over, girls," he said. "No Germans. There was an explosion at the paper factory near the Muski that frightened everyone to death, but our orders are the same. The embassy are very jumpy, things are on the move, they want us out as quickly as possible. The lorry will pick you up tomorrow afternoon.

"And so, our work begins." Bagley seemed to be relishing his own Richard the Third moment. He looked at Arleta and Janine, who were standing as far away from each other as possible. "The most important thing for us now is to work as a team." He looked searchingly at each one of them. "Pack your bags, girls, check your papers are in order, don't leave any portable props behind, and the best of British luck to all of you. Knock 'em dead."

CHAPTER 14

Telling his mother he was going to North Africa was awful. He'd kept the secret for days, feeling ghostlike and fraudulent in his boyhood home, as if he was a bad understudy pretending to be a son. What made it worse was she'd been so very happy and lit up at having her boy, not only home but at a loose end for once. She'd cooked all his favorite meals, they'd gone through the family albums together. One night she'd even consented to play the piano for him: Joplin and Liszt and a faltering Chopin etude that had wrung his heart and made her wince with frustration. "I used to know this so well."

She was standing in the hall when he told her. She was wearing her dog-walking coat. Bonny, their old Labrador, was on a lead. He said the good news first, that there was the possibility that he would soon be promoted to flying officer, and then she listened quietly and obediently to the rest—that he was about to join a wing of the Desert Air Force in North Africa. Their camp was in the desert midway between Cairo and Alexandria. An amalgamated squadron full of Aussies and South Africans and Brits. They'd mostly be flying escort to medium bombers and attacking enemy airfields.

"They're very short out there at the moment, Ma," he told her. "And I'll be learning to fly Kittyhawks. I've never done that before." All true; there was never any point in lying to her; she was an intelligent woman, an avid newspaper reader. "They're quite busy there, too." He saw her eyes widen. "There's a push planned."

She bent down and stroked Bonny's ears. "I thought you might be off soon," she said.

She'd heard his complaints in the last few months about how quiet things were at his new station, an Operational Training Unit at Aston Down. They did nothing but training runs there now, and putting your life in the hands of a windy or reckless new pilot was hair-raising—every bit as dangerous as being in combat. That's what he said. It was partly true.

Bonny started to whine. Time for his walk, she said. He watched from the window as she headed briskly toward the woods. She was thinner than he remembered her—almost childlike in the gumboots she'd worn in case the weather changed.

She was gone longer than usual. Her eyes were red and swollen when she came back. She went upstairs to her bedroom and came out before supper with fresh lipstick on and wearing a pretty frock.

They met on the stairs.

"*Such* a lovely night," she said, as if nothing had passed between them. "I think we should eat on the terrace." Much to the relief of the local farmers, who were haymaking, the rain that had threatened all day had not fallen. The sky above the Severn estuary had burst into a recklessly beautiful sunset.

"That sounds wonderful, Ma," he said. "Thank you," as if she had magically procured the night.

"I can't say it yet," he heard her throat click as she touched his face, "but I am proud of you." Her own father had died of a sudden heart-attack, aged thirty-six. "I really am. It may take a little while to show it."

"Nothing to be proud of," he muttered, and meant it.

In the kitchen, he helped her mash the potatoes. She gave him a tray of cutlery and plates and told him to set the table on the terrace.

"For two or for three?" he asked out of habit, although he usually knew the answer.

"Well, set for him but don't expect him." She stood in a cloud of steam checking the spinach.

It was warm out on the terrace, where she'd lit a candle. The air was full of the peanutty smell of cut grass. In the far field they could see the bobbing light of a tractor working its way up and down the field, anxious to get the hay in before the weather changed.

They were eating her wonderful game stew when they heard the sound of his father's little Austin spraying gravel in the drive. He'd put the bigger car, the Rover, up on blocks in the stable; it was too heavy on petrol.

"He knows your news," his mother said quickly. "I told him earlier, but please don't talk about it before we eat." Her face haggard in the candlelight, working against tears.

His father stood for a moment under the porch light, gaunt in his dark hat and dark suit. There was a bulging briefcase in his hand.

"Honestly, *men.*" His mother stood up in a sudden fury. "Why do they always come late?"

She went into the kitchen, leaving her own stew to go cold.

"So, old chap," his father said, giving him an awkward pat on the shoulder. "Off again, I hear. North Africa, is it?"

"Yes," Dom said. "I—"

"Frank, what have you been up to? Let's hear something about you for a change." His mother came charging back with the plates; the air volatile around her. Her old dog jumped as she banged the tray down, and glanced anxiously at his mistress and then at Frank.

"I'm hungry, dear one," his father said in a strained voice. "So perhaps you'll allow me to take my hat off and eat first? I've been operating since nine o'clock this morning."

His mother took a deep jagged breath; she sat on the edge of her chair, her meal untouched, her eyes staring. When Dom saw his father squeeze her hand under the table, he felt both relieved and guilty. The baton must be handed on. He'd taken on the role of her protector for too long, and there wasn't enough left of him now, but still it was sad to see tears held in check all day roll down her cheeks, and to see her brush them away like an angry little girl.

For dessert they had the stewed damsons she'd bottled the year before, followed by the real coffee his father had been given by a grateful patient. She'd gathered herself up again, and although it was a brittle performance, he admired the way she talked about the weather, about plums, about a lovely concert she'd heard on the radio, as if she hadn't a care in the world. His father sat silently, picking his teeth discreetly with a toothpick. At ten o'clock, looking half dead with tiredness, he retired to bed.

"He's a good man, you know," she said when the light went on in the upstairs bathroom and they could hear the gurgling of water as he cleaned his teeth. "It was his single-mindedness I most admired when we first met." She lit a cigarette, and looked Dom squarely in the eyes. "I can hardly blame him for that now, can I?"

The most she'd ever said to him about her marriage.

They watched the tractor's wavering light go down the track toward Simpson's farm next door and stayed at the table on the terrace and talked until their clothes were damp with dew and the light had all but faded from the day.

When the candle wavered and guttered, she pinched it between her fingers and it was then he felt the urge to confide in her. They hadn't done well on this score before, both of them performing some semblance of what the other wanted, but not really laughing or talking or letting their hair down.

"I have another reason for going to North Africa," he told her shyly. "Well . . . maybe. At least I hope I do. It's partly ridiculous."

"Hang on."

She went inside and got a rug. She huddled inside it listening intently.

"I've grown up an awful lot in the last two years, Ma," he told her, making her smile—as if she didn't know! "I think I was a conceited ass before. I took so much for granted, you, this," he lifted his glass toward the house, dark now the light in the bathroom had gone out, "Cambridge, my friends." When he stopped suddenly, she grasped his hand.

"Tell me about it," she said. "If it would help. You must tell someone."

"No! No, no." He shook his head. "I don't want to. I'm not talking about that."

He felt the thumping in his heart, and wanted to stop already—why not accept the soul's loneliness and get on with it. Why bother the poor woman?

"Please, Dom. Sorry." She touched his hand tentatively and then took hers away.

He downed his whiskey.

"I'm talking about someone else . . . I . . . Look, it's not important."

He was about to tell her about Saba's singing, but it suddenly felt ridiculous, because there was nothing now to tell, he would sound like a lovelorn loon.

"What happened to Annabel?" she said, in a brave spurt. "I thought she was such a darling girl." Her face was tense; she'd been steeling herself for this.

"Nothing."

"But it can't have been nothing—she was mad about you."

"I told you before, Mother, she didn't like the hospital; she said it was nothing personal. I don't blame her."

"Well I do." Her face tightened like a fist. "I think it was perfectly bloody of her. Darling, sorry, I know you hate this, but you look so good again." His poor mother, terrified of him, miserable and shrunken in the twilight, huddled in her rug. "Couldn't you try again. Write to her or have her down for a few days?"

"No," he said. "Absolutely not."

"Why not?"

"Because I don't want it."

A silence fell between them, rigid and dark with unsaid things, and he wondered, as he had many times in hospital, how much honesty it was kind to burden your parents with.

"There was someone . . . a girl in hospital," he blurted out. "It will probably sound completely ridiculous . . . but I felt for her." As soon as he started he regretted it.

"No!" She turned to him, her eyes shining. "No! Not ridiculous at all." She took a tremulous breath. "Who was she?"

"She came to sing for us."

"Any good?" His mother had her sharp professional face on.

"Yes."

She gave him the strangest look.

"I'm happy for you," she said at last, "because I . . ." When she swallowed hard, he thought, I've never seen her cry before, how odd that today it should happen twice.

"Because I . . . think . . . I sort of know that . . . well, I think that everyone should die knowing they've had one great passion."

"Mother . . ." He wanted to stop her right there. She was jinxing him; stepping into his dream.

"It may sound silly and schoolgirlish, but I believe it. It gives you a tremendous confidence, a sense that you haven't been cheated even if it does go wrong, and you mustn't let anyone talk you out of it," she added fiercely. "If you get it wrong, at least it's your mistake."

She'd squeezed his hand so hard, he'd felt some great secret iced up inside her, and hoped profoundly that she wouldn't tell him what it was. He knew her well enough to know she would regret it later.

"It's nothing yet," he muttered to himself.

"Is she really good?" she asked again. "As a singer, I mean."

He smiled sardonically to himself at the sharpness of her tone. She liked people with a center to them, and had treated one or two of the pretty girls he'd brought home before Annabel not exactly coldly, but with a certain drawing aside of skirts that had infuriated him at the time.

"She's very good," he couldn't stop himself. "It's so impressive."

"Well now listen!" she warned. "Don't get all foolish and romantic about her. If she's like that, her life will be as important as yours. You will have to understand this and it will be very, very hard for you. I'm afraid you're rather used to being the center of attention yourself."

"Oh thanks, Ma," he mocked her. "A fascinating bighead, is that it? Anyway, I like her passion. I'm not frightened of it." It was too late now, an act of cruelty almost, to tell his mother about how badly that first and last date had ended.

And looking at her son, Alys Benson had a piercing sense of how much war had already taken from him: his youth, his two best friends. She told herself to remember him like this, tonight, his dark hair wet with dew, his eyes so bright.

"Anyway," he helped himself to one of her cigarettes and lit it, "North Africa is where everything's happening at the moment, and I'm," he shook his head, "I'm a fighter boy now." He bunched his fists and struck a Tarzan pose—her silly schoolboy again. "And we're not getting enough of it at the moment. I can't stay doing nothing forever. It will drive me mad."

"I can imagine," she'd said, thinking, *I hate flying, I wish your father had never told you about it.*

And he thought, *No, you can't.* Only another fighter pilot could know how shockingly addictive the whole thing was. It was the way he formed friendships with other men far deeper than anything he'd ever experienced before; the way he frightened himself, defined himself as a man. Could any woman possibly understand this? He had no way of knowing, although he'd thought about it recently in connection with Saba. He'd written one more letter to her but heard nothing back. With her, he would have to fly blind.

CHAPTER 15

As the morning progressed, Arleta's hair grew greener and her mood darkened until it was positively dangerous and it was imperative to get her to the hairdresser's before they left town.

Willie, desperate to help, had dashed over to Cicurel's, the so-called Harrods of Cairo, to see if they stocked Tahitian Sunset, or, failing that, any other cure for green hair, and drawn a blank with the smart French woman who ran their cosmetic department. He'd fared no better with the snooty, heavily powdered English girl behind the makeup counter at Chemla's, another fancy emporium, who told him in a fake Home Counties drawl it was madness to try and dye your own hair, particularly out here. In desperation he ran back to the barber's shop in the bazaar and came back with a pot of black goo that the proprietor highly recommended, and which Arleta looked at dubiously, particularly when she learned its source. When she snapped, "He sounds like the same idiot that sold me this," Willie slunk off to the corner like a dog that had been badly beaten but still longed to please.

Then Arleta had a brainwave. Why on earth hadn't she thought of it before?

Scrabbling through her knapsack, she said a friend of hers on the last Cairo tour with the Merrybelles had highly recommended a hairdressing shop on Sharia Kasr-el-Nil, not far from the office. Where in the hell was it? She thumbed through her address book; here it was: The Salon Vogue, number 37, proprietor Mitzie Duhring.

"Go with her," Willie softly pleaded with Saba. "I'd offer, but she'd bite my head off. You could have your own done there."

Saba needed no persuading. She felt sorry for Arleta, who suddenly seemed so vulnerable, and besides, her own hair had grown remarkably in the heat and had had no attention since her last cut at

Pam's of Pomeroy Street. Willie said there was plenty of time between now and leaving.

An hour and ten minutes later, they both sat wrapped in towels, sipping tea in a discreetly furnished, softly lit salon that felt like a private sitting room. The owner of the salon, a severely dressed, quietly spoken woman, more doctor than hairdresser, unwrapped Arleta's turban and was closely examining the damage. She rubbed the hair between her fingers; as she held it for inspection under the light she murmured in a guttural voice, "*Gott in Himmel,* good God! What have they done to you?"

Saba and Arleta glanced quickly at each other. She couldn't be . . . surely not—even in the topsy-turvy world of Cairo. But her name was Mitzie Duhring, which sounded pretty German. Saba's heart started to pound. If she told Cleeve about this so early in her employment, he might think her ridiculous, like an overeager schoolgirl on her first day at school pumping her hand in the air. But surely she should say something.

In a silence conspicuously lacking in the usual *Going anywhere nice tonight?* and *Where have you come from?* Mitzie ordered her assistant to wash Arleta's hair thoroughly four times. Next, she silently cut Saba's hair—her efficient, bony hands winking with diamonds, her face in partial shadow in the mirror.

Saba, pretending to read an old copy of *Vogue,* watched her carefully when it was safe to do so. She estimated that if she left the salon by four o'clock, there would be time to get a taxi to Cleeve's and be back at the flat to get her packing done.

Arleta, visibly relaxing in Madame Duhring's calmly professional hands, winked at Saba when she caught her eye. She was in the middle of telling Saba that Mitzie had just told her she could so easily have gone bald again, just like in Malta, when a small brass bell over the salon door jingled, and a stunning young Egyptian woman walked in—pale-complexioned, with almond-shaped eyes and dressed in high heels, silk stockings, and a beautifully tailored blue silk suit. The two long braids that hung to her waist swung as she walked and so did her hips, giving the impression of a knowing and provocative schoolgirl.

The assistant, who was washing Arleta's hair, let out a gasp when she saw her. This was someone of importance. She excused herself, rinsed her hands, and ushered the highly scented stranger to the chair beside Saba's.

Saba watched Mitzie's reflection in the glass. She heard her greet the woman, first in French then in English. The braids were released, the thick black hair combed and discussed with the same muted seriousness with which Arleta's problems had been addressed. Five minutes later, the woman sat down again—her hair wet and wound in a turban. When Saba caught her eye in the mirror, the exotic stranger smiled at her.

"Do you mind if I smoke?" she asked. She took out a mother-of-pearl cigarette holder.

"Not one bit." Saba pushed the ashtray toward her.

Sabas ears were on stalks as the assistant wound the woman's hair into an elaborate series of pin curls. Mitzie addressed the woman formally as Madame Hekmet. When she complimented her on how well her skin was looking, the woman dimpled prettily and said she had her own mother to thank for that. She had been very fussy with her ever since she was a child. Lots of fresh vegetables and fruit and nuts and seeds. "And of course the dancing helps," she added. "It keeps me healthy."

So Egyptian. A dancer. A successful one, judging by the impeccable handbag, the pale suede shoes. Saba wondered if she was a belly dancer—the ones Willie called "gippy tummies."

Mitzie was combing out the woman's heavy cloud of hair now—it came almost to her waist.

"So, cut it all off?" Mitzie smiled at what was obviously an old joke between them.

"We'll keep it for now." The woman's voice was husky and self-satisfied. "I'm giving a party, for some of your people."

Mitzie's scissors stopped snipping.

"Ah." She raised her eyebrows and glanced quickly at Saba.

The dancer looked older in her turban and with her hair scraped back. She moved her finger along her eyebrow. "So, I want something special."

"One second."

Mitzie walked over to Saba, and with an automatic smile, tested the dryness of her hair with a finger; she put her under a hair dryer, and flicked the switch.

Saba, inside its deafening hum, wondered if her own imagination was overheating. If this German-sounding person was really German, was she allowed to run a business here when the rest had gone? And if she was German, why had the dancer said *a party for some of your people,* so openly and in English. It made no sense.

Half an hour later, Mitzie turned off the hair dryer switch and again, without conversation, combed her out. Saba was delighted: her hair fell in a brilliantly shiny, sophisticated Veronica Lake–ish swoop over her right eye. Mitzie definitely knew her stuff.

Arleta did a mock double take and put her two thumbs in the air.

"How long are you going to be?" Saba mouthed, tapping her watch.

"One hour," said Arleta. There was a tray of coffee beside her and some petits fours.

"I'm going back to pack." Saba pointed toward the clock on the wall.

Arleta beckoned her over. "What's the verdict?" She lifted the corner of her hairnet. "Still a gremlin?"

Saba peeped under the hood. Arleta's new hair was a hot white-blond—much blonder than she'd been before.

"Sensational," she said. "You're going to love it."

"Listen." Half an hour later, Saba was sitting on Cleeve's sofa. His lift had broken down; she was breathless from the stairs. "I have no idea whether this is important or not, but I thought I should tell you anyway."

She told him about the green hair, the Salon Vogue, the possibly German proprietor. "At least I'm almost certain she was, although she spoke mostly in English."

Cleeve sprawled and clasped his hands behind his head. He looked at her approvingly.

"Full marks," he said, "for picking up on that one. I know Mitzie well—everybody does—she's a fixture on the Cairo social scene."

Saba flushed with embarrassment. She'd made a twit of herself thinking this was hot news.

"No, your instincts were spot on," Cleeve said. "And she is an interesting anomaly. Lady Lampson, the ambassador's wife, is one of her clients, also or so I've heard Freya Stark, the explorer, when she's not off on some donkey somewhere, but her most famous client, and the one she owes her liberty to, is Queen Farida, the wife of the Egyptian king."

Saba was totally confused: the wife of the English ambassador having her hair cut by a German? It made no sense at all.

"Here's the thing," Cleeve said. "The embassy would love to see Frau Duhring interned with the rest of the Germans in Cairo, but they dare not come between a woman and her hair because Queen Farida adores her. Funny when you think of it, the fate of a nation resting on the queen's curls."

"But is she a Nazi?" Saba felt a crawling up her spine.

"No, because she and her husband refused to join the Nazi party. They've been cast out by the German community here, but her situation is precarious. Her husband has already been interned and Sir Miles Lampson, an awful twit, would love to send her away; he doesn't like the idea of a German national snooping on all that juicy hairdressing-salon gossip. But he can't afford to. We're desperately unpopular with the Egyptians at the moment, and this, silly as it may sound, could be the straw that breaks the camel's back. We simply can't afford to upset Farida—the king adores her, he's said to buy her a new jewel every month.

"Any other good nuggets while you were there?" he threw out casually while he was making tea.

"Well, maybe, I don't know. Probably nothing."

"Say it."

"Well, only this, there was another woman there, very beautiful, a dancer, Madame Hekmet they called her; I thought I heard her say something about a party for German people. It sounded as if she thought Mitzie knew who was going to be there, but I couldn't hear all of it—Mitzie put me under the dryer."

"Hmm . . ." Cleeve drummed his fingers against his lip. "Nothing else?"

"No."

"Could be a hole in one, could be straight into the rough—you simply never know."

She had no idea what he was talking about.

"Did she say where the party was?"

"No."

"Almost certainly in Imbaba, where the Cairo houseboats are moored. It's near the Kit Kat Club where she probably dances. Anyway," he added briskly, "we can easily check that out."

"How?"

"That's for me to know and you to find out." He smiled at her playfully. "Tea?"

"No thanks; I've got to run. We leave tomorrow. I'll get an awful scolding from Bagley if I'm late."

The lift was working again, clanking and complaining, its filthy yellow ceiling light stacked with more dead flies.

"You're quite the girl, aren't you?" Cleeve remarked softly before he shut the cage door behind her. He peered through the bars at her and smiled. "I had a feeling you'd be rather good at this, and if you are, we have something quite important coming up."

He pressed the button and, as the lift cranked down, she saw his face, his knees, his desert boots disappearing and then heard only his echoing voice coming down the dark shaft, saying something valedictory like farewell, or good luck, or break a leg, and hearing this, she got a great rush of almost unbearable excitement thinking that at last her life was truly taking off. They were leaving. Tomorrow.

CHAPTER 16

There was a mad dash the next day to pack up the flat and get their kit in order before their lorry picked them up at sixteen hundred hours. They were going, Furness had finally told them, to Abu Sueir, an airbase in the Canal Zone, about seventy-five miles northeast of Cairo.

Before they left, Saba wrote to her father.

Dear Baba,

We're leaving Cairo today to go on the road and start our proper work. I want you to know that if anything happens to me—which it won't!—I have done what I felt I was meant to do here, and that I am sorry that what has made me happy has hurt you so. I hope one day we will understand each other better. Where is your ship now? Please tell me, and please write. You can send a letter to me here at ENSA, Sharia Kasr-el-Nil. The posts are terribly slow but it would be good to hear from you.

Saba

There were other things she wanted to tell him, both trivial and large: how it had felt that night singing "Mazi," in front of the pyramids at the Mena House; how magical Cairo could be with its lurid sunsets, its feluccas sailing like giant moths down the Nile; the amazing shops, some far posher than any she'd seen in Cardiff; how awful, too, with its heat and blare and noise and stinks—the drains and camel dung, the spices from the markets, the jasmine ropes sold at restaurants at night, the indefinable smell of dust. She wanted to say that she feared for him. (Janine, whose brother-in-law was in the merchant navy, had spelled out for her in grisly detail the carnage in the shipping lanes at home.) She wanted to say that she missed him, that she hated him, too, for being so childish. Such a muddle in her head about him, such a stupid waste of love.

Her sweaty fingers made the letters of the address run. Pomeroy Street, Butetown, Cardiff felt like a million miles away. Searching for moisture in her dry mouth, she licked the edges of a yellow aerogramme and wondered if she'd ever see him again.

They left Cairo a few hours later in a battle-scarred bus and headed northeast to Abu Sueir. Bagley and some soldiers had gone ahead of them to set up the portable stage.

Saba sat by herself—in this heat a body next to you felt like a furnace, and there were enough empty seats for them to have a row each. Arleta and Janine, still no-speakies, were at opposite ends of the bus; the acrobats at the back; Willie, dead to the world, snored percussively under a copy of the NAAFI newspaper; and Captain Furness sat tensely behind the driver, his swagger stick on the seat beside him, hamlike knees stretched out in the aisle.

She made a pillow of her khaki jacket—it was too hot to rest your head against the glass—and though she already felt car sick from the fumes, tried to tell herself the adventure was beginning. Outside the window there was precious little to see but miles and miles of crinkled sand, a few dead trees, a heap of animal bones.

She was half asleep when Willie staggered toward her and dropped some paper in her lap.

"For you, my love. They came from the NAAFI earlier but you was asleep."

Two letters. For her! She woke up immediately. One was written in her mother's slapdash hand, and postmarked South Wales. The other's unfamiliar handwriting made her stomach clench. She turned it around in her hand and stuffed it in the canvas bag under her feet.

Her mother had written:

Dear Saba,

Everyone is fine on Pomeroy Street, apart from Mrs. Prentice, who went to Swansea to see her sister two weeks ago and got bombed. I'm still working all the hours God sends at you know where. Tansu was a bit mopey for a while without you but now is part of a knitting group at the Sailors' Hall, which has cheered her up no end. Little Lou has started a new school in Ponty and she is happy there and still comes home at the weekends. Did you get her letter yet? Your father is away again, working for . . . [a crudely cut hole from the censor's scissors here] *but I think he has written to you. I don't know what to say about that, so I will leave it to him, but if he hasn't written know that the posts are terrible and try not to worry too much, it may not mean anything.*

Your loving Mam xoxo
Post script [it was Joyce's habit to always write this in full]

I got a pattern off an old copy of Woman's Friend, and I've made you a dress out of cream parachute silk (They had a sale of it in Howell's and the queues were round the block, I got there early.) I posted it with this letter.

Mam. My mam. She held the letter to her cheek smiling, so glad to hear from her she could have wept.

She read it again—it hurt thinking about her mother standing like Switzerland now between Dad and her, also to picture her queuing for hours for parachute silk, her hopeful whirlings on the Singer sewing machine she was so proud of. The Schiaparelli of Pomeroy Street. Saba wished she'd make something beautiful for herself for a change. The dress had not arrived, and even if it had, she probably wouldn't want to wear it anyway, except out of sentiment or loyalty. How frightening it was how quickly things changed, even things you wanted to stay the same. All Saba wanted now was for them to stay alive, and for her mother to be happy while she was away—was that so terrible? Probably, she sighed, and looked out the window. She'd turned out to be a rotten daughter.

The other letter now. The buff-colored envelope poked out from the bag. She put her nail under the flap and had it half open when Willie appeared.

"Mind if I join you for a bit?" He sat down heavily beside her. "Sorry about the getup," he'd changed from his khakis into a dubious-looking green-striped pajama top, "but I'm baking. You've lost your little friend, I see." He pointed toward Arleta, who was fast asleep four seats ahead of them.

"Yes, well . . ." She showed him the letter. "I've just got these, my first, and I think she thought . . ." She hoped he'd take the hint, but Willie was not famous for subtlety.

"I hear there was a right old dust-up earlier." He pointed at Janine, sitting close to the driver, as upright as a startled ostrich, and drew so close that the hairs from his ears tickled Saba's chin. "That stuck-up madame needs a bit of a seeing-to," he said, "if you know what I mean. One of the acrobats said he'd do it. Lev, I think. Lovely job."

"Willie!" She sprang away. "That's naughty."

"It would help her dancing and all. I mean it. Arleta almost lost her hair." Willie grabbed his own bald pate and looked anguished. "I hear she nearly went mad." He gave a wheezy laugh and looked back at Arleta. "Very spirited, that one," he said softly, and then he sighed.

"I hope they make up," said Saba. "It's so boring if no one's speaking."

"Arleta's as good as gold," Willie said. "She'll get her out of it," he added self-righteously, "It's bad for the company if people can't get along. We've got to stick together." He mopped his damp face. "None of us have a clue what's round the next corner, now do we, girl?"

"No, we don't, Willie," she said. Both of them stopped. The bus suddenly swerved to avoid a team of camels crossing the road. The men who led them looked up at them—their eyes expressionless, faces swathed against the dust. Behind them stretched miles and miles of sand shimmering and dissolving in a heat haze. "We certainly don't. Thank you for pointing that out to me."

When Willie went back to his seat, she pulled the buff-colored envelope from her bag again. The heat inside the bus was now 120 degrees; her wet hand had dissolved part of her address.

. . . *ear* . . . *aba.* Damn it! The censor's vigilance meant the letter hung like a paper chain in her hands—she couldn't even work out the date. She put the flimsy aerogramme against the window and, in daylight so bright her eyeballs flinched, made out part of a word at the top of the letter: *une* and then *42.* A hole above the date where the address might have been. His address, or her crazy thinking? All she knew was part of her had leapt into life like a flame when she'd seen the letter, and that now she was shocked at how disappointed she felt, and annoyed with herself, too. Why would he write to her now?

Some food came round in a cardboard box: bully-beef sandwiches and warm water, a sickly smelling banana turning black and wilting in its own skin. After it, to block out the heat, they tried to sleep again, and when she woke, the dust had cleared and she saw more sand stretching out to the horizon like a limitless sea. If you were not in a good state of mind, the scale of it could make everything look stunningly pointless; their little lorry a piece of thistledown blown by any random wind.

When Furness stood up to brief them on what to expect, dried saliva had caked in the corners of his mouth, and his face streamed with sweat. For the next ten days, he said, they would be whisked from place to place to perform at RAF camps, field units, and hospitals in what he described vaguely as the Canal Zone; after that they'd be moving west to follow in the footsteps of the Eighth Army. Some of these camps would be secret, or too small even to have proper names. Sometimes, Arleta had whispered, they didn't even tell you where you were, especially if you were near enemy lines.

When Furness had stopped talking and gone back to his seat, Saba lay stretched out over two seats, feeling the juddering desert road beneath her, thinking about Dom and their exciting, painful evening together. It annoyed her to still think of him, but that evening, its disappointing ending, had got stuck in her mind like the pieces of a mismatched puzzle she needed to solve.

She thought about the gentleness of his hand holding her foot when she'd sat down with the blister from those blasted shoes. He'd rubbed her toes between his fingers, and even though she'd been embarrassed, hoping her feet weren't sweaty from the audition and the dancing, she'd honestly wanted to purr like a kitten because it was so sudden and shockingly intimate. The wet pavement; him kneeling, his brown eyes looking at her under a lock of dark hair, the light in them tender, that was what she thought of. It was so unexpected after their wisecracking, it had seemed to iron out all the sharp angles of the day, and she'd believed in it.

And the next bit ruined everything. She'd definitely seen him kiss that girl in the club. Their heads had stayed together for a long time, talking intensely like lovers do, and all of it had made her think her own instincts were hopelessly wrong, and it got her goat to think of how she had let him spoil what had been such a marvelous day.

Oh God, she woke enraged and breathing heavily and with a raging thirst, having already drunk her pint of chemical-tasting water. Sweat trickled down between her breasts as the bus was rocked down a rough bit of road. Opening her eyes, all she could see was flipping sand and a skinny goat, eating a thorn bush, that leapt away in terror at the sight of them.

"Please, I am sitting?" A pair of well-muscled thighs slid into the empty seat beside her. Boguslaw the acrobat.

Bog, Boggers, Bog Brush—he answered to all of them—brought nerve-racking news. While she'd been dreaming, the plans had changed: tonight, instead of the small first concert planned, they would perform for up to a thousand troops, RAF personnel and medics at a transit camp near Abu Sueir. The portable stage, the piano, the props and the costumes had gone ahead; they were setting up now.

"Please gods, they don't expect a big company and a big show," Bog grimaced. Max Bagley had made no secret of the fact that they were spectacularly underrehearsed, and they'd all hoped for a day's rest first.

Saba hadn't seen Bog for the past few days. The acrobats had been billeted in another part of town, and Arleta, the girls' expert on the dark side of life, had whispered that the boys had been out on the razz.

"I'm not trying to shock you," she'd said in her husky, thrilling voice, "but the boys like to play, and there's this street they go to in Cairo called Wagh-el-Birket that caters for all tastes: young girls, dogs, sheep, chickens. And I'll tell you true story," she added, her eyes green slits, "early this year, a young naval officer was caught stark naked in the Shepheard Hotel. He was had up for indecent exposure and got off by quoting from the rulebook: 'an officer is deemed to be in uniform if he is appropriately dressed for the port in which he is engaged.' Ha, ha, ha, isn't that wonderful?"

Janine's beautifully plucked eyebrows shot up to her hairline. "Well, you see," she'd said, "I don't find that even remotely funny," and up they'd shot again when Arleta said that she personally thought the British army should do what the French and the Italians did and set up legal brothels for soldiers. They were young and lusty; it was inhuman to expect them to do without creature comforts for so long. At which point Janine had removed a damp flannel she kept in her handbag, and wiped her hands very deliberately.

"I am watching you earlier." Boguslaw cozied up to Saba, his left leg so close she could feel the tickle of the hairs against her leg. "Does your letter make you sad?" He gave a deep sigh.

"A little," she said.

His leg moved closer.

"You're too pretty to be sad," he said. "Is a man?"

"Yes. No."

"A strong man?" A biceps appeared like a giant cobra in his arm. "Strong like this."

"Very, very strong." It was much too hot for flirting. When the bus slowed down, in an effort to divert him, she pointed to a fruit stand on the side of the road. A man, his donkey; a veiled wife sat passive beside a pile of dried beans, some sugar-beet stalks, some dates. The woman was swatting flies from a sleeping baby on her lap. Two other children played in the dirt beside them.

"Are you married, Bog?" she asked him—she'd teased him and taught him songs but they hadn't talked properly yet.

"Not now," he said. "I was." She heard him inhale sharply. "They're dead," he said at last. He moved his leg away from her. "Wife, daughter, mother, family . . . My family." He took a deep breath. "We all lived in Warsaw before the war. Mother, father, wife, children, us boys, circus." He did the shadow of a cartwheel in his seat. "Always working. Not good, not good. One day, we are away doing a show, and when we come home, the Germans have been." He threw up his hands, a look of deep disgust on his face. "My family is all gone." He clicked his fingers. "Now, I can't go home.

"I hate the fucking bastard Germans," he said at last, "and the fucking bastard Russians, too. I can't forgive them."

Saba clasped his hand, horrified at having asked her question so carelessly; Arleta had warned her the boys had a sad background.

"I'm sorry, Boguslaw," she said. "I should . . . I would never . . ."

"No, no, no, no. It's okay." He stood above her, eyes shut. "I wanted to tell you, it's not your fault." He was sweating. "I go and sit with my brothers now."

They arrived at their destination late in the afternoon, so covered in dust they looked like porcelain figures. A harried subaltern marched them down a dusty track and showed them the female quarters—a four-man tent. Janine moaned softly when she saw it. The tent stank of DiMP and the camp beds were so close they touched. There were three rusty nails on a post to hang their costumes on; a cracked mirror on the wall would serve as their dressing room. Arleta took the mirror down immediately saying it was bad luck, and hung the framed four-leafed clover she carried with her on the nail.

In a small hut outside there was an Elsan and a roll of lavatory paper that had crisped up in the heat, and a jerrycan containing their water, which was severely rationed—one pint a day for drinking, one to wash in. When Arleta joked there'd be no face-splashing that night, Janine's lips thinned.

"Come on, love." Arleta patted Janine softly on the arm. "Let's get on. I'm no good at sulking."

"I'm sorry, too," Janine said in a tight voice. Her eyes filled with tears. "Sorry I came." Her chin wobbled violently for a moment. She told them both in a violent rush that her fiancé had given her the push before she came on tour, and she was so upset she couldn't talk about it yet. She was sorry to have been such a pain. She'd hoped the tour would take her mind off it, but she really wasn't strong enough for it yet.

"Oh love! Say no more!"

"No, no, no, don't." She wasn't ready yet for Arleta's lavish sympathies, and physically backed away, one delicate hand in the air.

She was incapable of a clumsy gesture, even two feet from an Elsan. "But I did mean to say earlier," she ventured timidly, "your hair looks nice."

Which it did—a dazzling white-blond now, quite spectacular. The boys had all done double takes and whistled when they'd seen it, which had cheered Arleta up no end.

"I expect we're all on edge a bit," Janine said. "It feels so terribly disorganized, I'm not used to that." She looked down at the narrow camp beds, with their stained mosquito nets. "We're supposed to check under them for snakes and scorpions," she said, getting down on her hands and knees. "It's all so sudden." Her voice was shuddery as she straightened up. "I'm never going to do this again," she said.

An hour later, Max Bagley's voice, strained and disembodied, came through the canvas flap.

"One hour till showtime," he said. "If the piano goes flat, ignore it—it was damaged on the way here. Keep your shoes on," he warned, his voice scarily monotone, "the stage is very uneven and the floodlights near the front are still not working. No plummets into the audience, *s'il vous plaît.*"

"This will be a disaster," Janine predicted when he had gone. She was lying under a sheet with an eye mask on. "No proper piano, no costumes, no flaps." The props lorry had broken down earlier—it was touch and go whether they'd get the stage up in time. To block her out, Saba spat on her sponge—they were already low on water after a quick cup of tea—and began her makeup. Her scared-looking eyes swam into view in Arleta's mirror, and then her reflection wavered, turned yellow and went out.

"Blast it." Arleta lit their acetylene lamp again—the generators were temporarily on the blink.

"Thirty minutes, ladies." Bagley's voice again. "The spots are working now."

"Good." Saba only half heard him. She was humming her songs in her head.

"Darling," said Arleta, bobbing down beside her, back pearly with sweat. "Be an angel and do up my top popper." She looked very pale.

Saba clicked it into place.

"Thank you, sweetheart." Arleta kissed her, a faint whiff of gin on her breath.

"All right?" Saba said.

"Terrified—thanks for asking," said Arleta. Her first number was a Josephine Baker send-up and she was putting a plastic pineapple on her head. "A real old attack of the collywobbles; I get it sometimes, especially at the beginning of a tour."

"Crepi il lupo!" Saba said, squeezing her hand.

"Come again?"

"My old singing teacher used to say it before the curtain went up," Saba explained. "It's better than break a leg. First he'd say to me '*In bocca al lupo*,' that's Italian for 'in the wolf's mouth,' then I'd say '*Crepi il lupo*,' which means 'the wolf dies.'"

"Well my lupo is alive and bloody kicking, but I'll give it a whirl." Arleta put her arms around Saba and said in a muffled voice. "Thank you."

"What for?"

"For being a wonderful friend."

Half an hour later the call came.

"Ready, girls?"

"Ready."

"Ready, Janine?"

"Hope so." Janine balanced on the camp bed, voice muffled as she chalked her shoes.

Arleta stood up, pineapple securely fastened to her head with a double row of kirby grips. *"Crepi il lupo!"* She strode toward the desert stage, and their first proper concert together.

The portable stage looked not bad considering. Its red lights pulsed like a swollen heart in the middle of the drab huts, the barbed wire and the rows of tents. Saba walked up the steps to the back of the stage. She peeped around the dusty curtain and saw rows and rows of soldiers waiting like patient children beneath a starlit sky. There were uniformed nurses from the base hospital in the aisles, their patients dark mounds on stretchers beside them.

The running order was written on a blackboard in the wings. She checked it again. The Banana Brothers first, then Willie, then her first two numbers. Her mouth and eyes felt gritty with sand, her heart beat faster. This was the high-board moment. Bagley was waiting on the other side of the stage to start the show. When he looked at her, she lifted her chin and stood straighter, blocking out everything he'd said about her shortcomings—she couldn't afford to think of that now; that way lay the sick bucket and the leaping wolf.

Bagley lifted his hand. "Five minutes," he mouthed. He smiled at her, moving with fluid grace between the portable generator and the lights and the curtains. Arleta came up beside her and linked arms. She did a little running dance on the spot.

Bagley's arm came down. The band struck up, Willie dashing onto the stage to some jolly farting and squeaking circus music, pretending with his butterfly net to catch the dancing insects in front of the spotlights. They were on.

"Ladies and gentlemen, hold on to your hats because we're here, the marvelous, the incomparable razzle-dazzles, live from Cairo and Orpington. Tonight there are but eight of us . . . but good things come in small packages, so prepared to be amaaaaazed!!!!"

Bog came first, in a blue spangled suit, leaping high into two amber-colored pools of light. Roars and laughter from the audience as Willie, trying to follow him, did rickety handstands near the wings. Bog cartwheeled hectically, one two three four five times across the stage. Lev appeared and flung Bog into the air like a juggling ball. Hey!! And now a triumphant Bog tossed on top of a shouting human pyramid, beaming and quivering his legs and making anguished faces to show how brilliant they were. When he saw the girls in the wings he winked at them and they winked back.

"Bravo, Boggers," Saba said. She blew him a kiss. "*Magnificato.*"

Some of the stretcher cases were laughing now, their faces crimson-washed from the lights of the ambulances that would take them home. The able-bodied men sitting on uncomfortable tin seats were clapping wildly, the air thick with their blue cigarette smoke. Willie came back for a bit and rattled off a few gags, then Janine appeared, and he dashed after her with his butterfly net as she fluttered against the desert sky like a green moth, dashing hither and yon as if in frantic pursuit of another moth to mate with to the opening chorus from *Scheherazade.* The men looked wistful.

Saba, hearing the dying chords of violins, felt her own heart plucked hard. From where she stood, hidden by the curtain, she could see Janine waving and leaping as she flew off the stage, another person altogether. Her name was rubbed off the blackboard.

"*Ah nooooowa, the verrrra beautiful . . .*" Willie appeared in a huge baggy suit, clutching his throat and staggering. He glanced at her briefly in the wings to see if she was there, "*. . . the verrray alllarmingly charming, our own little desert song birdaa, Missa Saba Tarcaaaaan.*"

Arleta stood with her in the wings. She squeezed her hand, and gave her a push. "Knock 'em dead, girl," she whispered.

Saba felt a sluggish breeze as Bog and Lev lifted her through the red and yellow lights and placed her down in the center of the stage. They jutted their arms toward her like stamens toward a flower. Bagley appeared behind a battered-looking piano—the spotlight on him illuminating a fresh cloud of dark insects. He raised his hand, played a few notes and they leapt together into "Get Happy."

You could see so much from the stage: the faces of the nut-brown men softening, a soldier, raised up from his stretcher, beaming and waving. Saba flung herself into the song, loving the syncopated rhythms that Bagley slyly threw in so as not to make it too ordinary and corny, and loving, too, her own wide-throated ending when she threw her head back into a cloud of stars and gave it all she could. By the end of the song she was steaming with heat, the audience roaring and stamping, and when she glanced at Bagley sitting in a pool of light at his piano, and saw him put his thumbs up, she felt a hot surge of triumph. Not so bad, hey?

When Bagley swung into a larky version of "You Must Have Been a Beautiful Baby," the men moaned, hollered, and stamped as she danced and sang about driving young girls mad. Bagley, in spite of a personal dislike of the saccharine, constantly reminded them to sing sweet.

"These men don't fight for democracy, freedom, or any of that guff. They fight for their mum or for their girl, and as far as they're concerned, you're it for the ten minutes you're on stage."

The night air felt still and soft around Saba's face. Max had told her if things were going well to sing a third song, and they were, so she could relax now. She waited for the low rumble of a plane to pass high above the stars, and then felt a deep silence descend on the men as she told them she was going to sing her favorite song, "All the Things You Are."

Insects obscured Bagley now. He played the opening bars, and when she sang, part of her could hear she was too soft. Bagley had warned her that when she was singing outdoors in a large space she would have to learn to throw her voice differently. Also, technically, it was harder to hold a line in a slow song than in one of the perky little numbers she'd started with. But she loved this song so much, she stopped caring, and after a few tentative notes hit her stride, remembering to use her microphone, as Bagley had taught her, as the confidential friend you told your secrets to, and as she and the song joined up, she felt a deep and creamy kind of contentment move through her veins. It was almost a shock at the end of it to remember where she was, to look out and see tears sparkling like diamonds in some of the men's eyes. As she left the stage, the men roared and whistled and stamped.

"Oh you little lamb. Well done, darling." Arleta, slick with sweat and scent, hugged her as she came off stage. "Brilliant, brilliant girl! You were nervous and you did it."

She added something else that Saba couldn't hear because the crowd were still clapping and shouting. She pointed toward the dark desert, the tin huts.

"Darling, do me a huge, huge favor," she said. "Go to our tent and get me some face powder. I'm sweating like a pig. Hurry! Hurry! Hurry! I'm on next."

Still high as a kite from her performance, Saba took the torch and ran along the forty yards or so of dirt road that led to their tent. From a distance, the portable stage glowed like a huge lit-up butterfly wing and felt like the magnetic center of the night. She could hear the boom of Willie's voice; he was on fire now:

"*Are you all alllllllll riggggghhhhhht?*" And the answer: "*Yyeeeeesssssssss!*"

The desert night was bright with stars. When she got to the tent, there was a dim light shining inside the canvas, a dark silhouette. She pulled back the flap; Dom was sitting on a chair waiting for her. When she first saw him, she tripped on the guy rope and almost fell into his arms.

CHAPTER 17

As he stood up, a shock of dark hair fell over his eyes.

"You!" she said. "How on earth . . . ?"

"I'll tell you later." His smile was mischievous.

"Do you know Arleta?" Her mind was struggling with this; her heart bounding.

"I do now."

"Oh God," she suddenly remembered. "She's on—"

"Don't bother," he said. "That was a put-up job—we're both guilty."

"I've got to go back in a minute for my curtain call."

"You must." His lips had a beautiful curve to them. After months of telling herself he was out of bounds now, she was shocked by how much she wanted to kiss them.

"I've borrowed a jeep," he said. "Can I take you out for supper after the show?"

"Yes." She was so relieved. "But I must dash back."

He said that he would wait here. He asked if she would get into trouble if she left the camp.

"No," she said, although she wasn't sure.

She flew down the dusty path and onto the stage, into a shrill blast of whistles, beaming and waving and blowing kisses. Arleta was waiting in the wings when she came off.

"He's here," she whispered.

"I know," Arleta's hug enveloped her in greasepaint and Shalimar, "and quite a dish if I may say so."

"Can I leave the camp tonight without permission?"

"No one's said we can't." Arleta's expression was perfectly bland. "No curfew I know of yet. And honey bun, if I may say so, you've kept *him* under wraps."

"He's a fighter pilot," Saba whispered, pulling her finger across her throat. Arleta had warned her to avoid them like the plague. They were conceited, she'd said, and unreliable, also a bad bet, because most of them didn't come back.

"Well, you old dark horse!" Arleta tugged a strand of her hair and gave her a kiss on her forehead. "Don't say you haven't been warned."

As they raced across the desert in a battered jeep, the risen moon was so bright it seemed to have turned the night into a photographic negative of day, and she was dazzled by it.

"What happened to you in London that night?" he said immediately. "When I got back to our table, you were gone, and this was a heck of a long way to come to find you."

"Oh, I had a ton of things to do." She couldn't bear the thought of him knowing how much it had hurt; how foolish it had made her feel. "I needed an early night, and you . . . you seemed to have your hands full." She glanced up at him.

"It wasn't what you thought." His voice was neutral, his eyes on the road. "She was the girlfriend of a chap from our squadron. It was the first time I'd seen her since he died. The timing wasn't brilliant. I'm sorry about that."

She stared at him, cringing at the memory of herself stomping out like a child, grateful he hadn't seen her, but there was another feeling, too, of sweet release.

"I was in a bit of a state myself," she said. "There was too much going on."

"Yes," he said softly. "Much too much."

"Was he a friend? The chap who died, I mean."

"Yep. We were at school together, and at university."

"How old?"

"Twenty-two."

He gunned the accelerator. The faint pinprick of the jeep's lights picked up nothing but sand and rock. Saba shivered and hugged herself—the vastness of the desert around them felt like a warning of how tiny they were and how quickly snuffed out.

"This feels like blindman's buff," she said, thinking one may as well be brave; it could all be over for all of them in a flash. "Where are we going?"

"My name," he said, "is Alish Barbour. I'm a white slave trader. I've already lost the map." She was relieved to see him smiling again.

He drove easily and fast, one hand draped over the wheel.

"I know a place where we can eat in Ishmailia—about a twenty-minute drive from here."

The gleam of his white teeth in the moonlight as he turned and smiled at her.

"Hungry?" he said. He put his foot down on the accelerator.

"Starving." Though she was too excited for real hunger. She could feel his heat beside her, a sense of heightened awareness that was almost unbearable. *Calm down, calm down*, she told herself.

"Where have you been?" she said, hoping to sound sensible. "I mean before you came here."

He said he'd been in Abu Sueir himself, a couple of weeks before she'd arrived. They'd been on a training exercise, on the new Kittyhawks, the fighter planes they'd be using from now on. Afterward, they'd flown south to Luxor and spent a couple of days going up the Nile on an old steamer.

"You could have come with me," he said with a swift glance in her direction.

"I could," she said, "but I was working."

On the outskirts of Ismailia, rackety music burst from a street that smelled of roasted sweet potatoes, and charcoal and old drains. There was a cafe on the corner where a group of men sat in the glow of an acetylene light smoking and drinking and playing board games.

He drove down another narrow street and parked the jeep there. He held her hand as he led her down a crumbling pavement to the restaurant he knew called Chez Henri. He stopped outside a heavily carved wooden door with a grille above it. When the door opened it was on to a simply furnished candlelit room where no more than six or seven tables were covered in white cloths. On each table there was a jam jar with a spray of jasmine in it.

"Ismailia is a town full of prisoners now," he told her, "Germans, thousands of Italians, but fortunately not Henri—he escaped from Paris. He had a restaurant there before the war."

"It's lovely." She closed her eyes, terribly happy suddenly, and inhaled the room—its smell of roasting meat, of jasmine, of cigarette smoke.

Henri appeared between them, portly and suave in his long white apron and wreathed in smiles.

"Monsieur, madame, good evening!" If they'd been babies he would have kissed them and pinched their cheeks. He led them to a table in the corner. He lit the wicks of two cork candles.

When the flames glowed, Saba saw this was not a proper restaurant at all, more like an ordinary sitting room with its simple furnishings and comfortable sofa and family pictures on the wall. Its door was open to the night; from the window of the shabby house opposite came the croak of a sleepy child, the silhouette of a woman staring down at them. The woman pulled behind the curtain when Saba looked up.

Henri brought a carafe of wine, and after her first sip she said to Dom, "How did you get here? How did you find me?"

"Elementary, my dear Watson. I went to Cairo and asked the girl at the ENSA office where you were." He smiled with the innocent confidence of a man women tell things to. "And I sent you a letter."

"This?" She took her purse out of her bag and showed him its tattered remains. "I didn't know it was you."

"Ah, well, the mystery is solved. Did you hope it was?" He raised his eyes and looked at her.

She looked at the menu. They think they're God's gift to women, Arleta had warned her—girls literally lie down at their approach.

"Maybe. I'll let you know. I still don't understand," she said. His hand on the menu was brown and beautiful. He had long fingers. "What are you doing in North Africa?"

"Oh, that part was easy," he said. "They're very short of pilots and a friend of mine is with the Desert Air Force. He fixed it. We're based between Cairo and Alexandria."

"Were you pleased—after what happened to you, I mean." She felt his slight move away from her. He was looking toward the door.

"Yes." He turned back with a polite social look. She had definitely strayed into enemy territory. "I was pleased—it was becoming a bore in England. There are only so many games of chess you can play in the mess."

And then a sudden shyness seemed to overtake them. Dom drew a pattern with his hand on the tablecloth and she, overwhelmed by the concert and the shock of seeing him, warned herself to slow down.

"Where are you staying tonight?"

"There are rooms upstairs," Dom said. "I'll stay here, after I've dropped you back of course." He slid his eyes toward her.

"Of course," she said demurely. His brown fingers were on the table playing with the salt pot. She could feel her own heart beating and took a quick breath.

Henri appeared again, followed by a plump child of about five wearing pajamas. Henri put a menu on the table, some flat bread, and two water glasses. The little boy put down their side plates with the fastidious air of an altar boy placing a chalice and was rewarded by a noisy kiss from his father.

"What would you like to eat?" Henri smiled at them.

"She's starving," Dom told him. "What's good tonight?"

"I propose roast duck served with honey, lavender, and thyme. It is delicious," their host said simply. "We have lamb cooked with preserved lemons, that's good, too."

They chose the lamb, and while they were waiting, Dom half filled Saba's glass and pushed it toward her. "How long have we got?" he said. He looked young in that moment, anxious, too.

"There's no rush," she said. It was already too late and she didn't care.

He touched her lightly on the hand.

"I want to say something . . . you were so good tonight."

"When?" She was confused.

"The concert."

"You heard me?" She hadn't expected that.

"Yes." His eyes had the large pupils of a child. There were tortoiseshell lights in them. He took her hand and this time kept it in his. "Tell me something. What does it feel like?"

"What does what feel like?" She thought for a moment he meant being with him, and was trying to compose an answer.

"Singing like that?"

She let his hand go. No one had ever asked her this before.

"Well, I don't know . . . it's hard to explain. Panic at first, especially tonight. We were so late, and it was our first proper concert, and all those men waiting, and then one of those beetles almost flew into my mouth, and then the music sounded so strange, that piano was a bit flat, but then . . . I don't know. There was a moment when I was singing 'All the Things You Are," when I . . . well, it's hard to describe how good it feels, it's like a wave that travels through you."

She'd given up trying to make it sound hard; the truth was she'd loved almost every minute of it, the sense of being part of the war effort, of being allowed to do regularly what she'd practiced for so long, of living way beyond her natural limits, of doing well at what she most wanted to do—it felt so good. Her entire body, her spine, the tips of her toes, her belly, her head, was still in the glow of it.

"A wave that you catch."

"Yes."

"Ooh, that does sound good."

"You're teasing me." She caught his wrists in her hands.

"No. I promise I'm not." He was watching her closely.

"For that moment, you feel complete, as if there's nothing missing. Does that sound batty to you?

"No." He took a sip of wine. "It feels like flying."

"Does it?"

"Yes, but carry on, you first."

They gazed at each other almost warily.

"And all those men, crying out in the night for you," he continued in a lighter tone. "I could hear them from the tent. How does that feel?"

"That's not why I do it," she said. The truth was that what she'd felt most earlier that night was not the thrill of being admired, but something more difficult to put into words without sounding too what her mum would call stuck on yourself—the pain of the men coming toward her, the pain of homesickness, of lost friends, of exhaustion and prolonged fright, changing as if by magic into delight and relief, and how that felt like turning water into wine, but of course you couldn't say that without sounding like a complete prat.

"You seemed very confident."

She felt exposed, as if she had said it.

"It's all right." His dark intelligent eyes gazed at her steadily. "I thought . . ." he seemed to choose his words carefully, "I thought you were tremendous . . . really." He was about to say something else, but stopped.

Henri was back flourishing a tray above his head. He'd brought them a selection of doll-sized dishes he called *mizzi'at*, filled with spicy vegetables and hummus and some olives; the olives he said were smuggled out of France.

"Tell me the honest truth," Dom said when they were alone again. He drew closer to her across the table, his gaze intense. "Is it the best thing in your life?"

"I don't know." Had he read her blasphemous mind? Then she said, "I do. Love it, I mean." She tore a piece of bread in half, and dipped it in oil. "I don't know yet if it's the best thing in my life, but it's where I feel most myself." She watched the expression in his eyes sharpen.

"What does that mean 'most yourself'? Do you think you have a self, I mean a proper self, not just a reflection of what other people want you to be?"

"I'm not sure." She felt in dangerous territory again. "But I have a lot to learn," she heard herself apologizing. "Max Bagley, our musical director, thinks I get some songs wrong."

"In what way?"

"He says I copy other people." The admission was still painful. She put her head close to his and sang a line softly. "When I sang it the other day, he said I was doing a Bessie Smith and trying to sound like some weary old black lady about to pick a bale of cotton, and I should sing it just like me."

"If you do that again, I'll have to take that old cotton picker to bed," he breathed in her hair. They looked at each other with surprise and burst out laughing.

"No, no, no." She was alarmed by how excited she felt and could feel the blush spreading from the roots of her hair. "This is serious! Talk to me!" But it felt good, so good to laugh with him. When he picked up her hand and kissed the palm of it, she didn't pull away.

"To return to Mr. Bagwash, or whatever his name is." Their hands were side by side on the table. "Surely what he said is partly rot. How do you learn anything without listening, copying, practicing? Sorry, it's definitely rubbish, ignore it altogether."

He talked passionately and seriously to her then about Picasso, who'd pinched from everyone; about T. S. Eliot, who he'd studied at Cambridge; of the steady building up of technique, the learning from other people, the final drawing together of all these influences to make a whole. Charlie Parker, he added, was laughed off the stage the first time he performed.

"Who he?"

"Ah! So I have a discovery for you. I'm going to buy you a record. He had to practice for hours before he dared to play in public again. It doesn't happen overnight, I'm sure it doesn't; don't let him stomp on your dream."

When the roast lamb came it was sweet and tender, and after it Henri's boy, half asleep now, brought a homemade ice cream served in a glass and flavored with rosewater, and then a bottle of sweet-tasting wine on the house.

"Have some of this." Henri was smiling at them as if they delighted him. "It's from Alexandria, it's called zabib." He poured Saba half a glass. "It's better than Beaume de Venise."

"This is delicious," she said, and it was, sweet and flowery. "I'll be drunk," she told Dom.

"I'll look after you," he said. "I have to see you again." He looked at her steadily. "I have an important package for you."

"A package?" She narrowed her eyes, mock suspicious. "What's in it?"

"Ah, you'll have to wait."

"Why?"

"Some things have to be earned."

"Yes?"

"Yes. It's from your mother."

"Liar."

"You'll see—and I want a full apology when you do."

Over coffee, Dom became serious again. He told her about his mother's career as a pianist, and how angry it had made his father. One of the abiding memories of his childhood had been watching her come home alone after a concert—her first—that his father had been too busy, or too disapproving, to attend. He remembered her smart suit, the taxi, and her leather case with the music in it. How lonely she'd seemed to him, letting herself into the house that had gone to bed. Not long after that she'd given up. He'd been too young at the time to understand why, but it was wrong, he felt, to have a passion like that and to shut it down.

"It's almost as if everybody in life has a river running through them, let's say like the Nile," his eyes were flashing now as he expounded his thesis, "a river that gives you your own particular life. You dam it up at your peril."

"All that water pouring out your ears," she teased him. But she liked him talking like this; he was by far and away the most interesting man she'd ever met.

"What about you?" she asked over a second glass of zabib. Earlier, when the candle had flared and she'd seen the scar on the side of his face she'd remembered the hospital, the other young men with their skin grafts like elephant's trunks, their ruined faces. "Are you flying a lot?"

"Yes."

"Is it busy?"

"Honest truth?"

"Yes."

"It is quite busy up there." He shifted in his seat.

"Busier say than the Battle of Britain?" She narrowed her eyes. "And none of that Boy Biggles landing like an angel's kiss stuff."

"Well . . ."—he lit a cigarette—"it is quite hot," he said softly. He didn't expand, except to say their aerodrome was out in the desert, not far from enemy lines. That he shared a tent with a chap called Barney, someone he knew from school, who had got him the transfer in the first place.

"But what do you do?"

He said they were flying missions, sometimes as escorts for bombers or supply lorries, and sometimes in direct combat. He looked at her, and was about to say something else when she interrupted him.

"Why did you come to Egypt? Did you have to?"

"Yes," he said quietly. "I had to. This awful girl stood me up in London."

"Be serious. Why?"

Several expressions seemed to move across his face.

"It's complicated. I'll tell you some other time."

"Tell me one," she urged. While they'd been talking, the restaurant had emptied. The boy was curled on the sofa asleep with his thumb in his mouth; Henri, folding napkins, closing the shutters. Dom put a cork back on the bottle of zabib.

"All right then," he said. "Just one: flying. You know what you said earlier about feeling most yourself when you were singing. That's how I feel in a plane. Free."

She pictured him spinning in space miles above earth, and felt sick. If she hadn't been to the hospital she would never have known what could so easily come next. There were other things to ask, but she was frightened she'd jinx him.

"So, both misfits," she joked instead. "No feet on the ground here."

"Antigravity," he said. "Well, that's always a risk. Oh God!"

Henri was blowing the candles out. He put the bill on the table and shrugged regretfully. Their supper was over.

As he drove her home across the desert, she fell into that kind of dark and dreamless sleep that feels like falling into a pit. When she opened her eyes again, she could see his brown fingers on the wheel, the dark outline of his hair, his straight nose, and felt glad in a way to be going home. She longed for him in a way that frightened her: it was too much, it had happened too quickly, she would have to give it some sort of more serious attention later.

While she'd been sleeping, her body had scooted up against his as if to a magnet; her head was resting against his shoulder, and she could smell him again, the same woody smell, but this time mingled with the faint aroma of petrol and dust. When she moved herself back to a respectable distance, she opened her eyes wide and looked out at the stars. High above her, like a cluster of sapphires, was the brilliant blue of the Seven Sisters, and there, the cloudy Milky Way. Her father, who knew them like old friends, had taught her their names when she was a girl. Five minutes later she saw the faint glimmer of red-brick buildings, the tracer lights around the transit camp, leaking out into the night.

"Saba." His voice came to her out of the dark. "We're nearly back. I've been thinking. I have some leave at the end of the month. Do you know where you'll be?"

A convoy of British army lorries trundled past them—a long glowworm drowning out her reply. In their taillights she saw a thorn bush, a mound of rocks. "I can show you fear in a handful of dust"—he'd said that earlier. The fact that he knew such poems, and about Charlie Parker and other things, was already part of his attraction for her: they were young, they could learn together. Over supper, he'd told her that he hoped to be a writer when the war was over, and to keep flying.

Half a mile from the transit camp, he stopped the jeep and turned to her. He took her hair in both hands and held it behind her neck as he kissed her.

"We could meet in Alexandria," he said. "Or Cairo."

"Oh God," she murmured into his hair, "I don't know."

"Don't be frightened," he said.

"I'm not frightened," she said, which wasn't true. "I don't know where I'll be," she gasped. Her whole body felt soft and yielding—it was terrifying to feel it leap toward him. "That's what I meant. We never seem to know."

Dom glanced at her and drew back.

"You can write to me. You can write to me and let me know."

"It's not that . . ." She could hear her voice faltering. "Of course I'll do that . . . but . . ." Thinking of Cleeve, his warnings about boyfriends.

"If there's someone else," he moved away from her and looked in her eyes, "tell me straightaway. I shall have him killed, of course, but at least I'll know."

"It's not that." She felt overwhelmed by everything. The nearness of him, and all that lay ahead.

When he put his arm around her and kissed her again, she could feel him thinking; a slight chill of separation between them.

At the high wire fence on the outskirts of the camp, they stopped at the guard's hut. A soldier checked Dom's papers.

"Lovely concert, Miss Tarcan," the soldier said, not bothering to check hers. "Our first for over a year. Would it be cheeky to ask for your autograph here?"

She scribbled her signature on a torn piece of paper. The guard folded it carefully and put it in his top pocket.

"Will you be on tomorrow?" he asked.

"We don't have a clue yet," she said. Everything was so up in the air. "But they'll probably put a sign up near the NAAFI."

The soldier thanked her again; he said he had only been married for three weeks when he came here, his first kiddy had been born while he was away. His wife was finding it hard. "I hope she's still there when I get back," he said in a jocular voice.

"Oh, hang about." They were driving off when the guard called them back. "Forgot to tell you: Captain Ball dropped by to see if you were back. Something about a party at the officers' mess tonight. He seemed very keen for all you ENSA girls to go." He twitched the corner of his eye, a modified wink, out of respect for Dom maybe.

Ludicrous to feel so immediately flustered, but she did. "It's part of the job," she told Dom with a shrug. "The party."

His expression didn't change. "You don't have to explain yourself to me," he said. "I'm sure you've got lots of admirers."

And then he left her, after a quick peck on the cheek, a ruffling of her hair that made her feel like a younger sister or something. He said he'd write, and then he floored the accelerator and sped away in a ball of dust.

Later, lying in her canvas bed, she went through every detail of the evening, raging at herself for the awkward way she had ended it. Her rushed good-bye, her evasive answer when he'd asked when they could meet again—it sounded so furtive, jarring. She didn't want to start by having secrets from him.

CHAPTER 18

He took off at dusk in the Spitfire he'd been asked to deliver to LG39, the squadron's temporary base in the desert. Before he left, he went through the usual instrument and safety checks: oil, air pressure, oxygen feed, parachute stowed securely under his seat. The petrol gauge registered almost full, easily enough for the one-hour hop.

It was growing dark as the plane lifted off. The dust storm that had grounded all planes earlier had cleared, leaving a shimmering coppery patina in the air. At twenty thousand feet, flying down a corridor of cloud, he heard himself singing and then laughing. It was mad, it was crazy and impossible, but he was completely and utterly in love for the first time.

When he pictured her standing in her red dress in the pool of light singing "All the Things You Are," he felt with alarm all the carefully suppressed emotions of the last year burst into life again like a desert landscape after rain. She'd felt like the magnetic center of the night. Later, in the restaurant, when she'd confided in him how much she had to learn, he'd felt like her protector already—there were too many old farts in life who couldn't wait to slap you down, and she didn't deserve it. She was too original, too free. He increased the engine speed, felt the little plane lift, flew above and then through a few cottony clouds, and when he came out the other side he was still thinking of her. Saba, asleep in the jeep, curled up like a child, her flood of dark hair over his knee.

And then, in the middle of all this euphoria, as sudden as an engine cutting out, he located a new feeling for him in connection with a woman: she frightened him. He felt like someone who'd been given some strange, beautiful, semitamed animal with no idea yet how to handle it. She was powerful. If emotions were weather, she could stir up a tornado.

He'd felt it the first night he'd met her at the hospital, and even more intensely this time. He'd almost stopped breathing when she walked on the stage for fear something would go wrong. She'd stood in the spotlight owning the night with a reckless bravado he found both touching and admirable. When she was singing, the men on either side of him had leaned toward her and exhaled a kind of group sigh. One or two of them had groaned softly, a few muttered obscenities. He understood it—of course he did: strip away all the bravado and the false cheer, they were all lonely men stuck in the middle of nowhere, bored or scared shitless most of the time, hungry for wives or sweethearts. But it disturbed him already that they should think of her like that. In fact, face it, he was already having to wrestle with a feeling of deep dismay about her, a feeling that disturbed and weakened him. He was jealous.

He gunned the engine, glanced at the darkening sky beneath him and the few faint stars winking on his starboard side, and then at the wavering lights below. One of the many dangers of night flying was that it was possible to get distracted by random stars and mistake them for airport lights, the perfect metaphor, he suddenly thought, for falling for the wrong girl.

Half an hour from the landing ground, he stopped thinking of her altogether as he tapped the altimeter and glanced down again. This was a tricky little runway, lit only by feeble gas flares and deliberately concealed. Concentrate!

One of the many things he loved about flying was that it did stop you thinking in an everyday way. Up here, miles away from the hectic, scurrying earth, you became as alive as any wild animal to its moods and changes: what clouds were forming, the shape and texture of rain, the dips of valleys. That fluffy gray cloud that had just sailed by might, on another continent, hide a mountain wall that could kill you, or the wingtip of one of the Messerschmitt 109s that flew in regularly from nearby Sicily and Italy.

He was looking for them now as he descended. Before he'd flown east, three days ago, he'd been warned by his flight commander, Paul Rivers, that if he became tangled up in a "show" on the way home, he was to get himself down as quickly as possible.

"The planes are more important than you mate," he'd joked. "We can't afford to lose any more, and besides, I want to go home now." He'd stuck his finger in his mouth like a baby. "I miss my mummy."

Rivers, like Dom, had flown in the Battle of Britain. The plan was that as soon as Dom had got his bearings he would replace him.

On their brief tour of the airfield a few weeks ago, Rivers, his blunt, pug-nosed face covered in dots of calamine lotion from his desert sores, had told Dom that things had got pretty hot out here recently, and that he was bloody grateful that he was to be tour-expired. He'd had enough sand in his bloody underpants and his bloody coffee and his fucking ears to last him a lifetime. He also had a wife and a new baby waiting for him on his parents' property in Queensland.

"Yeah, it will be quite nice to see the little tyke," he agreed with an unconvincing show of reluctance, which made Dom smile. For a brief moment he'd envied him his settled future and guaranteed life.

Rivers had told him over a disgusting cup of chlorine coffee that the Germans now outnumbered them by four to one. They were well supplied with bases in Greece and Sicily, had better and more numerous planes. Young pilots like Dom had flown in from all over the world to help the Allies with this final push. "We reckon," the Aussie had drawled, "it's going to be like a second Battle of Britain here soon, only hotter and longer and harder."

That was another thing Dom hadn't told her. Another major offensive, in five days? A month? Two months? The whole place seethed with rumors, no one ever really knew.

From the air the small runway looked as insignificant as a toenail. He steered down gently, and after he'd landed, reached under his seat and grabbed his kitbag. An hour or so later, as he walked toward his tent, a young man with the broad shoulders and easy lope of an athlete stood up and walked toward him smiling. "Dom, you old bastard. Where've you been?"

Barney got a Stella beer for Dom from the sandpit where the ice had melted hours ago. He didn't have to ask. They'd been part of the same gang at school. Barney was the captain of the cricket team and about to get an England trial before the war bounced that one.

It was Barney who helped him get the transfer to the Desert Air Force. They'd done their basic training together at Brize Norton what seemed like a lifetime ago.

On the day they'd both flown solo from Coggershill to Thame, a feeble hop in retrospect, they had gone out together and got royally plastered at their local pub, the Queen's Head. If either of them then had declared over a pint that they were fighting for England or for their fellow men, they would have died laughing. Flying was the thing. It still was, different now. There was a new wariness, a hardness that Dom saw in Barney's eyes that he recognized in his own. They had both been shot down and hurt badly, they had both killed and wanted to kill again. Most of the pilots in the squadron were like this: fiercely competitive in a languid, don't-give-a-damn way. Parts of them frozen in shock. They had lost half their friends—Jacko the worst for both of them. They never talked about him except in a kind of distancing code.

They drank a couple of beers each outside their tent, and then Barney, not known for his sensitivity, glanced at Dom and said:

"You look different. You all right?"

Dom said never better.

Barney said he'd spent the morning flying with the air reconnaissance boys, having a snoop at the German aerodrome at Sidi Nsir, trying to locate exactly where their runways were. All their boys got home safe and sound. They'd spent the afternoon in Cairo, swimming at the Gezira Club, had a meal and come home. That was the way of their confusing lives now: war in the morning and fun in the afternoon.

"So how was your trip, old cock?"

"Not bad. Rather fun actually."

He couldn't tell Barney about Saba, not yet. He wanted to keep the shining feeling for a little while longer; couldn't bear the thought of the inevitable ribbing that would follow—"An ENSA singer, oh for God's sake, we all fall in love with them."

Their tent stank of curry and Barney's old socks. It was lit by a gas torch. It was boiling, boiling hot.

"Gotcha, little bastard." Barney walloped a cockroach on the wall with his grimy pillow. "Well, glad it was fun, because there's a rumor that all leave is going to be canceled for the next ten days," he said.

Dom slung his kitbag on the floor and sprawled on the camp bed, exhausted.

"They're sending us off to some deep desert place for extensive training. We had a briefing this morning from Davies. The rumor is there's a push planned in the next ten days."

"When will we hear?"

"Don't know; when they feel like telling us, as per."

Barney said this in a humorous drawl, a look of concealed excitement in his eyes. Dom felt it, too: a surge of pure adrenaline that stopped him sleeping for an hour or two even though his body was worn out. He was half waiting for the jangling telephone call that could wrench him and the rest of the squadron from their beds in the early hours of the night and have them sprinting toward the already shuddering planes. He was half listening to fragmented parts of "All the Things You Are," playing underneath him now. It was new to him, this jumbled, jazzed-up feeling. It felt like falling off the edge of his known world.

When sleep finally came, he dreamt that he and Saba were lying in each other's arms on warm sand somewhere. A motorboat with sails like a felucca was chug-chug-chugging across a calm blue bay. She loved him; he could feel it like a transfusion of light in his veins. They were floating together in some warm and womblike state. It was so simple.

He'd gone to sleep without undressing; his head was resting on his kitbag. The motorboat with sails, which was a Junkers Ju 88, rumbled above them and disappeared into cloud.

CHAPTER 19

The day after the concert, Saba was driven back to Ismailia and to a grimy apartment block where Dermot Cleeve was staying. They sat on rattan chairs drinking bottled lime juice in a dismal little room with cracks on the ceiling and a naked bulb overhead. Cleeve, his face pink and freshly shaven, wore new-looking linen trousers. Before he sat down, he folded a tea towel and placed it carefully on his chair with the air of a man decidedly not in his natural habitat. He said he'd being driving around all week trying to put together a program for the troops. No more ENSA artistes were allowed into Cairo until the situation improved there, and the difficulties of getting actual shows to remote desert areas had become so great, he said, they were relying more and more on broadcasts.

"But enough dreary shop talk." He stretched out his legs, and put his hands behind his head. "Because I now know two or three things about last night. First that the concert went well, which is splendid, and also that you were out rather late," he added playfully. "May one ask who the lucky young man was?"

She felt a childish urge to say *None of your business.*

"He's a friend."

"Quite a pretty friend, I hear," he said archly. "And if by chance he becomes more than a friend, may I warn you not to tell him about our conversations."

She jumped. "Did you follow us?"

He took a silver cigarette case out of his top pocket. "May I?" He lit up and took a sip of his juice, looking disdainfully at the thick glass it came in.

"No. But you do remember what I said to you in Cairo?" he said in a low voice. "Not a word to anyone, and get a pass next time, or ask permission. I can sometimes swing it if you want to ask me."

"We're allowed out," she whispered back. "I haven't taken Holy Orders and no one said we needed a pass to have a drink after the show."

"Oh, fiery girl!" He pursed his lips. "Of course you're allowed out, of course you are, you'd go mad without it, it's just that I have two exciting bits of news for you, and I'd prefer that you didn't get court-martialed before it happens."

He'd found out that for the next two weeks the company would be traveling west, more or less in the footsteps of the Eighth Army. In early August they would join up with a large company, The Fearsome Follies, and then God and the British army willing, do one week in Alexandria at the Gaiety. A darling little theater, although appalling acoustics. Did she know it?

She didn't.

Cleeve arranged the crease in his trousers and looked around him.

"If that happens, you'll do two shows with the company, and then we have another job for you—the one I mentioned." He looked at her significantly. "Quite important, actually, if it comes off. Zafer Ozan wants to book you for a short engagement at the Cheval D'Or in Alexandria for two nights in the middle of August." She'd surely heard of that?

"Yes," she said. Arleta had mentioned it.

"Well, it's an incredible honor. I can't remember another ENSA entertainer on tour ever being asked to do it."

The club, he explained, was on a plum spot on the Corniche, close to the Cecil Hotel. Some wonderful artists had played there before the war: Django Reinhardt, Maurice Chevalier, Tina Roje, Asmahan. Had she heard of Tina Roje? No, she hadn't heard of her either, but her heart was beating with excitement.

"Who do I have to get permission from?"

"No one," he said softly. "You can leave that to us. It's all arranged. But at some point, if things go as we hope, you'll be asked to go to a party at Ozan's house. He's a great party man, and he'll want to show you off. The house, I hear, is heaven, like something out of *One Thousand and One Nights.* He has some important friends coming for supper and you'll sing a couple of songs."

"A couple of songs?" she asked. Her stomach was churning. "Will anyone else be there? From the company, I mean." They felt like family now.

"No, but Madame Eloise, the wardrobe woman from Cairo, is living there temporarily. I think she has, or had, a small shop near the Corniche. I've arranged for you to stay with some friends of hers. She's a delightful person. She knows Ozan, not well, but she'll look after you."

"Does she know? About me, I mean."

"No. Your cover story is that you've been given a couple of weeks' leave to do some broadcast work and that you've been asked to sing for Mr. Ozan. I've told her how talented you are." He gave her a quick sincere smile; he seemed as excited as she was.

"Thank you." She hardly heard him. "So I just have to sing at the club and this party?"

"That's all." He drained his glass and put it down on the table. "For the time being the party is the most important thing—some businessmen, politicians, relatives of the royal family, movers and shakers will be there. Your job is to throw your teeth around and sing."

"Throw my teeth around?"

"Charm them, get to know them. Men love to boast to pretty girls. We're not asking you to be Mata Hari, but if anyone should drop information helpful to us . . . Asmahan, for example, is a gorgeous Syrian singer, rumored to have liaisons with two high-ranking German officers. She may not be there, of course."

"And that's all?"

"For the time being." He started to put papers away in his briefcase. "There might be another, much bigger job later. I don't want to talk about it now, so . . ." The quick bright smile was switched on again. "Anything else you'd like to ask me before we wrap it up?"

"Yes. Couldn't Arleta come too? She's hardworking, she's loyal; wouldn't it seem more natural, particularly as she knows him?"

A shadow passed over his face, whether of irritation or impatience she couldn't tell.

"We've been through this," he reminded her. "Arleta can't sing in Turkish, can she? That was the thing that melted Ozan's heart about you, actually," he whispered roguishly. "To be perfectly frank, I don't think she can sing at all."

"I don't agree," Saba said loyally—it pained her to understand what he meant. "The men love her."

"A little too much," he replied tartly. "A bit of a reputation, if you know what I mean."

"For what?"

He gazed at her steadily.

"You must know by now."

"I don't."

"Don't look so cross. It's a fact of life that gorgeous girls like you get more offers, the same way as powerful men do. It doesn't mean they're depraved, just luckier; some can resist, some can't, but this . . ." his larky look disappeared, his voice dropped, "is too important to take risks."

He grimaced as a bomber flew low over their heads, drowning out his next sentence.

"I think it would be polite to reply to Ozan soon." Some dusty birds flew in a cloud past the window. "They're a kind of kite," Cleeve said. "Disgusting creatures, God knows what they're doing around here.

"Oh, and by the way, Madame Eloise has agreed to lend dresses again, and Bagley will rehearse your tunes. He was thrilled to hear about your possible booking at the Cheval D'Or. In the quaint little sphere we inhabit, this kind of thing doesn't happen very often."

"Was he?" She felt a surge of triumph—maybe not so bad after all? "So, everything is arranged."

"It is. Am I to assume your answer is yes?"

"Of course," she said. One of the birds let out a jarring shriek at the very moment she was trying to look calm and collected. "So, when will I see you again?"

"In August, in Alexandria, *inshallah.*"

He said good-bye to her with a courteous touch of his panama hat. He was going to spend the rest of his day, he said, recording a marvelous composer and oud player, Mohamed El Qasabgi, for posterity.

That wasn't the kind of thing, he noted regretfully, one could play for the troops, who, of course, adored sentimental music, but it kept one sane.

Later, back at the camp, and walking toward her tent, she wondered if it was possible to die of excitement. Cleeve had insinuated that she was about to join some exclusive club, and that her singing could, just possibly, help change the way the war went. What a thought! She imagined her mother rolling around with laughter at it, her father apologizing with tears in his eyes—yet who would not feel proud?

And Dom. He was close to Alexandria, too. Her mind had locked onto this while Cleeve had been talking. She had to think of a way they could meet that would not be too dangerous for either of them.

She was deep in thought and almost at the tent when she saw another kite streaking across the sky with a stolen sausage link in its mouth.

And then the bothering bit crept into her mind again.

At the end of their meeting, Cleeve had warned her to keep her mouth shut about why she was in Alexandria, so what to tell Dom? She was not someone who enjoyed or was good at lying—her Mum had once pointed out that she always signaled a whopper on the way by putting her right hand over her right eye, like one of those *see no evil* monkeys. But she had given her word, and she would try.

CHAPTER 20

When Saba walked into the tent, Arleta was washing her blue silk nightdress in a canvas basin.

"Darling," she wrapped Saba in a soapy embrace, "where have you been, you wicked creature? I've been having kittens!"

"Not many kittens," Saba teased, kissing the top of her head. After she'd said good-bye to Dom she'd gone back to the tent and found it empty. About three in the morning, Arleta's head had poked through the canvas flap and Saba had listened to the sparkling crackle of her hair being tended, her teeth being brushed, the delicate jasmine and rose puff of Guerlain's Shalimar without which Arleta claimed she couldn't sleep a wink, silly as that sounded, the click of the torch going out, and finally the luxurious sigh that signaled that Arleta had had rather a good night of her own.

"So! Last night." Arleta abandoned her laundry. "What on earth was going on?"

"Well, the show seemed to go well." Saba felt wary—the rule in the company was tell one tell all.

"Oh don't be ridiculous. The beautiful man, who was he?"

"Well . . . he came unexpectedly to see me."

"I saw that, stupid."

"And he's . . ." Saba closed her eyes. "Look, I don't know, I don't know . . . oh." Her happiness spilled out; it was very hard to keep things from Arleta, it felt like meanness. "I met him before in London, and before that in hospital—and yes, he's a fighter pilot!" She curled her fingers into a pair of devil horns. "And please don't tell me what you think about them, because I already know." She tickled Arleta under the arm.

"If you have beans to spill," Arleta's eyes were glowing, "spill them now. It's only fair."

Saba couldn't resist. As she sketched out briefly how Dom had come to the audition, how they'd walked the streets of London that evening, how he'd driven her across the desert last night, she felt a rising elation.

"I mean, he's just so beautiful, and we have such interesting conversations together already, and he makes me laugh and . . . oh bugger, in a way it feels so simple and uncomplicated, as if he's been there waiting. . . . Does that sound daft?"

"Oh dear, oh dear, oh dear." Arleta dried her hands properly and sat down on the bed. She pulled Saba into the camp chair beside it. "She's got it bad. And by the way, it's never simple and uncomplicated. Did you sleep together?"

"No, but last night, I wanted to so badly. I've never felt so . . ." she gazed around her wildly, "completely out of control."

"Gosh." Even Arleta was impressed. She did a stage fall onto her camp bed and then sat up and hugged Saba. "Oh little lamb," she murmured into her hair. "Do be careful. It's so exciting, but he *is* a fighter pilot, enough said, or should be."

"But all of our lives are dangerous here," Saba said passionately. "And I know I'm definitely going to see him again." Oh God, she thought, what a hopeless spy she was going to be; she'd already said more about him than Cleeve would probably approve of.

"Of course they are and of course you will." Arleta patted her on the knee. "Of course you will."

She blew out air and jumped to her feet. She tied a piece of string across the tent and pegged out the blue silk nightdress and a pair of frothy matching knickers.

"And your night?" Saba poked her in the side.

Arleta narrowed her cat's eyes.

"Well, I was doing my bit for the Anglo-American alliance," she said. "I'll tell you all about him later."

"Sounds interesting."

"It was, and a little bit alarming, too. I'm too tired to give it full throttle now, I'll tell you later."

* * *

Lunch was bully-beef sandwiches and prunes. After it, Saba, Arleta, Janine, Willie, and the acrobats were rounded up and put into what Willie called a wog wagon, a small converted lorry with scalding metal seats shaped like bedpans arranged one behind the other.

They were followed by another lorry carrying rolled scenery, the stage, their kitbags, and Willie's fez, chicken feet, and Hitler mustache, accompanied by Max Bagley, Captain Crowley, and two soldiers with pistols in their holsters. The only information they'd been given was they were bound for a field hospital approximately fifty miles into the Western Desert.

The sun shrank their eyeballs as it swept across the cloudless sky, and the desert was so full of glassy mirages that it looked like a flat sea. The temperature rose to 125 degrees in the nonexistent shade, and everyone in the lorry felt ratty and disinclined to talk.

After two hours' traveling they stopped at a settlement where the only visible signs of life were a scattering of flat-roofed houses and a rust-colored watering hole by the side of the road. A house made of red mud was open to the street and a few wooden tables were scattered outside. A barefoot man served them flatbread, a tiny piece of white chewy cheese and hot, sweet mint tea, which Willie told them in a cheerful whisper tasted like camel's pee. This annoyed Janine, who hated coarseness. "Oh touchy, touchy," he said as she removed herself to another table and fell asleep, her delicate head like a drooping flower in her hands.

Their host was refilling their glasses when shouts came from outside: some trouble with the chassis of their lorry, parts of which now hung down like sheep udders. Crowley, who liked to show off about all the countries he had served in, was shouting at two bewildered-looking men in oily robes in the language they had all started to imitate and call Lingo Bingo. "Come on, you bastards, *jaldi jow*, chop, chop. Under lorry bang bang."

"God, what a rude sod he is," Arleta murmured. "One day he's going to get himself shot."

But the men smiled. They lay down under the lorry with their spanners while the cast rested. They had two performances ahead of them that night.

The acrobats took their bedrolls, did a bit of play wrestling and then fell asleep under a thorn tree beside the water hole. Janine, who hated putting her fair skin in the sun, stayed inside the restaurant asleep at the table. Arleta and Saba lay under a juniper tree looking up at the patterned sky through its branches. Beside them, a donkey was lashed to another tree and hee-hawed at the sight of them.

"Poor little thing." When Saba offered it bread, it nibbled her hands with velvet lips and gazed at her with kindly eyes. "Why do they treat their animals so badly here?" she asked Arleta. "No water, no food, no shade."

Arleta said that life was hard on these people, too; on her last tour of Egypt, she'd seen men walking round and round and round in the blazing sun all day pushing a wheel just to get the water out of a well. "They probably think that donkey has a whale of a time."

"Well, I don't think so." Saba jumped up. "The poor little thing can hardly move its head. I don't think the owner would mind if I lengthened the rope."

"I wouldn't interfere if I was you," advised Arleta, but Saba ignored her. She jumped up, loosened the rope, patted the donkey's neck and gave it another piece of flatbread. "There you are, dear little man."

"You're a shocking softie," Arleta said drowsily. "You'll get yourself hurt one day, and you'll be crawling with fleas tonight."

When Arleta fell asleep, Saba, watched with mild curiosity by the donkey, got a writing pad out of her kitbag. She shook the sand out of its creases, and wrote:

Dear Dom,

I'm going to Alex in August. Any chance we could meet there?

Now she must think of a safe way of getting the message to him—one that Cleeve would approve of.

Closing her eyes, she had an almost photographic image of Dom flying alone over the desert, with its tanks and hidden aerodromes and landmines.

She shook her head. He would live, she must believe he would, else there would be no peace from now on.

A fly woke Arleta up.

"Sod off." She brushed it away. "How long have I been asleep?"

"Twenty minutes."

"*Yalla yalla*, girls," Crowley was waving his swagger stick in their direction. He made a cone of his hands and bellowed, "Lorry fixed, get mobile in ten minutes. Don't leave anything behind. Got that, Willie boy?" he roared at Willie, who he treated like a halfwit. "Ten minutes. Don't forget your hat." Willie was dozing on the veranda; his knotted handkerchief had fallen into the dust.

"Sabs," Arleta said quickly, "before we get on the lorry, I want to tell you something about last night. I wouldn't feel right without passing it on."

It seemed that while Saba had been out with Dom, Arleta and Janine had gone to the officers' mess to have a drink with some of the bigger wigs on the base. These included an air commodore who had flown in from Tunisia, an army doctor with the worst case of desert sores that Arleta had ever seen, and a padre who banged on a bit about Willie's rude jokes, so it was no contest at all really, she continued, when her eye lit on an American colonel: a full colonel, mind, and awfully handsome with blond, blond hair, broad shoulders, honey-colored skin; a real southern gentleman in spite of his striking good looks. Arleta's voice grew low and husky.

"And I do so like Americans." When she threw back her hair, Saba saw a bruise on her neck. "We had a lovely talk and then he smuggled me into his rooms and we made love. I think he thought all his Christmases and Thanksgivings had come at once."

Arleta, as always, was strikingly unrepentant about such matters, and if she felt guilty about betraying her Bill, she showed little sign of it. Once, when Saba had asked about this, she'd said they had an arrangement—she'd said it in the French way, which made it sound more fun—he'd written to her saying she should take her pleasures where she might, because he was going to.

"Oh grow up, darling," she had said to Saba's shocked face. "There's a war on. I don't want him to live like a monk and he knows I'm not cut out for nun-dom or whatever you call it. This way is much more sensible."

"Anyway," she continued now, "shut up for a moment because this is what I want to tell you. Later, much later, when we were having a brandy and a cigarette, the lovely Wentworth Junior the Third—that was his name—told me something that he said he shouldn't have. He has some kind of intelligence job, and in his opinion the war here will be over very, very soon." Arleta took a deep breath and shook her head vigorously.

"Over! Are you sure?" Saba was shocked to find herself a little disappointed.

"No, silly, course I'm not sure, nobody is, but here's the point: he said there is going to be the mother and father of all battles soon."

"But they're always saying that."

"He was convinced this was the one. He was actually shocked that we hadn't been sent home already."

"Where will they be fighting?"

"Didn't say, wouldn't, but it's bound to be near the coastline, that's where all the Germans are, and the various supply lines; that's where they're bombing mostly."

"Near Alexandria? Near Cairo?"

"Alexandria. He says it's an open secret among the men that the battle will happen in the next few weeks there. And if we're sent there, we should jump ship, it's just too dangerous."

Arleta went on to say that she knew for a fact that they'd just moved another ENSA company, The Live Wires, out from Alex to Palestine. "I actually worked with one of the girls in it—Beryl Knight, a dancer, awful frizzy hair but a very nice girl," she added loyally.

"So, will we have to go soon?"

"No, this is the point. Wentworth's good buddy," Arleta slipped into an unconvincing American twang, "is Captain Furness. I swore to him this morning I wouldn't say anything, but apparently we're not going to be sent away—we'll be following the Eighth Army into the desert."

"Heavens."

They exchanged a strange look.

"Do you want to do that?" Saba asked.

"Girls, come on! *Jaldi jow.*" Captain Crowley, red-faced and shouting now.

"Do you mean keep going?"

"Yes."

"I do. You?"

"Yes," said Saba. "I couldn't bear to go home now."

Arleta just looked at her.

"We must be mad," she said. She squeezed Saba's hand and they laughed shakily.

For the next leg of their journey, Bagley got on the bus with them and said they were going to have another rehearsal of the doo-wop song. He'd explained to them before that doo-wop was a kind of African music he'd heard in a club in Harlem before the war began. The song was called "My Prayer," he said. He couldn't remember the exact lyrics but it was about the kind of promises you make when you're in love and you want them to be sacred and bind you forever.

"The chorus is fabulous—come on, Bog, you try it, and Arleta. The melody goes like this, *Umbadumba umbadumb ummmmbbbuumm.* You should see the negro men who sing this stuff—they beam, they strut, they shoot their cuffs." He did a bit of portly strutting up the center of the bus to demonstrate. "So, you sing the line, Saba, and the rest of you do the *umbas.*

"What's so fascinating about this new kind of music," Bagley continued, "is that it has distinct echoes of the madrigal. *Now is the month of maying, when merry lads are playing,*" he sang in his clear, high voice. "*Fa la la la la la la*—you get it—*de wop de wahhhh,*" he ended in a black voice.

Beside him, Crowley sat rigid with alarm and embarrassment. He never knew where to look when they were messing around like this.

But Bagley was on fire, and so were the rest of them, magically transformed by a song.

Which ended in a roar of laughter. Bagley told them to shut up now and save their voices for that night. Saba, who had slipped into the seat beside Willie, was shocked when she glanced at him to see two great tears running down his cheeks like marrowfat peas. She looked at him more closely—the whites of his eyes were red with crying; with his knotted hankie on his head again he looked like a sad fat baby.

"What's the matter, Willie, is it your ticker?" she whispered. When she put her hand in his, he gripped it hard. Usually he hated being asked about his health—he was terrified of being sent home—but this felt different.

He gave a small snort and a shuddering sigh.

"In a way," he said at last, "your fault. You'd better not sing that 'My Prayer' to the troops; you'll have them in floods."

"Willie, come on—there must be something else."

He glanced around to check it was safe to talk.

"Tell me." She squeezed his hand. "I won't blab."

He looked across at Arleta, who was fast asleep, her blond hair spilling into the aisle.

"It is my ticker, but it's not in a medical way." He swallowed noisily. "It's her." As he spoke, Arleta's tumbling waves shifted from side to side, picking up reflections from the sun.

"Arleta?"

"Yes."

There was a long, fraught silence.

"D'you remember," Willie said at the end of it, "what a wonderful surprise it was seeing me at the auditions in London that day and how we'd worked together in Malta and Brighton? Well, it's no coincidence. I've tried to get on every tour she's been on, but she's killing me, Saba." As he said this, the faded irises of his eyes floated under their lids and another tear rolled down the side of his face.

Saba clutched his hand. He must have seen Arleta leave with her blond American the night before.

"But, Willie, has she ever given you any reason to think . . . ?"

"Well, you tell me. She's always telling me I'm wonderful and she loves me and I'm the funniest man she's ever met. She's so beautiful . . ." he ended brokenly.

"Yes, but Willie . . ."

"I know, I know, we all go on like that in the business, and I'm the silliest old man that ever lived for thinking she really meant it." He stopped suddenly. More tears rolling down his face, and a large *whoomph* into his handkerchief. "Sorry, love, I'm not much fun, am I?"

"No, no, no, no, it's all right, Willie, but not being nosy or anything, I thought you had a wife and that she passed away a few months before we went on tour. That's what Arleta told me."

"Well, that's another can of worms," he said. "So to speak. Arleta puts a lovely slant on it, but the truth is, we were married for over thirty-four years, and I hardly knew her, and that was my fault, too. I love all this," he gestured around the dusty lorry, "the touring, the performing, I can't seem to stop." He added that he had two girls, now grown up, and he hardly knew a thing about them either.

"My dad's a bit like that," Saba said.

"Performer?" he asked, picking up a bit. "If he is, he should be very, very proud of you."

"No, to both parts. He hates me doing this. We didn't even say good-bye."

"Oh blimey, that's a bit serious, can't you make up?"

"Can't," she said. "He's at sea."

"Well send a letter home," he said. "He must go home sometimes."

"Umm, maybe." She hated to talk about it—it felt so shameful.

To cheer them both up, Willie got a couple of melted peppermints from his pocket, which seemed to have a calming effect.

He said she was young enough to take a bit of advice from him, because, in his opinion, there was good and bad excitement in life, and the excitement of performing could turn around sometimes, and bite you on the you-know-what. It was too much, it was unwise, and it skewed other things in your life.

"I'll tell you a little story," he said. "One time I went home to our house in Crouch End—I'd been away for ages doing a wonderful pantomime in Blackpool and I was as high as a flaming kite and very taken with myself. But when I got home the missus was livid. I hadn't seen her for two months and I hadn't even remembered to tell her what time I was coming home, so she leaves a note on the doorstep saying 'Baked beans and bread in the cupboard, I'm out.'

"But she'd forgotten to leave the key under the mat, so I tried to climb through the cloakroom, and I'm so fat, I got wedged in the window, and looking at my house from this angle I thought, *I can't do this anymore, it's too small and too cramped. I can't do it.* But you have to do it sometimes, don't you. You have to be ordinary and learn to like it."

He was so het up he had to look out of the window where light was draining from the day and the desert sand was drenched in a brilliant geranium red.

"You all right now, love?" Willie asked. "Arleta says you were homesick at first."

"I'm getting a bit addicted myself, Willie," she said, mesmerized by the sunset, and upset to have seen Willie crying. "But I do miss home. It's the first time I've been farther than Cardiff on my own, so a bit of a step."

He patted her hand softly. "I'm here if you ever need me, don't forget that, gel."

"Thank you, Willie."

"Two concerts tonight, then. A bit of shut-eye in order."

"You all right now, Willie?" She gave him a quick kiss on the cheek.

"Course I am." He tried to wink at her. "That'll learn you to sing songs to silly old men." He held his Adam's apple between his fingers, wobbled it and warbled: "*Because I love yoooouuuuuuu.*"

When he extended the last note into a small dog's trembling howl and everyone in the bus burst out laughing, except Arleta who was still asleep and Crowley who was frowning over the maps again.

CHAPTER 21

Dom had never known that love could feel so like fear. But that night as he lay in his camp bed and conjured up her image, he recognized fear's physical sensations—the powdery limbs, the pounding heart. He pictured her glossy hair, the playful twist to her smile when she teased him. How in the restaurant, when they'd been talking, she'd fixed her big brown eyes on him and seemed to drink him in.

And now he saw her—it almost made him furious to do so—with that tiny band of performers racketing around desert outposts and transit camps and aerodromes, all of them sitting ducks for the Germans, who were circling closer and closer. There were land mines in the desert—one of their aircrew had had his leg blown off the week before—and serious supply shortages already. What if a lorry they were on broke down in the wrong place? There was always now the distinct possibility of a sudden air-raid attack by the Germans, and lately, the Italians.

Saba had told him a German Stuka had hit part of the stage before the ack-ack could get it during another ENSA group's performance near Suez. They'd got to the chorus of "A Nightingale Sang in Berkeley Square" when *boooom!!!!* It had shot through part of a comedian's baggy trousers—she'd made a funny story out of it.

They'd kept on singing of course—well bully for them—but he didn't want her to have to take part in these kinds of heroics, and he was furious at the authorities for not sending them away to safety, although he would never have dared tell her that.

And so, on the borderlines of sleep, when you're free to think anything, he pleaded, *Send her home; let the troops do without music. She's too young for this.*

* * *

Six o'clock the next morning, a field telephone woke him. The usual instant boggle-eyed awakeness.

Paul Rivers wanted Dom and Barney to report to the crew room after breakfast. Four new pilots had arrived for retraining before the big push. They were to take them shadow flying that afternoon.

After breakfast, it was overcast and humid and they waited until the last possible moment to climb into the flight suits that made you sweat like a pig. Six of them made their way to the sand airstrip where the ground crew were preparing their aircraft.

The new boys were Scott, an awkwardly hearty Canadian whose hand squelched with sweat and made whoopee-cushion noises as it pumped Dom's, and his friend Cliff, a silent midwesterner, whose massive, impassive face looked like a rock carving. Scott said he'd learned to fly as a crop duster in the States. The other two would join them after lunch.

They were waiting for take-off in a tin hut at the end of the runway when Scott said, "So, what's the situation here, fellows? Do we have a snowball's chance in hell of winning this thing?"

"Well, on the whole, snowballs don't have much of a life expectancy out here," Barney said pleasantly.

"Oh very English, pip-pip and all that." The Canadian scowled and looked at Dom. "But what's the score?"

Not an unreasonable question.

"Well, the Hun have aerodromes now in Tunisia, in Libya, and scattered around the Western Desert, and they're moving east, or at least trying to. If they can capture Alexandria and Cairo we're stuffed, so the next bit is not to let them do that."

When he stopped to spit some sand out of his mouth, Barney took over.

"The fighting here is not the old Battle of Britain man-against-man stuff," he said. "We're mostly covering bomber patrols, escorting tanks, protecting supply lines. We haven't had any major offensives yet, but that could change at a moment's notice.

"One of their main problems, ours too, is running out of water. You may have noticed," he rubbed his bristling chin, "it's not in plentiful supply here." He screwed up his eyes against the sun and they followed his gaze toward the miles and miles and miles of desert behind him. He was getting irritable; it was time to fly and stop talking.

Dom felt it, too, a craving to leave the ground.

Half an hour later, he climbed into the tight mouth of the Kittyhawk, put the parachute under his seat, plugged in the oxygen, turned it on full and then squeezed tubes to see if it was coming through. At the RT command of *All right, chaps, off we go,* they rose into the air.

The new pilots had been briefed about shadow shooting. Now Dom and Barney flew in formation together, elegant as Ginger and Fred and showing off to the new boys just a bit as they dipped and spun and glided across the desert, letting their shadows drop like giant ink spots.

It was boiling hot as usual inside the Perspex and tin universe of the aircraft, but already he could feel the fears of the night and the petty worries of the day recede. He was flying again.

"Okay now, watch it now! Watch it! We're coming over," Dom told the new boys through his radio transmission.

And then *boom! boom! boom! boom!* Each aircraft had been given three rounds of ammunition to unleash. Dom could hear Scott laughing, and the taciturn American whooping and hollering as he emptied his guns into their black shadows.

Once, such moments were the high points of Dom's life, the times when he forgot everything—lovers, parents, home—to play the most dangerous and exhilarating game devised by man or devil. He'd loved all of it then: the feeling of mastery, the freedom from petty earth, the danger, the fear, but now a smear of shame was mixed into the exhilaration. Nothing he could talk about yet, to anyone—not to his parents, not to his living friends, certainly not to a woman—but always there.

The first shadowings had come in the early days of the Battle of Britain. He'd gone up in a Spitfire, misread the altimeter, and the plane had plunged down at top speed toward the coast of Norfolk. The earth had come hurtling toward him. His stomach hit his brains. It was only at the last possible moment that he'd managed to swerve and climb again.

That was the day when he'd sworn to himself that if he got down in one piece, he'd go straight to his flight commander and say he would never fly again. He'd passed out for a few moments after landing and woke tasting his own vomit in his crash helmet. But on his way back to the mess, walking on jelly legs and staggering under the weight of his parachute, he'd changed his mind again. He simply couldn't stop. It was what he needed to feel alive.

And then, much later and much worse, he'd persuaded Jacko to go up again even though he knew Jacko was struggling with the mathematics of flight. There was something about coordinating hand, eye, foot, maps, controls, and the altimeter that didn't come naturally to him. He'd tried to tell Dom he was windy and Dom had teased him out of it, or tried—a moment of casual cruelty that would stay with him for the rest of his life.

What happened next was the rock under the sunny surface of things. But he mustn't dwell on it; they'd been warned about that. "Be economic with emotion," the wing commander had told them on day one at flight school. "Look at the chap on your right, and now at the one on your left; soon one of them will be dead."

He must forget his joke; forget Jacko's face on fire, the plane spinning toward the sea like a pointless toy.

His new priorities were clear: flying, fighting, and seeing Saba again.

CHAPTER 22

When Willie collapsed on stage, ten days later, it was Janine who saved his life. They were performing at a fuel depot close to an infantry camp near Burg el Arab; Arleta was pretending to be Josephine Baker dancing the famous banana dance that had enchanted *tout* Paris; Willie was the ravenous little boy eating her bananas while she leapt around blissfully unaware. It was very funny and Saba loved it. She was roaring with laughter in the wings when she saw Willie's eyes go blank and float up into his lids. She thought it was a stunt, until he crashed heavily to the floor and the curtain came hurriedly down.

He fell on a rusty nail in the wings that shot into a hand that instantly spurted blood. Janine whipped off her tights, twisted them into a makeshift tourniquet, and then ran on muscles of steel toward the much-derided panic bag for emergency iodine and bandages, all applied with ice-cool efficiency.

The cause of his initial faint was diagnosed as jaundice, possibly contracted from food from one of the flyblown street stalls he insisted were far safer than the jellied-eel stands in London. He was now in a military hospital on the base looking yellow and uncertain, but still alive. Saba and Arleta had gone to see him every day, with Janine, who was shyly the heroine of the hour, until Arleta had herself gone yellow and come down with jaundice. The eight-piece combo that was supposed to arrive from Malta hadn't. Janine, who'd been offered a transfer to India, delayed her departure, and sometimes read to Willie in the afternoons. The last time Saba had arrived she'd been brushing his hair and blushed bright red at the sight of her.

"Do you want to do this?" Bagley asked when the official request came through for Saba to transfer to Alex and do a week of wireless broadcasts. "With Willie and Arleta off, there's sod all to do here, and a couple of nights at the Cheval D'Or would be quite a feather in your cap." His forehead had wrinkled as he'd read the order again. "But I hear it's pretty hot there—I mean, you could probably go home now if you pushed it. I'd certainly help you."

She'd looked at him in amazement. Stop now! Was he completely mad?

But four days later, stepping off the plane in Alexandria, she felt a complicated mix of emotions: orphanish to be sure at leaving the company (both Willie and Arleta had cried; Bog had offered to marry her), excited about the possibility of performing at the Cheval D'Or, desperate to get some kind of safe message to Dom. If they were ever to have a chance of meeting, it would have to be here.

"Darling." Madame Eloise stepped out of a sea of dun-colored soldiers to meet her, looking like some cool and exotic flower in her white linen dress and pale primrose hat.

"Madame." Saba tried to sidestep the little groaning kisses on both cheeks. She'd been sick again on the plane, and Madame smelled delicious—a tart fragrance like grapefruits and sweet roses.

"Oh don't bother with all that Madame business." Madame's voice had a faint cockney twang Saba hadn't noticed before. "That's for my shop customers. Call me Ellie."

As they walked across the road, Ellie explained the fortunate coincidence that had led her here.

"I happened to be here on business," she said, "when Captain Furness, an old friend, asked me to step in. The other chaperone got stuck in Cairo, where all the wretched trains have stopped. So we're orphans together. Doing what, I'm not entirely sure." She stopped smiling and frowned; it made her look older—Saba guessed at least forty.

"To be honest with you, Ellie," Saba said, "I haven't got a flipping clue either. I was whisked out of the desert this morning and told I'd get my orders when I arrived here."

"Well, all to be revealed soon." Ellie put up a parasol. "I hope."

A taxi took them down a desert road littered on both sides with wrecked tanks and burned-out jeeps, and when they turned toward the city Saba was shocked. Arleta, who'd once done a three-week tour here, had waxed eloquent about its fabulous beaches, and shops as good as London, and cosmopolitan street cafes, and perfect climate, but as they drove closer, Saba saw shattered pavements and charred houses, an old woman with a bandage around her head scavenging for food.

"This looks like a dangerous place to live," she said. She found it hard to imagine that there would be a nightclub open here.

"Don't worry, pet." Ellie patted her hand. "We're staying in a staff house that belonged to a Colonel Patterson, in Ramleh, in the eastern part of town, away from all this. God it's bright outside."

The black shadows of flowers moved across her face as she pulled the taxi's homemade blackout curtains.

"People are on edge here, naturally, after the flap," she continued breezily, "but life goes on, people are swimming again and partying, and most of them say the Germans will bypass Alexandria."

"We've been living inside a bit of a bubble lately," Saba said, thinking how easily this battered town could be circled by a line of German tanks, "and traveling so much." When she peered around the curtain she saw a group of men staring helplessly at a collapsed shop window in which a few stained dresses and cardboard boxes remained. "It's hard to know who to trust."

"Keep that closed." Ellie jerked the fabric and made it dark again. She patted Saba's hand and crossed her legs with a sucking sound. "I hear you girls have done heroic work in the desert, and if I may say so, you look absolutely done in," she said. "Look at you!" A circle of dust had formed around Saba's feet; the laces in her shoes were clogged with it. "A bath first, I think, then a decent lunch. Tomorrow you've been asked out to lunch with Zafer Ozan, which should be fun. Have you seen his house?"

"I met him once. He heard me sing in Cairo."

"Oh well, glory, you are in for a treat. I hear it's stunning."

"Are you coming?" Saba hoped she was.

Ellie hesitated. "Not sure yet; let's wait and see."

The charming villa they were staying in had iron grilles on its windows and blackout curtains inside. When the taxi stopped outside it, a *suffragi* took Saba's dusty kitbag from the back of the car and led them toward the house.

"The house is lovely and cool, you'll be happy to hear," Ellie said. They had stepped into a tiled hall. Her heels clattered emptily into a sitting room smelling of furniture polish that looked like a dentist's waiting room with its half-empty bookshelves and old copies of *Country Life*. "We keep all the shutters closed during the day, and use the fans at night."

The Pattersons, it seemed, had gone for longer than a holiday. There were gaps on the wall where pictures had disappeared; the teak floor had a pale square in the middle of it where the rug had been. When a servant took Saba to the guest room on the second floor where she felt a dizzying wave of tiredness at the sight of the clean white sheets, the mosquito net, the soft-looking bed. All of the company were exhausted now and she hadn't had a decent night's sleep for what felt like a long time. In a saucer beside her bed, someone had lit a Moon Tiger—its green coils of insect repellent gently smoldering, dropping ash on the floor.

"Bath first, then bed." Ellie padded into the room in her stockinged feet. She had a jar of violet-colored bath salts in one hand, towels in the other. She followed Saba into the bathroom where the water was already flowing. She handed Saba a green silk kimono and said she must use it while she was here.

"You're very kind," said Saba. Her limbs were aching for her first proper bath in a month.

"Not kind, happy to see you." Ellie opened her mouth to say something else, but left it at that. "Hop in," she said. "I'll see you at supper."

The water was hot and smelled so good. Saba, scrubbing herself with soap, was astounded at how much dust and sand had stuck to her skin. The day before, they'd all been caught in a dust storm as they'd left the rehearsal tent. For ten minutes the sand had lashed and stung them; when they got back to their tents they laughed at each other—they were so coated in dust that Saba said they should be on a plinth at the Cairo museum. The pint of water they'd shared to wash it off had left them all with grit in their underwear, their teeth, their hair and made them feel irritable and out of sorts.

Sunlight bounced off the water. Bliss! A whole bath to herself without Janine's wretched egg-timer or her damp sighs behind the door. It was only when Saba was washing her hair with the shampoo thoughtfully provided that she felt a wiggle of loneliness. Arleta usually rinsed her hair for her, and helped her dry it in a way that made her feel like a cherished baby. Before she left, Arleta had hugged her tight; she'd pinched Saba's cheeks and said she wanted her back soon: they were family now. Even Janine had pecked her on the cheek.

When she'd gone to see Willie in hospital, he'd pretended to bawl his eyes out like a fat baby. Arleta said she didn't think he'd last long.

The water was almost cold when she woke. She heard the grumble of aeroplanes overhead, the gurgle of pipes from the kitchens below, and, for a moment, had no idea where she was.

She dressed and went downstairs. "Well, you had a good one," Ellie said. She'd changed into a pair of pale gray silk lounging pajamas and knotted a long rope of pearls around her neck. She was drinking a gin and tonic. She went over to the window and checked that the dark blue blackout curtains were fully drawn, and told Saba that after supper they would have some fun trying on clothes.

"Ozan throws a great party, or so I've heard." She closed her eyes ecstatically. "Marvelous music, rivers of Bollinger—wish I'd kept up with *my* singing lessons."

"What did you do before the war?" Saba asked quickly. Ellie's hints made her uneasy—she still wasn't sure what she was doing here, or whether it was safe for her to go to the party. She wished Cleeve was around to brief her again.

"A long story." Ellie took a sip of her gin. There was a taut perkiness about her tonight that Saba hadn't noticed before that made her wonder if she was more nervous than she was letting on. "Which I'll nutshell: went to Paris when I was young, instantly fell in love with the city—an absolute *coup de foudre.* In those days, no interest in clothes whatsoever—lived in jodhpurs and twinsets—but one day, shopping in a local market, a man saw me, great gawky thing that I was. He asked me to be a house model for Jean Patou. They made me lose half a stone, taught me how to use makeup, and then I did three of their collections."

She stood up and walked in a haughty way toward the blackout curtain: "Feather on the head, tail on the derriere, that's how they taught us to walk."

"Numéro un—une robe blanche," she imitated the gloomy voice of a vendeuse, and then *pring pring* she played an imaginary piano. *"Numéro deux—une robe noire.* Dead boring, but suppose it was a start. The main thing was, I lived independently for the first time. That was wonderful."

They ate supper together in a sparsely furnished dining room, where the only light came from a fringed lamp on the sideboard.

Ellie had organized a local dish called kushari, a cumin-scented mix of lentils and onions and vegetables smothered in a spicy sauce. She apologized for serving peasant food. "The Egyptians call it a messy mix," she said, "but I adore it, much better than ghastly tinned sausages and all that bully-beef rubbish." They washed it down with a glass of French wine. Ellie said it was a present from a new boyfriend, a French-Egyptian wine merchant.

"He's Free French and I'm quite taken," she said, her eyes lighting up. Saba was surprised; surely forty was too old for passion?

Saba ate heartily; she loved the food and said so. It reminded her of the dishes Tansu used to make. She told Ellie, a good listener, about Tan: how they used to lie in bed listening to music on the wireless together, how brave Tan had been arriving in Wales from Turkey with nothing but her suitcase. Ellie smiled at Saba as if she were her own child.

"I'm feeling quite nervous actually, Ellie," Saba said when they were eating tiny pastries and drinking Turkish coffee. "I've never sung at a proper nightclub before, or at a really posh party like Mr. Ozan's. I don't know what songs they'll like even."

Ellie leaned forward; she grabbed both of Saba's hands and held them between hers. She looked her intently in the eyes. "They'll love you," she said. "Dermot Cleeve says you're a real find."

Saba looked at her. So she did know Cleeve.

"I thought he might be here tonight," said Saba. She was aware of how her voice bounced in the empty, rugless room. It almost felt as if they were on a stage.

"Don't worry," said Ellie. "Everything is falling into place. While you were in the bath I got a telephone call from Furness. You're to rehearse with a woman called Faiza Mushawar; her husband used to own the Café de Paris, not the real one of course, but the one on the Corniche. She is a fine singer herself, although more in that moany, waily Arab style than is to my taste—have you ever been to one of their concerts, darling? Well don't. Hideous. They go on for absolutely days. Anyway, I hear they have a first-class band there." Her diamond ring flashed as she patted Saba's hand. "A lovely change from singing in the desert. That must have been depressing."

"It's not," Saba said. How to explain how shockingly alive it had made her feel, and proud, too, to be doing her bit. "When do we start?" She wanted Ellie to say immediately so she could stop feeling nervous.

"The day after tomorrow at ten."

The business part of their conversation seemed over, and now, as darkness deepened outside the house, Ellie babbled on amiably—about the dresses she'd brought, how she'd help with makeup if necessary. She'd done the models at Patou and still had her kit with all the old favorites in it. Tangee's Red Red was fabulous under lights. Saba tuned her out. She was thinking about her songs. "Stormy Weather," her head nodded as she silently sang it; the doo-wop maybe for a bit of light relief; "My Funny Valentine" definitely, she loved singing that. It would be a treat, she thought, not to sing the relentlessly chirpy songs ENSA insisted on even to men who looked half dead.

The tray of coffee cups rattled as the servant left the room. There was a distant boom, followed by the rat-tat-tat of antiaircraft guns. The servant stopped and waited expectantly. Ellie listened hard, her eyes wide open, her nostrils flared.

"There's an air-raid shelter behind the courtyard," she said, "if we need it. Personally, I can't be bothered to run out at every single thing. It's nothing like as bad as London was, I can assure you." The flame of her match caught her tense smile, and Saba felt fearful and dislocated again. In Cardiff, when the bombs were this close and she and Tan couldn't be fagged to go to the shelter, they'd lie under the table in the front room together. They'd hug each other and sing songs, the mountainous upholstered bulk of her gran as solid as a sofa or a building.

The antiaircraft guns stopped; she heard the shrill sound of a rocket. To distract herself she picked up the photograph on the sideboard of the sensibly departed Pattersons, they stood in front of a large gray slab of a building next to a flag at what looked like a passing-out parade. Gray English sky above them. The colonel's pleasant long-jawed face bent toward Mrs. Patterson, smiling rigidly at the camera.

"Amazing, isn't it." Ellie took the photo from her. "How scared some people get at the slightest thing. Ever since I've been in Egypt," she stretched her feet and admired her toes, "they've gone on about the big push. I'd have been gone eight or nine times if I believed them, and to what? Some awful little flat in London, where thousands and thousands of people have been killed already."

"So, will you stay after the war?" Saba asked.

"If a certain someone wants me to," Ellie said with a cat-that-got-the-cream smile, "I'd definitely stay." She added softly, "I love it here, I really do."

The bombing had stopped. The doors were double-locked; the servants dismissed. Saba took the plunge.

"Ellie," she said, "you know, in Cairo you asked us about . . . you know . . . men friends?" She used the phrase shyly, but "boyfriend" sounded wrong, too. "Well, there is someone I'd like to see while I'm here. He's in the Desert Air Force, and he has some leave coming up."

"Does Dermot know about him?" Ellie asked pleasantly. She pushed a box of Turkish delight toward her. "Have one—they're delish."

"No."

"Ummm." Ellie put her sweet down on a saucer, her teeth marks clearly imprinted. "Gosh." Her thoughtful expression had changed. She leaned forward and clasped Saba's hand. "So funny you asked me this," she said quietly.

She got up and poured them both a small brandy even though Saba had not asked for one. She paced around for a bit with her drink in her hand taking small excited sips, and then she sat down.

"Saba," she said. "Listen." She drained her glass and then explained in a low voice that her new boyfriend mentioned earlier, whose name was Tariq, was actually in Alexandria that week and she was absolutely longing to see him. Not that she had minded, of course, but she'd had to cancel a weekend away with him to be Saba's chaperone. He was a very passionate man, and they'd had rather a bust-up about this, but now, well maybe . . .

"Saba," she added, in an urgent whisper, "will you promise me not to breathe a word of this to Captain Furness or Dermot Cleeve or any of the ENSA gang for that matter. But I don't want to lose this man and I wasn't sure I'd have time to see him. He's off himself next week to Beirut." She looked carefully at Saba. "Tell me your friend's name again."

"His name is Dom. Pilot Officer Dominic Benson."

"Shall I see what I can do?"

Saba sank to her knees, and clasped her hands together in mock prayer. "Please."

Ellie chewed her bottom lip and stared thoughtfully at Saba.

"If I do this, you must keep mum. People are frightful gossips here—it's very easy to lose your reputation, so the fewer people we tell the better," by which Saba assumed she meant they would tell no one. Which was fine with her.

CHAPTER 23

The next day, a uniformed chauffeur drove up to the house in a Bugatti, the most beautiful car Saba had ever seen, with a blue china evil eye swinging from its front mirror.

The chauffer delivered a note on elaborately engraved paper requesting the pleasure of Miss Saba Tarcan's company at Mr. Zafer Ozan's house near Montazah at one o'clock. He hoped she would honor him by staying for lunch.

If Ellie was miffed at not being asked she hid her disappointment generously. After breakfast, she took Saba up to her bedroom and told her to take her pick from the row of beautiful and expensive dresses hanging like highly scented corpses in white cotton bags in her wardrobe. After some consideration, they chose an exquisitely simple blue silk that Ellie said she'd picked up in Paris, at a Christian Dior sample sale. She insisted Saba take the matching bag as well—a bright blue feathery thing that lay like a dead bird at the bottom of the wardrobe in a shoebox lined with tissue paper.

During these procedures, Ellie became electric with excitement. She insisted on a ladylike waspy corset, and a stole; she darted toward her jewelry case and produced a pair of pearl earrings, which she clipped on Saba's ears, murmuring *of course, of course* as if she had reached the end of some daunting religious crisis; she grabbed a brush and pulled it through Saba's hair, saying she had fabulous hair and should thank her lucky stars for it. Fat chance anyone had of finding a decent hairdresser in Alex at the moment.

Saba forgot to answer. She was thinking about her songs again and found Ellie's bright stream of chat distracting. She also disliked being prodded and poked like this. It made her feel like a doll.

"Gorgeous. Beautiful!" Ellie squinted at her in the mirror. "Now." She opened a glass bottle with a tassel on it, and dabbed Saba's wrist.

"It's called Joy and the occasional free bottle was one of the perks of working with Patou, and now of course I'm addicted to the ruddy stuff. If you like it, I can give you some."

Saba sniffed her wrist and wrinkled her nose. Ellie's eyes had closed and her expression become stagily ecstatic. "Let it settle," she commanded. "Every ounce of its essence is made with twenty-eight dozen roses and ten thousand six hundred jasmine flowers. Can you imagine!"

In the same reverent voice she said that after the stock market had crashed in America, Patou had made the perfume for women who could no longer afford his clothes. "He called it the gift of memory," she said. "So sweet of him. It's supposed to be the most expensive scent in the world."

Saba was beginning to find Ellie's world confusing. A present to cheer poor women up that was the most expensive scent in the world. It had cost the lives of twenty-eight dozen roses and ten thousand six hundred jasmine flowers; that seemed quite a high price to pay for some decent pong.

Later that morning, Ozan's extraordinary car stopped outside their house again and Saba felt as if she had taken up residence in another life, and not one she was sure she wanted. While she and Arleta had had some good laughs at the expense of the ENSA uniform, with its laughable knickers and khaki brassieres, it had given her a comforting sense of doing the right thing, of belonging. Now, standing in the dusty street outside the Pattersons' house—powdered, scented, silk-covered, and with the bird bag—she felt like a made-up thing, a toy.

Her driver, a handsome Egyptian, was separated from her by a glass partition. As they moved off, she noticed him glance at her sharply through his rearview mirror—a hard sexual stare after the earlier smiles and bows. In his own world, she imagined, few women would travel alone like this.

The mainly European suburb of Ramleh came with smart houses, green lawns, carefully tended borders, and roads that led down to the beach that were tarmacked and well maintained. But then she saw opposite them in a scruffy native quarter a sandy street covered in the footprints of mules and donkeys, like a road breaching two centuries.

Out of town, their beautiful car purred past white-robed men riding bicycles or donkeys and, at one crossroad, a Bedouin family with camels tied nose to tail. To their left the Mediterranean dazzled like smashed pieces of blue glass; to the right was a wilderness of sand studded with the wrecks of jeeps and the occasional airplane.

A group of English soldiers, bare-chested and standing by a broken-down tank, shaded their eyes and goggled at the magnificent car as it drove past. When one of them blew her a kiss, the driver's eyes narrowed to murderous slits in the rearview mirror.

"We are nearly there, madame." He spoke for the first time. He put his foot down on the accelerator. She glanced in the direction in which he was looking, at the bright sea and a ring of green vegetation where she imagined the house to be.

Over a supper the night before she'd asked Ellie what she knew about Mr. Ozan, because she didn't really know a thing. Nerves had taken away her appetite and her rice and chicken fell like a stone in her stomach.

"Well that makes two of us." Ellie had carried on eating. "I know nothing, apart from what Tariq tells me."

"What does he say?"

"Well, he only supplies him with wine, he's hardly a bosom friend."

"And?"

"Well, all I really know is common knowledge: that the man owns lots of different businesses and nightclubs and that he's extraordinarily rich and well connected. I'd love to see his house." Ellie tucked her feet up and grew conspiratorial in the lamplight. "Apparently he has houses everywhere—Beirut, Istanbul, Cairo. Funny to think of a little Turkish man doing so well, although he may well be half Egyptian, too, I'm not sure. Can I get you another drink, darling?"

Ellie had walked toward the sideboard and poured herself one. "I can't wait to hear what you make of it all." She sat down again and swirled her ice around with her finger. "Tariq says that his parties are quite spectacular. He says Ozan has a rival in Cairo, another impresario, and the two of them are like children, always trying to outdo each other."

Ozan, Ellie continued, was one of the biggest collectors of Islamic art in the world. She imagined that the most valuable stuff would be locked away at the moment, but even so . . . "God, how I'd love to spend a day looking through it."

Saba, seeing Ellie's body go slack with pleasure at the thought of this, remembered the conversation she and Dom had had that night about people and their passions; how they flowed through you like some secret river that you dammed at your peril. For Ellie, dresses, bits of china, jewelry; for Dom, flying; for his mother, her piano. Her passion for it had not died, he thought, but been diverted, unsuccessfully, into a search for some unattainable domestic perfection that was exhausting, ridiculous. For instance, if the tray of roast potatoes she was cooking weren't the right shade of brown, she would chuck the whole lot away and start again. Her photo albums were so rigorously maintained that the family were filed and labeled almost before the camera had been clicked.

Saba, thinking about her own mother's wonky efforts with the sewing machine, the box of unsorted photos under the bed near the potty, had felt an unexpected surge of gratitude for her. There was something sad and unsettling about the wrong kind of high standards.

She was deeply into this train of thought when the driver had to tap on the window between them. They had arrived at Mr. Ozan's and he didn't want her to miss a moment of it.

In fact she was disappointed. From a distance, there seemed nothing special here—just a sprawling flat-roofed house with iron grilles over its windows. The windows, partly camouflaged by palm leaves, gave the house a sneaky eye-patched look.

An armed sentry waved them through iron gates and up an imposing avenue of trees with well-tended gardens on either side. There was a high wall around the garden with bunches of barbed wire on top of it. The driver's back was sweating now; he drove up a strip of gravel toward the front door, pulled aside the glass partition and said gruffly, "We stop."

A servant wearing a uniform of no recognizable country opened the door. He led her into a large marble hall that had a chokingly rich smell, somewhere between perfume and charcoal. It was only when she was standing inside the hall that Saba saw that the house was like biting into an expensive chocolate, and far more spectacular inside than out. In a magnificent reception room with a gold-leaf ceiling and marbled floors, gorgeous low velvet sofas were arranged, Arabic-style, around the edges of the room, and piled high with jeweled cushions. One wall was entirely covered by painted cabinets, lit with soft lights and stuffed with what looked to Saba like all the treasures of the Orient: marbled eggs, masks, exquisitely inlaid boxes.

She was sitting on the edge of a sofa, trying not to goggle too obviously at all this, when another servant appeared to announce that Mr. Ozan could see her now. He was waiting for her in the garden.

The servant led her toward a heavily carved door at the end of the marbled corridor. Before he opened it, he smiled at her, almost furtively, as if to say *Don't miss this; it's special.* And it was. When he stepped aside, she stepped over the threshold and into a garden like a vision of Eden in an old-fashioned Bible print. In the foreground was a series of mazelike water channels that led to beds of roses and lilacs, and then to trees that filled the air with the scents of almond, cypress, and Arabian jasmine.

In the middle of this vision, both artless-seeming and brilliantly contrived, the eye was drawn toward a huge and beautiful alabaster fountain carved with birds and fishes. The water flung so recklessly into the air seemed to laugh at the desert in the distance, at the huge blue sky above it and at the distant sea sparkling like an amethyst.

She sat down on a stone bench near the fountain. It was baking hot here after the dim coolness of the house. A noisy bird was singing extravagantly in the jasmine bush and, in the distance, she heard a telephone ringing, the scattering of feet, what seemed like a world away.

"Miss Tarcan." Mr. Ozan burst from the house, plump, bustling, beautifully groomed in his well-cut European suit and expensive shoes. He bounced down the path, hand extended, beaming at her like a favorite uncle. "Great pleasure for me." She caught a whiff of some pungent perfume as he shook her hand. "I am very happy to see you again. But bad news for me, too." He glanced at his watch. "Something unexpected has come up. I have to fly to Beirut this afternoon, but you are in my house now, I can explain some things to you—my hope is you will stay for lunch then I must go." His smile was protective and warm.

At a table near the fountain, a tray had been laid out for them: tea served in little glasses, small dishes of dates and pastries.

Mr. Ozan took a sip of tea. "So, do you actually remember me?" He looked at her teasingly over the rim of his cup, his eyes so thickly lashed they looked as though they were ringed with kohl. "We met before at the Mena House."

"Of course," she said.

"That's right." He snorted with laughter at the memory. "And you sang some Umm Kulthum. I thought that was very brave of you. She is our national treasure."

"I didn't know that." Saba grinned. "I learned bits of it from my father. He's an engineer on ships. Lots of crew were Egyptian. I don't think I got all the words right. Did I?"

He shook his head fondly. "Not all of them, but it was very charming," he said. "So I wanted to meet you. And now, here is the thing—forgive me for coming so quickly to the point, but my plane won't wait. I have some big parties coming up soon. Some important people: we make good food, we have dancers, singers, some of the best musicians we can find." His eyes sparkled at the thought of it. "And I would like you to sing for me. Would you do that? If it works well, I can prepare for you a proper booking at one of my clubs."

She was flattered. How could she not be? Arleta had told her that Ozan, before the war, went to a famous nightclub called Le Grand Duc where he had talent-spotted great artists—Ellie called it a rich man's hobby. But there was something else about him that stirred her on a deeper level; the sight of his dark eyes twinkling at her reminded her of her father. Not her recent furiously disapproving dad, but the baba from earlier days who'd chased her around the backyard laughing.

"I know some other Turkish songs," she announced eagerly, for that moment the child who'd stood on the table singing. "I'm half Turkish."

His expression softened. "Me too, with a bit of Greek and Egyptian thrown into the pot, but what part of you is Turkish?" he said gently.

Without thinking, she put her hand over her heart.

"This part."

Mr. Ozan burst out laughing, showing beautiful white teeth.

"I meant your mother or your father." His English was excellent, but he had a way of adding a soft purr to the end of *motherrrr, fatherrrr*, just as her father did.

"My father."

"And where does he hail from?"

She told him briefly about the farm, the plane trees, about his father the schoolteacher—surprised all over again at how little she knew—Ozan listened raptly. He closed his eyes as if in pain.

"Did they have to leave their farm?"

"Yes."

"Do you know what happened?"

"No." She felt tears come to her eyes. "He didn't talk about it."

"It's hard to leave your land." He looked at her sadly. "But we can talk more about this later. This is not forrr the idle chat." Again he purred his r's like a cat.

She watched him crumble a sticky pastry between his fingers. He told her that he had been educated at a Jesuit school in Cairo, and also in London for one year. He said that although he was a successful businessman, "I am in here," he'd clutched his chest, "a musician—but one, I am sad to say, who cannot play for toffees or sing." What he'd most enjoyed before the war, he told her, his eyes gleaming, was to go to a big city like Paris or London and listen to the best singers there. "Everybody thinks people in this part of the world only like the *aaaahhhhh*," he twisted his wrists around and wailed like an Arab singer, "but I have heard Piaf and Ella Fitzgerald, Sarah Vaughan, Jacques Brel, all of the great ones—I like them as much as Umm Kulthum."

One of the pleasures of his life, he said, was to discover good young singers. He mentioned a few names, none of them familiar to her, and talked tantalizingly of the tours he arranged for them across the Mediterranean in the nightclubs he owned: in Istanbul, in Cairo, Beirut, and Alexandria. "I have learned that all great singers need practice," he said. "Not just practice to sing, but practice to perform. And we make the perfect place to learn, for many of these people," which he pronounced *bipple*.

"But now," he gave an eloquent shrug, "there is a big drought on talented artistes in Egypt, so when I heard you sing, it made me very happy. I saw something in you, something exciting. In our language we would call you a Mutriba, she is one who creates *tarab*—literally enchantment—with her songs."

The blue silk dress had made her feel all cool and sophisticated, but now she could feel herself grinning.

"What kind of songs do you want me to sing at your parties?" She knew she would do it now. "I need to practice."

"I've been thinking about that." He gave a powerful snort. "We need tact. The parties will be in Beirut, where some of my clients dislike Western music very much indeed. They must be happy, too. So two, maybe three Arabic songs. Can you do this?"

"I'll need to rehearse," she said. "I don't want to make a fool of myself."

"I have arranged for Faiza to teach you at the club. She's old now, but she is still considered one of the best singers in Egypt. It will be interesting for you."

"Count me in." She put her hand out, he shook it.

"So, we have a deal," he said. When his eyes lit up like that, she saw what a sweet child he must have been.

A bottle of Bollinger appeared in an ice bucket with two exquisite champagne flutes. She'd never drunk during the day before, but the occasion felt so odd and special she let him pour her a glass.

Ozan waved; a servant appeared at almost a jog trot, setting down on the table a mass of small alabaster dishes. When the lids were whisked away, she saw a dish of tiny birds no bigger than budgies covered in herbs and oranges; some rice covered in almonds. The servant danced around them placing pickles and small salads and olives and bread in a semicircle around them.

"It's a picnic today." Mr. Ozan tucked his napkin in. "When you come to my party, I make a proper feast for you."

He helped Saba to a portion of the baby quail, watching her fondly while she ate a dish so delicious it was all she could do to stop herself groaning with pleasure. It was overwhelming after the ghastly food in the desert.

Mr. Ozan seemed a hearty eater, sucking his fingers and chewing noisily and picking up the small bones of the bird to crunch them. While he was thus engaged, his eyes went distant and blank, and he occasionally gave a small grunt of pleasure.

He was wiping his chin with a napkin when a servant brought a telephone to him. There was the rat-tat-tat of conversation and then Mr. Ozan ripped his napkin out of his shirt and started to breathe heavily and sigh. Heavy footsteps in the hall, a dark-suited man stood at the door. When Ozan saw him he stopped talking and stood up.

"Forgive me." He took her hand. "This is unfortunate but the plane is already waiting, there is some mistake. I'll be in touch when I get back from Beirut. Sorry for the rush. Please be my guest and stay for as long as you like." He bowed slightly and disappeared into the house.

A lovely woman appeared in the doorway almost as soon as he was gone. She smiled shyly at Saba. "I am Mr. Ozan's wife," she said. "My name is Leyla."

Leyla was a classic Turkish beauty with high cheekbones, thick black eyebrows, and shining hair that she wore loose. The sight of her, cool as a mountain stream in her green silk dress, made it almost impossible to believe in the harshness of the desert that surrounded them, or that Rommel's army might be as close as forty miles away.

"Zafer is very sorry he had to leave so quickly," she said. Her English, like his, was excellent. "If you will please wait here, the car comes in ten minutes," she added. She bowed and left the garden, still smiling.

The champagne and the hypnotic sounds of the fountain made Saba feel drowsy, and she closed her eyes after Leyla had gone, happy to have a few moments' peace. Half in a dream, she heard more heavy boots walking across the marble floor. The soft voice of a woman, a door closing.

"Madame," a servant stood at the door, waiting for her, "the car is here."

Reluctant to leave the enchanting garden, she followed him through the heavy doors and across the marble hall. She was almost out the front door when, damn! She remembered she'd left Ellie's blue-feathered bag on the sofa in the reception room.

"One moment, please," she told the servant. "I have left my . . ." She pointed toward the room that lay somber and stately behind the carved door, its precious objects flashing and winking.

When the door opened a fraction wider she saw two men in gray uniforms sitting near the window. They were clean-shaven with very short hair. Their legs were sprawled in front of them as though they were at ease here. When the man closest to her stood up, she felt a jolting fear—she was looking into the eyes of a German officer. He was less than a foot away. He clicked his heels and bowed.

"*Das Mädchen ist schön,*" he said to his friend, who looked her up and down appreciatively.

Saba froze for a moment, and then smiled at them while her brain slowly began to function. She mimed a handbag, and shrugged helplessly.

The younger man stood up. He had fine intelligent eyes. He dug under a cushion and held up the handbag by its delicately feathered strap. He handed it to her with a pleasant smile.

"*Shukran,*" she murmured.

"*Ellaleqa.*"

She returned his slight bow, turned, and walked with her heart pounding toward the waiting car.

CHAPTER 24

"Mr. Cleeve's here." Ellie was standing at the door when Saba got home. She looked pale. She pointed upstairs toward the bedroom. "He came suddenly on the Cairo train. He's having a little rest upstairs." There was a warning note in her voice. "Don't forget to keep *schtum* about our other arrangements," she whispered, steering her into the sitting room. "It could spoil everything and I have some rather good news for you.

"A big gin or a tiddler?" Ellie pushed her gently into a chair. She drew the blackout curtains and lit a small lamp. "I'm going to have a big one—it's been quite a busy day, and I'm dying to hear," she added in her more social voice, "about yours—do tell all."

Saba looked at her and made a rapid calculation. If Cleeve were here, it would be safer to tell him and no one else about the Germans. Ellie was still such a new friend.

Ellie took a sip of her gin. "Saba, I'll say this quickly before he comes." She lowered her voice and glanced toward the ceiling. "Damn!" The sound of a chair moving across the floorboards. "I'll have to tell you later. Dermot wants to talk over songs and recordings and things with you, so I'm going to make myself scarce." She stood up. "Can't wait to hear what the house was like," she resumed in a brighter tone as Cleeve loped into the room carrying a briefcase in his hand.

"My goodness." Cleeve put his head on one side in mock admiration and smiled at Saba. "What a stunning frock. I can see Madame E has performed her usual magic."

"Drink, Dermot?" Ellie said quickly. "Then I'll go up and change for supper and leave you both to it."

"Gin and tonic, sweetheart," he said. "Oh what heaven to be back in civilization." He sank into a chair. "I sat on that bloody Cairo train for four hours," he complained. "They were loading all these cars for the big brass. One of the porters eventually switched on the wireless in one of them so we could listen to some music, otherwise I would have been a mad person by now. Which reminds me." He gulped some gin and opened his briefcase. "Pressie for Saba," he said. "A Hoagy Carmichael recording. It was smuggled over from New York. Quite superb."

The package sat in Saba's lap.

"Well open it," he said, crinkling his eyes.

"Thank you," she said woodenly—Ellie was hovering at the door. "Perhaps later."

"Darlings, I'm off," said Ellie quickly. "See you at dinner. I'm glad you like the dress, Dermot." They could hear her scampering footsteps going upstairs.

"She doesn't know anything," Dermot said when the door had closed. "She's only your dresser, and I would have arranged to meet you somewhere else tonight, but it was impossible to arrange transport. Are you hungry?" he added in his conversational voice. "I'm starving. I could call for something."

"No," she said. She pulled her chair so that it faced him and looked him squarely in the eye. "I'm not hungry, and I don't want to talk about dresses, and I don't want to talk about Hoagy Carmichael. What I want to know is why you let me go to Zafer Ozan's house on my own when you knew what was going on there."

"I don't know what you're talking about."

"You must know," Saba exploded. "There were two German officers there." She wanted to spit with fury. "One of them was trying to speak to me. I could have been captured, I could have been raped. Why didn't anyone warn me?"

"Darling." Cleeve was almost pleading with her. "What a nasty fright, I'm so sorry about it. Hang on . . ." He stood up, placed his finger on his lips and put Hoagy Carmichael's "Stardust" on the Pattersons' gramophone. "I do so love this man," he said mildly, lowering the needle. "He knows the notes, he knows the melody, but best of all he knows how to make a tune swing. She thinks we're rehearsing," he whispered.

"Now listen." He leaned toward Saba. "It's important you understand this: someone like Ozan doesn't see the Germans as the great boogeymen that we do. Half the shopkeepers in Alexandria now have signs in German underneath their counters saying '*wilkommen*' in case it goes the other way. It's human nature, darling. Point the second," there was a signet ring on his little finger, "Ozan is Turkish, or most of him is. Turkey is neutral. He is an international businessman, he can ask who the hell he likes to his house. If you're a guest of his, you are perfectly safe."

"You don't know that."

"I do."

"How?"

"I just do." Cleeve took a long sip of gin and rattled the ice.

"Now listen, settle down and talk to me, because I'm leaving shortly—what did these Germans say to you?"

"I don't know. I don't speak German."

"So what did you say?"

"To whom?" She glared at him still.

"To the man who talked to you. The German."

"Nothing, I answered him in Arabic."

He blew out air.

"Good girl. Quick thinking. How well do you actually speak Arabic?"

"Hardly at all," she said through gritted teeth, "that's the point—only the few words a friend taught me at school. If that man had spoken the language he would have been on to me in a flash. I could have been killed or captured."

"Darling, darling." He held up his hand to stop her. "I think we've gone right off into the realms of melodrama here. There are several things I need to explain to you."

He steepled his hands under his chin. Pashas like Ozan, he said, were largely oblivious to the war; they ducked and dived, their lifeblood was business and they would sell to the highest bidder. "And a lovely man, of course," he added quickly. "Passionate about music. But having said all that," he opened his cigarette case and seemed to select his words as carefully as he did his cigarette, "I'm somewhat surprised to hear that our German friends are so blatantly there at the moment. I'm going to have to discuss this with my superior. We need to work out a careful strategy."

"Who is your superior?"

"I can't tell you that just yet." A fly caught in the lampshade momentarily distracted him. He picked up a *Parade* magazine, rolled it, and whacked the insect dead. "I'm not trying to be deliberately evasive, it's just that I need time to brief him on the situation. What did Ozan ask you to do?"

"If you tell me more about why I was there, I'll tell you about today." This seemed her only bargaining chip.

He sighed and placed the dead fly in the ashtray.

"We have a strong suspicion that Ozan has changed the location of his party from Alexandria to either Beirut or Istanbul; it's important for us to know, as soon as possible, which place he decides on. If it's Istanbul we may have a little job for you to do there that could turn into rather an important job. I won't waste time by discussing it now."

"And the parties are important because . . . ?" She was not going to let him off the hook now.

"Some of the key people in the Middle East go to them, and you might just pick up something of vital importance. The point is," he leaned forward, his face sweating, "his lot hold the keys to victory."

"What lot?"

"The suppliers. Ozan, thanks to the parties and the nightclubs, has a large network of friends and business acquaintances, some of whom control the supplies of oil and now water, and without oil and water, we may as well all go home now."

"Is there anything else?"

"My, what a terrier." He looked at her in mock alarm. "I wouldn't like to be interrogated by you."

Patronizing twit. She felt like thwacking him over the head.

"Radar," he said simply.

"The British want to make use of Turkish airbases. Strategically, they are absolutely vital, and it so happens that Ozan's family own the land around one of them, about fourteen miles from Ankara. It would be helpful to know which way he's going to jump."

She heard the drone of distant aircraft, and from upstairs the faint splashes of Ellie performing her evening toilette.

"Listen, Saba," he said. He opened his arms as if he were freeing a bird. "If you don't feel like doing any of this, you can go home now. Right back to England if you like."

She sat in silence, a million conflicting thoughts going through her head. There was a kindly, understanding look in Cleeve's eyes when she looked up—the usual look of amused curiosity.

"I'll do it," she said.

CHAPTER 25

As soon as the front door clicked behind him, Saba raced upstairs.

"Ellie," she whispered urgently through the keyhole of her bedroom. "He's gone. What did you want to tell me?"

"Come in and close the door behind you.

"Well now," Ellie's kidney-shaped dressing table gave back three smug reflections of herself, "I think you're going to be rather pleased with me. You see, I've found him." She powdered her nose in a spirited way. "Your Pilot Officer Benson."

Saba sank to the floor beside her.

"Is this a joke?"

"No." Ellie swiveled around and looked at her seriously. "But it's a secret, and you've got to swear to keep it."

Saba saw her own flushed face in the mirror.

"How did you find him?"

"I'd like to claim some great victory," Ellie said. "But I can't. I was having a drink this afternoon in Pastroudis, a group of pilots were there on leave, I asked if they knew him and of course they did. Easy-peasy."

"And?" Saba's body was literally vibrating with excitement.

"They said they'd get a message to him, that, as far as they knew, he was in town. If all goes to plan, he'll be down at the Cheval D'Or tonight. Tariq's sending a taxi for us at around nine thirty, which just about gives you time to have a bath and get dressed."

"Did you tell Mr. Cleeve? He mustn't know."

"Of course not, you twit." Ellie stood up and smoothed her dress down. "Listen, Saba," she said, "I am supposed to be your chaperone, but don't you ever get sick of the boys making all the rules?" She gave a little wink. "We don't have much time, so let's discuss this later," she'd gone back to her chaperone voice, "over a drink at the club. I'd have a bath now if I was you; it's been an awfully long day, and who knows what the night may bring?"

She stood up and opened her wardrobe door. While she rummaged, she told Saba that she'd meet Faiza Mushawar that night, too—the singing teacher. Faiza, although as old as God, would be dressed up to the nines, probably even to the tens, that was the Egyptian way.

"What about this little number?" She put a black sequinned cocktail dress on the bed. "Or this?" A green satin skirt was flung beside it.

"No," said Saba. She was quite clear about this; if Dom was coming, she wanted to feel like herself.

She stood in her half-slip and looked at herself in the mirror. Her hair was below her shoulders now, and she was thinner than she had been; her arms had grown brown in the sun. When she tried to put on her favorite silver bracelet, her hands were trembling too much to do up its fiddly catch.

After some deliberation, she chose the red silk dress that she had worn that night in Ismailia. It was a bit creased but she loved it; it meant something to her now.

A taxi drew up outside the house; Ellie's boyfriend, Tariq, had arrived, a short, powerfully built man whose wire-rimmed glasses and impeccable clothes gave him a serious, even scholastic air. He'd brought a string of jasmine for Ellie, whom he was clearly mad about. "Jasmine," he explained, "is the flower of love in Egypt."

Earlier, Ellie had seemed anxious to explain to Saba that her boyfriend was not, as she put it, "a typical native," but half French and half Egyptian; a civilized man of the world whose four passions in life were wine (he'd spent his childhood on a small vineyard near Bordeaux), music, women, and Egyptology. He'd first come to this city in search of buried bones, but when archaeology had proved an expensive occupation, he'd financed it by importing fine wines, which he'd done with some success.

He seemed to bring out a more kittenish, excitable side of Ellie's nature. They bounded together toward the waiting car and jumped inside it as if they couldn't wait for the evening to begin, and soon the air was full of everybody's combined scents: sandalwood from Tariq's side, Joy on all Ellie's pulse points; even their driver with his brass box of ambergris and frankincense on his dashboard added to the rich and frankly overpowering air.

Tariq, sitting close to Ellie on the backseat, apologized for the scruffiness of the car and also for the brevity of the trip he was about to take them on. "It would have been fun to show you Alexandria by night," he said, "but there's bad shortage of petrol here, so we must do it some other time."

Saba, drawing aside a blackout curtain, saw a city half in hiding. Empty roads bathed in shrouded streetlights; an empty tram sliding down potholed streets toward the sea, and, in dark cafes between burned-out buildings, the silhouettes of male figures drinking coffee or arak by candlelight. Tariq said, with a smile to hide the bitterness of his words, that the people of Alexandria had got nothing out of the war except inflation and darkness. "You are seeing Alex in her widow's weeds," he said protectively. "The bombings have been horrible, but it will pass. She will recover."

He told Saba that this city that he loved had been planned by Alexander the Great and laid out like a gigantic chessboard. It was called the pearl of the Mediterranean. Before the war, he said, there were taverns everywhere, and some of the smartest clothes shops in the Middle East.

"Here is for your antiques, some wonderful shops, very expensive some of them, and just as good as Paris; here"—he pointed toward the sea—"for your fish markets. There for your banking. Up there in the alleyways"—he made a vague gesture out of the taxi window—"is where all the bad girls live."

"Of which there are plenty," Ellie added.

Tariq wondered if it was possible to have a city that was really a city that didn't have the promise of something sinful there. Otherwise why would young men bother to leave home?

"Don't listen to him." When Ellie covered Saba's ears, she heard the boom of laughter. "He's wicked and depraved. She's a nice young girl," she told him.

"My favorite streets," Tariq explained, "are down by the sea. Normally it has shops and cafes and peanut sellers and all kinds of fun, but the people are very nervous to be out too late after dark now."

"I'm not." Ellie's scented presence stirred beside her. Saba saw her squeeze Tariq's hand. She heard her breath quicken.

"I'm not either," he said. "Everywhere in the Middle East is dangerous now, so let me be in Alexandria with two beautiful women."

"Flatterer!" Saba heard the huskiness in Ellie's voice, then the light sipping of kisses, like cats drinking milk, a rustling, a deep sigh. Tariq stopped talking for a while, and Saba, so close to them, felt both embarrassed and aroused and slightly shocked. Wasn't Ellie too old for this?

Ten minutes later, their taxi slowed down. Tariq came up for air and said they'd reached the Corniche; it was a shame she couldn't see it in all its glory, on summer evenings glittering like an enormous necklace, and full of people, not just soldiers. Winding down her window, Saba caught the fresh smell of the sea and heard its slap.

A black horse clip-clopped beside her, making her start. The only light came from a small charcoal brazier underneath the carriage that moved like a ruby through the darkness. Behind its half-drawn curtains two figures embraced.

A small boy ran beside them, a tray around his neck.

"Big welcome for you, Mrs. Queen." He thrust a tray of cheap pens and bracelets through their moving window. "English good." Skinny little fingers covered in cheap rings made the "V" sign. "German no good. Churcheeel good. Hitler very bad boy. Please have a look." He gazed at them winsomely, head on one side.

Tariq laughed, gave him a coin. "The perfect diplomat meets the real world economy."

"Very sensible, too," Ellie said. "When you have absolutely no idea what side your bread is buttered on.

"Now, darling, can you see it?" Ellie gave Saba a sly pinch. "It's over there. The club," she whispered. She pointed toward a faint strip of light in the middle of a row of dark houses.

"I try never to look at the ships," she said as they walked toward it. "Too depressing. Men and their fucking wars." Her curse word leapt out of the darkness, startling Saba. It seemed so out of character with Ellie's meticulous makeup, her reverence for Patou.

"'Scuse the French." Ellie gave her elbow a little wiggle. "It slipped out. What I really meant was let's have as much fun as we can while we can. There's nothing wrong with that."

A shiver of anticipation ran through Saba like electricity. Ellie was right: nothing wrong with that at all. The fear would come back soon enough.

A Nubian doorman smiled at her as she walked through the door of the club, his teeth lit blue by the painted-over lamps. She could hear the wail of a jazz trumpet, the clink of glasses, the solid blare of conversation just out of reach. She checked her watch. Nine thirty-five.

"He's coming at ten," Ellie whispered. "At least, he said he would."

"Who?" It was childish to pretend she didn't know, but the thought of being stood up now was unbearable.

"Don't be daft." Ellie play-pinched her. *"Him."*

"Oh *him*. Well, that would be nice." As if he was just an ordinary man, and this an ordinary day, but some things felt too overwhelming to be shared. Particularly now, and maybe never with Ellie. She didn't know enough about her yet, or for that matter about him.

Tariq walked ahead of them, parting cigarette smoke with his hands like waves. Inside, there were many tables lit by tiny candles in glass jars. The tables were crammed with soldiers, some with girls on their laps. A babble of voices: French, Greek, Australian, American.

There was a bar in the corner. Beside it, a small stage where an overwrought Egyptian singer, lassoing his microphone cord about himself, sobbed his way through "Fools Rush In" in an accent so heavy it might have been another language. An old lady sat behind the stage, her face half lit by the spotlight. She watched the singer closely with an expression of deep disdain.

"Faiza," whispered Tariq.

Faiza wore a brilliant purple evening dress. Her hair was brightly hennaed, her lips a red slash. On her lap was a splendid gray Persian cat, as impeccably groomed as its owner and wearing a jeweled lead. It watched the couples dancing cheek to cheek with a look of faintly nauseous contempt.

In the car coming over, Tariq had been keen to impress on Saba that Faiza was almost as famous as Umm Kulthum, a singer he worshipped. Like Umm, she was the daughter of a poor family, and when young, she'd disguised herself as a boy to sing. Faiza was, he said, a proper artist, not a common crooner: she sang verses from the Koran, her training had been long and arduous; she was also a great friend of Mr. Ozan.

When the song had reached its last wail of agony, Faiza looked around her. When she saw them she beckoned them toward her with a regal wave.

"I know who you are," she said to Saba. She stared at her intently—her huge black eyes were ringed with kohl, a little smudged in the heat—and then she shook her hand with a great rattle of bracelets. "You, come upstairs. You go and dance," she told Tariq and Ellie.

She took a kerosene lamp from the corner of the stage and made her imperious way through the packed club.

"I have apartments upstairs," she said. "We can talk there."

The cat dashed in front of Saba as she followed the old woman up the steps. She felt the shiver of its fur on her calf. At the top of the stairs, Faiza put a key in the lock and opened the door, onto a candlelit room where there was a piano and a number of comfortable-looking sofas, covered in silk cushions.

"This is where we have our proper parties now," she said. "Please, sit down. Something to drink?"

"No. No thank you." There was a clock on the wall behind the old lady's head. It was already nine forty-five.

The cat purred like a little motor as Faiza moved her fingers up and down its spine.

"We don't have much time before I sing again," she said, "so I will start right away. Mr. Ozan cannot be here tonight, but he tells me that you are a very good singer. The authorities have forbidden any of us to employ foreign singers for the past two years, and honestly, it's very, very boring for all of us." She smiled warmly. "We are artists, we want to hear everything, see everything," her bracelets jangled as she sketched out the world, "so the curfew is one great big bloody bore. Sorry for the word." They beamed at each other like people who shared a secret.

"And you want me to sing here?"

Faiza shrugged. A shrewd expression came into her face.

"Not impossible. We cannot make a living without new people," she pronounced it *bipple*, too, "but now we must be more discreet.

"Before the war, my husband worked with Mr. Ozan, we go everywhere to find the best people. We have here Argentinian dancers, French singers, Germans, Italians, such a wonderful place. Now . . ." The old girl's shrug was dismissive.

"And your husband?"

"Dead. A heart attack last year." She scooped the cat up and held it against her breast.

Downstairs, Saba could hear the sound of the band playing Arab music: drums, violin, oud, tabla, their wild, bounding rhythms ripping through the night. Also, the sound of a plane, close enough for the rotations of its propellers to be heard quite distinctly.

Faiza stopped talking to listen, too. As the plane passed, she shrugged eloquently, as if to say *who cares.*

"So," she resumed, "Mr. Ozan wants me to teach you." Her expression brightened.

"Do you mind?" Saba said. "I know your own training took you ages."

"No." Faiza looked surprised. "Of course not. I am very happy to try. Mr. Ozan is a wonderful man. We make lovely parties for him whenever he wants them."

"You see, I don't have very long here," Saba explained. "I'm with an ENSA company." Faiza looked confused. "We sing songs for soldiers in the desert. I'm in the army."

"Our songs are not easy to learn." The old lady had not understood her. "They are very beautiful, but you will have to learn a new technique." She pointed to her nose, her chest. "We sing from here, too."

"I know one or two songs," Saba said. "My grandmother, she's Turkish, loves the old songs."

She sang a snatch of "Yah Mustapha"; the old lady laughed and sang along.

"Ya Allah!" she called out softly. "I will teach you. Come tomorrow, here? Tea first, and then our first lesson."

"I'd love that," Saba said, and she meant it. "Tariq says you're famous." The old lady inclined her head modestly to one side, but did not deny it. "I love learning new songs."

"I'm old now, and my voice . . ." Faiza mimed herself being strangled. "But we will have some fun. Come tomorrow at ten thirty here. Don't be late, I have a hair appointment at lunchtime."

She glanced at the clock; Saba half rose. The time was ten to ten.

"Wait! Wait, wait." Faiza took both of Saba's hands in hers. "Come with me. I have something to show you."

As they walked across the room, Saba felt tango rhythms vibrate through the soles of her feet. The hoarse cries, the clapping, the stamp of shoes. She followed the old woman into a small room lit by a kerosene light in its corner. There was a sequinned costume hung on a hook; a dressing table littered with makeup. And sitting on a chair near the window, there was Dom.

"Saba." He stepped out of the darkness and put his arms around her.

"Oh my God!" Both of them were close to tears.

Faiza stood at the door. She was smiling.

"I will leave you now," she said. "If you want me, I am singing downstairs."

When the door closed, they kissed each other savagely, and then she cried with joy. She'd had no idea until then how frightened she'd been.

She stepped back and looked at him. It seemed that they had already gone beyond a place of self-control and she didn't care.

He was wearing a scruffy khaki shirt and trousers. His hair needed cutting. His skin had turned a deep nut brown since she saw him last. He was beautiful. After a long, slow kiss, a kind of claiming, he pushed her away.

"Let me look at you." He pulled her down on the sofa beside him. "What in hell are you doing here?" He couldn't stop smiling. "Do you understand this?"

"You first," she said, playing for time. How much was it safe to tell him?

He ran his hands through her hair as he spoke.

"Did you get my message, my letter I mean, I wrote it over a week ago?"

"No. Did you get mine?"

"No. I got a message from your friend Madame whatever-her-name-is; she said you'd be here tonight. That was all."

They kissed again. These details were trivial. There was a war on, messages got lost all the time.

When they stopped, he put both arms around her and hugged her tight, and she felt his heart beating against her and happiness ran through her like a river, as if every cell in her body was saying thank you for the miracle of him—here, and alive.

He told her that for the past ten days they'd been out in the desert south of Alex training. He didn't tell her what the training involved, or what it was for, only that it was over now, at least for the time being, and that the whole squadron had been given a week off because it had been pretty flat out and they wanted them rested. For the next month, all leave was canceled.

He gathered her hair in his hands, smoothed it back from her face and looked her straight in the eyes.

"I can't believe this," he said.

She stroked his face. "Guess what?" she said. The tip of his finger was exploring her dimple. "No, really, *guess what*? As far as I know, I'm here for at least a week, and pretty much on my own. I have to do some work, but we can see each other."

"What work?" She saw a look of confusion in his eyes. "I don't understand. Where are the others? Your friend Arleta? The acrobats?"

"They're not here." She hated having to start like this. "They'll probably come soon." Her right hand was covering her eye. "I'm going to do a couple of broadcasts. I didn't write to you because I didn't know I'd do them here, it was a very sudden thing." Too much, she was talking too much.

He took her hand down from her face, turned it palm upwards, and kissed it.

"Whom does it depend on?" he said. "Your staying, I mean."

"I honestly don't know."

"You don't know!" Oh, not a good thing to say, more confusion.

"But it's bloody dangerous here, most people have been evacuated. I don't want you to get hurt."

He was about to say something else when the music from downstairs reached a straggling halt, and then the woop-woop-woop of an air-raid siren broke through.

A muddle of voices out on the street below them now, the patter of feet on their way to the air-raid shelter. They decided to stay.

"At home, my gran wouldn't go to the shelters," she told him, "so I used to lie under the dining-room table with her. She's thirteen stone. I've still got the dents." When he laughed, she felt his breath on her cheek. "And afterward, we'd lie in bed together listening to the wireless."

"Well, now I'm insane with jealousy." He tightened his arms around her. "Listen," he said, "there'll be no gran and no wireless in our bed."

Our bed: he'd said it.

A wonderful laughter bubbled through them: the laughter of being young, of knowing something you'd longed for was happening.

Our bed. It would happen tonight, she knew it. She stood beside him at the window, shimmering with happiness. She loved how he just assumed it would. No holding back, no false coquetry; the wave had caught them and they would ride it.

When he pulled back half an inch of blackout curtain she saw his profile etched on the wall, clear and distinct like a silhouette—the straight nose, the tousled hair, the shadow of his arm around her. A wash of light moved over the bay and the dark blue sea, and then the rat-tat-tat of antiaircraft guns. In the heartbeat of silence he pulled her closer, and then from downstairs she heard the music again, jolly and impertinent, two fingers to the war.

"Let's get out of here," he said.

CHAPTER 26

There are rooms you know you won't forget; they are like songs that are part of you.

Number 12, Rue Lepsius was such a place: an old apartment building with an elaborate balcony that overlooked the street. Walking toward it, she saw, by the light of the moon, animal heads—lions, dolphins, griffins—carved into its walls.

As they drove there, Dom explained that the Desert Air Force rented three rooms here for overnight stays in Alexandria. "It's nothing special," he told her, helping her out, "but it's quiet, and as safe as anywhere. Are you all right?" he asked. "Not frightened?"

"No."

"I'll look after you."

"Yes."

The ground floor was deserted and dark.

"Here." He clicked open a lighter and led her upstairs. On the first-floor landing he kissed her softly, unlocked a door, and led her by the hand into a whitewashed room with high ceilings. When he lit two candles, she saw a white bed in the middle of the room, a mosquito net draped around it. There was a washstand, a chest of drawers, a half-drawn curtain with a bath behind it. The sight of his clothes—desert boots, shirt, trousers—flung carelessly on a wicker chair alarmed and delighted her.

He put the candles into two red glass bowls attached to the wall by an iron sconce and closed the wooden shutters. The window glass behind the shutters was crisscrossed with strips of tape in case of bomb blasts. The breeze from an overhead fan ruffled her hair as she stepped out of her clothes. There were no words, no preliminaries. She got into bed and waited for him in the dark like a hungry young animal. The brown gleam of his chest was lit by the candlelight as he lay down beside her.

"Here." He pulled her to him, and the kissing began again, and when he entered her swiftly all she could think was *Thank God, thank God at last.* It was like riding the curve of a wave; nothing in her life had felt so absolutely right and unstoppable.

They laughed when it was over. A laugh of triumph and possession.

He lay gasping, one hand on her breast, one tanned leg over the sheets.

"At long bloody last," he said, and they laughed again.

When she was a girl, she'd read other people's descriptions of falling in love: the tears, the madness, the irrational laughter, the melting, the raging, the burning, and she'd worried because she'd never felt even remotely like that. But when she woke the following morning, her first thought was: *It's happened. My first miracle.*

He was still asleep, lying on his back, one arm flung in an arc above his head. She looked at him, her body still singing from the night before: at the tuft of dark hair under his arm; at his lips, which were soft and clearly carved; there was a small scar underneath them. She must ask him where he got it. He breathed out, his lips slightly parted, teeth white against tanned skin. There was a faint depression under his eyes where the skin was paler than the rest of his face, maybe where his flying goggles had been. His left ear was slightly bigger than his right ear, and below it, when she examined the miraculous skin graft, she saw that it was now almost imperceptible: that the scar which ran from the bottom of his left ear down to the hollow of his neck had faded but you could see, if you looked closely, the raised skin of the surgeon's neat stitches. Gazing at those stitches, thinking about the hospital, she heard her breath come jaggedly. How could she bear it if it happened again? She ran her hand down the side of his ribs. She stroked the curve of his hip bone, saw the point beneath the rumpled sheet where his suntan ended and his whiter skin began.

"Umm." His eyelashes flickered as he stirred. "Lovely," he murmured, and went back to sleep again, and slept, and slept. He was exhausted, she could see that; they'd hardly slept a wink the night before, and before that, endless nights on call in the desert.

When he woke up, he looked at the clock and groaned.

"What a waste, come back to bed." She was half dressed and about to leave a note.

"Can't," she said, "I'm busy."

"I'm starving." His voice was sleepy; his hair stood on end. "You're dressed. Do you want breakfast? There's a hotel next door: eggs, coffee, falafel, omelet. I'll get up in a tick."

"Told you, I can't." She sat down beside him on the bed. "I'm off to work." She watched his expression change to one of confusion.

"To work?" He dropped her hand. "I don't understand. Where? Why? You said there were no concerts here."

She sat down on the wicker chair and put one hand over her eye.

"Down at the club. I'm learning new songs."

"Can't that wait?"

"No. I'm supposed to be doing a broadcast soon."

"Oh. So, will you come back? Can we have dinner tonight?" Their voices stilted now.

"Of course." She got down on her hands and knees and buried her head into his chest. "I'm sorry."

She copied down the number from the telephone in the hall, so she could phone him as soon as she got there. She told him to promise not to move until she was back.

"I'm going to move." He'd got out of bed like a fluid whip. "I'm going to find you a taxi so you're safe; I'm going to pay the driver so he returns. Saba," he looked at her, "I don't want to sound like your Great-uncle Sid, but I'm not sure you really understand how dangerous this city is at the moment."

She said that she did, but she didn't, not really. She was becoming more and more aware of the innocent and isolated bubble that she had been moving in. To be sure, she'd seen the victims of this war, the haggard faces of the men, the hospital stretchers lying in the aisles, but they had been kept apart from any concrete news. And that morning, before Dom woke, the door of the wardrobe that held his clothes had swung open. She'd got up, gone toward it like a sleepwalker, and stared inside it, at his dusty kitbag stained with oil, at a streak of what looked like rust-colored blood on his overalls.

She laid her head against his chest.

"Let me take you to the club." He stroked her hair. "Please. We can come back here afterward."

"No," she said, ruffling his hair. "I'm a big girl now." The risk that Cleeve had missed the Cairo train, or that Ozan might appear, was too great. "I'll only be a couple of hours. I'll rehearse and then I'll come back in a taxi and you can take me to lunch."

He smiled at her, thinking *Damn, damn, damn!* A whole day eaten up, what a waste.

Please God, she thought, hearing her own voice assert all this so confidently, don't let there be any complications, or holdups, or extra events that nobody has bothered to tell me about. I don't think I could bear it now.

"Oh thank heavens! You're back, you're safe." When Saba walked through the door of Colonel Patterson's house an hour later, Ellie sprang from her chair. She was in the living room, still in her evening dress; in the early-morning light her face looked gaunt, and there were dark circles under her eyes.

"I tried to find you last night, but I think the air raid confused everyone. It was bedlam, wasn't it? And I knew you were with your young man, so I assumed you were safe. I mean we both took a bit of a risk last night." Her eyes anxious as the words tumbled out.

"I was safe." Saba felt herself grinning, almost in spite of herself. "I was fine."

She declined the drink that Ellie offered, and the chance of breakfast; she was suddenly exhausted.

"So, a lovely time was had by all?" Ellie's sly look made it clear she was waiting for girlish confidences.

"Yes," Saba said. "A lovely time." Even if she'd wanted to she couldn't describe how wonderful. Her body felt so light, her mind in a state of bliss.

Ellie's eyebrow shot up. She wanted more.

"A lovely time?"

"Yes." Saba looked her straight in the eye. "Thank you. Look, I'm sorry you had to wait up for me, I hope you're not too tired." She heard

Ellie sigh and saw her sag, at which point she might have asked about her evening with Tariq, but she knew already this was not on the conscientious-chaperone script Ellie was reading from.

"If you don't mind," Saba said, "I'll shoot up now, have a bath and change. Faiza's expecting me at ten thirty; she has a hair appointment at lunch, I can't be late."

"Shall I pick you up then?" Ellie seemed to be testing the waters. *Is this too far? Is this?* It was clear she was longing to see Tariq again.

"There's really no need," said Saba. "I've made an arrangement to meet Dom for lunch. He only has five days here."

"And do you have any leave owing to you?" Ellie was thinking hard.

"None of us have had a holiday since we came."

"And so you're insisting on this—making your own arrangements at the club," Ellie had her shrewd expression on again, "because you want to be on top form for the wireless broadcasts and for Mr. Ozan's party." They were back on the script again.

"Exactly."

"Well." Ellie kicked her shoes off and walked around, her stockinged feet leaving pawprints on the floor. "As long as we're discreet, I think both of us can be at ease for a few days, if you get my drift. You can stay here if you like. Both of you." She'd dropped her voice to a whisper.

"Dom's got an apartment on Rue Lepsius," Saba said. "He'll look after me. It's quiet and private and close to the club. We're all trying to save petrol." They exchanged another look.

"Yes, we're all trying to save petrol, but you must promise not to say a word of this to Cleeve. Do you know that he forgot to pay me for the last two weeks; I don't imagine he thinks I can live on air. If it wasn't for Tariq, I'd be destitute, honestly destitute; if he ever finds out, you're to tell him that."

"Don't you get paid by the government like we do?"

"For some jobs, yes . . . it depends . . . it's complicated. Anyway, not a word to Cleeve, and if you see Tariq at this house, not a word about him either." Ellie winked. "He'll be off again soon."

She gave Saba some bath salts and a fresh towel; she hugged her. She said she would make it her business to sit in on some of Saba's rehearsals at the club—this with an ostentatious protectiveness, as if it was now her sole aim in life. And by the way, it would be better not to say too much to Faiza about Dom—Egyptians were shocking gossips.

Saba, in the bath, puzzled again about Ellie. In some ways, her presence in the city was as mysterious as her own. And then she forgot her; she was in love and gloriously happy.

CHAPTER 27

Dom was waiting in the flat at Rue Lepsius when she got back from her rehearsal. She bounded upstairs and into their room, thrilled to see him and a little shy. She'd never lived with a man for consecutive days before and it made her feel as if they were playing house together.

He saw the flush of her cheeks, her dark hair swinging as she walked into the room, and thought: *I'm sunk.* He'd missed her all morning and resented every second she'd been away. He wrapped his arms around her and said he could make her some tea—he'd discovered a tiny kerosene stove behind the floral curtain in the corner of the room. When he asked if she was hungry, she said she was starving and had eaten neither breakfast nor lunch that day.

"I'll take you to Dilawar's," he said, happy to feel more in control of things again. "It's the best cafe around here, and it's quiet."

Hand in hand they went downstairs together, and out into the street and down a narrow alleyway with chairs on either side that spilled out from an almost hidden cafe where people were drinking tea and eating pastries as if the war had never come. The warm air was full of the scent of jasmine from an old vine planted against a trellis. There was a fountain. On the marble counter inside the cafe was a huge old Russian samovar.

He chose a seat behind a screen where they could not be seen. He said he didn't want to talk to anyone but her.

It was too early for dinner and too late for lunch, so they ordered cheese and flatbreads, which came with doll-sized bowls of hummus and spicy vegetables. While they were waiting, he took both her hands in his, and kissed them softly.

"Did you miss me?" He put his fingertips inside her dimples. "I love these things."

"Didn't give you a thought," when she was aching to kiss him. "My day was really exciting."

"Even more exciting than the night before?" His voice was husky. She felt a huge surge of sexual desire leap through her.

"Almost."

He gave her a questioning look. "Really?"

"Really." She kissed the palm of his hand. "Almost."

In truth, it had been a wonderful day for her in every way: the memory of their lovemaking, in her body all day like a melody underneath the surface of things, had made a fascinating lesson with Faiza even better.

"Tell me what you did." He leaned toward her. "Tell me everything about you."

"Why should I?"

"Because you want to." When he narrowed his eyes like that, she felt another jolt of desire, and thought, *Slow down, be careful, anything could happen in the next few weeks.*

She took a deep breath. "Well . . . she's a funny old bird, but wonderful. You saw her last night. She looked like a little Christmas pudding: huge earrings, great big sparkly dress, no, don't laugh, that's how she was, but today she was plainly dressed, quite strict—she's so passionate about what she does."

I don't want you to be passionate about anything but me. The thought was so instinctive it shamed him.

He watched her eyes sparkling as she described how Faiza spoke fluent French, English, Arabic, and Greek, and before the war had worked in Paris at the Le Gemy Club on the Champs-Elysées. She'd been booked by a man called Louis Leplée, who'd discovered Piaf on the street, and done her first recordings with her. Mr. Leplée had been murdered. There was another bit to this story that Saba kept to herself even though it was interesting. Apparently—Faiza had told her this with much flashing of her kohled eyes and clutchings on the arm for emphasis—the rumor was that Piaf was a frequent performer for the German forces' social gatherings, but that she really worked for the Resistance.

"Do you believe this?" Saba had asked.

Faiza's shrug had been immense; everybody's at it, it seemed to imply. "And then what?" Dom tucked a strand of hair behind her ear.

"Well, she started to sing for me, and it was wonderful. She sang this . . ." She put her mouth to his ear and sang a phrase of "Yar Nar Fouadi," the song they'd been working on with much laughter and some difficulty that morning. "But she's a jazz singer, too—Ella Fitzgerald, Dinah Washington. She's brilliant, Dom, so alive. I can really learn from her."

"What did she say? What did she say that was different?" He had stopped teasing; he was excited for her.

"She told me that when she was a girl she had a flawless voice, a gift from God that could span five octaves quite easily, and it was wonderful. Now, technically, she's diminished, she has to change the keys to make it easier."

"How sad. To know you once did it so much better." He wasn't jealous now, this was quite interesting.

"She wasn't sad—that was her point. She said that if you listen to your true voice you get better with age, but to find your true voice you have to really work to find the space inside you. Is this boring?"

"No, no, no." He threaded his fingers through hers. "Keep going, I like it."

"She says her voice is better now because she's less keen to please everyone, because she's suffered more: her husband is dead, two of her children have died, one in a bombing only nine months ago. Even having a baby, she said, lowered her voice by an octave.

"Also, she is a follower of Sufism; she explained all this to me first, she said it was very important that I understood this about her because everybody has their song: it's like a message from God that speaks directly to them, and that part of the singer's job is to find their song. Does that sound ridiculous?"

"No," even though it was the kind of talk he would have scoffed at during his Cambridge days, "not at all, but do you believe that? Here, come, eat." He had made a sandwich for her with the flatbread while she talked.

"I do." She held the bread in her hand, gazing directly at him. "I never quite understand it, but there are songs that go through you like a rocket. They're frightening."

"Ah, now that I do believe," he said quietly.

"At home, I used to listen to Tansu singing her Turkish songs; she'd have a cigarette clamped between her teeth, and then she'd put it down on the hearth and sing her heart out. She was back home then, completely connected with who she was."

"I used to feel that about my mother," he told her. "At home, her piano was right under my bedroom, I'd lie in bed as a child and listen to her. She was good, very good, and for a child it was comforting, too—I could feel her back in her own natural element; the strength she got from it."

"Did she really give up."

"She gave up," he said. "She used to sing all the time when I was a child, but she stopped that, too. For years I didn't understand why. When I asked her once she said that she never wanted to do anything that she was second rate at—that seemed to me such a bad thing to say, cowardly and falsely grand. You have to be humble about these things, don't you, to be prepared to live in suspense, maybe for a long time. But go on, what else did this Faiza say?"

He found that he was riveted—he'd never had a girl like this; usually you had to get the talking over before the fun part began.

"So many things: how she had to fight to be a singer; how her family hated it—she had to dress as a boy at first. She also told me I must never worry about looking ugly when I sing."

"Ugly! What a strange thing to say. How could you?" He looked at her in amazement. "When you walked into the ward that night, you were like a vision. Maybe she got the word wrong."

"No, no, no! That's not what she meant. Yes, of course I must dress up and look nice, but it was more like . . ." she squeezed up her face at the effort of getting the words right, "I must learn to forget myself and be the song."

"To forget yourself. That's quite a tall order." He leaned across the table and took both of her hands in his. "At least for me."

"You're teasing me."

"No. I was thinking how sweet you'd look in glasses."

"You are teasing me and I don't care." She mock-biffed him around the ears. "I expect you think you're too clever for me."

"No, I don't."

"Yes, you do."

And she was thinking how she didn't usually go on like this. With Paul, her last boyfriend, conversation had felt like some sort of heavy chore, like housework, or a lever that had to be planned for and manipulated and got jammed on certain topics with agonizing silences in between.

"Let's talk about you," she said when they had settled down again. "I mean, how long, seriously, do you think it would take me to really get to know you?"

"Ten minutes, fifteen maximum." He poured her a glass of wine. "You know what they say about the Brylcreem boys."

"No," she said, although Arleta had told her this exactly. Conceited, self-centered, God's gift, et cetera. "Oh, very cynical." She pulled one of his ears.

"Well maybe, but there is a point to disguises," he told her. "Do you know that poem by Yeats called 'The Mask'?"

"No."

"A woman tells a man to *put off that mask of burning gold with emerald eyes.* She says she wants to find what's behind it, love or deceit; the man tells her it was the mask that *set your heart to beat, not what's behind.* I think your man has a point there."

"I don't care about bloody old Yeats," she told him. "I want to know what happened to you."

"What do you mean?" He blinked and looked away from her.

"The hospital. We haven't talked about it."

"Oh, the hospital." The smell of old meat was what he thought of when he thought of it, the smell of living and dying flesh, warm and sickly and sweet and cut with just enough Dettol to make it bearable; at other times he remembered Annabel's *It's not you, it's all this*, her regretful smile, damp, sympathetic hand on his brow. Nothing he could joke about yet, nothing he could share.

"What a vision you were." He pretended to be lost in a reverie: "Red dress, dark hair. I wanted to take you to bed right there and then."

"I'm not talking about that." She put her hand over his mouth and said softly, "What happened to you?"

"What happened?" She felt the soft rasp of his teeth against her fingers while he thought.

"I'll tell you one day," he said at last. "I do trust you."

He felt he must tell her soon—he'd been on the verge of it several times—that he'd wanted to see her again so badly, he'd taken the train to Cardiff, had seen her house in Pomeroy Street. Something stopped him—pride maybe, or training, a sense that he might have trespassed on her secrets. Life wasn't a childish game of show-and-tell, and easy confidences that made everything better before bed. It felt too early to take the risk.

"I want you to trust you," he said. "Am I right to?"

"Yes." She put her hand over her right eye. "I think so."

"You think so? Not know so?"

"Well . . ."

"You're looking very serious," he said. "What's the matter?"

"I don't know. Nothing. It's the war sometimes."

"Well, I can offer three possible cures," he said. "A, we could order an ice cream. B, drink another bottle of wine and sing some Arab songs. Or C, go back to the Rue Lepsius and make mad passionate love."

"I feel greedy tonight," she grinned at him, "so, ice cream at Rue Lepsius."

"And I feel greedy, too," he said. "I want you to lie in my arms and sing to me."

"Any special requests?"

"'Smoke Gets in Your Eyes.'"

She often sang to him in bed during the four days that followed; the days she counted as the happiest of her life, the most exquisitely painful, the most complete. The sounds of the war, filtered through shuttered windows, the occasional groans from ships in the harbor, the droning planes above, the whooping of the air-raid sirens, all of it made life feel almost unbearably precious. They would snatch every bit of it, take nothing for granted. They would be lovers, have a future—however short.

They made a pact not to have any solemn war talks, but they knew what they were going back to now. Total amnesia no longer possible. Everything felt so clear here: in this room with its whitewashed walls, their rumpled bed with its mosquito net, the whirling fan above, the comforting clutter of domestic items behind the floral curtain—the kettle, the stove, their cups, the lapis-blue pen she'd bought him in the market. Their temporary room was home.

There were sudden starvations after they'd made love that could only be sated by running down to Dilawar's—their cafe now. At night, candles were lit in little glass jars and put deep inside the cafe where they would not draw any attention to themselves, and a group of old men with carved faces gathered in the dimmest recesses to smoke their nargiles or take falafel from Ismail, the owner's son, a handsome, smiling boy who was teased because he wore a gas mask to cook falafels in, to stop the fumes going up his nose.

When the falafel smoke had cleared, the scent of jasmine permeated the alleyway. The sturdy old vine grew and grew up the trellised walls. Ismail gathered its flowers after dark, when the scent was more powerful; he sold them in long ropes, which they took back to their room.

In the mornings they drank tea in bed together like sensible old Darby and Joan types. "Here you are, Mrs. Benson," Dom said in an old man's whistle, doing a bandy walk to the bed to make her laugh. "There's your cuppa."

He ran around the corner to get fresh rolls from the baker. They were warm still when he bought them, and they would eat them in bed together, or if it was too hot, they'd sit side by side on the floor.

After breakfast Saba would wash and get dressed and on limbs that felt sunlit run to catch the tram down to the club. She and Faiza were making progress now: she had three Arabic songs she could sing with some fluency, and Faiza had taught her how to ululate with her tongue vibrating behind her teeth; also the different ways she had to take her breath (more of a cat's sip than a bellows breath) to accommodate the new rhythms. When she came back to Dom she would sing them for him, sometimes standing up, sometimes lying with him chest to chest, cheek to cheek. He'd pull her toward him without a word.

"I like that 'Ozkorini' best," he told her.

"I only know a snatch of it," she said.

Umm Kulthum had been sent away from Cairo now—both sides frightened she'd be used for propaganda purposes. Saba didn't tell him that. She told him instead that Ozkorini meant "Think of me. Remember me." Faiza had told her it was one of the few Arabic love songs addressed directly to a woman, most dealt with the pain of longing.

"What are they longing for?" she'd asked Faiza.

"For God," came the simple reply. "Or another country, or to be happy again. Life is hard for many bipples here." As she was saying this, it flashed through her mind that "Ozkorini" was one of Ozan's favorite songs, too, and wished it wasn't. She wanted it to be her and Dom's song. She loved him. It was such a simple shock to know this. It wasn't just that he was so beautiful to her; there were other things more difficult to name: a particular sympathy they shared, as though they were tuned to the same frequency. The way they laughed at the same things, the way they'd listened to each other as though on tenterhooks as each laid out for the other the important events of their lives, and the trivial: she knew now, for instance, that he had once in a fit of rage thrown a lamp at his sister's head after she'd put his teddy down the lavatory; that he felt guilty about frightening his mother, and sorry for her, too, feeling her loneliness and isolation; that he and his friends at school had once teased a boy because a girl had written a poem to him saying "and I love your long white neck"; how it felt to go night flying for the first time: the terror and the magic of flying half blind beyond the earth's crust.

And that was about all he'd said to her so far about flying; some unspoken agreement had been reached that the subject would not be discussed. There was no wireless in their room, and they didn't want one. They had shut down the outside world for a few precious days. But every morning, as she made her way down the Rue Lepsius, down the Rue Massalla and toward the innocently glistening blue sea, she saw more sandbags stacked on half-ruined streets, more airplanes making marks on the clear blue sky.

One afternoon, while he was cheerfully splashing in the bath, she went to the cupboard, opened it as quietly as she could, and took a closer look at his things. There was a pair of desert boots in the corner, the suede scuffed at the toes and covered in dust. In the toe of the left foot she found a map of North Africa; in the right foot she felt the cold steel of a revolver. Underneath the boots, a pair of khaki overalls covered in dust and oil. They belonged to another world and made her stomach somersault.

"What are you doing?" His voice came from behind the curtain; the slap of water as he moved.

"Looking in the cupboard."

"My stuff's normally in my locker," he said, as if that would make them safer. "I came here straight from the aerodrome."

When he walked into the room again, there was a towel around his waist and his hair was wet. He looked, so alive, she felt, for one moment, almost crazed with fear for him.

When he saw her face, he took her to bed without words and they made love. Later that night, over dinner at their cafe, he told her that she was easily the most interesting, the most wonderful girl he'd ever met, that when the war was over, he was going to learn to smoke a pipe and they'd buy a cottage with roses around it, and they were going to make lots of babies together, in between her doing concerts all over the world.

"That's ambitious," she teased him in order to hide her intense pleasure. This was the first time he'd talked like this. "So what are you going to be: a kept man?"

"I want to fly and write," he said it quickly, "but I can't think that far ahead."

"Superstitious?"

"No. Maybe."

The white bed, the purple sky, visible through the shutters before the blackout curtain was drawn. The ruddy glow of two candles before the last breath of day was blown on them. His miraculous brown body beside her in the mornings. His heat, his gaiety, his clever mind. She had not known you could have all this at once.

Four days, then three, and a terrible last day when everything that had seemed so wonderful went wrong. It began with a signal from the duty officer saying Dom was to report to Wadi Natrun. They would be flying again next week.

CHAPTER 28

On their last but one day, Ellie turned up unannounced at the club. She looked pale and out of sorts. She wore flat shoes and no jewelry, and had left the back of her hair unbrushed.

"Darling, listen," she said. "I have an urgent message for you. A man called Adrian McFarlane from ENSA has just phoned and left a message. He's staying at the Cecil Hotel. You won't say anything, will you, about our arrangement?" Her lip was trembling with nerves. "They want you to take the train back to Cairo. Apparently the company are re-forming there. They've sent a ticket."

Saba's heart sank. "When?"

"I don't know yet. I may have to go with you." Ellie looked glum. "Promise not to say a word about Tariq?"

Saba promised. "But what about Ozan's party?"

"He asked me to lend you a couple of evening dresses, so I assume it's still on. I thought I'd pack the blue dress, and that gold and silver sari dress that you wore at the Mena House. Does that sound right to you?"

"Well . . . but . . . they're yours. I can't just take them." Her mind was racing. What about Dom, how to explain this to him.

"Don't worry about that. I won't be out of pocket." Ellie seemed quite sure about this. "Let's just do exactly what they say."

"Is that all?" Saba said.

"All that I know. Don't forget," she almost snapped, "I'm just the wardrobe lady."

Half an hour later, she came back with another new message. The man from ENSA wanted Saba to report to a recording studio on Mahmoud Street at seven p.m. the following night for a Forces' Favorites program called *Alexandria Calling*.

"Well, you're a very popular girl," Faiza beamed.

"Yes." Her heart sank to her boots. The timing could not have been more terrible.

He thought it was a joke at first.

"A recording?" he said. "On our last night? Surely you can change it?"

She went silent, then said she couldn't.

And looking at her he believed her, and thought: this will drive you mad; leave her now while you can.

"Well, thanks for letting me know." He heard the coldness in his own voice.

"I didn't know myself until a few hours ago."

"Really?"

"Really."

It was mid-afternoon. They were lying in bed in each other's arms at the time, sated and slick with sweat. He'd just run a bath. A moment or two before, they'd been joking about his socks, which she'd insisted on washing the day before and hung on a hanger. Watching her rinse them so inexpertly, he'd felt sadness close over him like dark water—a sense that they were trying to cram a future that might never come into a few short days. And this was the problem: everything seemed so heightened and raw.

He disengaged himself from her arms.

"Can't you change it?" How hard would it be? he asked himself indignantly.

"No."

"That's ridiculous." He leapt out of bed and faced her. "It's a wireless program. You'll be singing a *song*. It's not like opening night at La Scala blooming Milan."

"Yes, a *song*." She got up on her elbow and glared at him. "Nothing but a bloody song, very unimportant. Candy floss. Let's cancel everything to suit Dom's arrangements."

"My *arrangements*?" He scowled. Oh the things he could have frightened her with had he chosen to.

"Yes, your arrangements."

They both had quick tempers, had already made each other laugh with cheerful warnings of the bad behavior that would inevitably come. He confessed to kicking his mother once when he was six years old when she'd made him practice too long at the piano. She'd kicked him smartly back; Saba had inspected the scar on his knee and said he'd deserved it. Saba owned up to several dramatic exits from Pomeroy Street with a packed bag dating back to when she was a toddler.

Now he watched the bomb he'd ignited explode. She stormed around the room like a clockwork toy, telling him he was selfish and thoughtless and mean and overbearing, too, and she was fed up to the back teeth with men telling her what to do. She stamped her foot and, after a few moments of this, collapsed into the bath behind the floral curtain in a flood of tears.

He'd run that bath for himself. His last bath before going back to the desert; possibly his last bath ever. The sound of her thoughtless splashings had enraged him.

"Overbearing? Me?" he bellowed through the curtain. "That's a bit rich coming from you."

"I am not overbearing," she yelled.

And then, he could hardly believe the words were coming out of a mouth twisted with rage. "I mean, I let you go off and sing for hundreds and thousands of men who don't even know you."

"You. Let. Me. Go. Off!" The voice behind the curtain was low and incredulous. "What a bloody cheek! You don't own me. You hardly even *know* me."

"No, I don't, and thank God for that. Spoiled and self-centered," he'd muttered. "An idiot."

"What did you say?"

"Nothing."

He'd heard her gulp. She filled the bath with more water and thrashed around in it like a netted fish. Breathing heavily, he put on his shorts and sat down near the window with his head in his hands. After a few moments of savage self-pity his temper went out as quickly as a summer storm, but the splashing in the bath continued, and then low gasping sounds.

"Saba." He felt stranded, and wanted a way back. He lit a cigarette.

"Sorry, can't hear," she said. "I'm too self-centered."

"A very grown-up thing to say." His voice softened.

And then he scribbled a note to her that read: *Ben bir eşeğim*, the Turkish for "I am a donkey." She'd written the phrase on a napkin a few days before, when he'd asked for instruction in curse words. He wrapped the note around a piece of Turkish delight—the kind she liked, pale pink and full of pistachio nuts. The kind she normally ate with a sensual, eye-rolling relish that made him laugh. He lowered it on a string over the curtain and into the bath.

The splashing stopped as she read the note. When he heard her chuckle, his eyes filled with tears of gratitude.

"Come here," she said—the sweetest sound he'd ever heard.

When he drew back the curtain, he couldn't believe how cruel he had been, how selfish. She looked so young lying there, hair wet, eyes swollen with weeping. So beautiful, too, with her brown skin gleaming, her black hair shifting like seaweed in the water. He took a flannel and washed her face and her shoulders, her belly; he gathered her in his arms and they went to bed together, mingling their tears and telling each other they were stupid and sorry and had never meant to hurt each other and never would again.

The following day, while she was asleep in the crook of his arm, he lay tense and watchful as he listened to the unmistakable roar of a Spitfire engine moving overhead; for the first time, he recoiled from it.

When he opened the shutter, a flock of birds flew through the vaporous air the aircraft had left behind, and Alexandria, battered, abandoned, came into focus again, and he was frightened for it. Nobody could say with any certainty how much of it would remain next month, next week even. All the talk now was of one final push.

"Are there a lot of them?" She'd been watching him.

"A lot of what?" he said cautiously. He combed her hair with his fingers.

"Airplanes."

"A few." It was unusual, he thought, to see aircraft moving so flagrantly over the city, and wondered if some were being delivered to LG39. They were desperately short now.

"Are you worried?"

"No." He hesitated, knowing what he said might stay with her for a long time. "Please don't worry about me. I've had a wonderful time. I'm sorry I nearly spoiled it last night." He got up, closed the shutter, and got back into bed with her.

"Saba, no!" He put his arms around her; she was howling, but without much sound, just deep breaths and swallows, a look of vivid distress in her eyes as she tried to control herself.

He dried her eyes on the corner of the sheet.

"This has been the best week of my life," he said. He buried his face in her hair and they clung together as if it were their last moment on earth.

Their breakfast on the following day was curiously formal, as if part of them had already gone. They went to Dilawar's and ordered coffee and croissants that she toyed with and half ate. They arranged to meet between her rehearsal and what she now called "the blasted broadcast."

"I'm sure you'll enjoy it once you're there," he said, diplomatic today. "It'll cheer the troops up."

"I hope so," she said softly. "I'll be back as soon as it's over." She looked at her watch and said she'd better go.

Before she left, they said good-bye to Ismail together—the handsome youth often stared at them from behind the beaded curtain that separated the cafe from the kitchen. A hungry, unabashed stare. A few nights earlier, during a general conversation with him about the war and Egypt and his life, he'd told them he thought they were lucky. He could never afford to get married; he lived with his mother.

They'd glanced at each other shyly during this outburst, pleased that he thought they were husband and wife.

They shook his hand, gathered their things, and walked out into the blare and glare of the street. As Saba's tram moved off, Dom stood and waved at her from the street corner. He had no fixed plan yet for the rest of the morning—he had hoped he would spend it with her. He felt sick with fear as he watched her go.

CHAPTER 29

As Saba wove in and out of the trinket sellers down by the Corniche, she was thinking of Dom in all his manifestations. There was the brown-skinned Dom whose body, both predatory and tender, claimed her at night, eyes gleaming in the candlelight; the silly schoolboy who sang to her from the bath and made her helpless with laughter; the kind and fatherly man who brought cups of tea in the morning and separated oranges fussily on the tray into neat segments; the clever one who challenged and mocked her, and who every now and then withdrew into an intense silence that frightened her; there was the ghost in their wardrobe who wore oil- and bloodstained overalls, who knew how to use a revolver—who refused to talk.

He still hadn't spoken about the day he was shot down, which made her wonder if friends had been killed or if he'd made some irretrievable mistake that haunted him. Sometimes she wondered if he felt unmanned by her having seen him too vulnerable for masculine pride in hospital. She couldn't tell. When conversation strayed in this direction a shuttered look came to his face and she got nothing.

But last night, sitting opposite him at Dilawar's, their toes touching under the table, she'd thought, *You can't die. I love you too much*, as though intensity of thought could stop it, and then a strange sort of rage at him for frightening her so, and now a terrible hollowness inside her because he was leaving so soon, and so was she. But there was something else, too, almost too confusing to contemplate, or was it simply self-protective, the almost automatic and balancing and surely wrong thought that their parting left her free to work again. Could all these separate parts of her ever be smoothly joined? She somehow doubted it. Even on a morning like this, it was comforting to slip, like an animal into some secret pond, into the half-light of the club and know that for the next two hours she would only think about her singing lesson with Faiza.

The chairs were up on the tables when she walked in, and the air was stale and redolent of the previous evening's cigarettes. From upstairs the muffled sound of tango music, the kind of staid European tango that Faiza liked, not the wild South American brand, next came Ella Fitzgerald. Faiza's taste in music was broad; you could say her soul was in the East, but her head, or wherever it was a sense of style resided, was in the West, and Ella was her favorite jazz artiste. She liked to gossip and tut about the singer's awful start in life—the brothels, the homes—as if they were close friends, and it was Faiza who had made Saba pay attention to her idol's musicality, her impeccable timing.

Faiza was jiggling around to "A-Tisket, A-Tasket" as she opened the door, a pencil stuck behind her ear. During the day she wore a faded robe and large unfashionable specs and looked like anybody's auntie from Alexandria; it was at night that the garish frocks and heavy makeup, the brilliantly dyed hair (a wig as it happened) appeared.

Saba knew more now about Faiza's plans, which were ambitious. Before the war, and thanks to Ozan, she'd had a successful career singing on the Mediterranean circuit—in Italy, Greece, France, and Istanbul. Now, having gone down well with the GI's and British audiences, her grand plan was an American tour. She might sing at the Apollo, or meet Ella Fitzgerald in person—Faiza lit up like a girl when she discussed all this, and although Saba privately felt that at fifty-five she had one foot in the grave, she had been helping Faiza with her English pronunciation, in return for help with the Arabic and Turkish songs.

After rehearsals they'd drunk tea and already talked of many things—music and food, poetry and men. Faiza admitted that her husband when young had beaten her. Like many Egyptian men he'd believed that virtuous maidens did not sing in public—it was neither proper nor respectable. It had caused her much pain for many years and a great split inside her. But in the end, she said, she'd been right to insist on doing what she knew she was put on this earth to do. Now, she didn't give a damn—sorry for the word—what other people thought or said about her. And eventually, she said with a shrug, and a cynical twinkle in her eye, she'd made enough money for husband and children to forgive her.

The other big love of Faiza's life was Mr. Ozan's father, another rich businessman, who had discovered her, a rough-and-ready girl, singing at a Bedouin wedding. He'd heard something special right from the start, and later encouraged her to dress properly, to learn languages, to listen to artistes from all over the world. Thanks to him, she now had the kind of life she'd once only dreamed of: enough money to buy herself and her widowed mother a very nice house in a village near Alexandria, even a motor car.

Today, they were working on getting the words right for "Ozkorini." Umm Kulthum's recording of this song had swept the Arab world.

Faiza showed Saba, with many terrible and exaggerated grimaces, how she must learn to use the frontal bones of her face to sing this well. She needs nasality, Faiza calls it *ghunna*, also an intentional hoarseness (*bahha*) that is hard to do and indicative of huge emotions. "Listen to how her voice cracks at the end of this song, too." Faiza darts to the gramophone, young in her enthusiasm.

Umm is, in her estimation, a far greater singer than all the Piafs, the Fitzgeralds, and the Washingtons rolled into one. She had already implied that Saba ran the risk of performing a kind of blasphemy when she sings her songs; that she would never in her lifetime learn the whole thing for herself. Even if her Arabic was good enough, English people did not listen to music in the same way. In Egypt it was like worship, like prayer. In old classical Arabic singing a performer would often repeat a single line over and over again, and by doing so rouse the audience to an almost orgasmic and ecstatic state. A single concert might go on for four to six hours. When Umm Kulthum sang her radio broadcasts, bakers stopped baking, bankers banking, mothers let their children lie on their laps. People flew in from all over the Arab world to hear her; both the Allies and the Axis had used her in their radio broadcasts. That was power. The kind of power that made demands on an audience.

This was not the first time Saba had heard this encomium, and today she desperately hoped Faiza would nutshell it. Downstairs, Faiza sat in a circle of light near the piano, Saba waiting for the nod of her head that said she could begin. They were working on the middle portion of "Ozkorini," a song that had already stretched its tentacles deep inside her. When the music started and Saba began to sing, her voice was throbbing and raw with pain. She was begging Dom to stay alive.

"This is the best you have sung," Faiza said when she stopped. "You did it from here." She made a circular swirling movement with both hands in the direction of her guts. "You are nearly ready to sing her."

The sound of clapping made them jump.

It was Ellie, in a white dress and the usual perfect coiffeur. Her shadow flew across the wall as she walked toward them.

"Sorry to burst in on you, Sabs," she said, "but I need a quick word. Marvelous music, by the way. You sound just like the real thing."

Saba, still in the song and vulnerable, blinked toward her. She could hear Faiza's cat underneath the table, the sound of its rough tongue mixed with its purring.

Faiza's smile was lemony—she disliked being interrupted during rehearsals and being seen without full makeup by people who didn't know her well.

"Five minutes," she said. "I'm going upstairs to get dressed."

"Saba, for God's sake, where have you been?" Ellie said when they were alone. A sweat shield had worked loose in the arm of her dress. She snatched it away and put it in her handbag.

"You know perfectly well where I've been." Saba was fed up with this charade. She'd seen Tariq's suitcase at the Pattersons' house and knew he'd stayed there while she was away. "You said the broadcast was tonight."

"You really should have told me," Ellie continued shamelessly. "Anyway, a new man from ENSA phoned this morning; he wants to see you right away. He's staying at their offices on Karmuz Street. There's a taxi outside. The driver knows where it is; I've paid him and tipped him, so don't get stung again. When you've seen him, come straight back home to the Pattersons', and I mean it. No more running off. Honestly!"

But there were no ENSA offices on Karmuz Street, or if there were they'd been burned down long ago, along with the other miserable ruins. Instead, the driver drove fast down a nondescript road two hundred yards ahead and stopped next to a street stall that sold lurid, flyblown sweets threaded onto strings.

He gestured to her to get out; he led her across a crumbling pavement and banged on the front door of an apartment with a green grille outside it that was padlocked.

Several locks were clicked, Cleeve opened the door. He was wearing glasses, had darkened his hair and was dressed in a shiny dark traveling salesman kind of suit.

"Sorry about the Charlie Chaplin getup," he said. His breath smelled of cigarettes and mints and something staler. "I'm traveling incognito this time."

He glanced quickly up and down the empty street.

"Upstairs," he muttered. "I've got some news."

He took her to a scruffy room, with overflowing ashtrays and a stained mug of coffee on the table. His suitcase was on the floor, half unpacked.

"Sit down." He pointed at a sagging sofa.

"Quite a bit to fill you in on. How are you, darling, by the way? You look marvelous." He drew the blackout curtains; the lamp he switched on stained his face in a strange hallucinatory wash of green light.

"Thank you," she said, thinking that sometimes too much happening in your life was worse than too little.

"Right." Cleeve lit a cigarette and stretched his legs out. "I'm catching the train back to Cairo tonight, so I don't have long, but let me bring you up to date.

"Ozan has definitely decided on Istanbul for his party—he has a house there on the Bosphorus—much safer and more fun. He wants you to go with him for the party and for a limited run at his club. We'd like you to do this if you can, and frankly, you'll be much safer there—perfectly natural for a half-Turkish girl to go home and sing in the country of her birth. Are you happy to do that?"

A crash of conflicting thoughts went through her head. The desire to be brave and do good things for her country, excitement at singing in a foreign place, the fear of putting the Mediterranean between her and Dom—although his leave, it was true, had been canceled for the next month, the arrangement felt precarious.

"How long will I be away?"

Cleeve gave his charming, lopsided smile.

"No more than a week at the absolute most. Ozan has promised to pay you well, you'll be put up in a nice hotel, and we'll keep an eye on you from a distance."

"Should he pay me? It doesn't feel right."

"It's the safest way. If he doesn't, it will look suspicious."

"What do I have to do?"

He looked at her in a friendly way. "Again, the answer is maybe nothing, maybe a lot. We simply don't know yet."

He spread a map on the table. "At the moment, Istanbul is the most important neutral city in the world because it's roughly equidistant from Germany, Russia, and the Western powers. The country has become very popular with German secret service agents on large expense accounts, which is where our friend Ozan has cleaned up at his clubs. Some of these chaps are jokes, they're just keeping their heads down until the war is over, but there are other people there with vital information to share.

"There's a young man in Istanbul, a pilot we believe could be of great interest to us; we hope you'll meet him—I'll brief you on this later." Cleeve's foot had started to jiggle up and down. "What we need is to collect any kind of intelligence we can about which way the Germans are going to jump. The British have been making plans to move in to German-occupied Greece. If this happens, they will want to make use of Turkish landing strips, which will mean Turkey cannot remain neutral for long."

He stubbed his cigarette out, and fixed her with an intense look. "Can you take all this in?"

"Yes, I can." She held his gaze, certain she couldn't, but determined not to show him that.

He opened a pigskin notebook. "Ozan looks after his performers well. You'll probably stay at the Pera Palace, which is charming, or the Büyük Londra. The usual run at the club is two weeks. If at any point you want to come back, or feel you have something you need to tell us, all you have to do is phone me in Cairo. My number is . . ." He started to scribble. "Phone me and say: 'Could you book me at the Gezirah next week?' I'll know what you mean. Otherwise, I'll be in Istanbul on the second of September. I'll be staying at an apartment on Istiklal Caddesi under the name of William McFarlane. I'll leave a note for you at the front desk of the hotel; I'll sign it from your cousin Bill. Got it?"

"Got it."

He smiled at her, a fan again, his eyes glistening sincerely. "D'you know, I think people are so wrong to imagine that showbiz types are fragile; we've found you marvelous to work with on the whole—fearless and patriotic. I suppose you excite people, they want to tell you things, or maybe for you to make them feel things they might not feel by themselves . . ." He trailed off almost sadly, as if he were talking to himself, and switched off the green lamp.

He looked at his watch. "Got to go, sorry, I must always seem so pressed for time," he said. This hadn't occurred to her—almost everyone you met now seemed either bored or madly rushed.

Before he left, he warned her that when she was in Istanbul she must not meet anyone she didn't know in a place outside of her hotel. He gave her an envelope with a wad of Turkish lira in it. The equivalent of £100, he told her. She must keep a careful note of what she spent, and if Mr. Ozan wanted to pay her, too, why not? She'd been working hard and he was as rich as Croesus, and a man like him enjoyed rewarding people.

And then, after some hesitation, he delved into his suitcase and brought out a small gun.

"You won't need this, but they're always useful."

"I don't know how to use it," she said.

"You don't need to," he twinkled. "It's like baby's first gun, all you have to do is point and shoot, exactly like a water pistol. The bullets go in here."

She took the gun and held it in the palm of her hand; for the first time, she was afraid.

She asked him again what day she might be leaving. He said he didn't know yet. Mr. Ozan would tell her. It would probably be at the end of the week.

"Don't look nervous," he said. "It should be fun."

CHAPTER 30

While Saba was rehearsing, Dom wandered for a while, trying not to resent this other life that took her away from him. He already recognized that when she was performing she was quite startlingly someone else, someone he shared and was in awe of, someone not quite normal in the way she was able to seem so natural, so zestful, and alive in front of thousands of strangers. What had felt precious about their last few days was that this faintly troubling double image of her had disappeared and their life together had become simple.

With two hours to fill, he walked down the Rue Fuad where he found a small jeweler's shop that sold exquisite enamelwork. After careful deliberation he spotted, in its dim interior, what he hoped would be the perfect present for her: a blue enamel bracelet, carved in fine silver lines with the outlines of gods and goddesses, each one encased in its own delicate link.

The store owner was fat and expansive with one cloudy eye. He brought Dom a chair, patted his knee, and insisted they share a glass of mint tea, or maybe some Stella beer, together. He put the bracelet on some velvet and explained each symbol to him with the eagerness of a man introducing a bunch of old and much-loved pals to a new friend. This was Horus, he pointed toward the one-eyed god of protection; Osiris, god of resurrection and fertility; Isis with her magic spells; and ah, this—the man's fat finger caressed the slender waist of a goddess with a pair of silver horns growing out of her head—this was Hathor, goddess of many things: love and music and beauty. She also represented the vengeful eye of Ra, goddess of drunkenness and destruction. The man laughed uproariously.

Oh the joy of finding the perfect present at the right time for the person you loved. Dom, who'd never gone beyond chocolates and flowers before, was so happy. He asked the jeweler to engrave her name on the back, and then, in a flash of inspiration that pleased him, *Ozkorini.* Think of me.

When the present was engraved and wrapped inside a pretty box, smelling faintly of frangipani, he longed to give it to her immediately, but there was still time to kill before meeting her. He decided on a beer at the Officers' Club, which was within walking distance, but felt a strange reluctance to go there. Usually he was excited at the thought of joining the squadron again. But today would soon be tomorrow, and tomorrow would mean men and only men, apart from the odd ATS girl, sand, tents, reeking latrines buzzing with flies, the telephone hurling them from bed at all kinds of ungodly hours, and all the rest . . . the bone-jarring exhaustion, the cauterizing of feeling and emotion. The dread of letting his flight down in some major way.

Thoughts leading, inevitably, to Jacko and the flash picture of his screaming face behind the Perspex of his Spitfire, before the flames ate him.

Stepping from the pavement's shade into stunning heat, he thought about the awful meal with Jacko's parents after the funeral—his mother's sudden wild look of *j'accuse* as she passed him the gravy, swiftly modified into a hostess's smile. Jacko would never have flown had he not met Dom, and she knew it.

"Sorry." He'd bumped into an old lady who glared at him.

Pay attention. *Stop it!* There was a war on. What did he expect?

"Heil, Dom! Old fucker!" When he walked into the bar, the tall figure of Barney unfurled from a leather chair and walked toward him. He was so glad to see him, the height, the heft of him, he could almost have cried. People didn't tell you how exhausting new love could be, thought Dom, sitting down beside him. The fear it brought.

"Where have you been?"

"Can't talk!" He clutched his throat like an expiring man. "Parched."

Once, he thought, watching Barney slope off to get a beer, he would have made a funny story out of the row with Saba the night before—her spitting rage, his own stupidity—but the walls had shifted again.

In the middle of the night, at around three, he'd got up for a glass of water, and when he'd got back into bed, he'd lain propped up on his elbow and looked at her. And watching her like this, the candlelight flickering over her face as she'd slept, unguarded as a child, what he'd most felt was a humbling of himself. He loved her—he knew that now without a shadow of doubt. Her fierceness, her talent, her vitality. He wanted to be loyal to her, to keep her safe. His own sharp tongue, his quick temper, his impatience must be curbed. He must not hurt her.

"Sorry, old cock, they've run out of Beechers, they've only got Guinness." Barney put the drinks down between them and grinned. "God, I'm glad to see you."

He took a long, noisy swig. Most of the wing, he said, when his glass was mostly froth, had opted to go to Cairo for their last leave, it was safer there. He'd been bored shitless, reduced to playing bridge with some brigadier and the matron from the local hospital.

He opened a second bottle and poured it. "Cheers!" They touched glasses. "Enjoy it while you can," Barney told him. He'd been at LG39 the day before to see if there was any news; the signals had been coming and going like tart's knickers.

"I saw some planes flying over the harbor this morning," Dom said. "I wondered if they were for us."

"Let's hope," Barney said tersely. "I was talking to a fitter the day before yesterday—quite a few of ours are kaput, something about sand bunging up their backsides."

While they were talking, four Australian pilots strolled into the bar wearing new uniforms with ironed arm creases that showed how scruffy the rest of them looked in their dusty khakis. Drinks were bought, they sprawled in the leather chairs exchanging names, squadrons, brief biographies, all affecting a nonchalant indifference that none of them felt now. Theirs was a stick insect's reaction: camouflage, fear, prudence. More and more men were being drafted in now, according to one of the Aussie pilots; they'd heard the big one would come in less than ten days. The man sighed after this announcement, as though telling them nothing more thrilling than a railway timetable.

This news went straight to Dom's brain like a drug of delight and confusion. Only an hour ago, sitting in the jeweler's shop, captivated by the goddess talk and with her present in his hand, he'd felt so changed, so pure, and yet this urge to fight, to fly, he felt he couldn't control it, any more than he could control wanting her, or his growing sense of wanting to be her protector.

He ate a horrible cheese sandwich, drank another beer. In some ways, yes, it was a definite relief after the exhausting heights of the last few days to be back, so to speak, at base camp and in the company of men—to be laughing about Buster Cartwright's hairy landing, so close to the hangar it had swept the turban off a nearby Indian fitter, or even listening to a long-winded account from one of the Aussies, a tall redheaded man with white eyebrows, about why he always attached his own car wing mirror to his own aircraft to give him an extra pair of eyes.

But halfway through his second beer, Dom thought with a rush of emotion about Saba in the bath: her body gleaming, the swirling mass of her hair underwater. She'd be singing now, focused and happy. In spite of her tears last night, she had a strong center, and he was glad. She would need it.

A couple of beers later, he put the jewelry box in his top pocket and decided to go down to the Cheval D'Or and surprise her after her rehearsal. When Saba had warned him with a firmness that surprised him not to go there again without an invitation, he'd felt both amused and resentful. He wasn't used to a woman giving him orders. But today, their last together, was surely different. The important thing, he reasoned as he walked toward the Corniche, was not to spoil it all by getting too morbid or sad, for he had felt dangerously close to tears himself when she'd cried the night before, and that wouldn't do.

A swim, he thought, seeing the dazzling turquoise sea ahead of him. The perfect thing. They could go down to Stanley Beach, hire costumes from the club, and drink afterward at one of the beachside stalls; a taxi back to the flat would leave her time to wash and get dressed and get to wherever she was going to do the wireless bloody thing. Although he'd bent over backward to make amends for his rant about the program, the lizard-brain part of him was still thinking *Damn and blast it.* Tonight, he wanted her for himself.

* * *

She must have gone straight to the recording, he thought. He had arranged himself casually against a lamppost across the road from the Cheval D'Or, waiting for the door to open. Either that, or it had been an exceptionally long rehearsal. In the harsh sunlight of early afternoon, the club with its faded awnings and dusty shutters looked spectacularly unglamorous. When he strained his ears to hear her singing, all he heard were the ordinary sounds of the Corniche, the clip-clopping of a few exhausted gharry horses, the faraway babble of foreign voices melting in the heat. Watching a pye-dog sitting in the gutter, absorbed in a fierce hunt for fleas, Dom's delight at the prospect of seeing her went away and he felt unpleasantly furtive—this was her territory and he was encroaching on it. He stood in the blistering sun and then grew disgusted—stick to the plan, he told himself, it was undignified to stay like this, skulking now behind sandbags like some sort of cut-price spy. Walk back to the Rue Lepsius and wait for her there. It would give him time to pack.

Walking back, the houses seemed to jump and blur. From now on, he warned himself, feeling sweat trickle down his back like an insect, he must close down his emotions. It was a near cert, when he got back, that he would be promoted to flight commander. Paul Rivers, exhausted now and longing to get home, had told him that, and now the lives of many men would depend on him; he couldn't afford to behave like a hysterical girl.

Also, Alexandria was now, officially, the most dangerous city in Egypt. The evidence was all around him—the scared-looking people, the charred houses, the wild cats and dogs roaming the streets. True, a few diehards refused to leave and were still swimming at Cleopatra Beach, or drinking Singapore Slings in deserted hotels, but it wasn't all that long ago that lines of panicky people had queued outside embassies and banks, desperate to leave. It had been madness to meet her here, with Rommel planning to take over the city any day now. He would advise her, more forcibly than ever, to leave.

Some street children swarmed toward him shouting, "Any gum, chum?" in excruciating American accents, begging him to relieve them of cigarettes and "first-quality whisks."

"Meet my sister, mister," said one with an unpleasant leer and the beginnings of a mustache on his top lip.

At the next street corner he watched a peasant farmer and his donkey pass, the beast piled high with bundles of sugarcane, the man shouting.

In their room on the Rue Lepsius, he sat for the first hour smoking, listening for the light skim of her tread running upstairs, the burst of song, but all he heard was a muddle of foreign voices from the street outside.

He started to pack his kit: his desert boots, his pistol, a couple of shirts; he took his socks down from the hanger where she'd left them. He smoked another cigarette, and when he got hungry, left her a note, dashing down the stairs to buy a foul-tasting falafel from a street vendor. It was then, standing in the street and seeing a large yolk-colored sun beginning to set, that he started to panic. What if she hadn't gone to the recording studio? Or had been held up there and not able to contact him, or caught by a stray hand grenade and was lost and bleeding in some dusty street somewhere; maybe their stupid row had upset her more than she'd admitted and she was punishing him by making him wait.

He walked around for hours trying to find her. First to the ENSA offices, where a note on the padlocked door said they had moved to Cairo, then to Dilawar's, empty except for the three old men who were regulars there.

He walked up shuttered alleyways, where blue lights shone eerily from wrought-iron lampposts. As he walked, he wondered if jealousy had driven him a little mad. (For he was jealous, had been almost from the moment he'd first met her, without really understanding why.) And he thought about mirages. It was part of a pilot's training to understand how a mirage could conjure up lakes and rivers, whole mountains out of nothing but desert sands. A confusion of perspective, a longing for something that wasn't there. He'd seen her work the same kind of magic on the men she sang for—their tired faces lit up with hope and happiness; her songs the mirror that gave them back their life. God help him if he'd mistaken four days of blissful lovemaking for something solid and real.

He was certain now she was gone. At six o'clock, he ran wildly down the street in the direction of the club again. Someone must know where she was.

Late afternoon was fading as he ran into dusk: the sun setting over the harbor in a molten furnace of ochre and peach–colored clouds that seemed to mock him. Fool, fool, fool for thinking you could contain her. When he got to the club, he stood gasping for breath on the pavement outside it. He banged on the locked door for five minutes and then he kicked it. An upstairs window opened; an old lady scowled down, he saw the pink of her scalp through wet hair.

"Where is she?" he shouted up. "Where is Saba?"

She told him to wait, ran downstairs and after an interminable scraping of locks opened the door. It took him a few seconds to see that this was Faiza Mushawar minus makeup. In the yellow light of sunset, her skin looked jaundiced. The line of her eyebrows had been drawn artificially high with a wobbly brown pencil.

"What is it?" she said crossly. "Who are you?"

"Dominic Benson," he said. "You must remember, I was here with Saba. We met in your room."

She stared at him, her brown eyes bulging. "No." A green-eyed cat was trying to force its way around her. She blocked its way with a slippered foot. "Many men come here."

"Please," he said. "Where is she?"

He told her he had to leave in the morning, that he was going back to the desert, that he and Saba had arranged to meet for lunch, that he'd waited all afternoon for her. While he talked, she sucked in her mouth and shook her head.

"I don't know where she's gone." She glanced over his shoulder. "Another city, another concert. People don't stay long." Her shrug saying *What do you expect? She's a singer, there's a war on. Things happen for no meaning.*

"Do you have any idea when she is coming back?" he asked as gently as he could.

She shrugged again—"She is working, is never sure"—it seemed to him her accent grew thicker by the moment. "Ask British peoples, I don't know." Soon he felt she would be denying even knowing her at all.

"Can you tell me the names of the people she has been staying with in Alex?"

This had driven him mad all afternoon: Palmerston? Petersen? Mathieson? In all the excitement of meeting her again, he hadn't paid proper attention. The old lady's eyes rolled a little.

"No."

Stop messing about, you bloody old fool, I know you speak English.

"Listen." He heard his voice pleading, when he really wanted to shout. The cat blinked at him, the red glow of setting sun reflected in its eyes. "Mrs. Mushawar, please help me. You taught her. She respected you. You must know." In a matter of hours, the lorry would come, it would take him back to the desert; he might never see her again. "Please."

Her skinny eyebrows rose. It seemed she might be on the verge of some sort of explanation or apology when she drew back and said, "Sorry for this, but I don't know. She here this morning, very nice, she not here now." She closed the door in his face.

He had come to the end of anything that could be called a plan. He spent the next few hours visiting the usual watering holes for the English, hoping by some miracle that she might be there. The Cecil bar was full of ATS girls. One or two of them crossed their legs and smiled hopefully as he walked in. Another said, if this Saba was still in Alex, she needed her head read. It was a deadly dump, give her Beirut any day.

It was dark by the time he got back to their room. From the harbor he heard the long, mournful blast of a foghorn. He sat on the chair, his head in his hands. He was meeting Barney outside the Officers' Club at seven o'clock the next morning. Barney had arranged a lift back to the aerodrome in a supply lorry. He had to go, he wanted to. On the following day, the whole squadron would be briefed on what they jocularly called the big one. This would be their last leave for a long time; from now on the fighting would be fierce and relentless. He could die without saying good-bye to her.

He felt mad with frustration at wasting this precious time. He told himself to calm down. He shaved, he made the bed, and he put the rest of his stuff, his khaki drills, his map, and the socks she'd washed, into his kitbag. It was then he saw her note.

Gone away suddenly for more concerts. So sorry. I love you. I hope to be back soon.

Love Saba

He read it several times, unable to believe his eyes—so brief, so offhand. No address, no proper information, almost a brush-off. And she'd been back, he could see that now, her hairbrush and soap gone, clothes, too, apart from her red dress, which she'd left in the cupboard. He took the dress from its hanger and lay on the bed with it. He inhaled its faint scent of roses and jasmine, and gave an anguished cry. He'd never imagined love could hurt this much—he felt winded, wounded, as if he'd been kicked hard in the stomach.

CHAPTER 31

As their plane roared through the night toward Istanbul, Saba had the nightmarish feeling of slippage, of things happening too fast and out of sequence. Ozan lay asleep three seats ahead of her, with his usual air of plump contentment, but she had not envisaged being on her own with him like this. Where was his wife? His entourage? What was Dom doing now? She hated the thought of hurting him like this.

She and Ellie had had a fierce row about it before she'd left Alexandria.

"I can't go without telling him," she'd told Ellie. "He's waiting for me. He's going back to his squadron tomorrow. I'm going to run down there straightaway."

Ellie had been doing what she called Hollywood packing—hurling clothes into an open suitcase with none of her usual tissue-paper-and-folding malarkey. At the end of it, she opened her arms wide in a curiously wild gesture.

"There *is* no time," she said. "I know it's mad-making, but they're picking you up in twenty minutes, and your plane leaves tonight and there's not a damn thing I can do about it." Her eyes looked nakedly red without their usual careful coating of mascara. "I'm not happy about this either," she said, "because now I have no job, and nowhere to live. And I'm sick of other people making all the decisions . . . and Tariq's furious and I was hoping he'd propose this week, so it's all a real mess, isn't it?"

In the end, they'd compromised.

"Listen, darling," Ellie had coaxed. "Write him a letter. I'll take it down to him the minute you've gone, and then at least he'll know."

Saba had gone blank with alarm. Given Cleeve's warnings, what could be safely said? So in the end, a hopeless, scrappy, heartless-seeming note—her mind lurched with shame when she thought of him reading it. What would he think of her now?

"May I join you for one moment?" Mr. Ozan, dressed superbly today in a pale suit and pearl-gray tie, had woken and decided to be sociable. He came swaying down the aisle and wedged himself beside her. His powerful, fat little body felt oppressively close—she was starting to feel airsick as well as everything else.

"Are you happy about our change of plan?" he roared over the engine noise. "Have you been to Turkey before?" He half turned to gauge her reaction to what he obviously felt would be a great treat. "You were telling me your father was born there."

"They left when he was young," she had to shout back. "My father wanted to travel . . . *wanted to travel.*" She hoped he'd shut up now.

"And, remind me, what town . . . *what town* did he hail from?" He was relentless.

"A small village called Üvezli," she said. "They didn't talk about it much."

"I know it, I think. It's on the way from Üsküdar to the Black Sea coast," he said. "A pretty place, we can show you when we get there. Don't look worried," he added gaily, "you are going to have the life of your time." He corrected himself: "The time of your life."

The plane's engine had settled into an easy hum. Through the small windows she saw clouds, and miles and miles below, the desert quietly filling up with the pinks and golds of the setting sun.

"I forgot to ask," Mr. Ozan said. "Your lessons with Faiza—did you like them?"

"Very much. I'd only sung a few Turkish baby songs before, but never in Arabic."

Ozan shifted in his seat. He shook his head.

"You won't need those songs now—Arabic is the official language in Beirut and my friends there are very sensitive about it being the language of song. In Istanbul," a proud curve came to his lips, "people are more Western-looking. We don't care so much."

She felt an odd mixture of relief and anticlimax, like a pupil who has worked hard only to find their exam has been canceled at the last moment. He'd been so passionate about the songs before; now they sounded about as important as whether to have cheese straws or peanuts at his party.

"So is there a band in Istanbul?"

She warned herself, *keep your mouth shut.* She was here for a reason, with a job to do. She mustn't mess it up. If she didn't keep this firmly in mind, she would lose her center and start to feel completely out of her depth; also, she would miss Dom more than was bearable.

"Yes, and they are first rate," Ozan assured her. "Every time any good new record has come out in Paris or in London, I have collected it for them, so they are bang up to the minute, too."

He grinned at her. "I am excited, are you?" And in a way she was—a sick kind of excitement that seemed to have bunched every muscle in her body.

"And of course, the other thing is . . ." Ozan stared down at the now dark and crinkled sea beneath them, "it will be nice to be away from this ghastly business for a while. Things are really hotting up. We are the lucky ones."

Dom, waking the following morning, reached into an empty space beside him. A phone was ringing in the hall downstairs, half dressed, he sprinted down and got the usual mild electric shock as he grabbed it. His face in the mirror above it looked so fraught he hardly recognized himself.

"Oh good, still there." A faint voice at last through the crackles. "Well, it's Saba's friend, Madame Eloise, here. Damn, dreadful line, sorry." More static, the faint hootings of her voice.

"Did you get the letter from Saba? Yes . . . good, she had to shoot off rather suddenly. But anyway . . . I understand you're off tomorrow, or is it today? Anyway . . . yes. No . . . sorry, what? Oh blast this . . ." The line cleared for a few seconds.

"She was in too much of a rush to give me any details—something about a party somewhere, or another concert—but she wants you to know she's safe and well and that she'll contact you as soon as she knows where she's going, if that doesn't sound too Alice in Wonderland. An address for her? No, sorry, no clue. I'm just the wardrobe lady. I think the best thing to do is to send letters to ENSA in Cairo; they'll . . . oh blast this awful line . . . they'll send them on. I didn't get the impression she'd be gone long. Good-bye then. Good luck! Sorry about this."

Barney's lift had fallen through, so he thumbed a ride back to the aerodrome in a supply lorry. He sat on his own in the back and gave himself a severe talking-to. A fighter pilot, Barney had told him once, only half-facetiously, was good for three things: eating, flying, and killing, and that was the way it had to be now. With things hotting up, he must simply close her down, seal her off like an engine that wouldn't function, otherwise she would kill him.

When he got back, he played a game of football with the lads in the dust, and for several hours felt a consoling and enveloping blankness.

Next he had a beer with his flight commander, Rivers, who as expected, said he'd completed his two hundred hours' flying time, and was now tour-expired. His weary face, swollen with desert sores and pink circles of calamine, could not hide its relief.

"So, Dom, they want you to take over, at least for the time being, so whizzo," he added flatly, "tons of fun ahead."

A feeling of something that might under other circumstances have been called pride in his accomplishment struggled through the humiliations of the day, like a bright fish in an ocean of grime. It was an honor, something solid and worth fighting for, something which under other circumstances he would have felt proud to tell her about.

It was Barney who handed Dom a warm Worthington's to celebrate, and Barney who later, during a game of chess, held a queen in his silvered hand and said, "I've been meaning to ask: did you hear from that ENSA girl again?" wrecking his small moment of pleasure.

Dom forced a smile. "Not a dicky bird." They finished the game in silence. He hadn't meant to, but he'd told Barney a little about Saba after their meeting in Ismailia. He'd been high as a kite and unable to stop himself. Barney, who'd had a few, had immediately sung, "I'm Dreaming of a White Mistress," and then had put his hand on Dom's arm and added with the solemnness of the half-cut. "Now listen! Listen . . . listen, very important announcement to make, and I want you to listen very hard to me: everyone falls in love with those ENSA popsies, so be careful." He'd made it sound so trivial, so ordinary, Dom was furious with himself for telling him.

When the light faded, about eight p.m., they packed the chessmen away in silence and went to bed. Barney was exhausted; Dom, too. He lay down on the damp camp bed, pulled up his blanket, and before he closed his eyes felt her absence with a physical ache like a kick in the guts. He was too hurt to feel angry, too old to cry, but he wanted to. She was gone, just like that, and he had no idea where.

There was a briefing on the following morning. An important one: Air Commodore Bingley, a rangy man with a headmaster's stoop, came from Advanced Air Headquarters to tell them the long wait was over. The training, the shadow fighting, the cross-country recces, the forced landings, the sitting in sweaty flying suits waiting for take-offs canceled at the last minute. They were on full squadron alert now.

Dom sat and listened in the middle of the dusty group of twenty-six young men. They lounged in their chairs in the boiling-hot dispersal hut without any visible display of interest or enthusiasm, but everyone's heart was pounding.

Bingley told them sharply to pay attention now. British Intelligence had discovered a fact of singular significance. On the night of 30 August, a full moon, General Rommel planned a surprise attack on the southern section of the Allied front near El Alamein. He would attack by night, and as far as they knew, through a gap between Munassib and Qaret El Huneunat, a place he believed was lightly held and lightly mined. If the attack succeeded it would open up the road to Alexandria, and then God knows what would happen. "Our job, bluntly put, is to try and shatter the Luftwaffe in the next ten days."

And Bingley, gazing at the young men, had a private moment of anguish as he said this, wondering who would be spared and who taken. He barked out that he sincerely hoped they'd all had their beauty sleep, because for the foreseeable future their job would be to fly as escorts to the Vickers Wellington bombers based at LG91. They would be on permanent call. All leave was canceled for the foreseeable future, he added, and Dom, for complicated reasons, was relieved.

"Any questions?"

"How many days do you estimate it will take?"

"Hopefully it will be a short mission," Bingley continued. "A few days and then out, but this could be the big one." His eye traveled up and down the lines of exhausted young men. "If Rommel manages to break through our lines and occupy Egypt, he'll have the perfect launch pad for more attacks on the Mediterranean. If we stop him, I think we'll have a very good chance of ending this war."

"Thank you, sir." Dom got up after this short speech was over. "We'll do our best."

Walking back to the mess together, Bingley confided that he'd heard a worrying rumor that some of the new Kittyhawks had an operational fault—their oxygen refurb system opened without warning and sometimes choked with sand. Also that they only had ten serviceable Spitfires left, six of these on the battle line, and a couple of them definitely approaching retirement age.

When he asked Dom if he would be prepared to fly back with him the next day and pick up a repaired Spit, Dom said yes immediately. It would be something to do, something to take his mind off things.

CHAPTER 32

In Istanbul, another beautiful car throbbed away on the tarmac, waiting to carry them away. This one, Mr. Ozan told her, was a 1934 Rolls Bentley, with an aluminium body, very rare, he said, his plump hand caressing its low, sleek sides. He suggested a brief tour of the city before they drove out to his summer house in Arnavutköy, which was some seven miles from the city and a lovely drive.

It was dusk, and as they drove toward the heart of the city, the Golden Horn was soaked in a peach-colored light. From the backseat of the Bentley, Saba saw ferry boats crinkling the waves, mosques, palaces, weird wooden buildings, and felt as if she were part of some elaborate hallucination.

Passing through the Roman walls on the edge of the city, the potholed street made the car lurch from side to side for a few moments like a paper cup in the ocean. She stared out at two women sitting in a dim alleyway peeling vegetables, surrounded by scrawny cats; an old man selling sesame rings under a kerosene light.

Closer to the center of the city, it surprised her how elegant and Westernized these Stamboulis looked: the women in their smart hats and silk stockings, the men in sober dark suits and white shirts. She'd imagined this place would be full of unsophisticated Tan-type people, but this was much posher than Cardiff. Ozan watched her reactions playfully. "So what is your verdict on our town?" he said.

"It's beautiful," she answered in a low voice, thinking *Stay calm, stay calm.* She had not prepared herself for the shock of being in her father's world again. There were so many men here that had the same erect bearing, his dark intense eyes. When they looked at her, part of her shriveled, as if he'd found her here and would shortly snatch her away.

They drove back toward the Bosphorus and left along the coast road. The moon was high and so bright it darted ahead of them through the trees, shedding light over branches and occasional gleams of water.

His summer house at Arnavutköy, Ozan said, was the relic of a life that was gone now. The year after Turkey had become a republic, in 1923, all members of the Ottoman Imperial Dynasty—the princes, the princesses, spouses, children—had been booted out. Many of his rich neighbors who were related to them had fled to Nice, to Egypt, to Beirut. A relative of his—he said with that proud little twitch of his mouth that came when he was boasting—had married into the Egyptian royal family; a few like him had been allowed to stay on and run successful businesses. She didn't know whether to believe him or not, but one thing was clear: he was a man who enjoyed an audience, and she for the time being was it.

She was woken by a gentle pat on her arm.

"We're here," he said. "My house."

She looked out of the car window at one of the most beautiful houses she had ever seen. Bathed in silvery moonlight, it stood right at the water's edge, and was made of interlocking panels of exquisitely carved wood. High windows gave back the shifting patterns of the sea, and with its many dips and crevices and elaborate moldings it had the look of a carved wooden puzzle or a magic ship in a child's fairy-tale book.

Ozan gave a deep sigh. He stepped out of the car and loosened his tie.

"Pretty, no?" The night air smelled of lemon trees and jasmine and the faint salty tang of the sea. He inhaled it with a satisfied snort. Such houses, he told her proudly, were called *yalis* by Stamboulis and were much prized because of their position right on the edge of the Bosphorus. Underneath his balcony—he pointed toward the water—his boats were moored.

He said she would sleep here for two nights and then move to a room at the Büyük Londra Hotel, close to the club where she would rehearse.

"But don't think about that tonight." He'd seen her try to stifle a yawn with her hand. "Tonight is for a good night's sleep. We have put you in one of the front rooms, where you can hear the waves."

* * *

Leyla was waiting in the marbled hall to greet them. Her face lit up when she saw her husband, and although she didn't kiss him, the atmosphere between them was charged as she placed a gentle hand on his arm. The three young children who peeped out from behind her skirts had Ozan's dark-rimmed eyes and the beginnings of important noses. They beamed at Saba shyly and hugged their father.

"So, Miss Tarcan, this is a great pleasure for me to meet you again," Leyla said, extending a cool hand. "I hope you will be very happy with us here. My husband," she said with a humorous look in his direction, "says he is going to make you a star."

It was Leyla who showed her around the gardens and the house on the following day. These were the moments Saba longed to share with her mother, so unpredictable in so many ways, but constant in her wistful, indignant love of luxury. "Never!" she would have muttered, examining the glorious house that seemed to float this morning on calm waters. "Oh for God's sake, look at that!" at the solid marble in its hall. Saba, absorbing this place, its sunlit rugs, its exquisite walls and windows open to the sea, hoped she could take some of it back—a small bone to comfort her mother's large hungers, but something.

What struck her later, as she followed her hostess down the sun-warmed paths, was the extreme neatness of the very rich, their attention to detail. The beautifully planted terraced gardens were a chessboard of sweetly scented herbs and shrubs; the small vineyard was laid out with mathematical precision; the immaculate stables where Ozan kept ponies for the children, and his own purebred Arabs with their pretty turned-up noses and long-lashed flirty eyes, had identically knotted ropes hanging outside each door, each one attached to scarlet halters on brass hooks.

As they left the stables, three peacocks picking their way through cypress trees made Saba jump when they squawked like a bunch of cats whose tails had been stamped on.

When Leyla laughed, it seemed to Saba to be their first natural moment together. Though faultlessly polite, in a hostessy way, Leyla had been more constrained today, so much so that Saba wondered if she longed to be alone with her husband, who, it seemed, was rarely in one place for longer than a few days; or maybe it was the thought of all the parties he had planned in the coming weeks, and she was tired of his habit of collecting people, which she alluded to very gently. "We've had lots of singers staying here," she told Saba. "From all over the world," she added—like Ozan, keen to emphasize their cosmopolitan credentials.

After lunch, Saba was told she could rest in her bedroom, which overlooked the Bosphorus and was large, light, and airy. The high brass bed, covered in an exquisitely worked silk and gold bedspread, was placed so she could see the sea without moving from her pillows—it felt like being inside a sumptuous barge. Above the bed was a rose-tinted glass chandelier, and at the end of the room, all for her, a wonderful bathroom made of Carrera marble, with a shower and brass taps. Ozan had boasted at lunch that he'd employed a French architect "of the highest quality" to modernize the house and install the plumbing, and that it was far more up to date than most of the now crumbling but still beautiful houses where the other grandees of the Ottoman Empire had once lived.

Lying half dazed in this room, propped up on her elbow and looking at the sea, Saba felt as if she'd wandered into the pages of *One Thousand and One Nights.* It was so far away from Pomeroy Street with its lino floor and chenille bedspreads, and Baba's suitcases stored above her one narrow wardrobe. For a brief moment a song felt like a magic carpet, one that could land you splat for sure, but also take you to places never dreamed of.

The only bad thing was Dom, and her stomach was in knots about him.

She slept for two hours. When she woke, the moon was shedding its light on black water, in the distance, pinpricks of light from houses on the dark shoreline of Asia. She heard the splashing waves, and snatches of music from the ferries going back to the Galata Bridge. She was so far away from anything that could be considered normal that she felt she was dangling on a fine thread between dreams and nightmares. She thought of the stories Tan had told her once, of the bodies of murdered harem girls smuggled out to the Golden Horn and drowned. She thought about Dom and the miles and miles of sea that separated them now. He was flying again, in danger.

She almost couldn't bear to think of the house on Rue Lepsius now. On the morning she'd gone, she'd opened her eyes first and felt him beside her, awake. She'd felt his hand on the nape of her neck, his mouth on her hair. When she'd turned to face him, they'd looked at each other with wonder—a steady look, no jokes this time, no evasions. And then a long, slow kiss.

What must he think of her now?

On the next day, after a fine breakfast of fresh fruits, yoghurt, croissants, eggs and hot coffee, she was taken upstairs to Ozan's study for their first meeting. The large marble desk he sat at commanded a magnificent view of the sea. The smell of his sharp lemony aftershave filled the room.

"Sit down," he said. In Alexandria, her impression had been of an ebullient, hospitable man: a back-slapper, a topper-up of drinks, a pincher of babies' cheeks. Now, with his black eyes magnified by a large pair of horn-rimmed glasses, he was all business and keen to get on.

He opened his diary. "We are moving you today," he said, not unkindly, but not waiting for her answer either. "To a hotel in Beyoğlu, a lively part of Istanbul. In three days' time, we make a party at this house for business friends of mine and maybe some of their girlfriends." He looked at her briefly. "I'd like you to sing some songs for them. Cheerful things.

"After that, you will sing at the club called the Moulin Rouge, and after that maybe Ankara—I have some businesses there. I will check all the dates today." He started to scribble in his diary with a gold pen.

So not the week *at the absolute most* that Cleeve had predicted. She had that uneasy feeling of slippage again, of being out of control.

"How many rehearsals?" she asked. She didn't care for him rapping out orders to her as if she were some sort of mechanical toy. "I can't just sing cold for your friends. I want it to be good."

"I know, I know." His stern expression softened as if to convey he understood and respected that art had its own rules. "There is no need for you to worry about that; the band, as you will see, is top class, so let me see . . ." He pursed his lips and consulted his diary again.

"Today you rehearse with them, but before that Leyla will take you shopping—she knows all the best shops in Beyoğlu. You can buy some dresses, I will pay."

"I have dresses," she said.

"I know," he said. He removed his glasses and looked at her. A look that for the first time gleamed with possibilities. "But you can have some more if you want," he said softly. He adjusted his weight in his chair and carried on scribbling in his book. "There will be lots of parties. I want you to look good."

"I'm honestly fine, thank you," she said, thinking *Damn you, Mr. Cleeve, you said this wouldn't happen.* "I brought my own clothes."

"Ahhh." With his chair at a precarious angle, he leaned back and appraised her, like a man at an auction deciding what to bid. "Are you one of those new women?" He gave a quizzical smile. "What are they called, suffragettes?"

"They're not so new," she said. "We've all moved on a bit since then." She smiled to show him no hard feelings. "And by the way, you don't have to be a suffragette to want to wear your own things."

He ignored this. "Well, if you see anything you want, talk to Leyla, who will show you around. She is also a liberated woman," he added. "But happy here, too." He opened his arms to include the room, the view, the glittering cabinets. From the room downstairs came the gurgling sound of a child laughing, its scampering feet.

"I'm not surprised," she said. "It's beautiful."

Again that strange proud curve of his lip—almost a smirk. "And when the singing is over," his paternal look had returned, "it will be my great pleasure to take you to your family's village—it's not far from here. Maybe you will find some of your people there." When he said that, she had a vision of herself as a tree—a tree like one of the ancient cedars that grew around the *yali*—that might grow another root in the ground. It was oddly comforting, but seemed unlikely, too.

"Thank you," she said, "I'd like that."

* * *

Back in her room, she saw that a walnut-wood gramophone and wireless had been placed there—a monster of a thing with green lights shining from its control panel, and pleated material in its front. Beside it, Ozan had left a pile of the records he frequently alluded to that he'd collected from all over the world: Fats Waller, Duke Ellington, Billie and Ella, Dinah Washington. Two by Turkish singers Saba had never heard of. When she turned on the radio, she heard the crackling of static like flames, and then a burst of tango music.

She twiddled some more, her heart in her mouth, and at last an English voice saying, "and this is Béla Bartók's Romanian Folk Dances" bled into by the Arabic wailing. While she dressed, she kept the wireless tuned to the same station, hearing the sounds coming and going, and eventually, on the hour, the pips, and a calm Home Counties voice saying: "This is the BBC coming to you from North Africa. Today the Desert Air Force and five infantry units engaged with the Luftwaffe sixty miles west of Alexandria, on the edge of the Western Desert. We have no news yet of casualties."

She almost stopped breathing, terrified of missing a single word. But that was it: *We have no news yet of casualties.* Loss of life was a forgone conclusion.

When the caterwauling music swept on again, she switched it off and lay on the bed, and felt, for the first time in her life, a powerful dislike of herself and her work. Being a singer had once felt so simple, so pure, so natural to her; now it felt like a cannibal that might eat her heart out. For there must be consequences, she saw that now. They would split her apart and cause other people pain, and it was stupid of her not to have thought of this before.

To stop herself thinking, she switched on the wireless again. Turkish tango music again—bounding and impertinent with its swooping rhythms, its stops and starts. Ozan said there was a craze for it in Istanbul and she'd soon be singing some. She turned it up, went into the bathroom and took off all her clothes.

In the shower, she laid her head against the cool tiled wall and closed her eyes as the water flowed over her. The bugger of it is, she thought, that what I most need now is to work. I'm no good to anyone without it.

Leyla drove her to her first rehearsal later that day.

They were early. In the elegant lobby of the Pera Palace Hotel, they sat drinking coffee and eating featherlight macaroons while a uniformed chauffeur waited patiently on the pavement outside.

Leyla, dressed today in a severely cut Chanel suit and row of double pearls, was greeted by the headwaiter with bows and twinkling smiles.

In the middle of a bland conversation about clothes, and all the wonderful tourist attractions Saba should see, Leyla blurted out, "Do you like your life?" She dabbed the corner of her mouth with a napkin and waited with watchful eyes for the answer.

"My life?" Saba was startled. Their conversation in the car hadn't strayed much beyond the polite formalities. "Well, yes. I do . . . at least I think so."

"No problems within your family?"

"How do you mean?" Saba had already been conscious of Leyla's confusion about her, the darting looks as if she were a puzzle she was working on.

"Well . . . so . . . well . . . they don't mind you singing or anything like that?" Leyla took a black Sobranie from a pearl cigarette case. "Or traveling alone. Here, have one of these, please!" She pushed the cigarettes toward her.

"No thanks." She'd given it up because they made her cough.

"We live in Wales." Saba made a quick decision not to tell Leyla about her father; she didn't know her well enough and it would make her feel too vulnerable. "People like a bit of a singsong there."

"And we like it, too." Leyla's manicured hand patted hers reassuringly. "It was only before Atatürk that women were silenced." Atatürk, who'd died four years ago, was, she said, their leader and pro-democracy, the great modernizer of Turkey. Before him, women could only really sing and dance for each other, in the *hamam,* the Turkish baths, but at a stroke he had let them out of their cages—they could sing and dance in public after centuries of it being forbidden. What relief! What joy! Except that in some poorer villages, "sorry for this—and no rudeness intended—but a singing girl is still a great disgrace. Some girls are beaten by their fathers if they do. In Anatolia there are whole villages still where only men are allowed to sing."

"Goodness!" Saba felt the surge of a blush spread over her face. Her father seemed to have missed this revolution, but what Leyla had said explained so much.

"And how did you meet Mr. Ozan?" she asked to break the awkward silence that followed.

"In London, before the war." Leyla stretched out her legs and studied her impeccable shoes. "Actually, I was studying to be a doctor."

Saba tried not to look surprised.

"A doctor! How wonderful—do you do it now?"

"No, I never did."

They glanced at each other warily.

"So, did you like London?" Saba asked after a while.

"No, forgive me. Not at all." Leyla smiled and shook her head. "I was very, very lonely, and I felt so sorry for the wife of the man I lived with. An English woman, a friend of my father's, but so busy all the time! Flowers, servants, cooking—no peace! And she was lonely, too, I think, with no aunties at home, and her children at boarding school, her husband working all the time. I don't think she knew what to do with me."

"So you must have been happy to meet Mr. Ozan?"

"It was like a miracle. He was over there going to the theater, the music, doing a hundred and one business things exactly like now." She smiled fondly. "I was at St. Thomas's Hospital for my first year. The first person in my family to do something like that. My grandfather was very unhappy about it, he hardly ever spoke to me again, but my father was progressive."

It made Saba feel queasy to remember that she should probably be paying close attention to these confidences: writing them down, pinning notes to her knickers. Part of her knew already she wasn't a natural spy.

"Zafer and I met at a party with some other Turkish people, friends of my family in London. We fell in love, we married the next year."

Leyla's voice had become somewhat mechanical. "No, no thank you," she snapped at a simpering waiter who had appeared with a new tray of pastries.

"Did you mind? Not finishing your studies, I mean."

"Not at all." Leyla said it so quickly Saba was frightened she'd overstepped the mark. They both drew in a breath and looked at their shoes.

"Well, sometimes . . . maybe . . . not so much." Leyla laughed without rancor at her own contradictions. "I did enjoy medicine but my parents were very pleased, he is a very good man, very successful, too. I have my children, my family." Her eyes were sparkling. "Never a dull moment as you would say. Now please, a bit more coffee, or shall we look at the shops before your rehearsal? By the way," she murmured while they were picking up their things, "I don't think you should tell Mr. Ozan I have talked to you of such things."

The two of them exchanged a look.

"I don't think he would exactly mind," Leyla shook the crumbs from her skirt, "but we have never spoken of these things, and I hardly think of them. It's almost as if it never happened."

After coffee, they went to the Londra hotel, where Felipe Ortiz, the bandleader, stood waiting for her beside an enormous potted palm tree near the front desk. Ortiz, a small, neat man with brilliantined slicked-back hair and a thin mustache, explained as they walked up the marble stairs that he was half Spanish and half Jewish, and had, like many Jews, fled to Istanbul two years ago. Before that he'd played all over Europe—France, Berlin, Italy, Spain. Hearing the sounds of a saxophone in an upstairs room, her steps quickened.

Felipe, though small in stature, was a man who gave off confidence like a lamp gives light. He told Saba they would rehearse for two hours each day in the morning. They had a lot to get through. The clientele at Ozan's parties and clubs were varied: Spanish, Jewish, Greeks, White Russians, and the Free French. The Turks, who were tango mad, tended not to like the new jazz; the French adored it; the Germans were sentimental and loved oompah music, of course. And here Felipe had an unsuccessful stab at a cockney accent, "blooming old 'Lili Marleen.'" He gave Saba a stack of sheet music to study later, and then they briefly discussed tempos and keys, the songs they liked, and Saba sang a few songs a cappella for him.

A fat drummer with a bulging paunch and sleepy eyes shambled into the room. His name was Carlos. Saba was briefly introduced, the band tuned to an up-tempo version of "I've Got You Under My Skin" and they were off.

When the song was ended, Felipe looked pleased—pretty good, his immaculate eyebrows indicated. Next came a jolly bouncing Turkish tango song called "Mehtapli Bir Gecede," which Carlos said meant "on a moonlit night." Saba tried to follow it but couldn't. For her, the highlight came after a break, when Felipe, fiddling quietly with his guitar, resolved the notes into a jazz version of "Stormy Weather."

"You." He looked at Saba, who sang along with him. Claude, the piano player, added a few soft touches.

And not for the first time, Saba was shocked at the sense of relief that singing brought to her. Nothing else would do sometimes. "At the end of the song," Felipe instructed the pianist, "I think when she sings about it raining all the time, you must," he put his finger to his lips, "bring it up on the last bit." He demonstrated on his guitar—a silky progression of notes that gave Saba goose bumps. The band was good. Ozan was right about that. Felipe was pleased with her. For that moment, nothing else mattered.

After the rehearsal, they went down to the heavily ornate bar and drank Turkish tea in small glasses, and laughed at the two ancient parrots that sat in a cage in between the heavy drapes, like old and bitchy women muttering Turkish threats together. Felipe told her that when the war was over, the band hoped to tour again and would be looking for a vocalist. North Africa, Europe, maybe America; they'd had an offer from the Tropicana in Cuba where he'd played before the war, a magical time, he'd said with his sad, sweet smile. The names affected her like a drug. "Mr. Ozan is keen to help us," he'd added. And now to complete the complications of the day, she felt herself shiver with excitement; she couldn't wait for the concerts to begin.

CHAPTER 33

He read the letter again, tore it in half, and burned both halves in his lighter flame.

Arleta had written, in her slapdash hand,

Dear Dom,

I hope you don't mind me calling you this. No, not a word have I heard from Saba either since she left us, so I've been worried, too. I think she must have joined another tour, or gone away, maybe gone back to England. She was sent to Alex to do some wireless broadcasts. I wrote to her, she didn't reply to me, and our little lot has broken up anyway, because of illness, accidents, etc. I don't think she even knows that our poor old comedian, Willie, died suddenly on stage, poor love, which is how he'd have wished to go. I tried to contact Janine, a dancer on our tour, but she went off, I believe to India. It's hard to keep in touch at the mo as you yourself probably know.

Sorry can't be more helpful. If I do hear from her I will definitely let her know. I miss her dreadfully, she was great fun and really talented. If you hear from her, please do contact me.

All the best,
Arleta Samson

He'd taken a comfort he knew was both unpleasant and snobbish in the schoolgirl handwriting. Performers were superficial, uneducated, unreliable, and forgettable. He'd got himself lost like a man in a room of funhouse mirrors. It would never have worked.

As a pilot he'd been trained to see that human beings had one big design fault in their brains. They saw fragments of reality and tried to build a whole world from them. When he, Barney, and Jacko had sat down to learn the first rules of navigation, their instructor had roared five words at them—compass, deviation, magnetic, variation, true—and they'd bellowed back the mnemonic Cadbury's Dairy Milk very tasty. But the principle was sound: what seemed real could trick you. The mountain, hiding behind those gorgeous fluffy clouds you were flying into, could shatter you into a million pieces. That line of stars on your starboard side masquerading as the welcoming lights of a runway or dancing like native girls waving strings of white flowers. Never mistake what you wanted for what was there—as she so clearly wasn't.

And so, a casual face-saving letter back to Arleta:

Thanks for contacting me. Do let me know if you hear anything. For the foreseeable future I'll be moving around with the DAF so safest to send letters to me either to the NAAFI in Wadi Natrun, or to the Wellington Club in Cairo. Good luck with your tour.

Dominic Benson

And that was that.

CHAPTER 34

On 1 September, as Saba walked into the Büyük Londra's lobby, the desk clerk handed her an envelope with the sheet music to "Night and Day" in it. Inside the front cover was a penciled note:

> *Can we meet tomorrow at 43 Istiklal Caddesi. I'm directly opposite the French pastry shop on the first floor. Take the lift and turn right. I shall be there from 10:30 a.m. onwards.*
>
> *Cousin Bill*

And she was relieved. She had been brought here for a reason, and would be back in North Africa soon where she could explain things properly to Dom. For that morning, lying in the scented luxury of her hotel room, she'd stopped breathing when she heard the calm voice of the BBC man announcing: "Today, there was more heavy bombing in the Western Desert where the Desert Air Force have been in action."

The news as usual was deliberately vague, but her mind had raced to fill in the gaps. Dom could be anywhere now: desperate, suffering, and here she was in a room with a rose crystal chandelier above her bed, and Persian carpets, and thick white towels in her own bathroom. From the window she could see ferry boats crossing the Golden Horn, the mosques on the skyline behind it. She would drink fresh orange juice for breakfast with fresh coffee and buttery croissants, and all the time—no point in fibbing about it—excited in a queasy way about rehearsing with the new band.

Because the confusing thing was that if she could forget about the war, which of course she never could, and Dom, this had been, professionally speaking, one of the most interesting weeks of her life.

Felipe, notwithstanding the sleepy eyes, the spivvy mustache, the slightly drunken manner, was the most exciting musician she had ever sung with. He'd been discovered playing flamenco in a bar on the back streets of Barcelona, and could play just about anything—torch songs, jazz standards, sad old folk songs—with a sort of elegant insouciance that hid the precision and verve of his technique. The band worshipped him, longed to please him, and forgave his occasionally ferocious outbursts when they didn't live up to his demands. Before the war, he'd told her in his voice cracked and glazed by the constant little cigarillos he smoked, he'd moved to Germany and raised a family there. Ozan had first heard him at the Grand Duc in Paris, and later pulled the necessary strings to get him out of Paris before the Germans arrived—hence their mutual love affair.

And it had given Saba a surge of confidence, particularly after her rough ride with Bagley, to find that Felipe seemed pleased with her, almost to accept her as an equal; someone capable of learning and going far. No words to this effect had been exchanged, but she'd seen it in his eyes when they did a duet together, and the more she felt it, the better she sang.

At their last rehearsal, he'd accompanied her on piano for "Why Don't You Do Right?" and she'd had a very strange experience with him, a moment that probably only another musician would know or recognize. For four or five bars they'd slotted into a rhythm that was so perfect that it felt like sitting inside a faultlessly constructed puzzle, or like dancing together in perfect rhythm. Nothing you could fake or force, but Felipe, who was generally quite reserved, had closed his eyes and yelped with pleasure afterward, and her blood had sung for hours. She was dying to try it again in concert that night.

After breakfast, she read Cleeve's note again, memorized the street number on Istiklal Caddesi, and then, feeling faintly absurd, taken a box of matches up to her room and burned the note over the lavatory. As she watched its charred remains swirl away, her mood improved, but the stomach churning did not go away. The thought of seeing Cleeve again had made her unexpectedly nervous, and then in less than nine hours from now—she counted out the hours on her wristwatch—she'd be at Ozan's house for the band's first performance together. Even Felipe seemed het up about this. Yesterday, after their last rehearsal, she'd seen a look of strain in his eyes as he'd warned them that Ozan, for all his easygoing ways, was a perfectionist; if the band did not please him, they'd be sent away. When he'd tried to smile, his mouth had twitched—apart from Istanbul and Ozan, Felipe had no home and no job now.

She spent the day wandering alone in and out of the narrow passages of Beyoğlu. She loved this old part of town: the dim alleyways where vegetables, tomatoes, aubergines, fat bunches of parsley were laid out as lovingly as flowers, the butchers' shops with sheep's heads in the window, their entrails neatly plaited beside them, the shop where preserved fruits lay like fat shining jewels in big glass jars.

She lingered for a while watching two old ladies prod potatoes and glare at apples with the same severe and forensic attention that Tan gave hers in the Cardiff market, and then moved on to Istiklal Caddesi, a wide thoroughfare filled with fashionably dressed people, where she hopped onto a tram. She got off at the wrong stop, walked for half a mile, then found it: Cleeve's temporary house—a narrow, ramshackle old Ottoman building with stained-glass windows between a shoe shop and an elegant French patisserie. She had no idea what she would tell him tomorrow, or what he wanted from her; this part of her life seemed precarious, unreal. I don't like being whatever it is I am to Cleeve, she thought suddenly. It doesn't suit me. I don't like shades of gray.

She ate at one of the more modest establishments on the street that served only *börek*—soft envelopes of pastry stuffed with either meat or cheese or vegetables—her father's favorite meal. She often saw faces like his now, in the streets, on trams—darkly handsome features with heavy beards that needed to be shaved twice a day. Yesterday she'd watched one man chasing his little boy in the street, and felt a sharp pang of regret. She and Baba had had good times once; the singsongs, the secret trips to buy ice creams on Angelina Street, all ending with that groaning shameful tussle in the bedroom. Her slap—she'd hit him!—when he'd torn the ENSA letter, still so shocking even when she thought of it now, would not be forgiven, not in this lifetime, and not by her now. She was fed up to the back teeth of waiting for his approval, for letters from him that would not come. Sometimes it seemed you just had to stop yourself going down an old mousehole where there was no cheese.

Istanbul, whether she liked it or not, had brought him into sharp focus again, raising questions. Why had he left this beautiful place with its mosques and scented bazaars, its bright glimpses of blue seas and distant shores, for the cold gray streets of Cardiff, where once, no one spoke his language? Why had he never come back? What was the source of the simmering anger she'd felt in him that had driven her away?

Later, back in her hotel room, alone, a singer again, her father was banished. She stood in front of a mirror in the blue dress Ellie had loaned her, shaking with nerves at the thought of Ozan's party, only a matter of hours away now. This is horrible! she thought. Why put myself through this?

A kaleidoscope of thoughts flashed through her mind as she spread panstick over her cheeks and stretched her mouth for lipstick. Tonight would be a humiliating failure, she was sure of it now, underrehearsed, embarrassing, a jumble of mismatched songs that would bewilder an audience whose tastes she had no clear idea of. Tonight would be a triumph. Ozan would love her; Paris and New York would follow. Dom would surprise her—he'd suddenly show up.

Later, in the back of the chauffeur-driven car Mr. Ozan sent for her, her eyes were closed and she was entirely oblivious to the moon rising over the Golden Horn or the fishermen dropping their lines over shadowy bridges, to men going to the mosque to pray, the shoe cleaner outside the gates of the British consulate packing his things to go home. She was tuned to her songs.

At Taksim Square, Felipe and the rest of the band got in. Smart dinner suits, fresh white shirts, and lashings of brilliantine. Felipe kissed her hand and said she looked sensational. The car headed down the steep hill and then turned again, following the sea and the dying day. On their left-hand side were the dark shadowed woods, where Felipe told her there were wolves; on their right, the gleam of the sea metallic as beaten copper in the dusk, the lights of ferry boats cutting through the waves.

* * *

Ozan's house at dusk was a marvelous sight; with light pouring out from every window, it seemed to float in the moonlit waters of the Bosphorus, ethereal and glittering like some outlandish ocean liner. Walking toward it, Saba heard the steady pump of tango music coming from inside.

Leyla, ravishing tonight in emeralds and pale green silk, stood at the door to greet them. Ozan, she said, had been roaring around the house all day overseeing everything, the food, the stage, the guest list. She rolled her big black eyes behind her husband's back—what a man! A monster!

She led them to a small room on the second floor where they could store their instruments, then down to a kitchen where five extra cooks and fourteen waiters had been brought in to pluck quail and chop coriander and dill and pound walnuts and make up the dozens of delicious little mezes for the guests to nibble at.

The cooks made a big fuss of Saba as she poked her head around the door. They smiled and bowed and offered her little bits to taste, but she ate only a tiny bowl of rice and some kind of divine-tasting chicken stew. She was nervous again and very rarely ate before singing.

"Come! Come." Leyla was excited, too. She led Saba by the hand upstairs where they peeped around the door and saw a large handsome paneled room crammed with people talking and laughing. The light from dozens of small candles poured down like golden honey on silks and satins and long-necked women with diamonds around their throats. Through open windows a full moon shone over the dark sea.

Inside, food and much male laughter, the clink of glasses and piles of pink Sobranie cigarettes lying in crystal bowls for anyone to smoke. It was, thought Saba, the kind of party you dreamed about when you were young. Mum would have fainted at it.

"Who are they?" she whispered to Felipe.

"All kinds," he whispered back, his mustache tickling her ear. "Ozan's business friends, film people, writers and traders, embassy staff, journalists—nearly a hundred and fifty of them, or so Leyla says."

Mr. Ozan hove into view, portly and suave in a ruby-colored velvet dinner jacket with braid around the cuffs, moving like a giant whale through the glowing room, eyes skimming the crowd, smiling, kissing, patting arms, pinching cheeks, accepting many compliments with a dignified and neutral dip of his head, as if to say *What did you expect?*

He'd given them strict instructions not to start to play until the guests had settled in and had time to chat and have a couple of drinks. And then, at nine o'clock precisely, he looked significantly in their direction, tapped his watch and the roar of the partygoers fell to an expectant hush. The curtain opened, a spotlight fell on the stage. "Ready," Felipe said quietly, checking them all. He raised his beautifully plucked eyebrows at Saba.

Deep breath, shoulders back. Crepi il lupo!

And they were off. Their first song, "Zu Zu Gazoo," was a nonsense thing composed by Felipe as an icebreaker. Carlos set its rapid pulse, Felipe's hands raced over his guitar, Saba leapt in singing, scatting, dancing, losing herself in a feeling of almost ecstasy that didn't feel conscious until the song ended and she heard the audience roar and clap. Felipe's smile said *It's working.* All the small incremental moments of practice, of building technique, of making mistakes, of learning when to hold and when to let go had made the song feel effortless and the night magical, and Saba knew that if she were a billionaire, she could never, ever replace this feeling of satisfaction and delight.

Next, "That Old Black Magic," with Felipe furling his lip now and doing his Satchmo imitation and doowapbababbing on the chorus. Then a beautiful Turkish song, "Veda Bûsesi," "the parting kiss," and finally "J'ai Deux Amours." It was pure fun and she loved it.

The candles burned down, leaving a hazy glow in the room; outside, the moon sank like a giant ripe peach into the sea, and the fishermen who had lingered in their boats outside to enjoy the music went home. Sounds of muffled laughter came from an upstairs room where Felipe had told her the nargiles and the lines of cocaine were laid out. He'd gone up there once or twice himself during their breaks. After midnight, the band, purring along now like some well-oiled engine, began to play all the schmoozy old favorites: "Blue Moon," "The Way You Look Tonight."

And Saba, watching the dancers drawing closer, and stealing kisses, felt her moment of happiness change in a heartbeat to one of shocking anxiety. Every cell in her body longed to dance with him, to feel his soft shining hair, his cheek on hers.

Please God, keep him safe. Don't let him die.

"'These Foolish Things,'" Felipe whispered. She loved this song. In an earlier rehearsal he'd shown her a way of holding back some of the notes by half a beat. "Sometimes in order to make them cry you need to make them wait," he'd said.

When the song ended, one or two of the dancers turned toward her entranced. They clapped their hands softly. She blew a kiss toward them from the palm of her hand.

"*Mashallah*!" Mr. Ozan shouted as he clambered onto the stage. Felipe raised his thumbs and smiled at her.

"Miss Saba Tarcan, my half-Turkish songbird," Mr. Ozan said in a muffled voice in the microphone; the audience gave her a loud ovation, they whistled and clapped. For that moment, at least, she could do no wrong.

"Well golly, golly, golly. Tremendous!" Cleeve clapped his hands together softly when, on the following day, she told him about the party. "Safely over the first fence. The band likes you, Ozan is besotted, the rest should be a piece of cake."

They were sitting in his flat—an anonymous room, scruffy like the Alexandria one; his unpacked suitcase in the corner, a half-eaten kebab on a table whose wonky leg was propped up with a faded copy of *Le Monde*.

"But I've interrupted you." He leaned forward eagerly. "Carry on. What happened next?"

They were drinking Turkish tea together out of mismatched glasses. Saba looked at her watch. Eleven o'clock.

"I can't stay long," she warned him. "As a treat, Mr. Ozan wants to take Leyla and me for a drive. He's going to try and find the place where my family once lived."

"Really." Cleeve's smile was a quick grimace—he had no interest in this whatsoever. He pushed away the kebab wrapper. "This place is a dump, sorry, I've only hired it for a couple of days. It's better we don't meet in hotels."

"I wasn't even born then," she said. "It feels like I took no interest in them before I came here."

"Isn't that true of most people?" He dropped two discarded pieces of meat into the wrapper, and threw it into the wastepaper basket. "Your parents only really exist for you as your parents." He lit a cigarette.

I know nothing about you either, Saba thought. Only the twinkly smile, the jokes, the matey conversations about music.

"So," he said. "The party."

"It was the most glamorous party I've ever been to," she said. "I couldn't believe it."

"Some of these people have made colossal profits from the war," Cleeve said. "Chiefly from sugar, salt, fuel. They've never had so much money, and they're not shy about spending it. What happened?"

"We played for about an hour," Saba continued, "and when we stopped, Mr. Ozan asked me to dance with some of the men who had come. He seemed proud of the fact that I was Turkish, that I'd come home, kept telling them how much I loved Istanbul."

"And do you?"

"Far more than I'd expected."

"And did you mind? The dancing, I mean."

She hesitated.

"I don't like Ozan telling me who to dance with—it makes me feel cheap—but that's hardly the point, is it?"

"Did you say anything?"

"No—in case I heard something."

"Good girl, oh they'll give you a great big medal for this when you get back."

Patronizing prat.

"And some dolly mixtures?"

"Don't get cross, Saba, and please go on, this is all tremendous. Who did you dance with?"

"A man called Necdet, a Levantine tobacco trader; he speaks seven languages and he smelled of almonds. Yuri somebody or other, fat and jolly. He said that most of the ships going up and down the Bosphorus belong to him. A White Russian, Alexei something like Beloi was his surname—he's here to write a book on economics. He made a pass at me."

"A serious one?"

"No. He told me Istanbul was stuffed to the gills with spies, all waiting to see which way the Turks jump. He made it sound like a joke."

"Well, true up to a point. Anything else?"

"Yes. There were four German officers there. I danced with two of them. That felt horrible but I didn't show it." She looked at him anxiously. "I'm just used to thinking of them as people who drop bombs, who kill people . . . Anyway," seeing his neutral expression, "I wanted to spit in their eyes, but I smiled nicely, and they smiled nicely back. One was called Severin Mueller; he's something in the embassy but didn't say what. He only wanted to talk about the music."

"Ah." Cleeve's head jerked up. "Now he is quite important to us—he's a new attaché from the embassy in Ankara. Why did you leave the best bit till last? Did you say anything to him?"

"Only a few words, but I was frightened—what if they realize I am English?"

He gave her his sincere look. "There are lots of parties here, Saba, where the German big brass and the English are in the same room together. I'm not saying they're making beautiful love to each other, but they talk, exchange the odd frigid smile, that sort of thing. And also, when you're with Ozan you're as safe as houses. Anything else?"

"Nothing else. Some of the men got pretty drunk by the end of the evening. They asked me to sing 'Lili Marleen.' I'd rehearsed it with Felipe in German. But Dermot," she was determined to tell him this and make him listen, "lovely as it is here, I don't want to swan around indefinitely. When will I get back to North Africa?" She heard her voice rising and made an effort to control herself. "Do you understand what I'm saying? If you have a definite job for me to do here I will do it as well as I can, but I'm not a spy, I'm a singer."

He put his hands out and held her arms as though she had become briefly and unreasonably hysterical. "Darling sweets!" he said. "Saba, my love." He planted a paternal kiss on her forehead. "Of course you're a singer. And of course we'll have you back soon, but there is something very important for you to do first, which is why I've asked you here today—to bring everything, hopefully, to a happy conclusion."

He drew close enough for her to smell the faint tang of cigarettes on his breath.

"Right, ready. Now listen."

Somewhere in the building the lift thunked and squealed.

He steepled his fingers together and looked at her.

"Saba, my love, you are part of an operation that has been going on for months in Turkey. Felipe is a key part of it. While you were dancing with the Germans, Felipe was doing a little exploring in the guest bedrooms of Ozan's house."

"Felipe?"

"Felipe is one of our key operatives here. Last night he was checking to see if Ozan's guests had been careless about what they left on their bedside tables."

"Why didn't you tell me this before?"

"I'm telling you now. We had to see how well you worked first."

She felt a kick of satisfaction and fear: so there was a reason for this.

"Does anyone else in the band know?"

"No one. Now," Cleeve drew closer, his voice dropped, "here's the next part. Listen very carefully.

"One year ago, a German fighter-pilot ace called Josef Jenke was shot down over the Black Sea. A pilot who happens to be on our payroll, too. He was picked up by the Turkish police, brought to Istanbul for questioning, and in accordance with international law, he was not sent to prison but billeted in a small pension in Pera. He's been treated pretty cushily there—allowed out for much of the day on parole, fed nicely, even supplied with the odd girl.

"Over the months and weeks of his arrest Josef has become part of the German clan. There aren't all that many of them here and for obvious reasons they stick together. He is a charming fellow, handsome, brave, the ladies like him, and he often dines out discreetly on his fighter-pilot exploits—his longing to fly again and take another shot at Johnny Britisher, that sort of thing. The situation now is that he gets invited to most of the parties, and he has become very close to a man called Otto Engel, who is part of an organization called the Ostministerium—the Ministry of the Occupied Eastern Territories. Their main activities as far as we can work out are black-marketeering and having a rollicking good time.

"Now here is the point." Cleeve looked down, as if someone might be crouching under the scruffy table. "Because Istanbul is now the most important neutral city in the world, we need urgently to speak to Jenke—he's done some brilliant work for us, but we think his days are numbered. We suspect that someone inside the Ostministerium has started to smell a rat. Certain inquiries have been made to his squadron; it's possible that any day now they will discover that he was a deserter. We need to get him out fast."

Cleeve anticipated her question.

"Josef loves women and music. He's a regular guest at house parties held at a private house that the Germans use in Tarabya, which is close to their summer embassy. One of Ozan's cronies supplies music and alcohol and girls, but he very rarely goes there.

"These evenings are very informal; it's difficult to know exactly what night Jenke will be there, but he knows you are coming, he knows who you are. When you get there you will sing, and maybe dance with a few people, and at some point in the evening Jenke will ask if he can have his photo taken with you. If you pose with him it will seem like the most natural thing in the world, a fan photograph if you like, and then we can snip him off," Cleeve scissored his nicotined fingers and smiled briefly, "make him a false passport and get him out of the country as quickly as possible."

"All in one night?"

"Felipe is confident it can be done in one night—two at the very most."

"How will I know it's him?"

Cleeve took some sheet music from his briefcase. "Jenke will flirt with you, and at some point he will walk up to the stage and you will hand him this, so he can sing a few bars with you. It's the sheet music to 'My Funny Valentine.'" He rifled through the pages until he got to a paper clip and a loose page.

"The instructions he needs are all written here invisibly. All you need to do is to open the music at the right page—he's experienced, he knows what to do. He'll take it when he's ready. It shouldn't be too difficult; all the lights will be turned down low and everyone will be drinking."

Saba watched a seagull take off from the windowsill, and dissolve into mist. She heard the lift clanking through the building, the wheeze of its door opening.

"I can do that." Although she wasn't sure she could, she felt strong feelings stir in her.

"Do you love your country, Saba?" Cleeve said softly. He was watching her closely.

She went very still for a moment. Did she love it enough to put her own life up for grabs? She hadn't really thought about patriotism except to know that if there was a crowd bellowing. "There'll Always Be an England" or "Jerusalem," her heart would be swelling, but with Germans dropping bombs on your green and pleasant land, this was hardly an unusual emotion.

"Yes," she said at last. "I do."

"Good girl." He patted her hand. "Perhaps I should warn you that the parties at Tarabya occasionally get a little wild." Cleeve sucked in his cheeks and looked at her waggishly. "It's where the Germans go to let their hair down. But Felipe will be there to keep an eye on you, and of course none of them want to upset Ozan either, he's much too important to them."

"And what then? I mean after this job. I don't want to stay indefinitely."

"Absolutely not," Cleeve was indignant. "We don't want you hanging around either. As soon as Jenke has his photo and his papers, he'll be gone and you'll be on a courier plane back to Cairo. If you want to come back here after the war, I'm sure Ozan will give you work—so everybody wins.

"But listen, Saba," his smile became a kindly frown, "it has to be your decision. Are you sure you can do this?"

She bowed her head. Her worst nightmare as a child had her dashing onto a stage in front of a huge audience only to discover, she'd forgotten her lines, what play she was in and who she was. But to back out now was more or less impossible—it was too late, and her dander was up, and she had already climbed the steps and was on the high board with Felipe and the others looking down. She took a quick breath and looked at him.

"I'll do it," she said.

CHAPTER 35

When Dom woke up, Barney's size-twelve foot was thumping him on the ear. Rain pattered down on his sleeping bag. He'd been dimly aware of it falling when he'd woken in the night, but now it poured with a steady soaking sound, seeping under the canvas flaps, making their clothes clammy and damp; there would be a sea of mud when they stepped outside.

He shone his torch on his watch—4:30—closed his eyes and tried to go back into the dream again, a feat he'd managed quite easily as a boy in cold prep school dormitories, but no more it seemed. In the dream, he'd given birth to twins. His heart burst with love for them—these babies with their Buddha-like tummies, and deep dimples, and wrists that looked as if they had rubber bands on them. He soaped their plump little arms and held his hands over their eyes to stop soap getting in them. He lifted them out of the bath and blew raspberries in their soft flesh; he powdered them and wrapped them in warm towels, and then he handed them to a woman who put them in pajamas and jiggled them on her knee. When she tickled them with her hair, they made chortling sounds like the deep bubbling of a stream. When he'd propped them up on cushions in front of a fire, their clear blue eyes had looked back at him, entirely content. *We trust you,* they were telling him. *We're safe.*

Oh what a tit. He opened his eyes and, sighing, got up, lit a cigarette and smoked it under a dripping tarpaulin outside the tent. Gazing at the sea of mud around him, the gray skies, the rusty plates smeared with beans from last night's meal, he mocked the midnight dreamer.

Fat babies, fat chance. It was shameful, ridiculous how much he dreamed about her, or some version of her, of which you didn't have to be Freud to know that the twins were a part, and he was so staggeringly tired now; he simply couldn't afford to go on like this. Since

October, the round-the-clock bombing sorties had gone on with the regularity of seaside trains, and yesterday, flying between Sidi Barrani and LG101, dazed and hallucinatory, he had seen the desert as a huge piece of crinkled art paper on which his plane drew enormous lines back and forth, back and forth. When he saw he'd stopped working the controls and was simply gazing slack-jawed at this, he'd had to pinch himself and sing to get safely home.

They'd lost five Spitfires in the relentless raids of the last few weeks; two pilots, one fitter who'd crashed in a jeep in a dust storm. Today, weather permitting, he planned to fly down on his own to a temporary hangar, close to Marsa Matruh, to see if any of the old patched-up Spits being repaired there would be usable or whether they were death traps.

When Barney had heard about this plan, over supper last night, they'd fallen out about it, and gone to bed angry at each other, a thing he could never remember happening before—not at school, nor at university, affable old Barney, normally speaking, was a golden retriever of a man—but tiredness, it seemed, made even the best of them chippy and humorless.

"Forget it, Dom," Barney had advised flatly. "It's our first afternoon off in weeks." Barney had tried to tempt him with various pleasant Cairo alternatives: some cold beers for once instead of the warm rubbish they were drinking now; Dorothy Lamour at the Sphinx—Barney waggled his hips, outlined huge bosoms with his hands. It could be their last day off for a long, long time.

All true.

"We need the Spits," Dom said flatly.

Which was true, too—every single aircraft was needed now, because Bingley's confident assertion that they would banish the Luftwaffe from Africa during the August raids had proved a pipe dream, and now a new last push was planned. There had been no formal briefings yet, but the mess and the bars of Cairo were buzzing with rumors that the Allies were about to descend on North Africa in the biggest seaborne invasion the world had ever seen; that once the beaches and ports had been secured, the ground bases and airfields could be quickly established, and then tick, tick, tick, like a game of Chinese checkers, Italy would be open to invasion, the Allies would have dominance in the air, and the whole sodding thing would soon be over. Dom was in two minds as to how he felt about that. He wanted it over now, and dreaded it, too. How did one come down from this—this nerve-shredding life, this death. Life post-Africa. And life post-Saba, even though, as he often reminded himself, he hardly thought of her now.

When Dom didn't answer, Barney stopped his silly Dorothy dancing.

"You are not seriously thinking about it, are you?"

"Not thinking about it. I've said yes."

There was a long, tense silence.

"You're a silly bugger, Dom," Barney said at last. "You're exhausted."

"I'm not." Though he hardly slept now—his body felt the shudder and vibration of an aircraft all the time.

Barney tried again, screwing his face up in the effort.

"I don't know if you remember this, Dom, but my father used to train a couple of racehorses, and he told me once that there was a very fine line between the horse who was a wonderfully brave jumper and the one that was an absolute fucking eejit. You've stepped over it." Barney pronounced eejit in a jokey Irish way, to soften the words, but there was a flash of real fury in his eyes.

They'd looked at each other, breathing heavily.

"You of all people should know that," Barney said next.

Barney had seen Jacko go down, too; he'd taken Dom aside before take-off, and said, "Tell him not to go; he's too windy." He'd heard the fading screams as the plane twirled like a useless piece of charred paper until it hit the sea.

They never spoke of it.

"If you want to blame me for that," said Dom, "don't bother. I do a good job of it every single day."

"Dom, that's mad." It took Barney a moment to decode this, and now the expression on his face was one of sorrow and concern. "He was a free agent—we all were."

And Dom, looking down on Barney, whose enormous feet now dangled over the end of his camp bed, wished with all his heart he could subscribe to the free-agent idea, too, but it was not possible and never would be.

"So, shutting up now." Barney's face grew cold and dark. He reached for a cigarette. "Fly the bloody thing." When he looked like that, Dom saw how he'd aged. He seemed long-suffering, like quite another person.

"Great," said Dom. "Give my regards to Dorothy."

Dom had a brief conversation with a nineteen-year-old mechanic inside a hangar when he got to Marsa Matruh. The boy's face was waxy green with fatigue, he'd worked all through the night to repair the Spit. They shared a quick meal from a random collection of half-empty tins. After the last mouthful of beans, Dom put on his damp flying suit, stuffed torch, map, parachute, and revolver under the cockpit seat, and took off again as quickly as he could, hoping to be home before night fell.

Gray afternoon light, the desert a dun-colored porridgy mass below him, a bank of cumulus cloud in the west where more rain threatened.

He was flying at fifteen thousand feet and making good progress, concentrating hard on the engine's noise, when he heard another sound, insignificant at first, like a flyswatter landing on cardboard. Glancing through the canopy, he saw from the corner of his eye the black shadow of an Me 109, and then heard the rat-tat-tat of more bullets before the plane sped away.

His first reaction was to swear, and then the weary everyday thought, *Oh fucking hell, not again,* wondering how much he'd be hurt this time. In a heartbeat he heard his own voice, panicked, shouting *no, no, no*, then he was gagging, the wet of his vomit in the gas mask now, the cockpit full of choking cordite fumes and glycol that made his nose run and his eyes stream. Eight seconds, *eight seconds,* the words pounded in his ears—eight measly seconds in which to bale out, to tear off his oxygen mask, release straps, turn the plane upside down and get himself out.

He wrestled desperately with the controls for a moment, and then realized it was no good. He grabbed the parachute from under the seat, ripped open the canopy and flung himself into the air, crying out as the parachute bunched between his legs, refusing to open, and then the long swooning dive toward the tilting earth.

CHAPTER 36

They were driving toward the German party house for their first engagement when Felipe glanced at Saba almost coyly, and said, "Were you surprised when Mr. Cleeve told you about me?"

"Yes, I was, very," she said. "And relieved, too. I haven't done this sort of thing before."

"Don't be nervous, Saba." He patted her hand, the long fingernails on his playing hand scratched her slightly. "I don't think our pilot will come for a few days, and these men don't want to make trouble; they want to have a good time, to eat a lot of bratwurst, get a little bit drunk, forget about the war for one night. You have nothing to fear."

She sat watching the light fade from the tops of the trees, hoping all this was true. Felipe's usually excellent English seemed a little more garbled during this explanation. His red satin shirt had a ring of sweat around armpits that smelled of ripe fruit.

She asked, "Does Mr. Ozan know all these people well?" When what she really wanted to ask was: Do you trust him? Will he keep us safe?

Felipe glanced at her quickly.

"He knows everyone, all the politicians, most of the Germans. He is a very important man."

"How do you become so important?"

"In Turkey, if you want to be very, very wealthy, I mean *really* wealthy, you make deals with politicians, it's just the way it is," Felipe muttered. "This war is a nice earner for many of them."

"But—" Saba felt alarmed again, but Felipe cut her off.

"That's enough—he is a very good man. He is good to us, and we have our own other reasons for being here."

The car slowed down to avoid an enormous pothole. "Now, concentrate, please," Felipe said. "I want to run through the plan again. As far as they are concerned you are a Turkish girl singer, a friend of Ozan's, your folks came from a village near Üsküdar and you're new to my band. What is the name of the village of your father?"

"Üvezli."

"Üvezli. We need to know if they ask. I don't think they will. Tonight will be a getting-to-know-you night—is for the relax, the music, we have a good time." Felipe gave a shaky smile. "So, we will play two or three sets of music—you can leave all this to me—and when we're not playing, we will sit and eat and drink, you may be asked to dance and that is fine. When you are dancing, smile a lot and talk as little as possible—they'll expect you to be shy."

Felipe pulled at his bow tie.

"It's hot tonight, isn't it?"

When he opened the car window, she felt the sticky scented air move over her face and was glad of it.

"Hot for autumn; in winter the winds come down from Russia they cut like a knife."

The smell of his sweat and his cologne filled the car. He told her she was not to panic if he occasionally left the room where they would perform. Part of his work there was to make a detailed map of the house, and to check if any of the officers had been careless with the official papers they sometimes traveled with. During these breaks, he might be upstairs under the pretext of having a "pee-pee" or a smoke. If she saw him take a girl upstairs, or having a pinch of naughty salt with the Germans, she mustn't be shocked. It was important for him to be one of the boys. He would never be gone long.

The faint pinpricks of light they were driving toward became a small village. The scent of roasting meat and spices filled their car and made Saba's mouth water—in the excitement of performing, she had forgotten to eat.

On the outskirts of the village, a group of old men were drinking coffee outside a cafe lit by a kerosene lamp; further on a family sat eating a meal together under a trellis heavy with jasmine and vines. The young woman had a baby on her lap. A toddler rested against the side of a young man and waited for its food; a donkey, munching a bundle of fresh green leaves, looked pleased with itself. A family at rest with the world and each other.

"They looked happy," she said to Felipe. For that moment, it seemed like the most seductive thing in the world.

"Yes." He gunned the accelerator.

And the sudden thought came to her that she knew not a thing about Felipe's private life. He was not a gabby man, and though they had talked about various things—music they liked, future plans, other musicians—their moments of real intimacy came when he accompanied her on his guitar.

"Do you like this kind of work, Felipe?" she asked. "You know . . . the other work at the German house . . . not the music part."

She still found it impossible to utter the word "spying"—it sounded preposterous, like a child's game of pretend, or maybe too frightening to say out loud.

"No." His face glowed green in the dash lights. "No! I don't like it too much, but I do it. Mr. Cleeve says our man Jenke has important information—that's enough for me. We . . ."

His voice tailed off like a bag with the air punched out of it, then he said, "I hate the bloody Nazis. I would like to strangle them all."

The air between them seemed to thicken and become full of terrible things. After a silence he added, "I had a wife before . . . in Berlin . . . her name was Rachel. A beautiful woman," he said, "Jewish. I had a daughter, too—Naomi—as lovely as her mother, very musical. You remind me of her."

"Please don't . . . if you . . . I'm so sorry."

"No. No. It's all right. I should say these things before. I was on tour with the band, six months. Barcelona, France, Madrid. Good fun, well, you know. I came back to Berlin. Lots of presents." He took both hands off the wheel to show how full his arms had been. "Our apartment smashed, family gone."

"I am so sorry, I . . ." She could have kicked herself for her stupid question. Felipe was another heartbroken stray like Bog and the acrobats. She seemed to be making a specialty of these innocent inquiries that detonated a bomb.

The car filled with cigarillo smoke.

"Don't say sorry." He gave a great exhaling sigh. "No, don't. Is necessary you know why I do this. I should have told you before. I had a bad choice to make after it happened: I could stay and be arrested myself—I'm half Jewish, you see—or I could come to Istanbul. I don't know if I've made the good choice, the only thing I know is that without this"—he turned and touched his guitar on the backseat—"I would have killed myself."

He started to hum, either to end the conversation, or maybe as an expression of some relief at having poured out even a tiny bit of his heart. By the time they arrived at the white house in Tarabya, he had his work face on again.

Felipe looked for a place to park. Saba gazed around her. The house was set in a clearing surrounded by a screen of pine trees and bounded by a high wooden fence. Beyond the fence were some nondescript cypress and Judas trees, scrub, a dirt road, and no nosy neighbors, which was probably why the Germans had chosen it. Close enough, Cleeve had said, to their official summer residence to be convenient, but far enough away for it to function as a sort of unofficial officers' mess, where they could bring girls and have gambling parties and entertain local businesspeople without too much bothersome protocol.

A couple of cars were there already—a Buick with German number plates on it and an Opel. Inside the high white windows the curtains were drawn with a dim reddish light shining through them.

Felipe found a spot near a pair of iron gates. He pulled on the handbrake and checked the rearview mirror.

"If anything goes wrong while we're here, I shall tell you to sing 'Quizas, Quizas, Quizas.' It's an old Spanish song, so no one will ask for it as a request; after that we quietly leave. Our excuse will be we have to get the night air, or go outside to smoke a cigarette. No panic, no shouting."

He said he would always park the car as close to the gate as possible.

"I'm telling you this as a precaution; nothing bad will happen."

His satin shirt was soaked through now, and he put on his dinner jacket to cover it. He lifted his guitar from the backseat and gathered up their sheet music. His calmness seemed genuine and she needed it because her mouth was dry as they crunched across the gravel for that first party. When she thought of Germans en bloc, she thought of bogeymen—torturers, rapists, assassins—and in spite of all Felipe's reassurances, she was very frightened.

Otto Engels opened the door, a thick-necked, smiling man in a wine-stained satin smoking jacket. Felipe had told her earlier that Engel, a member of Abwehr, the German Secret Service, was nicknamed Minister of Fun. He and his cronies took lots of bogus trips, had mistresses, and of course gave parties. The German Secret Service, unlike the British Secret Service, was not centralized, Felipe said, but made of many divisions, all of whom plotted and organized vendettas against one another.

Engel's florid face lit up when he saw them; he clapped his hands and gave one of those booming, empty laughs that wiped the smile off your face. Felipe, whose German was fluent too, introduced Saba with the air of a magician pulling something lovely out of a hat. He said it would be just him and her for the next few nights; the other band members had picked up a stomach bug. Engel closed his eyes, nuzzled Saba's hand with his lips, looked at Felipe approvingly as if to say *Nice, well done.*

She stepped through the door remembering Ellie's *Feather on head, tail on bum. No panic.*

Otto was booming at her side and holding her arm as she walked through a low-ceilinged room blurry and blue with smoke. Twenty or so young men stood around laughing, talking, drinking. They looked taller than most of the young men she knew, some of the younger ones extremely good-looking with their high cheekbones and strong, athletic bodies. The two or three young girls there were mostly bottle blondes in cheap-looking frocks and high heels. When Saba walked in, there was a dip in conversation, a low murmur of appreciation as the men smiled at her or made quick sly comments to one another.

A small stage had been rigged up for them in a bay window at the far end of the room, but Engel wanted to feed them first from a table in the kitchen groaning with cheeses and hunks of pâté, German sausages, booze. He was sweating in his eagerness.

"First we play." Felipe was all winning smiles now; it was as if he'd never known a bad moment in his life. "Later we drink."

He straightened his bow tie and bounded toward the stage. "Let's go, babeee." He bared his teeth in the fake Satchmo grin that usually made her laugh.

Ten minutes later they leapt into "Zu Zu Gazoo." Saba felt tense to start, but after a while the galloping rhythms of Felipe's guitar claimed her. It felt good playing together like this—no drums, no piano, just them.

The two primitive spotlights that had been placed next to the stage shone too brightly. Before their next number, Felipe fiddled with them discreetly and made the stage more intimate by sitting them both in a circle of light surrounded by shadows. He smiled at Saba, a gentle conspiratorial smile that said *We can do this,* and began a silky version of "Besame Mucho." When he said something in German to the group of young men waiting silent around the beer keg, she knew he was saying this was a song about kissing written by a Mexican girl who'd never been kissed in her life. They suddenly roared their approval.

"*Besame, besame mucho . . .*" Saba sat on her stool loving the clever variations Felipe played. She narrowed her eyes, scanning the room. No monsters here, or none visible, just a crush of men, miles away from home, watching her with hopeful, hungry eyes. From here she felt like a large reflecting mirror that could control them and make them feel what she wanted them to feel—already one or two of them had their lips puckered up like children waiting for their night-night kiss.

One man in particular stood out. He was tall and blond with a sensitive suffering face, and she was aware of him watching her closely but discreetly. When she asked Felipe during the break if he was the pilot, Felipe said no. "That man is called Severin—Severin Mueller. You danced with him at Ozan's party? He works for the embassy in Ankara.

"Jenke won't come tonight," he added. He smiled suavely, half at the audience, half at her; he fiddled with his guitar. "In five minutes I'm going to leave you and go upstairs—you stay here and sing."

She did as she was told, but she was terrified. She sang two Turkish songs, and waggled her hips, aware that the tall blond man was slightly frowning at her as if to say *This is not my kind of music.* When she stopped singing he clapped quietly, and then in a gesture that seemed not to fit his anxious aesthetic face, he touched his lips with his long fingers and blew her a kiss.

They were an instant success—without much competition. The Germans loved them, begged them to come back. They needed, it seemed, some magic added to that anonymous house so far from home. But the two parties they went to there seemed so strange to Saba. Both times there were obscene amounts of food—bratwurst and smoked salmon and cheeses, hams and sausages; and booze, too—crates of Bollinger under the kitchen table, schnapps, German beer. Cocaine upstairs. Women—daring secretaries from local embassies, lonely wives, heavily made-up blondes; White Russians—pale girls with jutting cheekbones for whom the Germans seemed to have a particular weakness.

Her own drug was the joy of singing with Felipe, which made it almost disturbingly easy to forget where she was. As they raced through the woods on the way to the parties, he taught her new songs: songs by Brecht, songs by a Cuban composer, a lovely Spanish song called "La Rosa y el Viento," the black version of "The Choo Choo Train" that he'd learned in a club in Harlem. One night, he said: "If you make a mistake in a song, don't forget every breath is a new beginning and a new chance."

But the magic wasn't always reliable, and there were times when the room, with its mismatched furniture, flickering lamps, and poor acoustics, felt like some hastily assembled approximation of home on a stage somewhere, and the eyes of the girls sitting on the men's knees looked glazed and peculiar, almost as if they distrusted her, too, and the whole experience took on a nightmarish quality. Sometimes the men took the girls upstairs to snort cocaine or to make love in makeshift bedrooms where a red scarf was thrown over the bedside lamp to give instant atmosphere. On the nights when there were no girls, the men stood around a beer keg playing drinking games. And it was then that Saba almost pitied them: they looked like large lost children determined to have a midnight feast.

But what was good was that bit by bit, Felipe was managing to put a detailed map together, and the Germans, drugged by their music, seemed to suspect nothing. Gradually Saba began to get to know some of the principal players: Severin, the blond attaché from Ankara, and Finkel the Frog, as she and Felipe called Otto Engel, who stood too close to her, his protruding eyes working their way up and down her as he mentally undressed her.

When the other men flirted with her in a more respectful way, she replied with shrugs and helpless glances toward Felipe, her translator. They asked for requests. They often wanted their pictures taken with her, and she always agreed.

On the night it happened, Felipe parked the car for the first time outside the gates. He turned off the engine. "Jenke will come here tonight," he said softly. He pointed toward a gap between two cypress trees. "There's a broken piece of the fence there, do you see it? That's the quickest way out, if we should ever need it, but it won't happen like that." He shrugged. "It never has. I'm telling you just in case." And she believed him, because she wanted to.

"How do you know?"

"Cleeve. I met him yesterday."

"Thank God for that." She was growing impatient with the pilot and the parties. "What took him so long?"

"I don't know." Felipe's face was in shadow. "All I know is they want Jenke urgently back in North Africa. Cleeve said something about enemy airfields." The war, he said in a quick aside, was at boiling point over there.

She felt herself go cold. She couldn't bear to think of Dom.

"So, tonight. The passport. Let's go through the routine again."

Felipe turned and picked up a songbook from the backseat of the car. One of the pages was held with a paper clip.

"His name as far as the Germans are concerned is Josef Jenke. He's a medium-sized man, muscular, brown hair. He'll be wearing a red waistcoat. He will request 'My Funny Valentine.' You will get the nod from me. All the documents he needs are on page fourteen of this book." He placed it in her hands.

"After you've sung the song, slip the loose page from the book, but leave it on the music stand—he can collect it later when it's safe to do so. Don't hand it to him. Wait. After that, all you have to do is the nice smiley photo with him. He will take care of the rest. All very simple."

Felipe smiled at her. He looked especially elegant tonight—the thin mustache trimmed, the carefully folded black handkerchief in the pocket of his cream-colored dinner jacket. His skin shiny and freshly shaved.

"You look beautiful tonight." When the words flew out of her, she was embarrassed.

"You ain't so bad yourself, kid," he growled in his Satchmo voice. "Gimme some skin."

She leaned over and hugged him.

"I've had the best time singing with you," she said, and his wounded eyes looked back at her.

"Yes," he said softly and shook his head.

As usual, it was Otto who stepped out of the noisy crowd to greet them. He spoke to Felipe in German, which Felipe translated into a mixture of pidgin English and Turkish. When Felipe admired his latest smoking jacket—a gaudy affair in blue silk—Otto preened for Saba and told Felipe it was one of a set he'd got a tailor at the Grand Bazaar to run up for him. He kissed the back of her hand, leaving a little of the froth from the beer he had been drinking. When he laughed and licked it off, it gave her the creeps even though she tried not to show it. Tonight, he told them, they were celebrating some good news from Berlin: his brother had had his first child, and everyone was to help themselves to whatever they wanted to drink—champagne, beer, schnapps, kanyak, he added, pointing toward the Turkish brandy, although he personally—a roar of laughter here—thought it tasted like horse piss.

"He says no offense to you, little lady." Otto kissed her hand again and waggled his eyebrows. "He's an idiot," Felipe added softly, still smiling.

As the evening progressed, the roar of sound from the sitting room rose until it seemed to form a solid wall. At the end of the room, near the big bay window, a group of men stood around a wooden beer keg shouting "*Stein, Stein, Stein*," and then gulping down huge glasses of beer. Three young girls, drafted in from God knows where, sat on the sofa looking tense and expectant. Only one of them, with bare goose-pimpled legs and wearing a cheap thin frock, was laughing heartily as if she got the joke.

It was so hot that Saba could feel sweat coiling down her back like a snake. When Severin opened the shutters, a cool breeze flowed through the room. When Felipe started to play, it was Severin who shushed the drinkers and stared at Saba as if he could will her to begin. She'd noticed before he was hungry for music like a drug addict, in the way the others weren't. When she sang, she saw how his tense, finely boned face relaxed—how he seemed to visibly exhale as if some secret crisis was over.

Felipe, who'd made it his business to drink with as many of the Germans as he could, had told her that Severin was lonely. He was only twenty-six years old and had a wife in Munich and a child born while he was away. He hadn't seen them for three years. He missed them. Felipe said this with no warmth—*bastard,* he may as well have added, *it serves you right.*

Saba didn't feel like that. In certain lights, Severin's ascetic face looked both innocent and lost and there was a quick, intuitive sympathy in his glance. It was confusing to know that if he hadn't been German she would definitely have talked to him, had fun with him; become, at the very least, friends.

Felipe was adjusting his guitar for the next song when there was a small commotion near the door where more guests had arrived. Otto was clapping them on the shoulder; laughing his braying laugh.

Felipe turned to her and breathed in her hair, "The pilot is here—the one on the right. Keep singing.

"And for our next song," he announced in German, "a very hot Spanish love song."

The drinking Germans gave a drunken *wooohhhhh.* Those who were dancing put their cheeks next to the Russian girls. Saba picked up the microphone.

She glanced at the pilot; they briefly locked eyes and then he looked away. He had a pleasant, nondescript face: medium height, short military hair, a genial air. He was standing next to Engel, who was already drunk; he was laughing at something Engel said.

He looked so relaxed, so happy to be here that she wondered for an instant whether there were people who got a positive kick out of spying, the way some people loved secrets. She knew now she wasn't one of them.

A Russian girl moved toward him. There were tufts of damp hair under her arms when she lifted them up. She wanted to dance. Saba sensed Felipe frowning beside her. A girl might complicate things.

Saba sang a Turkish song now—one Tan had taught her as a child. Out of the corner of her eye she was aware of Severin watching her impatiently. This kind of folk thing bored him stiff—his requests were always for jazz, or the new blues singers. As soon as she'd finished, he walked up to Felipe and spoke to him in German.

Felipe looked at Saba and smiled. He played the opening bars to Bessie Smith's "Fine and Mellow" and she sang along, careful as always to add some Turkish-sounding English, which was never difficult—she simply imitated Tan. Felipe's supple guitar riffs were like calm waves breaking.

She glanced across the room again. The pilot had disappeared into the crowd; he was keeping his distance, biding his time.

She wanted Severin to leave now, to join the dancers to keep the coast clear, but he was sitting quietly near them watching her, watching Felipe, waiting for his next fix, and as usual the song seemed to affect him powerfully—she saw his young man's Adam's apple bob at the end of it as he turned away.

Otto appeared, waggling his finger, swaying his stout hips. He'd dropped a glob of sour cream on the lapel of his smoking jacket. He wanted them to play "Lili Marlene"—a banned song now in Germany because it was so popular with the English, but he loved it and so did the other men.

She sang the words in German as Felipe had taught her and when she got to the bit about Lili's sweet face appearing in dreams a cluster of men formed around the small stage. Every boy in the world, it seemed, had fallen for Lili—that husky-voiced tramp waiting under a streetlight outside the barracks. These men who, half an hour ago, had roared like hogs over their drinking games seemed so sad suddenly, as if they'd all been recently jilted.

"Noch! Noch!" Otto shouted in a kind of childish ecstasy before the song was even over, his scarlet face running with sweat.

Now the pilot was standing near the window. When she looked at him he shook his head slightly, and then joined in with the singing, which had become hearty and jarring, like trays of crockery breaking.

Someone had opened the terrace doors to let the smoke out. Beyond them she saw the shadows of black trees against a dark blue sky. A few stars. The pilot, still singing, started to move toward her. His left hand was in his pocket; he looked comfortable in his skin. He had all the time in the world.

When the song was over, he smiled at Felipe. Did they by any chance know the song "My Funny Valentine," an American song? He'd heard it before the war.

He hummed the opening bars; Saba took a sip of water, her mouth was dry. Felipe's fingers trembled slightly as they worked their way through a pile of sheet music on the chair beside him.

"Do you know this?" he asked Saba. Two lines of sweat trickled down his face into his thin mustache. He pushed the songbook toward her.

"I know it," she said.

"Let's go," said Felipe.

He picked up the tortoiseshell plectrum; he stroked his guitar. The crotchets and quavers on page fourteen jumbled in front of her eyes.

She sang the sad sweet words about the beautiful unphotographable girl. She smiled at Felipe, a radiant smile as she put her hand on the page and worked it free.

The pilot was watching her, so relaxed she couldn't be sure he hadn't winked at her.

She watched Felipe's fingers, his eyes. She briefly scanned the room. Severin was dancing with a blonde—she caught his brief agonized look over the girl's shoulder. Frankel was telling a story. When the song ended there was a smattering of applause.

The pilot stepped forward, one hand in his pocket, a cigarette in the other.

"Nehmen Sie bitte fotographie mit dem Mädchen?" he said to Felipe. He looked at Saba, and gave a slight bow. Felipe, who was often asked to do this now, took a Box Brownie out of his guitar case. The pilot put his arm around her and struck a swaggering pose. He took the loose page from the stand.

The camera clicked, the bulb flashed. *"Danke,"* said the pilot. He gave a proper wink now and she patted his arm. Watching him make his leisurely way through the partygoers, and leave through the side door with Engel, she felt relief surge through her like new blood. Why had she felt so nervous about this? It had been nothing in the end. The job was done, she could go home, the strangest period of her life was now officially over.

When the pilot disappeared into the fug of the crowd, Felipe turned to her and said softly, "I need a smoke. You stay here. I'll be back in twenty minutes. I think your boy would like a dance."

Marlene Dietrich was singing "Falling in Love Again" on the gramophone when Severin stepped out of the shadows and gave a short bow. *"Möchten Sie Tanzen?"* he said. He clicked his heels, smiled his gentle smile, and pulled her out of her chair.

It was too hot, and he was too close; she felt hemmed in by his intense gaze.

When the song ended, she pretended to be overcome by the heat, and excused herself with a fanning gesture. When he frowned, she pointed at her watch and help up five fingers, forcing herself to smile.

She had meant to go outside and sit in the cool for a while, but the door was blocked by shouting men, so she ran quickly up the short flight of uncarpeted wooden stairs to the bathroom on the right of the first landing.

Her face in the mirror looked pinched and tired. It was ten past twelve; she longed for home now, not the hotel room in Istanbul, but somewhere with Dom if he'd have her. She flushed the chain, stepped out on the landing, and looked up. There was a light on in the bedroom, and she saw with relief Felipe's patent-leather shoes gleaming, his trousered legs half visible in the doorframe.

"Felipe," she walked toward him, "any chance we could leave soon? I'm fagged out."

The door opened. Inside was a double bed covered with greatcoats. The bedside light, partly concealed by a silk scarf, cast a sludgy red glow over the room. One of Felipe's cigarillos was smoldering in an ashtray.

"Has our friend gone?" she asked softly.

"Yes," he said. "You did well."

"You're a good boy to tidy up here," she joshed him, he was about to reply when she saw the imperceptible shake of his head.

She saw it, too, now—a smudged face in the wardrobe mirror behind him. When it came into focus, she saw Severin at the door; he was holding a gun.

"So, you are here," he said softly. "My little Valentine. Your English has improved.

"Look at me," he said to Felipe, who was breathing rapidly. "Kneel down, and then empty your pockets. Put everything on the bed."

"Don't hurt her." Felipe's eyes had shrunk into his head. "She knows nothing about this."

"Empty your pockets, please." Severin's voice was polite, even regretful.

A silk handkerchief was placed on the eiderdown, three tortoiseshell plectrums, a packet of cigarillos, a photograph of a woman holding a child's hand.

"And now the inside pocket. *Danke.* I don't enjoy this, you know," he said in the same quiet voice. "My wife is a musician also."

A piece of paper with a diagram fluttered down; some numbers, figures, what looked like a list of names.

Severin groaned; Saba felt the gun prod her side.

"We're going to have to do something, you know," he said to Felipe. "I shall call the others up in a minute. I have no choice."

"Don't hurt her."

"I shall do what I have to do."

The rumbling surge of boots sounded like rock falling off a cliff. She could not bear to look at Felipe, who was shaking and moaning. From downstairs came shouting and Marlene still singing on the gramophone. For a few seconds the lights in the house were switched off and she heard the high-pitched scream of one of the girls, and then more shouting before several cars drove away in a wash of lights that swept over the room, and illuminated Felipe's masklike face in the mirror. He must have known he was done for.

When the lights came on, two men were holding him, and there appeared to be an intense debate going on about what to do with Saba. In the end Severin stepped forward; he was calmer than Engel, who was practically gibbering with fear and panic.

Felipe, still immaculate in his dinner jacket, managed to smile at her before a man she did not recognize came into the room. He put a gun to Felipe's temple and pulled the trigger. There was a look of mild surprise in Felipe's eyes before they went blank, and blood and bits of his brain began to splatter the floor.

She heard herself scream; in the moment of panic that followed, she stumbled into Severin's arms and shouted senselessly at him.

When she pushed him away, he fumbled through the coats and found a silk scarf, which he tied around her mouth, and then the world went black as a blindfold went on and a gun was pressed into her ribs.

The coppery smell of blood, and the dull thump of boots going into Felipe's sides, and the swish of his coat as they dragged him out of the room. Downstairs she heard shouting, as if a furious argument was going on, what sounded like a tray of glasses breaking, and all the while Marlene, stuck in the groove of a record, singing and singing; obscenely and endlessly singing, as if she were trying to deliberately drive them mad.

She waited for them to come upstairs and get her, but the next thing she heard was the crunch of gravel, and the receding sounds of their footsteps, a car engine starting up with a roar and driving off fast.

She felt Severin's mouth against her ear. A hot jet of air into the darkness.

"You're with me," he said, "until they come back."

CHAPTER 37

I'm blind, was her first thought when she woke up. There was a mattress under her, but she was hemmed in by total darkness. When she tried to touch herself to see what hurt, the bed she'd been tied to made a hollow rattling sound and she felt a stinging, burning sensation in her ankles and wrists, as if she'd been stung by a giant wasp.

Her numbed brain remembered running feet, doors slamming, the wash of car headlights leaping through the trees. She wiggled her feet as violently as she could without making any sound, but it was no good, they were tied tightly, and more awake now, she could feel her scalp, tight with terror. They'd be back soon; all she could do was lie and wait like a bound animal.

"Where is everyone?" she mumbled into her gag. It was deathly quiet in the rooms below with the partygoers gone. Her blindfold—a stocking?—smelled musty and faintly of cheese, and all she could hear was her own jagged breathing and the wind, and what sounded like the faint peepings of a far-off bird. She expected to die; it would now be obvious to all of them that she was Felipe's accomplice, and they would shoot her as they had shot him—the warm, meaty smell of his blood still filled her nostrils, the memory of that look of mild surprise in his eyes before they'd gone blank made her feel sick with disgust and sorrow for him. And if they shot her, too, none of the people she had known and loved would have the slightest idea she was here.

If she squeezed her eyes very tight, the darkness whirled and the faint pinpricks of light that appeared made her think of Dom's description of night flying: how you could feel on the rim of the world up there. Dom would think she hadn't cared, or, maybe, gone to meet someone else. *I'm sorry, Dom,* she said to him, *I'm so sorry.*

She slept for maybe an hour or so—time felt slippery in the dark—and waking and feeling tears leaking down the side of her face, she gave herself a fierce talking-to. The blindfold would make her hysterical—it was happening already. Something must be done. She tried, for a while, to turn it into a cinema screen on which she could project any kind of film she liked. She was sitting with Dom having lunch in a restaurant with checked tablecloths overlooking the sea. After lunch, they walked down to a pebbly beach; they sat there talking and eating ice creams. They took a bicycle ride down an avenue of poplar trees leading to a country pub; they walked into her parents' house at Pomeroy Street. Tan was there cooking lunch, she could smell it, roast lamb and rice and spices, every one hugging and kissing her, even her father.

She was playing this game when she heard, from the room below, the high-pitched screech of what sounded like a singing kettle coming to the boil, the scuff of a chair, the faint chink of china being moved. Someone was there; she wasn't alone. She lay listening to her own heart pumping; a few moments later a man's footsteps ascended the stairs slowly step by step, and then the lift and release of the door opening.

"Who is it?" Her voice muffled by the gag.

No sound, just the door closing, and the creak of floorboards, and then the soft exhalation of a cushion as a body sat down on a chair, maybe two feet from the bed, the sound of a deep sigh.

"Please tell me." She felt someone's breath rustling her face, her blindfold being adjusted by fingers that were neither rough nor gentle, and then the ropes that tied her to the bed being tightened, too.

She smelled coffee being poured, then heard the clink of a cup and a gentle, well-bred slurp, a discreet swallow, a man's cough.

Whoever it was began to chew slowly on what smelled like rye bread, and something sharp and sweet like jam. His chewing was not noisy. He swallowed more coffee, and she felt herself intensely stared at. She heard the cup being put carefully back on the tray, and a shuffling toward the door where the tray was set down, and then footsteps coming back toward her. The darkness was shrilling behind her blindfold now; the footsteps were more decisive.

She gasped, feeling his bulk sit down on the bed beside her.

"Who are you?" she mumbled into the gag.

Some hair tickled her ear; the heat of the coffee on his lips and its smell.

"Severin." His voice was low and uncertain. "Don't be frightened."

One night when she was young, a family of bats had flown through an open window and into the house. She'd seen a tiny webbed hand around the attic door, and felt the same kind of crawling dread now as his hand stroked her hair.

"I will take this off," he loosened the gag, "but not if you scream."

"I won't . . . but please . . ." she heard his stifled moan as his free hand gently kneaded the crown of her head, his fingers moving in circles, "please don't, and take this off, too." She twitched her face around the blindfold. "I can't see."

Calm down, calm down, else you're a dead duck: an almost jocular voice inside her. His hand moved toward the nape of her neck, probing the muscles there.

"Please, talk to me." No reply, nothing but a small shivery jet of air coming from his nostrils, as his hand moved down toward her belly. When the hand stopped, it seemed he was weighing up several possibilities at once, like a boy who has captured a bird and who is not sure whether he will hurt it or not.

"Severin," she said. "Please don't do this. I don't think you want to."

He loosened the blindfold, and pushed it back into her hair. In the ruddy glow of the lamp, his chest looked hairless and smooth like a girl's. She heard the soft clink of his belt as it hit the floor. The smell of charred cloth from the scarf draped over the lamp gave her the mad thought that maybe the house would burn down first.

A line of fine blond hair went down from his navel to the top of the trousers he was now unzipping. His neck, too long for a man, gave him a startled giraffe look.

"They've gone now," he said. "I will look after you until they come back." He bent down toward her. His eyes were red-rimmed—had he been crying?—and there was the strangest expression on his face, somewhere between compassion and menace.

"Sorry about all the mess in here and all the noise before," he said mildly.

To stop herself screaming, she bit the inside of her lip.

His voice was soft. "He was a good musician, your friend," he said.

She squeezed her eyes tight shut to block out the sound of Felipe's dying before they'd dragged him downstairs. The drip and slurp of his head emptying on the floor.

"Why have they left me here?"

"I told you, I will look after you until they come back." He stopped suddenly and wrinkled his nose, as if smelling the blood for the first time.

He untied her roughly and pulled her to her feet, then snatched the blindfold off. She saw the brass bed, a sagging sofa with a rug over it, all soaked in the rust-colored glow of the lamp. On the wall, above a chest of drawers, there were a couple of badly framed reproductions. Severin led her over to one in which a man in the foreground stood against a sea of mist with trees poking out of it. "I like this one," he said softly. "I studied art history, you know, before I was in the army. It's called *A Wanderer in a Sea of Fog,* the artist is Friedrich," he added in a mechanical lecturer's voice.

"A wanderer in a sea of fog." His voice broke suddenly. "I feel this at the moment, because I liked your friend, I admired him even, I didn't want it to happen like this."

He was holding his belt in his hands, lip stuck out, his eyes innocent-looking and sad; for one confused moment she thought he would burst into tears.

When he kissed her, his breath stank of sausage and cigarettes.

"No, no, please, no."

"This is pretty," he said woodenly. His hand squeezed her breast. "Your dress. It's pretty, I like it." They both stared at the green silk, Felipe's blood splattered on its hem. She began to thrash and push him off.

"Don't, don't." She crossed her hands over her breasts.

"I won't hurt you," he said, his Adam's apple leaping in his throat. "Just take your dress off, please, there is too much blood. Lie facedown on the bed, and rest, all I want to do is to look at you."

The zipper of her dress was on the right side. She pretended to struggle with it, her mind racing furiously.

"So you studied art history?" She forced herself to look directly at him. He was adjusting the silk scarf over the light, all fuss and long white fingers. "Where, may I ask?"

"In Berlin. My college is a heap of bricks now." He inhaled noisily.

"Take that off—I know the game you play." His voice was rough and would take no more nonsense. He jerked the dress over her head. She was wearing silk stockings and a garter belt.

"Lie down on the bed, take off your underclothes and brassiere."

Her mind went a complete blank.

"I'm not surprised to hear you were an art student," she said. She unhooked her garter belt, still looking at him. "You have a very sensitive face." She could hear her heart thumping.

He looked surprised.

"All I want to do is look at you," he said unsteadily.

"Like a model in a life class," she said. "One who would like to stay alive."

"One who would like to stay alive," he repeated. She could hear him thinking.

"So, if you are a model, let's say in a sculpture class, I must measure you to get the proportions right."

She felt something hard go down her spine—a belt buckle? A gun?—and suppressed a scream.

"First, north and south." The cold scratch of steel moving down her buttocks. "You have a beautiful back," he said. "Then west and east"—his voice slurred and he pronounced it *wessa* and *eassa*. "Whoops!" He stumbled against her. He was drunker than she'd thought. The smell of vodka combined with sausage as he belched. "Begging your pardon."

"Accepted. The others," she said. "When will they get back?"

"Not for a long time, shut up your mouth." His voice was petulant, she had spoiled his game.

There was nothing playful now about his hand shoveling between her legs. She could feel her hysteria rising; soon she would spit or scream or strike him.

"Severin," she forced her voice low, "you're too good for this. For your own sake, don't do it."

He was muttering in German, and then, "Shut up. You don't know me."

He turned her over abruptly, put the blindfold on again, and stuffed a pillow under her. "Keep quiet."

Her jaw went into a kind of rigor mortis as he climbed on top of her. For a few seconds he flung himself blindly against her, groaning and swearing, but then she felt the flop of him against her stomach like a rag doll.

"You can't do this because you're a good man," she told him, unclenching her jaw. She felt her head bang against the brass bedstead. "Your wife is a good person, you're a good person."

"Don't talk about her!" he shouted. "Don't say anything."

His fingers jabbed inside her.

"That is me," he shouted, "and that is me, and that is me."

It hurt, it felt horrible, and when it was over, even though she could feel his full weight on her, his fluid leaking down the back of her legs, she thought quickly: *It hasn't happened, it didn't. He didn't rape me.* Wishing she had her gun on her, so she could hurt him and hammer him, could shoot him dead.

His weight shifted; he grunted, an animal grunt of dismay, exasperation.

"I should have told the others about you," he said, as if this was her fault and she disgusted him. "They only know about Felipe. I should have told them." He stood up abruptly and left the room, slamming the door behind him. She waited, her heart jumping out of her chest, listening for his footsteps on the stairs, but there was only silence. He was standing on the landing, or so she imagined, waiting to pounce again.

A second or so later, the door opened. He came over to the bed and jerked her roughly to her feet.

"Get up, put your clothes on and do your hair."

Her legs buckled as her feet touched the bare boards. She dressed herself in a daze and patted her hair, bewildered by the sight of her face in the mirror. He led her barefoot around the patch of dark blood where Felipe's head had spilled, down the stairs and into the hall near the kitchen.

When she yelled, he prodded her sharply in the back. "Do that again," he said in a low voice, "and I will shoot you."

In the kitchen, the wreckage of the party lay on a worn Formica table—a plate of half-eaten cheeses swimming in wine; smeared glasses; a pat of butter covered in ash and old cigarettes. He locked the door behind them.

He handed her a tea towel after she had been sick. *Stay calm*, she told herself, *you must stay calm.*

"They've taken your friend away." Severin's face was pale and twitching. "They wanted you to go with him, but I said I would question you first."

His unimpressive performance in the bedroom had clearly rattled him. His gestures were muddled, jerky; he seemed to have trouble looking at her. He threw crockery and food into a half-full sink, shattering several glasses as he did so. He swooped down on her, and pulled her so roughly onto the table that her arms almost jerked out of their sockets. He picked up his gun; it was pointing toward her as he inched backward groping in the direction of a portable gramophone that sat incongruously on the sideboard surrounded by dirty plates and glasses.

He had several tries at lowering the needle onto a record.

"Don't move, Turkish girl," he said. "Stay there, and sing your songs."

When the music came on, she was concentrating so hard that the room seemed to tilt wildly. She felt filthy and defiled. She hurt. But she wanted to live—it felt like the most important thing on earth. The record was old and the first few bars crackled like forest flames. And then she heard the sprightly introduction to "Mazi," the song with a tango beat that had once made Tan sigh and roll her eyes. *The past is a wound in my heart. My fate is darker than the color of my hair.* Thank God she knew it.

"Sing it."

Her mouth felt sore from the gag, but she sang the first verse as clearly and confidently as she could, amazed at the sounds that came out of her—truly, it was like another person singing. When she got to the first chorus, though, her confusion was evident, and she felt giddy with fear—in a couple of bars she'd come to the end of the words she knew.

The swooping violins dissolved into silence. He took the needle off, and looked at her, shaking his head. His skin was so white that she could see the blue bulge of the veins in his temples as he spoke.

"I am a translator, madame," he said softly. "My Turkish, I think, is better than yours."

He poured himself a glass of brandy and drank it quickly. There was a kitchen clock behind his head; it was almost five o'clock. My last day, she thought; they'll know now for sure.

"Why didn't you tell them about me?" she said.

He put a piece of half-eaten salami into his mouth; he chewed it, still looking at her.

"I should have."

"Felipe's dead," she said. She still couldn't believe it.

"Yes."

A stray piece of salami rind hung from his lips; his tongue made a slapping sound as it pulled it back.

"What was your game with him anyway?" he asked almost mildly. "Were you sleeping together?"

"No, we've only just started to play together."

"Why did you come out here with him alone?"

"That's what we were told to do."

She looked at him blearily. It crossed her mind to tell him she'd been booked through Mr. Ozan, about ENSA, but they seemed to have reached a point where she could only say simple things.

"What about the others, when will they be back?"

"I don't know." He was drinking the dregs from several glasses. "You were not very kind always, you wouldn't sing the songs I wanted," he complained, pushing a heap of dirty plates aside.

"I'm sorry," she answered with the wooden politeness of a waitress dealing with a tiresome customer. "Which did you want? I could sing them now."

He squeezed his eyes tight shut.

"Yes." Some of his brandy had dribbled down his chin. "Something nice for me, for once."

He was staggering now and when he asked for two German songs, it occurred to her that he had confused her with somebody else. "This is a lovely song," she said quickly. She sang "J'ai Deux Amours" without taking her eyes off him.

"More songs," he said. He was sounding sleepy.

Behind him the hands of the clock slid to ten past five; it was possible the others would be back soon.

She sang "The Raggle Taggle Gypsies," the songs coming randomly into her head now with no particular meaning to them. *Tonight she'll sleep on the cold dark earth,* her own voice as thin and scared as a runaway child.

"A draggle toggle is a funny word," he said, his mouth lopsided. "What does this mean?"

"I don't know exactly." Her throat was sore now, she was giddy. "A collection of things with no meaning."

"All these songs, what do they mean?" He put his hand against the table to steady himself.

"I don't know. I don't know." She shook her head.

He asked her then if she knew a song by Purcell called "Dido's Lament," mumbled something about a sister.

She said she did not know it, so he sang it for her in German first. The melody was hauntingly sad, even though his voice was slurred.

"What do the words mean, Severin?"

She saw his lips quiver.

"In English it goes '*Remember me, remember me, but ah! forget my fate.*' They sang it for my sister."

"Your sister?" He was shaking.

"She was a musician, too, she was on her way to college; one of your bombers got her."

He started to cry; his blond hair poked through his fingers. He shuddered and groaned, and shook his head vigorously as if in violent dispute with himself. Then he looked up at her, shrugged, and they exchanged the strangest look—somewhere between wild hilarity and sorrow.

"I have a wife also in Germany," he told her. They were sitting opposite each other now, the wrecked party between them. "We are childhood sweethearts. I miss her . . . I want to go home.

"It was my wife who sang this at my sister's funeral; she was at college with my sister. She would be horrified . . ." His face convulsed. "They took me to concerts, they . . ." His eyes looked shrunken and red.

He reached out for his glass again; her hand stopped him.

"Listen," she said, "if one of the others had stayed behind, it could have been much, much worse for me. I know that. I'm sure of it."

He gave her a foggy look.

"I nearly did a bad thing. I was so close." He held his thumb and index finger together. "*This* close."

She felt the sting of sick rise in her throat just at the thought of it.

"I wanted to," he mumbled, his head on the table again.

She touched him on the crown of his hair.

"Listen. Do me one favor—just one! Drive me somewhere, anywhere. I won't say it was you."

He looked at her for the longest few seconds of her life, and then at the clock with a start.

"Oh my God! My God! *Dummkopf! Dummkopf!*" He banged his hand to his forehead. "Where are the keys? The keys." He pulled a drawer out of the kitchen dresser so violently that it fell on the floor. When he found them, he grabbed her hand and flung her out the door.

Dawn had come in a wash of dull gray light as they made their way toward the car. He made her sit beside him in the front, and placed his revolver between them, and then he abruptly changed his mind and tied her up again and made her lie in a fetal position in the boot, which stank of petrol. A canvas bag of tools dug into her cheek. He drove off in a skid of tires, and then it was like being a passenger on the worst fairground ride you could possibly imagine, as he drove on and on, faster and faster down the curving road, the car veering from side to side, the canvas tool bag bumping her face.

She was going to die now, she was sure of it, thinking of his pale sweating face, the brandy he'd taken in greedy gulps before they'd left.

She tried to think of some prayers from school: "Oh my God, I am sorry and beg pardon for my sins . . . forgive me, forgive me my trespasses. I'm sorry . . ." And then a cracking, tearing sound like a giant forest fire, a dull thunk as her head hit the spare wheel, a shriek of tires, and then the car left the road, and tumbled over and over and over again until it stopped.

CHAPTER 38

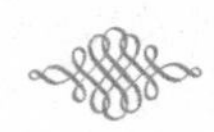

It was Barney's father Dom first thought of when he found himself facedown in the sand and rigid with shock. So good old Barney's pa was right, he reflected, absentmindedly picking bits of glass out of his wrist—one more effing overconfident eejit had bitten the dust. He turned over and lay for a while on his back, taking in with an expression of almost dopey wonderment the array of brightly colored lights jumping behind the shroud of his parachute.

He tried to work out how badly hurt he was this time. He wiggled his feet, he could feel them; he blinked, he could see. He mentally drew a line down his spine, no pain there, and he could feel earth beneath him—good, that was good—but then he smelled the strong stink of burning fuel, the taste of it in his mouth, and pulling back the parachute silk, he saw his aircraft on fire. And apart from one wing that had been flung clear, it was well on its way to a heap of pointless ash. He swore and would have gone on swearing but it hurt his rib cage. Crawling on hands and knees, too weak to disentangle himself from his parachute's run lines, he dragged himself toward the wing and lay down underneath it.

It had happened again, a strange, disconnected, jaunty voice inside him observed—only this time worse: he was in the middle of what looked like endless, fucking miles of desert, stretched out dreadfully all around him. He had no map—that had fried in the flames—no cheerful English ambulance staff arriving on the scene, no nurses waiting for him in hospital; he was completely and utterly alone, quite possibly behind enemy lines.

And joy! it had been raining here, too, just as it had rained for the last two weeks at the base at LG39, almost without cease. The sand his face was pressed against was a gritty mash, and at this time of year, when night fell, the temperature would dip to near freezing.

The pain, when he tried to sit up, was excruciating. "Don't! Don't, don't," he gasped, as if taking instruction from someone else. Maybe a couple of ribs smashed . . . maybe worse. He opened his eyes and lifted his head an inch or two; the desert, sodden and glistening after a recent shower, looked more like the sea. There was no chance, he estimated, that anyone would come and look for him tonight, if ever. Losing planes was a fact of life here, not an emergency; there were too many other things going on. Horrible to die in a place you didn't even know the name of—it was his last despairing thought before he went to sleep; and without her.

A shower of rain woke him just before dawn. He opened his eyes and looked up in confusion at the parachute silk that had blown over his face like a caul. He tore it off quickly, roaring in pain. He must not do that again. The fingers of his right hand were blistered, but at least he could see now. Above him a dense black sky, around him nothing but sand. There were wild animals in the desert, he knew that, foxes and hyenas, but here nothing but the faint rustling of wind and the sound of his own breath. He was completely and entirely alone.

He observed for a while the shape of his hands. When he lifted them to his nose they smelled of oil. He wished there was something practical he could do with them—open a map, wrap them around a gun, switch on a torch, something solid that would help get his brain working again.

He'd picked up the enemy plane at a landing ground close to Sidi Abdel Rahman, about twenty-three miles east of Marsa Matruh—that much he remembered. If his map and compass hadn't become kindling, he could work out exactly where he'd been shot down, but anyway, Marsa Matruh was one hundred and fourteen miles west of Alexandria. The desert between here and Alex was jam-packed with land mines, left from what had been German artillery outposts and some POW camps. It was also an area the Allies had attacked almost continuously. If the Germans didn't get him, his lot would.

He lay back. Enough . . . enough thinking . . . even this much had brought on a great urge to rest, to fall into a dreamlike state where pleasant, nebulous thoughts and images drifted through his brain—

thoughts of Saba and songs and Woodlees Farm, a barking dog in a meadow full of buttercups, the river at Brockweir. And while he slept, it rained, not heavily, and the parachute silk settled like a second skin on his ribs.

When he woke, hot and shivering, several hours later, he lay squinting at a sky whose dull gray made it impossible to work out the time. "Nothing has changed," he said out loud, surprised to hear how weak his voice was. A few moments later, he froze. He could hear the distant drone of planes in the sky somewhere far above the blank wall of cloud. They had come for him after all.

CHAPTER 39

Saba." Cleeve was there when she opened her eyes. "Thank God!" he said. He began to cry.

His face was all nostrils and wide eyes, he was telling her the trees had broken her fall, telling her she was lucky, lucky, lucky, and she mustn't be frightened now. She was safe, and sound. He'd come to pick her up when Felipe was so late.

"Felipe!" She started toward him in panic.

"Later," he said, "I'll tell you later—let's get you out of here first."

Everything was too fast. Having to sit up, having to try and walk up the muddy slope toward the road on legs that felt weak as pipe cleaners. Cleeve rolled up his trousers, his ankles white and skinny; his linen suit covered in her blood as he pushed her up the hill, bundled her into the back of the car and drove her at top speed back to Istanbul. She sat behind him, forehead on the window, gazing slackly at treetops whizzing by. There was pain in her head and it spread through her body like an oil slick. She slept, and when she woke she was sitting with Cleeve in a bright white room, where an English doctor said she'd been a very lucky girl, and where she was sick. They shone a sharp light in her eye; this won't hurt, the doctor said. He gave her an injection in the arm; she slept.

When she woke in the aircraft, it was like sloshing around in the guts of some large and noisy whale. The pain in her head felt worse. There was someone sitting beside her wearing a white skirt and smelling of Dettol. When they wiped her head with a cool flannel it was nice.

A clunk, and then a softness as she was lifted into bed. Lovely, lovely sleep at last, and strange flickering underwater journeys inside her head that had music in them. She was not unhappy.

Oh skylark, I don't know if you can find these things
But my heart is riding on your wings
So if you see them—

She was flying on a song when the nurse came.

"Saba."

"No."

"Saba, Miss Tarcan. Come on now, *come on*."

"No, no, no, safe here." Someone patted her face, but she wanted to stay on the ocean bed swimming in a golden patch of water.

Squeaking sound. Shoes. No, no, no! I don't want to come up. Nice here. Like driftwood, like bones.

Time . . . goes . . . Ouch! Her head hit a big rock and she slept again. A flicker of white light, a spider in front of her, ouch, ouch, ouch, it hurts to open your eyes.

"Saba." *Go away, go away.* The patting continues. "Saba, Saba, it's me . . . it's me."

When she opened her eyes, Arleta was sitting on the bed next to her. Saba was sick all over her and went back to sleep.

Arleta came again the next day. There was a bunch of wilted roses in her hand. She was crying.

"Saba, thank God, thank God. What has happened to you?"

Saba touched the swathe of crêpe bandages around her head; her hand felt wooden and separate.

"Someone hit me on the head."

"Well that's a statement of the bleeding obvious," Arleta said. They began to giggle weakly.

"Where am I?"

"You're in hospital, in Cairo, darling—the Anglo-American. You've been sleeping like a champion."

Arleta smelled beautiful; roses and lemons said the bells of St. Clement's. She was dressed in a brilliantly blue frock; her hair was so dazzling it hurt to look at it. It was like electric sparks coming out of her. When Saba put her hand out, Arleta's kisses left bright red wings all over it.

"Don't talk. I'm not supposed to be here; they'll kick me out." Arleta started blowing her nose. "Oh dear, this is so wonderful. I thought we'd . . . I was so worried . . . Oh I'm such a fool."

Squeak of shoes on linoleum, a loud voice—*ow!*—said cross things that she was too tired to listen to, and then *visiting hours* in an explosion of sound that made her head shrink. *No, don't go, help me,* but when she woke up she was alone again, and swimming through a long, shadowy stretch of water. Her heart felt waterlogged, her spine, her neck, her head ached in a dull, persistent way and the shadows frightened her. She kept swimming, trying to break through into the sunlit shallows where the bright fishes were, but the shadow got thicker and thicker, it was endless.

In the middle of the night, when most of Cairo was asleep, and everyone seemed to have gone, a moth rattling inside the shade of her bedside light woke her. She sat up, confused by the spartan room with its hard polished surfaces. In the corner of her room there was a child's wooden wheelchair, with a knitted elephant inside it.

She looked around her.

"Where's Dom?" she asked, her heart racing with fear.

She pulled a red cord above her bed.

"Where's Dom?" she said to the nurse when she came in.

"I don't know who you mean, dear, I was *asleep*." The night nurse gave her a beady look. Her hair was on end, her apron untied. "It's three o'clock in the flipping morning."

The nurse, seeing her wild expression, got her a drink of water, and made her take two pink pills that she said would help her sleep. "You've had a very nasty bang on the head, dear." The nurse had recovered her professional self. "You're bound to feel upset."

She held the pills in her mouth, and spat them out when the nurse was gone. She had to wake up, to pay attention now. Where was Dom? A sudden premonition that she would not see him again made sweat prickle all over her. He'd died without her, or at least the certainty of her. She'd thrown away the most precious gift of her life, and she was dirty now, too, thanks to her greedy determination to do and have everything. She understood her father's look of utter revulsion for her. She deserved to die.

Crying made the blood pound in her temples like a sledgehammer; the migraine that followed brought a kind of perverse comfort—she was being punished, and rightly so. Now she remembered that while she was unconscious, a conversation had turned on and off in her head like a faulty light, a question needing an answer. She was lying in water, somewhere beautifully calm and comfortable, waiting for waves to settle over her, but something else—she'd experienced it as a sharp object, as if she was pond life being stirred by a bullying boy—kept trying to rouse her, to call her back. *I was a fool*, she thought before she went to sleep. *I should have let myself die.*

The next day, Pam—the nice nurse—put her sensible English head round the door.

"A nice fresh eggie for breakfast? We got them from the market yesterday. Eggie and soldiers. You haven't had anything to eat for a long time."

"How long have I been here?"

"A week—no, hang on." She consulted a chart at the end of the bed. "Goodness! Ten days already—you *have* been poorly."

Pam put a cool hand on Saba's head. "I'll take your temperature later." She straightened the sheet with a snap. "And I'll do you a blanket bath, love. You've got a visitor today." She plumped one of the pillows that had fallen on the floor.

"Dom?" she said softly, but the nurse didn't hear. Felipe, she'd remembered, was dead. Cleeve had told her that, and she couldn't stop thinking about the gurgling sounds he'd made just after they'd shot him, the sound of water stuck in a drain, his eyes so gentle, so surprised. She remembered the tall German, the clunk of his belt, his breath smelling of sausages, his fingers. She'd sung for him like a wind-up doll, let him hug her. How could she? *How could she?* It made her want to vomit just to think of him.

"Yes, your ENSA friend has come every single day since you were admitted." Pam removed the dead moth from inside the lampshade. "Isn't she gorgeous! Not like you, disgusting thing." She dropped the moth in the wastepaper basket. "And so nice with it—she gave us all your choccies and flowers and she was so upset about you. The acrobats came, too, and Captain Furness. It was quite good fun really, although you weren't the best company, if I may say so."

"Arleta," she said weakly. "When can I see her?"

"You've seen her! Silly billy. You spoke to her yesterday and the day before that."

"How long have I been here?"

"Ten days, you've just asked me that. Oh, we are a dozy girl today."

When Pam closed the doors on the shiny world outside, Saba slept again. She and Mum were at home, it was summer and her legs were bare; a warm breeze came through the kitchen window. Tan was cooking up something spicy in the kitchen, and they were laughing because Mum was playing the chicken song on the piano, and Baba was there, too, warbling the chorus, vibrating his throat with his fingers: *"keep that chickie a peck peck innnnnnnnchick chock chicken I do."* And his laugh was so deep and happy, and she was happy too. *"Akşam yemeğiniz hazir,"* Tan called from the kitchen. "Get it while it's hot."

When she woke up, Arleta was sitting at the end of her bed, not blurred around the edges, but real and in focus. She'd brought a tiny paper fan, and a packet of humbugs from the NAAFI.

"Hooray." She put her hands gently around Saba's face. "You're back. You've had a rotten time." When they embraced, Saba could hear the grinding sound inside Arleta's jaw as she fought to control herself.

When Arleta released her, Saba said: "Dom. Have you seen him?"

Arleta glanced at her, and then toward the window.

"No," she said, "I don't really know him." She sounded genuinely surprised.

Saba watched her with fierce concentration. Arleta was never a very good actress, but she seemed to be telling the truth.

"Do you want me to try and find him?"

"Yes." Saba grabbed Arleta's hand so hard the whites of her knuckles showed. "Flight Lieutenant Dominic Benson, Desert Air Force. Wadi Natrun is where the transit camp is . . . he might be anywhere."

It felt like bad luck to even say his name.

"Sweetheart, darling, please, please, please don't cry. I promise I'll look for him tomorrow. It'll be all right."

But it wouldn't be all right. That was what Saba felt now; that there were no more safety nets, just as there hadn't been for Felipe and his wife and daughter, for Bog and his family, and for all the other hundreds and thousands of people whose luck had run out. Why had she thought she would be exempt from punishment?

"What's happened to you, my darling?" Arleta dipped a hanky in the glass of water. She wiped Saba's face, which was flushed and feverish again. "Try and tell me."

She pulled her chair closer to the bed.

Saba told her as much of it as she could bear—about Turkey, and the parties, and Felipe, then she remembered and clapped her hand over her mouth.

"Oh bugger. I'm not supposed to say any of this. It's a secret."

"Don't worry, my pet." Arleta calmly patted her hand. "My lips are sealed, and you've got a concussion, and I've done a little bit in that line myself, though nothing as dramatic, and the main thing is you're safe. But tell me, this German chap you sang for, it must have been *terrifying*."

"It was." Oh, the relief of holding Arleta's hand and talking: like pricking a boil and seeing poison spurt out.

"His name was Severin. He made me stand on a table and sing for him—it was the most bloody awful feeling, like being a chimpanzee in nappies."

Arleta started to splutter. "Oh you are a one, you still make me laugh. Not the having to sing, but the chimpanzee bit." She wanted this to be a funny story.

"He loved music," Saba continued. "Can I have some water, please?"

"Love, you're trembling." Arleta tightened her grip.

Saba's voice had become wooden. "He loved the music, that's what he said. He blamed me."

"Saba, I've lost you. Blamed you for what?"

"For making him do things."

Stale stockings came back to her, unwashed silk stockings tied tightly around her mouth; the smell of vodka and sausages too.

"Oh my God, my God!" Arleta was appalled. "What happened?"

"I had to stand on the table and sing for him. It was so creepy." Saba couldn't bear to tell her the whole story, not yet. Maybe never.

"Just that?"

"He started to cry and tell me how much he loved his wife."

Arleta's eyes were wide open. "Talk about being saved in the nick of."

"And then he sang a song to me in English—it's called 'Dido's Lament.'"

"Never heard of it—sounds a hoot."

"He drove off the road and into a tree . . . they found me by the side of the road . . . I don't remember . . . I think he's dead . . . I don't know for sure."

After a pause she continued.

"I've gone mad, Arleta. There was this lovely Turkish family Felipe and I saw on the way to the party. I keep having this dream of driving into their house and killing them, but we didn't, did we? Did anyone say anything about that?"

"No, love, no, that's not likely." Arleta put her arms around her and held her tight. "It's normal to have these peculiar thoughts when you've had a shock, but they're not real."

"I thought Severin was better than the others because he liked music so much. Can you think of anything more stupid? I hate the fact that I sang for him. It makes me feel so cheap," she added with a soft wail.

"Now that is a pile of steaming whatnot," Arleta said severely. "You were singing for your sodding life."

"If Dom was dead, you would tell me, wouldn't you?" Saba clutched her arm. "I've got the most awful feeling. Have the nurses told you?"

"No, love." Arleta had tears in her eyes. "Not a thing. But listen," she said quickly. Matron had just opened the door; she was tapping her watch significantly. "I'm going to make you a promise. Tomorrow I shall go out. I will scour Cairo for this young man of yours—if he's in town, I'll find him and bring him here." Her confidence was frightening, wonderful. "Is that a deal?"

"It's a deal." They hugged each other hard.

CHAPTER 40

Barney was sitting in a dark corner of the Windsor Club in Soliman Pasha Street when Arleta entered the men-only bar like a force-ten gale. She click-clacked toward him in a tight green dress, fair hair swinging. "Ha," she'd spotted his uniform, "the very man I wanted to see."

The air filled with her rich perfume as she sat down. She crossed her stockinged legs with a swish, and placed them at a fetching angle.

"I've just seen your friends at Shepheard's," she said. "They said you'd be here."

"Why are you looking for me?" Barney was unshaven. There were two smeared glasses on the table beside him.

"A friend of mine is looking for Dominic Benson."

"Wass name?"

"Saba Tarcan," Arleta was beaming, "and I have some wonderful news—she's alive. She's convalescing in the Anglo-American."

Barney looked up from his drink mumbling a string of words, two of which he'd never said in front of a woman before.

Arleta leapt up, eyes blazing. "I beg your pardon."

"A see you on Tuesday, I said—wass matter with that?"

"Don't you dare say that to me. I'll smack your silly head in."

"Sorry," he reached for a packet of Camels, "but I'm not a great fan of your friend." He shook his head and turned away.

"Dom's gone," he said after a while. "He's missing, presumed dead."

"Oh for Christ's sake." Arleta sat down beside him. "Not another." She took several deep breaths. "What happened?"

"I don't know. Look . . . I'm sorry, but I can't . . ."

He couldn't speak: first Jacko, now Dom. The blackest ten days of his life so far.

"What happened?"

"Not sure . . ." he said at last. "He went off to collect a plane . . . too tired . . . exhausted . . . they'll probably give him a posthumous DFC . . . so, bully for him." He toasted Dom bleakly with an empty glass.

"Barney, you're plastered," said Arleta. "I'm going to get you some coffee, and then we're going to talk, and then I want you to go to bed."

He was in no fit state to leer. It made him look sweet and a bit dopey.

"Sit there like a good boy," said Arleta. "I'll be back."

She returned with two cups and a plate of sandwiches.

"Come on, eat up," she said, "and have a big cup of coffee. Don't spill it now. Sit up, pay attention. There."

He drank half a cup, and when he slopped some on his saucer, he gave her a guilty look.

"I shouldn't have sworn at you," he said. "It's such a mess, though."

Arleta squeezed his hand. "Don't worry, don't worry," she murmured. "It's a horrible mess, and he was your friend, and that poor girl . . ." With a thunk, his head collapsed on the table and she stroked his hair.

"Poor girl." His head jerked up sharply. "No, I don't hate many people, but I hate her. She ditched him cold in Alexandria. He was so torn up."

"Now stop that right now." Arleta put her hand over his mouth. "Finish your coffee, I'll pay the bill." Her face had paled. "We could go to the Gezirah Club and walk in the gardens. You need to keep moving."

In the park, when he broke down, she lent him a perfumed silk hanky to dry his eyes.

"I haven't talked about him . . . not yet," he said with a whoop of sorrow. "You see, I've known him for such a long time and I liked him so much, he was . . . we were at school together, he was one of my best friends . . . we . . . and so many good people gone now, you know, people who would have been doctors, and lawyers, teachers, had children. Oh for God's sake . . . sorry about this."

He straightened his back, widened his eyes, gave a gasping sigh—

determined not to let the side down. It was one of the saddest things she'd ever seen.

"You don't have to stop," she murmured. "You must miss him like mad."

"I do," he gave a strange groaning laugh, "I do . . . it's as if there's a huge gap in the squadron now. He was such good fun—the men and the officers liked him, too. I'm sorry, I'm talking too much."

"Barney, for God's sake come here." She pressed his head against her bosom. "Come here," she murmured, "and don't be an idiot. Of course you want to talk about it. I would, too, if I were you. I have to ask you one thing myself. What did he say about Saba? She was mad about him, by the way."

"I didn't actually speak to him about it." His look was furtive and far away. "Oh damn it, what does it matter now anyway. I read his diary. They gave me his things."

"Tell me more." She gave him an encouraging squeeze. "I would have done the same thing by the way."

A green and red parrot flew down from a tamarind tree. It landed on the grass beside them and screeched.

"Hope he didn't see that." Barney disengaged himself from her arms; his dopey spaniel look had returned. "That bird, I mean."

"Oh stop that." Arleta fluffed her hair out. "Sit down for a moment." She pointed to a bench under the tree.

"I've met Dom," she said. "He came to a show we were doing, a show near Fayid. He'd come to see Saba. He was very determined—and very attractive, too, I thought."

"I wouldn't know about that," Barney almost smiled, "but girls certainly thought so. It was his bad luck to bump into your friend."

"Shut up! Right now." Arleta's eyes had narrowed into mean green slits. "I'll tell you about it later."

"A fat lot of good it will do him now."

"Tell me about Dom." She looked him in the eye. "Have you known him for long?"

"Since prep school," Barney cleared his throat, "and then at Cambridge we joined the squadron together. It was fun; Dom was a brilliant pilot—my father, who was an amateur jockey, says it has to do with the same things: nerve, and feel; quick reactions. Dom adored it, it was like a drug, for me, too. He talked us all into joining up—when things went badly wrong, it cut him up terribly."

He gave her a wild look. "I still can't believe it."

"Do you know what happened? Only say if you want to." She stroked his thumb.

"I don't know anything. He went to pick up a Spitfire, he didn't come back. That's all I know. I was in Cairo that day. When I got back I saw them rubbing his name off the blackboard, I was furious. It was too early. I've seen men strolling back into camp ages after you've written them off—bad things don't always happen. But that was two weeks ago, and I'm trying to . . . just . . . I don't know what." Barney ran out of words.

They stood up and walked again, down an avenue of large date palms that flung spiky shadows on the path. An English nanny, nasal, bored, called to two small children—"Rose, Nigel, play nicely else we'll go straight home. I shan't tell you again."

Arleta stopped. She looked at her watch and groaned.

"Blast." She put a hand on his arm. "Oh, sugar. Barney, I've got to go—we have a performance at eight—an outdoor number for the troops in the Ezbekiya Garden. Come if you like—we could have some supper afterward. I want to hear as much as I can before I see her tomorrow morning."

He looked momentarily stunned, like a man whose electricity supply had been abruptly cut off.

"Priorities straight—get the hair done." His attempt at a joke was not a success.

"Well yes, I do need to do all that, as it happens." She gave him a level look. "I don't suppose you'd fly without a helmet on."

"Tough lady."

"Nope," she smiled at him, "not really. Just a person doing a job, and if you want my advice, you'll go back to the club, have a zizz and a shave and meet me later at Londees—you've had a tough day."

"Right ho, nanny."

When she said she would probably be late, he said that would be fine, he would wait for her.

* * *

Later that night, as Arleta scissored her way across the terrace at Londees, every man in the room turned to look at her, except Barney, who was reading intently from the menu, embarrassed, it seemed, to have been caught out earlier in his emotional underwear.

"Supper's on me, darling," she said as she sat down, "because I asked you, and because I got paid today." She ordered lavishly and ate heartily—fried fish, fresh vegetables, a bottle of wine—and while Barney picked at his food, she talked brightly about the director of their show, a man called Bagley, who was back in town again and a bit of a bully. How he expected West End magic with two acrobats—one had done his tendon in—no comedian, no Saba, and three new recruits, shattered after a tour in India, was beyond imagining. When Bagley had called them all into the dressing room afterward and given them a real rollicking, she'd wanted to bite his eye.

"I'm sorry," Barney said politely, "bite his eye? That sounds a bit extreme."

"Sorry, love," she said, "an old Cockney form of endearment." He laughed for the first time since Dom had died.

Over coffee and liqueurs on a candlelit terrace overlooking the Nile, the mood softened and grew more intimate. "I'm sorry I swore at you earlier," Barney said again. "I've never done that before . . . and it was horribly rude. It's no excuse, but I'd just finished writing to Dom's mother. I used to spend summer holidays with them."

"You've said sorry already." She touched his hand gently. "You can stop now. What on earth did you say?"

"Well, I know them pretty well, so the usual guff," Barney's voice wobbled, "about how proud she should be, and how ghastly this bloody mess was, but what a good time he'd had out here until, well. It's true, you know . . . he said they'd been the best days of his life."

Rain had begun to fall on the Nile, dimpling the surface of the water, blurring and fading the colored lights on the pleasure boats. On the far shore, a peasant family lay like sardines under a tarpaulin.

"What's she like?" he said suddenly. "I mean really like. I'm not trying to be rude, but it's awfully hard to tell with people like you."

"What do you mean?" Arleta was laughing.

"Well, don't take this wrongly, but it's part of your job to get people to fall for you. You're the dream girls, but not really real, sort of like those pictures of country cottages with hollyhocks round the door and stuff that people buy to put on the walls of their flats when they live in London."

Arleta was silent, just looking at him, and then she shook her head. "You are such a twerp, Barney," she said at last. "Saba's lovely—she's my friend. And she's exciting because she's good at something, *really* good."

"Well . . ." His mouth turned down, he was not convinced.

"And it's not as much fun as you might think, the dream-girl thing. Men can feel very let down when they see how ordinary you are without your war paint on."

Barney grunted.

"Mind you, it took me a while to forgive her for being so good." Arleta stirred her coffee. "Not that she would have known."

"Really?"

"If I'm honest, I was jealous of her when we first met. Well, you know, or you probably don't, but when you're a dancer or a singer, people tell you all the time that talent is seventy percent hard work, thirty percent talent, all that stuff. And it's true, up to a point, until it's so obviously a lot of old cobblers. Because here was this girl, this *thing*, this funny little thing from *Wales*—awful clothes, no real experience, certainly no West End experience—with this terrific voice. Well, more than the voice, a real sparkle about her. What's that word? Caramba? Charmisma? Anyway, the *it* thing. Everybody recognizes it when they see it, and of course, she was younger than me. I'm thirty-two, you know—one foot in the grave in showbiz terms."

"Conceited, too, I expect." Barney gave another deep sigh and put his elbows on the table.

"No," Arleta took a swig of wine, "not particularly—no more than most of us—anyway, I got over it. She's a good one, and we've had so many laughs on tour and I hate feeling jealous, it's not me at all. I don't know why men always think women are such bitches to each other, it's mostly not true you know—it's the girls who support you."

"What a saint. Strange she jilted my friend without so much as a by your leave."

"Now listen." Arleta gave him her tigress look. "And shut up. I've had enough of that, so stop it." There was a long pause.

"Barney," Arleta lit a cigarette, "can you keep a secret? I'm serious now."

"Yes."

So she told him, in a low voice, as much as she could safely say about Saba's sudden departure from Alexandria and the Turkish assignment.

"She was warned not to tell your friend Dom. She was protecting him."

"Protecting him?" Barney was looking at her aslant, as if he didn't believe a word of this.

"Look, I honestly don't give a big rat's arse whether you believe me or not." Arleta's eyes were flashing. "It just happens to be true."

He stared at her, horrified, fascinated. He had no idea how to handle a woman like this.

"Don't bite my eye," he said softly. "This is quite unexpected, that's all. Now please don't take this wrongly again, but it's just I never think of women doing work . . . I mean like this . . . so . . . Oh Lord . . . give me a second . . . let me think about this." Barney sat with his head in his hands. He shook it several times. "It's possible I've been an idiot," he said at last. "And if I have, I'm sorry. I don't think I've ever hated anyone as much, I may have got it wrong. How did you find out?"

"I don't think she would have 'fessed up at all except she was badly concussed," said Arleta, "and she's still in quite a state and covered in bruises; she thinks it was a car crash, but there's more to it than that, I think. And the one thing she goes on and on about is seeing Dom."

Arleta's eyes filled with tears.

"Oh God, I'm going to have to tell her tomorrow, aren't I? That'll be fun."

CHAPTER 41

The new nurse said her name was Enid; she whipped back the curtains on gray sky, gray rooftops, a glum-looking pigeon sitting on a chimney pot. Rain was good, said Enid: those gyppo farmers, poor blighters, were absolutely desperate for it after the summer droughts. She left a cup of tepid tea on Saba's bedside table and said she would be back shortly.

"Personally speaking . . ." Enid returned with a carafe of cloudy red water in her hand; she couldn't wait to go back home now. Sick of the flies, sick of the heat in summer, murder it had been, this one; sick of not enough leave and now sick of the rain. You never expected to be cold in Egypt, did you, but it was horrible out and the houses never seemed to have enough heating, they weren't set up for cold, were they?

Enid snapped the coverlet taut and twinkled at her. "But you're going to have a nice day anyway. Your friend Arleta is coming to see you with a young man."

Saba stopped breathing for a moment. "Who?"

"Heavens. Hang on." The nurse put her finger under the rim of her starched hat and scratched.

"Let me think . . . a Pilot Officer somebody or other. I'm not sure but I think his name was Barney."

Fear shot through her veins like electricity. Dom's friend. He was coming to tell her something, and it would not be good.

"Thank you, Nurse," she said politely.

When Enid closed the frosted-glass door behind her, Saba lay perfectly still with her eyes closed. She'd lost him.

The door opened again. "Brekkie!" Enid walking toward her with her nursey smile on.

"I'm not hungry," Saba said. "You have it." She had seen Enid wolfing down leftovers in the ward late at night.

"Oh don't be so silly." The nurse put the tray down. "I won't eat it. And you'll never get better if you eat like a bird."

Saba smiled blankly, not hearing a word. When the door closed again, she got up and hobbled to a basin in the corner of the room and stared at her reflection in the mirror. There was a large crêpe bandage around her head; both her eyes were still swollen like bad plums, with yellow and purple bruises extending from the lower lids to halfway down her cheekbones. On her way back to bed, the room swung so violently that she had to cling to the child's wicker wheelchair in the corner of the ward. When its wheels slid across the floor she nearly fell.

Back in bed again, she looked at the clock on the wall. Nine o'clock. Usual visiting hours were between eleven and twelve. Soon the frosted-glass door that stood between the ward and everything else would open.

She wished her mother was here—someone to wait with, someone who knew her well enough not to talk. She'd thought a lot about her recently, what it must have felt like with a husband at sea for most of her married life, the terror of waiting, the memory of her mother's face frozen in concentration listening to the shipping forecast on the wireless every night, and then—*click!*—forecast over, jolly or angry depending on the mood, Mum again: shouting, cracking jokes, cooking, finding socks, always knowing she was one knock on the door away from disaster. Her cheerfulness felt heroic to Saba now; one more thing taken for granted.

Shortly before lunch, she heard the clickety-clack of high-heeled shoes coming down the corridor—quite different from the cautious squeak of the nurses' crêpe soles. The shoes stopped outside her door.

"Darling?" Arleta's voice muffled through the frosted glass. "Are you decent?"

The handle half turned. When the door opened, Saba sat up in bed white-faced.

"Yes. Say it quickly," she said when she saw Arleta's face. "I know what you're going to say." The dark silhouette of a man outside the glass door.

"I'm sorry," said Arleta. She kicked off her heels, got on to the bed and they held each other tight.

"Oh love," she said softly. "This is brutal."

A flash of pain went like forked lightning through her head when Arleta said it. She sobbed without sound for a while. He'd gone; she knew it. Enid, hovering sympathetically, handed her a sick bowl in case she needed it, a warm flannel, and one of her own mints to suck.

A uniformed man walked in—a big red-faced blank to Saba, a noise, standing over the bed.

"Do you want me to leave?" he said immediately. "I could come back later."

She nodded her head. She wanted to hide like a sick animal and howl. The roar of sound in her head was almost unbearable. The nurse said she could have a pill soon, a phenobarbital, if she wanted to sleep.

"It's nothing personal." Her words bounced off the walls. "Thank you for coming."

The man twisted his hat in his hands. He touched her arm.

"I'm sorry," he said before he left. He put a package on her bedside table and said something about Dom's locker, but she wasn't listening properly.

When Arleta left, a new nurse came in. She said how chilly it was getting now that the nights were drawing in; she left two painkillers for Saba's head, which was full of forked lightning again. "Night-night, then, love." The nurse drew the curtains; she switched off the overhead lights and closed the frosted door.

She'd been longing for everyone to leave, but now that she was alone, the night seemed to stretch out all around her like a dark sea in which she might easily drown.

She woke after midnight, parched from crying, and reached for the water carafe. When she turned on the light, her hand touched the parcel the tall man had left for her. She sat up in bed and opened it clumsily. Inside the wrappings there was a box filled with tissue paper, and in it a blue enamel bracelet with the outlines of Egyptian gods and goddesses carved in silver. She turned it in her hand and saw engraved on its back *Ozkorini.*

Think of me.

It was beautiful. It must have cost him every last penny of his pay packet. Tucked inside the box was a card engraved with the address of a jeweler in Alexandria.

She was throwing away the wrapping paper when she found the remains of a letter written on a torn and crumpled bit of paper. Adjusting the lamp, she saw that it wasn't a proper letter, more like a draft with words crossed out, in two spots so violently that the pen had pierced the paper. A letter written in high emotion, something he'd never meant to send.

The words floated senselessly in front of her eyes like cinders. She smoothed the paper out, pieced the torn bits together, and still couldn't take them in, until one sentence leapt out: *Maybe in the end, life is shoddier than songs.*

Her hands trembled as she pieced together the two bits of paper with numbers on them: August 2nd, 1942.

She moaned softly. So, no escape from it now. He'd bought the bracelet, his first proper present for her, full of hope and excitement; and died bewildered and disappointed, maybe even hating her. She would not forgive herself for this.

CHAPTER 42

After she left hospital, Saba moved in with Arleta, who had found a sublet on Antikhana Street. The flat, with its pentagon-shaped rooms and round windows, gave the charming illusion of living on the top deck of an ocean liner, and it was cheap, too.

Arleta insisted on paying Saba's half-share of the rent, and even cooked for her from her eccentric and limited repertoire: mess number one was rice, beans, and meat, boiled on a small gas ring in the kitchen; mess number two was rice, beans, fish, and whatever fresh vegetables were available. Sometimes there was a salad with a dash of gin added to the dressing. And Arleta was a firm believer in daily treats, too—a bringer of buns and cream cakes from Groppi's, the buyer of a lurid lime-green nightie with tassels on it from the souk with a twist of pistachio halva tucked inside it.

But best of all, Arleta was furiously busy for most of the day, with rehearsals, hair appointments, dates, parties (Cairo was crammed that month with young officers back from the desert with plenty of pay to spend), and for Saba it was easier to be alone as she felt such wretched company. There were whole days now when she felt so awful she could hardly be bothered to get out of her nightdress, when grief felt like a kind of flu of the soul that made quite ordinary activities such as eating and walking insurmountable. At other times, her feelings were so extreme it was as if someone had poured petrol on her and set her alight.

Grief had also rendered her dithery and weak and incapable of making a decision: sometimes the thought of leaving Cairo without knowing what had happened to Dom felt like an appalling act of betrayal; at other times, it felt pointless to stay and she longed for home.

On the day before she left hospital she'd been struck by another blow. Enid had waddled in with her nice nursey smile on, and placed an airmail letter on her bed saying that this would cheer her up anyway, which was unintentionally comical in its way. It was from her father, who knew nothing of her accident. He wrote:

Dear Saba,

It is with great pain and after much suffering that I send this to you, but your mother tells me that I cannot carry on not answering your letters. You have caused a great rift in our family and brought shame to all of us by disrespecting my wishes and going away. It is an insult to my honor, and one I cannot find it in my heart to forgive you for. Now it would be better, for your mother and me if you stay with your choice and don't come home. You have made your decision, and I have made mine. You are no longer a daughter to me. I am at sea at the moment, moving between . . . and . . . so I have not told your mother yet, but I will inform her of my decision when I get home. It would be better for us all if you did not see your mother and grandmother either.

I am sorry it is like this.

Followed by his careful signature: *Remzi Tarcan.*

Her first reaction after reading this was one of boiling rage. *Hypocrite, liar, jailer. Why could you choose a traveling life and not me?* She'd been part of the war effort, too. She knew now what a difference they had made to the men's morale: this was not flannel, it was true, and how dare he make it sound so trivial, so wrong. When the anger wore off, she wanted to bury her head in her mother's lap and say, "Forgive me." Her mother, she knew, would be in turmoil about this: longing to write, not daring to, in case it got her into a fight with her husband, who was perfectly capable of using his fists on her when he was roused.

And so it was that all the happiness about singing, and Dom, and traveling, and even the thought of home and Pomeroy Street, the simple marvel of being alive, now felt not wrong exactly, but like a form of extreme naïveté that deserved punishment. How could she not have seen the world's traps; nor felt the cruelty and randomness of war; nor seen that people were almost never who you thought they were? The hard truth was she'd broken up her family by coming here.

During the long days of convalescence in the flat, lonely and cut adrift from work, she began to hate the talents that had led her here. She'd gone around in this stupid bubble of self-regard and now the bubble had burst and she deserved everything she'd got.

After a few days' rest, she went to see Furness at the ENSA office at the Kasr-el-Nil to ask about a flight home to England. She'd more or less decided, when the war was over, to go back to Wales and get a sensible job, in an office, or perhaps as a nanny to some family. There was a peculiar atmosphere about this meeting. Furness had given her a sort of deaf smile before he'd said he was sorry to hear she'd been unwell. He'd fiddled irritably during their interview with the files on his desk as if he couldn't wait for her to leave. He'd do what he could, he said at last, with a shuddering sigh, but there were now vast numbers of ENSA entertainers stuck here with no exit visas, plus the flipping king was coming out for a royal visit soon, so anything else she'd like him to do for her?

And then Cleeve turned up. Cleeve who was usually so careful about meeting in anonymous places. Their first meeting since he'd lifted her out of the smashed car beside the road to Istanbul.

He strolled into her apartment, a civilized man again in his nice-looking raincoat and trilby. She was trying to light a fire with green wood, and the apartment was choking with smoke.

"Good God, Saba," he said, batting the fumes away with his hand. "What on earth are you trying to do—commit suttee?"

"What are you talking about?" She stared at him; she'd forgotten to lock the door and was thrown to see him in the middle of her sitting room.

"You know, those Hindu widows who throw themselves on the burning pyre."

He'd looked mortified.

"Oh God, how tactless! I came to say I was sorry to hear about your chap. Not a good start. Sorry."

"How did you hear?" She was staring at him.

"Well, you know, all part of the job? Look, can we go out for a cup of tea or something? I shouldn't really be here."

* * *

In the coffee shop he changed places twice and fiddled with his spoon. "Saba," he said, "I'm sorry it's taken me so long to come and see you. I was desperately upset about what happened in Turkey, but it wasn't safe for me to hang around."

She saw a new look in his eye, a crumpled look of hurt and what may or may not have been intense concern; who knew who to trust now? He cleared his throat.

"Where did you find me?" she said. "In Turkey, I mean."

"Under a tree, in a ditch. The car was burning beside you, you were jolly lucky."

He held his top teeth over his lower lip, which had begun to tremble. She looked away.

"It was horrid, Saba. I feel guilty about what happened. Ten minutes later and I don't like to think."

"Well don't." She couldn't stand the thought of him being emotional, or talking about Felipe, not yet.

"What happened to Jenke?" she asked him. "I'd at least like to know that. He had the documents. Did he get away?"

"Yes."

She waited for more.

"Is that it? Just yes, nothing else?" She could hear her voice rising.

"No."

"Was it useful, his information?"

"I think so."

Cleeve lit a cigarette and gave a little gasp.

"I think it was all right," he said faintly. He leaned over and took her hand and looked her in the eye in a way she found unnerving.

"Saba," he said, "are you really all right? I've been so very worried about you."

She felt his fingers close around her hand and hoped he would take them away soon.

"I'm not sure we should have sent you there."

"It wasn't your fault," she said. "It was mine. I wanted to travel, I loved the singing—everybody has their Achilles' heel, I found mine."

"You still have bruises." When he pointed in a hangdog way toward her forehead, she clenched her fists under the table—his sympathy was almost unbearable.

"Listen," she said. "I want to go home, you can help me with that. When I asked Captain Furness last week, he would hardly talk to me. He also didn't ask a thing about the accident, he couldn't wait to get rid of me." Her voice throbbed with rage. "Doesn't that strike you as odd that I—"

"No, it doesn't, Saba," he interrupted her, "because this could ruin his career: the ENSA setup is incredibly fragile. The brass hats resent the fact that they take up time and lorries and things, they think of performers as badly behaved children, so when things go belly-up, both sides rush to bury it."

"Dermot," she'd been steeling herself for this ever since they'd sat down, "there's one thing I really do need to ask you. My friend . . . the pilot . . . he's missing presumed dead. Is there any chance . . ."

"No." Cleeve pulled away from her. "None whatsoever . . . sorry, but absolutely none." His eyes were focused on a tatty poster hanging on the wall above her head, it showed a woman floating down the Nile and drinking Ovaltine. "Don't you think it's always better to tell the truth?"

"Surely someone can help me look—Jenke or someone?"

"No. Sorry, Saba . . . let's be clear right away. This work doesn't come with a quid pro quo. I shouldn't be here now." He fiddled with his raincoat belt.

"Well, give Jenke my regards when you see him," she said, standing up.

"I don't think I will see him again," he said softly. "That's how it is here. Ships passing in the night, although sometimes the consonant could easily be changed."

The following day, Max Bagley dropped by, so happy to be back in Cairo, he said, he could have cried. He'd been in the punishment zone, Ismailia, this summer directing a company that made their lot look like models of sanity. Half the dancers had gone down with foot rot because it was so hot; one of the comedians had turned out to have epilepsy.

He took her to Groppi's, ordered macaroons and ice cream, and after some small talk, and a sprinkling of compliments, he looked at her with his bright, calculating eyes.

"The shows I mentioned. We've got some absolute corkers coming up. No chance of you coming back, I suppose?"

His smile was as sweet and innocent as the ice cream that ringed his mouth, but she'd acquired, almost overnight it seemed, the habit of suspicion.

"No chance, Max, I'm afraid. I'm waiting to go home."

"So I hear." He pushed a macaroon toward her. "Try one of these, they're divine."

"No thanks, I've just had breakfast." A lie but she couldn't stand another lecture about eating up.

"Well, let me tickle your fancy with this, Super Sabs," he said, through a mouthful of crumbs. "Thing is, I've written a musical." Pause for a look of thrilling intensity. "It's easily the best thing I've ever done. I'll be casting after Christmas, should you change your mind."

"Thanks, Max," she said quietly, "but I won't change my mind. It's nice of you to think of me."

"Saba, may I say one thing?" He propped his chin in his hands and looked deeply into her eyes. "I know I was a bit sharp with you during rehearsals. I've got a nasty tongue sometimes because I want everything to be perfect, but I only do it with people I respect, and what I should have made perfectly clear to you is that you were . . . are," he corrected himself, "good, very good. I think you have a great future ahead of you. End of apology. More grovel to follow if necessary." He touched his forehead, mouth, and chest in a mock salaam.

There was no glow of pleasure when he said this. It all sounded like flannel to her.

"Sorry, Max," she said. "I'm not trying to be a prima donna."

He wiped his mouth with a napkin and stared at her.

"It's like being an athlete, Sabs, you can't let the muscles go slack."

"I know that."

"It's not just the talent fairy waving her little wand."

"Gosh. Really?" She pushed the crumbs into a little pile with her finger, and looked at him.

"Did that sound patronizing?"

"Only a bit, Max, but thanks for trying."

As he drained his cup in one gulp, she felt the click of his charm being switched off. She knew by now how Max's mind worked: the wheels would already be churning inside his brain about who to cast as her replacement; and later there would probably be a satisfying bitch to whoever was at hand about how that Saba Tarcan wasn't as good as she thought she was—how he'd put his finger on her unique flaws the moment he'd seen her—for there was a fire of ego inside Max Bagley that needed to be stoked more or less constantly.

"What happened to Janine?" she asked him while he was searching for his hat.

"She went to India and then, or so I gather, was sent home." He gave her a beady look. "Couldn't cope at all." There was a pause. "She was an awful drip, wasn't she?" he added. "Lovely line, but no sense of humor whatsoever."

"When I thought about her later," she said, "I mean after I left the company, I felt sorry for her. She told me once she'd been having ballet lessons since she was three years old, that every scrap of the family money went on her. She didn't have a childhood, and now she won't have a proper career because just when everything was starting to open up for her, the war came. She's sure she'll be past her prime when it's over; dancers are unlucky like that."

"Well, the war's ballsed up a lot of lives." Max wasn't the slightest bit interested. "So I can't feel very boo-hoo about that."

He did at least insist on walking her home; it had started to drizzle and the sky was thunderously gray.

"Funny, isn't it, being in a company?" he said as they picked their way over broken pavements. "One moment you're all madly cozy—you know all about each other's love affairs, the state of their bowels, what they like to eat for breakfast, their weaknesses, their breaking points—and the next, *pouff!* Gone. When you're in a show, it seems like the most important thing in the world." His voice trailed off wearily.

"What will you do when the war's over, Max?"

"Dunno. Another job maybe," he said grimly. "Go on tour again." She was shocked by how worn-out he sounded.

"Why not go home for a while and have a proper holiday?" He'd talked about a place in London.

"To my bedsit in Muswell Hill," he said in the same flat voice. "If it's still standing. Whizzoo! What fun."

Boggers next, en route to a job in India. The usual leotard replaced by a shiny ill-fitting suit made, he told her proudly, by a tailor in the souk. He stood in the middle of the room discreetly tensing and flexing various muscles and made a stumbling speech he'd obviously prepared beforehand. He told Saba that she was a very nice and beautiful lady, and that when the war was over they should move to Brazil and form a double act there. If she wanted it very much they could get married.

She stumbled through a speech of her own: so kind of him, wonderful opportunity, but going home, et cetera, and she was tremendously grateful when Arleta suddenly arrived with enough energy left over from a two-hour rehearsal to admire the suit, which had obviously been bought for the occasion, and pinch his cheeks, and ask him to share mess number one with them. Saba watched her in awe.

When he left, Arleta collapsed on the sofa like a rag doll and said:

"God, I feel *dire.* I'm practically certain I'm getting a cold or flu or something, which is why I have a huge, *huge* boon to beg of you."

She rolled onto the floor, clasped her hands together in prayer, and begged Saba to help her out the following night at a small concert to be held at a supply depot near Suez.

"Get up, you silly woman!" Saba didn't feel like joking, much less performing. "What do you have in mind?"

She knew she wasn't ready for work. But Arleta was persuasive. Only a couple of duets, she said. It would be fun. Good old Dr. Footlights would get her through.

But he hadn't. She'd done it for Arleta, who, red-nosed and even croakier than the day before, was thrilled to have her back. At the depot, Arleta did a very grown-up version of "Christopher Robin Is Saying His Prayers" (*Wasn't it fun in the bath tonight? The cold's so cold, and the hot's so hot*), and they'd sung a couple of duets together, lighthearted things: "Makin' Whoopee," done with two prams, then a spoof on "Cheek to Cheek," when they pretended to be GI Janes whose cheeks got stuck together by chewing gum. Arleta, radiantly restored to health, had chewed up the scenery a bit with some extravagant shimmying at the end of the choruses, but the men seemed to love it and they left the stage to a shrill blast of wolf whistles.

And Saba, looking down from the stage at the sea of khaki men with their lonely, eager faces, made an unhappy discovery: you didn't need heart or soul to make an audience cheer and clap—at a pinch, another part of you would take over like a well-schooled circus pony.

After the intermission, Arleta, who was about to do her solo, ran from the stage into the wings clutching her throat dramatically and pretending to strangle herself.

"I can't. *Can't.*" Her voice cracked into a faint whisper. "Voice completely gone."

Well, maybe it was a trick, and maybe it wasn't, but there was nothing for it but for Saba, unrehearsed and unprepared, to take over. She was doing fine, until a boy in the front row asked for "Smoke Gets in Your Eyes." The last time she'd sung it, they'd been in bed together, in the Rue Lepsius room, her face against his chest, his hand combing her hair.

Halfway through the song, she felt a wave of blackest misery sweep over her; her throat seemed to close down. The boy who'd requested the song—a skinny kid, with a new short back and sides—looked baffled as she left the stage early, the band still playing an echo of the chorus.

She ran down the steps that led from the stage toward the scruffy tented village, the Nissen huts, the row of rubbish bins. There were no stars that night, just black cloud, and miles of mud and barbed wire. Arleta found her in a gangway between two rows of tents, sitting in the mud sobbing her guts out.

"I'm so sorry, darling," Arleta said, sitting down beside her. "I got it wrong. I think it's time you went home."

CHAPTER 43

For several days Dom slipped in and out of consciousness. His wet hair was plastered over his forehead, his lips had turned blue, parts of his parachute were still wrapped around him like a grotesque half-hatched pupa with a human head.

A desert lark was singing its strange *choo eee cha cha wooeee* song on a leafless tree nearby. The pile of ashes that had been the plane was now a soggy mess with a few bits of wire poking out, and smashed pieces of glass.

From time to time a boy, like a figure in a dream, appeared, shimmering and unreliable, sometimes with goats around him. A skinny boy with a look of horrified disgust on his face who muttered at him and occasionally screamed, who feinted and retreated and seemed to want to kill him. This time, breathing heavily, the boy tied his donkey to the tree. He stared at Dom. He inched toward him, his heart pumping wildly, snatched the scattered objects around him, the compass, the razor, the bottled tablets from his escape kit, stuffed them in his pocket, and was about to ride off again when he heard Dom sigh.

When Dom woke, hot and shivering, several hours later, he lay squinting at a sky whose dull gray made it impossible to work out the time. "Nothing has changed," he said out loud, shocked at how feeble his voice sounded. A few moments later, he froze hearing the distant drone of planes in the sky somewhere far above the blank wall of cloud. They would see him soon; they would get him. As a boy, he'd listened one night breathless with horror as his grandfather, fueled by several whiskeys too many, recalled his time as a prisoner of war—captured in a ditch before Ypres—the chicken-cage beds, the claustrophobia, the beatings, the sense of utter degraded helplessness. Being captured was one of his worst nightmares.

His muscles were taut as violin strings as he listened. The white sky had changed, and he saw, sliding out from behind what were black blobs of reflected cloud, four planes flying in formation above him—five thousand, seven thousand feet? It was hard to tell from here. Four 109s, swastikas painted like large insects underneath them. The sound faded, grew louder. Then, above the German planes, he heard the unmistakable roar of Spitfires and stopped breathing as he pictured himself stretched out like a human target on the sand. Jesus Christ Almighty. Now what?

Facedown he lay, listening with his whole body for his own death, and then he heard the sounds of the planes flying away, followed by his own lungs creaking and retching as he coughed.

After they'd gone a wave of pure exhilaration swept through him. He was alive! He was alive. He rolled over on his side, gritted his teeth, took several deep breaths, and yelling, stood up. He was standing, squinting and swaying, watching the dissolving and loosening of solid reality, when he saw the boy again, this time on a donkey coming toward him from some way off. There was a man with him.

The man looked at him for a long time, scratching his armpit. He lifted the aircraft wing and he and the boy stared at him together—a pale, half-dead agnabi who had dropped from the sky. Dom started to cry, feeling the stag beetles crawling over him. Two vultures flew above him in a speculative way, and around him the desert stretched out, implacable, vast. It didn't care. When the sun came out it would roast the flesh off his bones, or if it rained, there were no trees for shelter. He would die within days, if these two people didn't kill him.

He was still raving as they bundled up the parachute and tied it to the donkey. Telling them to leave him, telling them he wanted to die. They threw him sideways across the beast's bony back, his flying boots dragging in the mud. They took him back to their temporary home—four ramshackle tents whose guy ropes were covered in tattered bits of cloth. In front of the tents there was a hobbled camel, and a small donkey, now honking furiously at its mother's return. A skinny dog, its tail at a crazy pipe-cleaner angle, barked at them.

Dom had stopped his noise. He ached all over now, he longed for nothing more than to lie down. They took him to the largest of the tents and unrolled a thin mattress for him behind a curtain. He lay all night in this windowless corner, breathing in the fumes of a tallow candle, and camel dung, and the goat's hair the tent was made of. His lungs squeaked, his face burned. While he slept, three toddlers came to the mouth of the tent, barefoot and in grimy pajamas, picking their noses, laughing nervously. From time to time a man's curious face appeared around the door and stared at him without expression. He called his wife in to look at Dom. They did not know if he was German or English, and it did not particularly matter because an agnabi was an agnabi and their war had ruined the land, the cotton crops, the price of fuel, and made their lives even harder than they already were. As soon as he was well, he would go.

The boy's mother, Abida, who was only twenty-eight and soft-hearted, felt differently. Her last job of the day was to check on the goats, to put fava beans on to cook for tomorrow's breakfast, and lastly to pull down the various bits of sacking that made their dwelling relatively watertight. Before she went to bed, she went out into the vast star-studded night, crept around to the side of the tent where he lay and, raising a candle over his face, sneaked another look at him. He was soaked with sweat, coughing and muttering. He was a handsome boy, and he was dying. It was the will of Allah, but it was sad.

CHAPTER 44

One Wednesday morning she was in the sitting room at Antikhana Street when Mr. Ozan walked in. He was plumply poured into a beautiful dark suit and held an enormous bunch of lilies in his hand. She jumped.

"Saba, my dear." His voice was stern, his eyes full of concern. "You are a woman alone, please lock your door in future."

He sat down and looked around him. Arleta, who had the occasional attack of neatness—Tiggywinkles, she called them—had draped the sofa with some silk throws and put a bowl of Turkish delight on the table to try and tempt Saba, who was still too thin.

"Nice, very nice," he said approvingly. "I've only just heard about your accident." Her hand went instinctively to her head. "What can I do?"

"You've only just heard?" Hard not to sound skeptical.

"Yes!" Ozan sounded angry. "I was traveling, and when I came back you'd gone and nobody knew where."

His eyes looked capable of murder as he asked for details, reminding her of her father during similar interrogations. Who was at the house that night? Who was driving her? Who did she blame most?

"That's all I remember," she lied. If she told him about Severin, she would have to think about it again, and male outrage would follow, and the thought of that exhausted her—she no longer cared.

"I would kill him if I knew." Ozan's dark eyes flashed. "The German house is boarded up now, and I've heard that Engel was sent back to Germany to go on trial there. The ambassador knew nothing about the party house, and was furious about it; some of them were even selling drugs from there. They stole the drugs from military hospitals. They were very bad men."

For a moment she thought he was going to cry. "I had no idea they were such bad men, Saba. You should not have been there—for this, I can never forgive myself."

"You heard about Felipe?" Her eyes filled with tears.

"They shot him. I heard that. Yes. This was a terrible tragedy. I was very fond of him. I should never have taken you to Istanbul," he said mournfully.

"No," she told him. "It was my fault, too. I'd heard all about your clubs. I must take some of the blame."

"If your father was here, he would blame me, and me only, but . . ." Mr. Ozan gave a shrug so big he seemed to be trying to turn himself inside out. "I wanted new singers, I thought you were good. I was excited."

"I don't think my father would care anymore," she said. Wearily she told him about the letter. "He doesn't want to see me again," she added, "he hates all this."

Ozan kneaded his forehead between his fingers, he made the clucking sound Tan made when she was upset.

"Well," he said at last, "you saw his village." As if this explained everything. "There was nothing there for you," he said, staring at her. "Was there?"

"No."

She felt a pinch of pain just thinking about it. They'd gone to Üvezli on a perfect autumn day—hard bright sunshine, the bluest sky imaginable—but Ozan was right: not much there, apart from a few whitewashed houses, a mosque, a primary school, a sleepy cafe beside a square, with cats snoozing under the tables. They'd taken flowers, presents, all the rich promise of Ozan's wealth and Saba's youth and beauty. The stage set for a beautiful reunion, except no one came: no cries of joy from ancient relatives, and no stirring of memories in the half-dozen houses they'd called at. Just a few old men sitting on wooden chairs in the dusty street, each one shaking his head. Closed as oysters. They either hadn't understood or hadn't wanted to, or they'd come too late.

On their way back home, Ozan had explained in a low, apologetic voice, as if he were personally responsible, that many of the people here were descendants of the Turkish Muslims from the Caucasus who'd fled from the approaching Russian armies during the Ottoman war with Russia in 1877. Others were driven out in 1920, first rounded up by the British and French who had occupied the area around Istanbul, then shot for joining the irregular Turkish nationalist forces. They were naturally suspicious of strangers. As her father had been, all his life. She saw this clearly now.

Later that day, Ozan, obviously still smarting, had urged her to write a letter to her father: *At least he'll know you tried to find him; he'll know you cared*, she had tried, but found it impossible to finish. There were too many barriers between them now, and she felt something else, too, something the war had taught her: that she had no God-given right to secrets he didn't want to tell.

Mr. Ozan was kneading his forehead again, trying to find some sliver of hope here.

"There is one thing I would say about your father's decision," he said at last. "It will set you free as an artist—just as Faiza had to be set free, and Umm Kulthum. It is hard for people like you to serve two masters."

She said nothing, because that part of her felt so dead now and because the word "artist" seemed falsely grand in connection with her. Hearing him sigh again, she passed the box of Turkish delight.

"Who gave you this?" He stopped her arm and looked at her bracelet.

"A friend. An English pilot."

He examined it closely. "It's beautiful. These two," he touched the tiny engraved figures with the familiarity of old friends, "are Bastet and Hathor, they are both the goddesses of music and other things. This one," he moved his fingers to the right, "is Nut, she is for the sky and the heavens. They call Bastet the Lady with the Red Clothes; do you know why?"

Because she could not talk, she took the bracelet off and handed it to him. While he was squinting at the inscription, she mopped her eyes hurriedly on the hem of her skirt.

"Ozkorini," he said. "How does an Englishman know these things?"

"Because . . ." he waited for her patiently, "he was with me in Alexandria when I learned the songs. He was interested in such things."

"He was a good man."

"Yes. . . . He died while I was in Istanbul."

She was training herself to say this now, it cut out speculation and false hope, and having to listen to stories about other people who'd walked into camp months after they'd been shot down.

Mr. Ozan closed his eyes. A muscle twitched in his jaw.

"I am sorry for this."

"I should have expected it," she said. "So many of them have gone."

"But these are such young men. How old was yours?" There was a stillness about Mr. Ozan, as if he had all the time in the world to listen.

"Twenty-three." She heard her own voice, watery and choked with regret. Without a word he handed her a beautifully monogrammed handkerchief.

"Saba, listen to me," his voice was gentle, "this is an awful thing for you, but you will meet someone else, *inshallah.*"

"I don't think so."

"Many men will love you because of who you are. They'll want to marry you."

"The thing is," she said, "I let him down."

"What happened?" His voice was gentle, so like her father's when he'd been kind.

She said more than she meant to: about the burns hospital, about Alexandria. He listened, calm and attentive.

"Who knows," he said softly when she was finished. "He may still come back—not always do bad things happen."

"No," she said, "I thought that for a while, I don't now. So many have gone."

Every breath is a new beginning and a new chance. Felipe's words. Not true. Not for him.

She suddenly felt exhausted by Ozan—his crinkled forehead, his big kind eyes, the large spotlight of his attention on her. She hoped he would leave soon.

"Would it help to find out how he died?"

"No . . . not necessarily . . . I don't know. Anyway, we've tried."

He consulted the gold watch nestling in his hairy wrist.

"I'm flying back to Istanbul tonight," he wiped his chin, "so forgive me, but I must ask you one more thing before I go. When the war in Egypt is over, which *inshallah* it will be soon, I make a big party for everyone: for Egyptians, for Turkish people, for the English, for everyone in Alexandria and Cairo. Faiza will come, and I'll get the best dancers, acrobats, jugglers. I want you to sing." He looked at her expectantly; this was supposed to be a great treat.

She stood up and walked to the window. Outside, the sky was gray again, the day drawing in; soon it would be Christmas.

"That's kind of you, Mr. Ozan, but I'm going home soon—at least I hope I am."

"Will your government fly you home?"

"Yes." She watched two dark birds flying above the wet rooftops and toward the sea. "As soon as they can."

"But there's still plenty of work here for artistes. I've never seen Cairo so full—your people, our people, Americans, lots of people under thirty wanting to have fun again."

"I know, but I don't want to sing again."

Mr. Ozan's jaw dropped. "You are a singer. You can't stop."

"I can."

He thumped his fist softly on the table. His voice rose.

"If you stop singing, you will hurt the best part of yourself."

"I don't think my father would agree with you about that."

"Well, sorry for the word, but the man is a twit. Not all men think as he does—not even all Turkish men. The world moves on. Listen." He leapt to his feet, gesticulating wildly, and for once his impeccable English let him down. "Think of other bipples," he said passionately. "When you have a gift like you have a gift, it's the honey you lay down, not just for yourself but for your children's happiness also."

"Well, that's a nice idea," she said. Beads of sweat had broken out on his forehead. "It's just that I don't believe it anymore." Severin's face flashed into her mind like a bilious dream.

"You are saying no?" Ozan clapped his hand to his temples, incredulous, heartbroken. "This concert will be tremendous—fireworks and horses, singers—like nothing these cities have ever seen."

"I'm saying no," she said. "I can't do it anymore."

CHAPTER 45

For the first four days he lay in a torpor in the corner of the tent, wheezing and coughing and sleeping, then sleeping again. Sometimes the boy, or an older man with spongy red gums and two teeth, came and held a rough cup to his lips with some bitter brackish medicine in it that made him splutter. Twice a day the boy fed him some floury-tasting grain, occasionally with vegetables in it. From time to time he was aware of the dull pitter-patter of rain falling, or the screech of a bird, or, from another part of the house, male voices laughing and the rattle of some game they were playing. Once, an airplane flew so low over the tent it almost took the roof off, but he wasn't frightened, he simply noted it in a kind of dim anesthetized way, as if it were happening to someone else and in another place.

When he woke up properly, with a thumping headache and a tight chest, the boy was sitting at the end of his bed. He looked about twelve, had a wild mop of black curls, and a pallid complexion as if he might have suffered from malaria, or bilharzia. The boy smiled at him shyly; he touched his fingers to his mouth as if to ask if he was hungry. Dom nodded his head, bewildered and disoriented. When the boy skedaddled on his skinny legs out of the room to get food, Dom took stock of the desperate poverty of his surroundings. The greasy pile of quilts he lay on didn't look as if they'd been washed for years let alone weeks. On a makeshift shelf at the back of the tent there were small amounts of grain, and dried food in sacks that spoke of frugal housekeeping and small rations.

The boy returned with an older man who wore a faded djellaba and whose flapping sandals were tied with string. He came over to the bed and patted Dom's arm, beaming with joy, as if his recovery had presented them with a tremendous gift.

"Karim," he said, pointing to himself. "Ibrahim." The boy beamed.

"My name is Dom," he told them. He had never felt so far away from the person who had that name, or more vulnerable. When Ibrahim handed him an earthenware bowl, he was surprised to find he needed help to feed himself. The boy held the spoon to his lips and dribbled in a thin lentil soup, opening his own mouth as he did so like a mother bird feeding her young.

When he had finished eating, Dom fell back on the pillows, rummaging around in his brain for the word for thank you. Instead he held up his fingers and asked in English: "How long have I been here?" When the boy held up four fingers he was amazed, and then the boy counted out five more and made a joke of it, counting out more. Dom closed his eyes, overwhelmed. He might have been here for weeks for all he knew.

When he woke in the night, scratching himself and very cold, he thought about what a burden he must have been to this poor family, who could barely afford to feed themselves, and how lightly they carried it. He already felt ashamed of the man he'd been when he'd first come to North Africa—God, was it less than a year ago—who'd looked at people like these from the air, and seen only toylike figures moving their animals around. They'd given up their land for foreign soldiers to fight in and he'd barely spared them a thought.

As a child, Egypt had been a vital part of his imagination and his games, the link formed during a bad bout of measles when his mother read to him every day from a book that obsessed him about the archaeologist Howard Carter. When his mother got to the point where Carter had walked down out of the sunlight one day in the Valley of Kings, taken a piece of clay out of a wall and *whoosh!*—the smell of spices, the feeling of hot air—found himself staring into Tutankhamen's chamber. Dom had jammed himself against her side, hardly daring to breathe.

He'd loved the drama and the anguish of the archaeologist's long and fruitless-seeming search. How, only a week before he found the treasures, an exhausted, heartbroken Carter had made the decision to go back to England, and live more sensible dreams. How he'd stumbled on a step that led to Tut's chamber and, looking up, seen the entrance. How he'd walked a couple more steps, found the seal covering the entrance of the tomb, and, breaking it and holding his candle up, seen huge gold couches, jewels, priceless treasures. How the friend waiting outside had asked, "Have you found anything?" and Carter, scarcely able to breathe, had said, "Yes. Wonderful things."

When he'd recovered from measles, Dom spent months scouring the countryside around Woodlees Farm, turning over damp leaves, going through woodpiles, looking for his own buried treasure.

But war had a way of making things squalid. The dun-colored phrasebook handed to serving officers on arrival contained mostly warnings about washing hands, boiling water, guarding wallets, and staying away from local prostitutes, and nothing to do with Egypt's extraordinary past, or for that matter the humbling hospitality of its people. Today, when the boy had fed him the last spoonful of lentil soup, he had placed his hand over his worn winter jumper and said "*Sahtayn*," which he knew from his phrasebook meant "two healths to you."

Later, Karim, the boy's father, came back carrying a battered wooden board. He threw some counters down on the quilt and became tremendously animated trying to explain to Dom the rules of a game, which Dom had never played and failed to understand. It seemed to be some distant relative of drafts, but he couldn't make out the rules, and both of them eventually smiled at each other, embarrassed by their mutual incomprehension.

To break the silence, Dom mimed writing, and paper, praying that this family was not illiterate.

Karim sprang up and fetched an old notebook from behind a jar of rice, which had a pencil and a string attached. Dom drew a picture of an aircraft, and then the sea—when lost in North Africa, the first rule of navigation was a simple one: turn north until you hit the coast. He pointed to himself, and then the sea, and looked inquiringly at Karim.

His chest still felt tight and wheezy, but he couldn't stay for much longer; he could see already how carefully this family eked out its supplies of rice and lentils and corn. He handed his map to Karim—who looked completely bewildered by it. At last he pointed to a spot that Dom estimated would be about forty miles south of Marsa. Dom then drew a train, wondering if one stopped near here. Karim shook his head, and looked confused. He held up four stained fingers, then drew a crude donkey on the page. Four days, or at least that was what Dom thought he'd said.

Karim padded out again, slip-slopping in his broken sandles, and Dom lay scratching himself vigorously. There were bed bugs—though he was used to them by now; mobile dandruff they called them in the squadron, and they didn't bother him unduly. Much more troubling was the thought of now what? He seemed to have reached some frightening state of spiritual and mental emptiness and the idea of going back to the squadron made him feel weak with exhaustion and a peculiar kind of sorrow he could not put his finger on. The curious life the pilots led here—the frantic drinking, the parties in Alex and Cairo then back to the desert for the killing, the bombing raids—had already created a kind of unhappy split in him that was widening.

Meeting Saba had healed the split. She'd made him feel so lucky, so sure, so rescued from the self he was becoming, even though she was not, in conventional terms, what his mother would call "marriage material." It wasn't just her lovely dimples, or her singing, or the way they both shouted with laughter at the same things; she had returned him to something essential in himself—her own passion and self-belief connecting him to the boy he'd been, the boy who'd dreamed of a long and arduous journey toward buried treasure. When he'd confessed to her his plan of one day being able to write as well as fly, that night in the restaurant in Ismailia—a dream he hadn't dared to confess even to Barney—she hadn't looked skeptical, or amazed, or made him feel pretentious; she'd gone out and bought him a pen and notebook. That was how it happened in her world: you did it and you did it until you got it right.

When Ibrahim came bouncing back later that day, he was followed by two toddlers with black curious eyes and runny noses. The boy pulled a long sad face, that mocked Dom's serious expression. He'd brought the board game back with him, and was prepared to try again with the dim *agnabi*. And this time Dom concentrated, wondering if this game was a distant relative of Senet, the board game played by ancient Egyptians, charting their journey toward a longed-for afterlife. An elaborately carved version of this game had been found inside Tutankhamen's tomb.

The boy was babbling passionately now, his dark curls bobbing as he spoke. He placed a bundle of grimy counters in Dom's hand and, pointing to the dark squares, grimaced and rolled his eyes to indicate the terrible disasters that would befall him should one of his counters land there. The pale squares were plainly the good-luck ones, and the boy's expression became secretive and calm as he reached them. Because he was enjoying himself, Dom did, too. A clear case of cheating was overlooked at one point, when the boy skimmed one of his counters over a bad-luck square, his face crafty, only to move it swiftly back, perhaps frightened of antagonizing the gods. And afterward, Dom, thinking he would teach him snakes and ladders, drew out a board on the piece of paper. The boy leaned eagerly toward him, his face bright with anticipation. When the lead in the pencil crumbled beyond repair, the boy gasped with disappointment. There wasn't another.

They sat in silence for a while contemplating this disaster, and then a strange look came over the boy's face. He put his hands to his lips to shush Dom, looked toward the door, and then rushed out.

He returned flushed and breathless ten minutes or so later. He shut the door carefully, sat down on the bed, and drew out of his pocket a stained piece of rag. Inside it were Dom's watch—the glass on its face smashed—his small compass in its leather case, and the pen that Saba had bought him. In the other rag he'd wrapped the three small bottles of tablets: the benzedrine amphetamine, the salt tablets, the water purification tablets—all standard issue in pilot's escape kits. The boy lined them up carefully on the dirt floor.

With a carefully neutral expression, he watched Dom seize the pen and hold it, thrilled to have it in his hands again. When he set the pen down, the boy watched him anxiously as he slipped his index finger between two narrow pieces of leather in the lid of his compass case, and felt for the twenty Egyptian pound notes all pilots were given in case of emergency. They were still there.

He didn't care about the watch. The pen was the most important thing. And the money—the relief he felt at being able to reward the family was overwhelming. He wondered when the right time would be to give it to them, and before he went to sleep that afternoon, tucked it under his pillow.

Daylight was fading into blood-red dusk when he heard the rackety cries of the goats returning, the hollow jangle of their bells. When the boy's father appeared in his room, Dom drew a picture of the sea on the notepad and pointed vigorously toward himself. The boy looked sad, but Karim looked pleased, and even more so when Dom peeled off some of the notes and gave them to him, banging his hand on his heart to show how grateful he was. He owed them his life, and with their help there was a good chance—land mines and bombs notwithstanding—that he could get to wherever home was now.

CHAPTER 46

The next time Mr. Ozan came back, the chauffeur kept the car engine running while he ran up her stairs.

"Now listen." His shrewd black eyes glared at her around the door. "I've been thinking of our talk the other day, and I am going to make you an offer that you may think is cruel. But I am a businessman. I have a show to put on and I want you in it. If you agree, I will help you look for him, and if he is dead," there was no sugar coating this time, "you will know." He glared at her again.

She stared at him. It was seven forty-five in the morning. She was still in her nightdress, which made her feel furious—her instinctive covering of her breasts when what she most wanted was to perform some violent retaliatory act of her own like screaming or striking him violently around the face. His bargain stood for everything she had begun to loathe about show business—its tin-pot values, its selfishness, its determination that the show must go on, no matter what the cost to other people.

"This sounds like blackmail to me," she said.

"It is," he said, discreetly ogling her. "I shall come back tomorrow and you can give me your answer."

"Don't bother, and don't come back," she screamed at him like a wild animal. "They've been looking for him, you stupid man. He's dead, and I'm going home now. My ticket came through last week."

The door slammed, he was gone. She threw on a raincoat and walked down toward the Nile, sobbing with fury. Gharries, cars, donkey carts swept by her, splattering her stockings with rain. Crossing roads, dodging traffic, ignoring wolf whistles from a passing army lorry, her mind flipped back and forth: Ozan was a bully—as bad as the rest of them. What he offered was sleazy and underhanded, a song for a life, or a song for death confirmed.

The stone lions on the Khedive Ibrahim Bridge shone with rain as she passed them; fishermen hung over its sides shrouded in tarpaulins or old newspapers, the Nile flowing beneath them, sluggish and gray in the rain, the twinkling fairy lights on the barges dead as fish eyes. *By the waters of Babylon, there we sat down, yea we wept*—she'd sung these words, set to music by William Walton, with Caradoc once. Her teacher flaming with passion, with something akin to a sorrowful joy, as he told her to feel it, feel it feel it to the nth degree and then rein it back. Looking down at the water, she thought about their first days here. The laughs with Arleta as they'd hurtled in a taxi on their way to that blue-moon night at the Mena House. The rowdy singsongs on the way home; peaceful breakfasts in the courtyard of the Minerva; her first sunglasses, left God knows where and never replaced; the concerts. The richest period of her life so far, in spite of all the hardships. Now she saw nothing but sadness in the expressions of the gaunt old men who sat by their braziers selling trinkets, the bored young soldiers prowling through the waterlogged souks looking for cheap souvenirs to take home. *Yeh, wept, wept! And hanged our harps upon the willow.* The words flew back disjointedly.

I want to die now. The thought was so familiar it no longer shocked her.

She was walking across the bridge with no specific destination in mind when she heard the pattering of feet behind her.

"Saba, stop!" Arleta shouted. Her hair lay in wet strands around her face. "Where are you going?"

"I'm all right—honestly, leave me, I'm fine."

She felt a sort of dispassionate sorrow for Arleta—grief was so boring, too.

"Balls," said Arleta, seeing her face. "Let's get in a taxi and go home."

They were soaked by the time they got back to Antikhana Street. Arleta made some Camp coffee and they wrapped their wet hair in turbans and sat in their dressing gowns in front of a single-bar electric fire.

"Saba." Arleta leaned over and took her hand. "This is no good, you know. You've got to talk to me. You frightened me to death."

She tried to fob Arleta off at first with vague talk about feeling low and wanting to go home.

"Is that all, Sabs?"

"No." She fiddled with the cups for a while. "I've decided not to sing again."

"Oh stop that! You know you don't mean it."

"I do."

"What?" Arleta sounded genuinely shocked.

"I've been thinking for a while, it's not worth it."

"Not worth what?"

"Well, you know, those few rapturous moments." Saba closed her eyes. "It's caused so much pain to the people around me."

"I must warn you, Saba, that you are making no sense to me." Arleta's eyes were slitty and mean.

"And you see, I had this all straight in my mind, that I'd go home, do something else with my life, something—I don't know, teaching or being a librarian or a secretary—that doesn't make you feel guilty, or vain, or stupid, and now Mr. Ozan has made me this offer."

Which she tried to explain even though Arleta's eyes looked lethal, and she was tugging her own hair.

"And you see, now he's left me with no choice," Saba said on a rising note. "I've got to do it: one concert in Alexandria, one in Cairo, and I can't tell you how much I dread it."

"I don't think it will be that hard once you start." Arleta's eyes were open and friendly again, her voice coaxing. "If I'm around, we could do our duet."

"And Ozan does know everyone," Arleta said. "If anyone can find Dom, he can."

"Yes," she said, thinking, *I wish people would stop pretending now.*

"And if you do do it," Arleta was quite lit up now, "I have one suggestion to make—don't get cross—that we track down Madame Eloise again, and that you start eating, that you get out of those blasted pajamas, and we go straight forth to the hairdresser's, because no one wants a girl who is dull with stringy hair."

And Saba smiled for the first time that day.

"You're an idiot," she said. "And I love you."

"Don't go all soppy on me."

"Don't worry, I won't."

They sat talking by the fire for the next hour, Arleta, who had a performance that night at the open-air cinema, winding her hair into pin curls. "Sabs," she said, neatly skewering one with a bobby pin, "since we are having a nose-to-nose, I have one more thing to confess and you mustn't be angry with me."

Saba looked at her.

"Don't hate me," Arleta said, "but I've got a new boyfriend."

"Why should I hate you? Listen, Arlie, just because of Dom doesn't mean I—"

"No, listen, shut up, it's Barney—Dom's friend."

There was a beat of silence while the news sank in.

"Dom's friend. When?" Saba felt a kind of swirling unreality.

"While you were in hospital." Arleta put down her toast. "We met and we talked, and suddenly we were sleeping together."

"Oh, come off it Arl, what do you mean, you were suddenly sleeping together—that's such a stupid expression." Saba was properly angry now. "You don't just *suddenly* sleep with people, like flies who collide in the air, so just say it out loud: we were making love."

"All right: we were making love." Arleta's cat eyes narrowed as she considered this. "Although I wouldn't call it that."

"So what would you call it?"

"A mercy fuck, if you'll excuse my French. He was in a complete state about Dom, and I was so worried about you."

"Oh. So you slept with him because you were worried about me? How very kind."

"Partly, yes. Look, no excuses, but I was in a state myself. I thought you were going to die." Arleta's eyes filled with tears. "And I'm quite fond of you really," she said.

And this was so obviously true now that Saba, trembling with rage, forced herself to calm down. She didn't know Barney, she didn't own him. Her response was unbalanced, like everything else in her life.

"Oh, Arlie, I'm sorry." She gave her a brief hug. "I'm so mean at the moment, I don't know what to do with myself. Do you love him?"

"I could, but it won't do me much good. He's a mess. Anyway, don't you remember, I'm spoken for, and there's the small matter of my little boy." She took the picture out of her pocket; her face crumpled at the sight of his blond curls, his sweet face.

"Ghastly little varmint," she said.

"Maybe you should tell Barney—wouldn't he be pleased?"

"I don't think so." It was Arleta's turn to sound bleak. "Men don't usually find other men's children a great aphrodisiac."

"But if he loves you . . ." She couldn't help it, she felt a deep dismay at this—it seemed so unfair. "He might. It would be nice to have a family after the war."

"No. Lovely thought," Arleta was quite decisive, "but let's keep our feet on the ground: the man isn't thinking of me as wife material; practically every friend he has ever had has died and I am like a sucky blanket for him, and that's fine. I'm ten years older than him, and he's in so much shock about your fellow, he can hardly think straight. There was another one, too, called Jacko. Did Dom talk about him?"

"No."

"They were all at school together?"

"Yes."

They both looked toward the window. A muezzin was calling out the evening prayers. The sky had flushed with the dying sun, and turned the tips of the houses opposite into rose-colored castles.

"Barney said he was shot down, and that Dom blamed himself for it, and that he shouldn't."

"Bit late for that. Poor Dom."

"Poor everyone," said Arleta. "War is so bloody awful. I don't know why men like it so much." She gave a huge sigh and put her hair net on.

"Tell me something else," Saba said. "Does Barney know about me?"

"A little, I think."

"He must hate me. Dom must have told him how I left."

Arleta's silence said it all.

"It was tricky," she said at last. "I told him what I could about your

Turkish adventure. I'm not sure he believed me. Come on, love." Arleta stood up abruptly, her face full of a sadness Saba had never seen before. She put the photo of her little boy into her vanity case. "Let's switch dem lights off and get you to bed."

When Saba woke, around two in the morning, it was pitch-black outside their window and she was thinking about Arleta's fiancé Bill, a man Arleta rarely mentioned now. She wondered if Bill was dead already, or comforting himself with someone else, or back home in pieces with his mum, and for those few moments she saw war as a vast fracturing mirror shattering all their lives.

CHAPTER 47

When he left the tent for the last time, the woman who had been cooking his beans and his flatbread appeared quickly in the mouth of the tent as a pair of liquid, curious brown eyes that stared, blinked, and, in response to her husband's sharp bark, hurriedly disappeared.

Karim and the boy helped Dom onto a donkey laden with saddlebags. Today Karim was wearing a pair of broken-down sandals patched from what looked like old car tire; Ibrahim, who led the donkey, had a definite air of swagger about him. He was wearing his best clothes: a spotless, perfectly ironed djellaba, on his head a long scarf wound over and around a woolen cap.

Karim waved his hands at the horizon indicating that this would be a long journey; Dom thought he heard him say Marsa Matruh, but could not be sure; the way the locals pronounced their words was so different, and the long discussion that had followed made him cough.

It was a bright, cold day. For the first hour he saw nothing but the desert stretching around him and the occasional blighted tree. He could feel the boy at his side, casting anxious, furtive looks in his direction. They were friends now—Dom had found a piece of paper in his pocket and made him paper airplanes, and after the first shy overtures, the boy had brought his board back and they'd made up all kinds of games on it together.

After nearly four hours' walk, the dust road became tarmac and he saw the dusty sign ahead of him. It was Marsa and quicker than he'd anticipated. There was a railway station there. He was back in civilization again, or some approximation of it.

He pointed to it, put his thumbs up, tried to smile, but what he felt most was a profound sadness and shame. On his way here, he'd seen through their eyes the destruction of the land all around: the charred jeeps abandoned by the roadside; the shattered pavements, the aircraft looking like a broken pterodactyl, half-buried in the sand.

The boy seemed excited at the adventure of going into town, but Karim, after looking around him, gave Dom the strangest look, a wry shrug, as if to say *What can you do? This is life and life only.* And Dom thought again of his own elation when he'd dropped bombs on a fuel dump not far from here; the time when the Karims and Ibrahims of this world were tiny toys on the ground. They owed him nothing.

The railway station was on the edge of the town. As they drew closer, Ibrahim's frail shoulders began to droop, and his eyes grew frightened. It was clear he hadn't been this far before.

When they reached the ticket office, Dom got down from the donkey. There were British and Australian soldiers walking on the pavements, some of them watching him, and he was beginning to feel self-conscious in the djellaba they'd given him to travel in. The boy was grinning and jiggling around in the dust; Karim touched him lightly on the arm.

And though already half-back in his world again, what Dom most wanted looking at them for the last time was to kneel at their feet and thank them over and over again for their incredible kindness.

"Here." He pulled out the leather compass case. The beautiful old-fashioned compass with its scratched leather case and faded mauve velvet lining had once belonged to his father. There were still fourteen Egyptian pounds inside its lid. He peeled off four pounds for himself and handed the rest to Karim—at least they would have a decent meal here and buy some provisions, and perhaps a bundle of alfalfa for the donkey who stood patiently by.

"This," he said to Ibrahim, "is for you." He handed him the compass and the case. The boy looked completely stunned. He bit his lip as he stared at it, then he looked at his father who was smiling. "For you." Dom closed the boy's fingers over his gift. "*Sukran.*" He held his own hand over his heart, and when they had turned watched the small boy, the man, the donkey get smaller and smaller until they'd dissolved in dust and heat. That was it. They'd said good-bye. Dom was saved; it didn't feel like it.

* * *

Inside the station, he bought a one-way ticket to Alex, a two-hour journey from Marsa. Alex was the last place on earth that Dom wanted to be without Saba, but he had no choice. He didn't have enough money to get to Cairo, and he would be close to the squadron there.

When he arrived, he found a cheap hotel near the Rue Nebi Daniel called the Waterloo. It looked like a dive from the outside, but the bedrooms were clean and quiet, and it was cheap and perfect for his purpose, which was sleep, which he did for close to thirteen hours. When he woke up, he gazed in bewilderment at a long flypaper, covered in dead insects, hanging from the ceiling; at the rough walls. He was out of time and out of place and the dust-covered robe that lay on the floor seemed to belong to someone else.

He was staggeringly tired. The early starts, the late nights, the shock of being shot down, the chest infection that had left him wheezing and weak, had caught up with him. His back still ached from the donkey ride, and he felt light-headed and unreal as he walked out into the street near his hotel. Two doors down, in a dim little shop whirring with sewing machines, a tailor sold him a pair of Western trousers and a white shirt. His flying boots he transformed into black shoes by ripping off the detachable sheepskin on the calf—grateful now for the clever bod at the MOD who'd come up with this idea of inconspicuous shoes for men on the run. Next door to the tailor was a Greek barber who shaved him with a cut-throat razor, heating the water in a little brazier next to his chair, and touching his face afterward with a cologne that smelled of sandalwood.

The clothes, the shave gave him a sense of being in slightly clearer focus. After two cups of coffee he returned to his hotel and phoned the squadron to tell them he was back.

"That's good news, sir," the voice at the end of the phone said with no notable surprise or emotion. When he was told that Barney was in Suez, training, and Rivers had gone, he felt relieved rather than sorry. He couldn't face them yet. Too bloody feeble was how he put it to himself, furious at his weakness.

He was about to hang up when another, more authoritative voice came on the line. A hearty, rushed voice, saying he was Dom's replacement, Tom Philips.

"Wonderful news you're back," the voice boomed. "I expect . . ." The line filled with static, so he couldn't hear the rest, but it sounded effusive. And then in a roar, "Do you need medical treatment? I repeat. Do. You. Need. Medical treatment? Over."

Dom said no. After the burns hospital he couldn't stand the thought of being incarcerated again.

"I'd like to take a week's leave," he shouted back. "I've got reasonable digs here." He gave his new address, received in another staticky roar.

Some version of the message must have got through. Two days later, the squadron's padre came to see him, a whispery, sympathetic man with bad breath. He'd had a wretched bout of pneumonia himself last year, he confided in an eggy blast. He advised Dom not to overdo it. He'd had a word with the CO before coming to see him, he added, and with Tom Philips. They both thought Dom should take a couple of weeks' leave. There had been a nasty outbreak of influenza at Wadi Natrun and several landing grounds, and it was pretty quiet here anyway now that the Germans had retreated to Tunis.

The padre brought a care package with him: some clean clothes, a month's back pay, and a copy of the *Bugle,* a forces newspaper that advertised local goings-on. Then he broke the wary silence that followed with what sounded like a warmed-up sermon.

"I think Alexandria has something to teach all of us about resilience," he said. "Nothing but invasions since Alexander came in 332 BC. First him, then the Romans, then, well, I've forgotten who next, but now look at 'em. Back on their feet again. New buildings going up already, roads being built, concerts, music, marvelous. I brought you this in case you want some distraction."

He pointed toward a line of advertisements in the *Bugle*'s entertainments section.

Dom skimmed his eyes down the page, desperate for the old bore to bugger off.

And saw her name.

Saba Tarcan.

The other names—Faiza Mushawar, Bagley, Arleta, Asmahan—scrambled in front of his eyes.

What a thing, he told himself, too shocked to feel angry. What a thing! She'd been here all along. Not posted, or gone home, or any of the other excuses he'd made for her. Here in Egypt all along, working and almost certainly with a new man.

He smiled and shook the padre's hand.

"Very good of you to come. Goodbye."

When he was gone, Dom needed to walk. On the steps of the hotel, he turned right, toward the tram station, watching people flowing in and out of it, from gloom to brilliant winter sunshine.

Not so bad, not so bad. He was testing himself like a man trying to walk on a badly broken leg. A train would carry him away soon—away from Alexandria, away from North Africa. He'd go back to England and start another kind of life.

He turned away from the station and walked down toward the sea. The padre was right, he noted pleasantly to himself, Alex was showing signs of speedy recovery. Although the blackout was still officially in place, some of the blue paint that had covered the streetlights had been scrubbed off. A team of gardeners were planting seedlings in the municipal gardens, workmen were banging their hammers again, restoring the charred buildings. He could fight it, too—all the dying and dead friends, the false hopes, the bogus emotions. He would not fall into the trap of useless nostalgia. When it was over, it was over.

At the corner of Rue Fuad a legless boy stretched out a hand to him.

"Long live Mrs. Queen and the Royal Dukes of England."

Dom dropped a coin into his cup, and walked on.

If it did hurt, he had only himself to blame. After his desert prang, he'd come undone for a while, he could see that now. Lying in bed in Karim's tent, he'd wanted to think his life out clearly, but all that time her songs had played underneath his conscious mind—like a bridge from one thought to the next, a way of talking, deeper than words. And he'd kept the songs playing because he knew he could not keep going without her.

Back there, with the desert stretching all around him, the vast sky above, he'd seen something so clearly. That all human beings were lonely and separated creatures who needed each other, as he'd needed her—whether a mirage or real hadn't seemed to matter.

At night, before he went to sleep, he'd focused the whole thing in his mind like a series of scenes in a film: Saba lying in the bath singing "Louisville Lou" to him; the sight of her inexpertly washing his socks and putting them on hangers; the sudden breathless joy of catching her eye across a room and seeing her face light up. Oh, and it had gone on: dreams about the twins again, a cottage in the country, friends around a table for dinner, the whole thing played forward, not backward, so they could have a future together.

Complete balls. He must stop that now. In the real world, mirages could kill you, they could eat up a life.

A light rain began to fall. He turned his collar up and, fixing his eyes on the sea, set off at a brisk pace, thinking he must build up his strength and go back to the squadron soon, but inside he was like a man stumbling from bog to bog, because everywhere reminded him of her. There was the shop where he'd bought the blue bracelet from the fat jeweler with the glass eye who'd told him about the goddesses, and there the cafe where they'd drunk wine one night, when the old man had played an oud and then, as a special treat for her, a record by Asmahan, and she'd listened, completely enchanted. And there was the corner of the street where they'd hugged each other before she'd disappeared into the crowd, as it turned out forever. And around the next corner, the house on Rue Lepsius where he'd sobbed uncontrollably on the night she left—a memory that made him wince with shame. It must not happen again.

Take it! he told himself. *Take it, take it, take it!* The hour had passed.

CHAPTER 48

When Mr. Ozan got permission to hold his gala concert in the grounds of the Montazah Palace, he let out a bellow of delight like a young bull let loose in a field of cows. The Royal Summer Palace with its fairy-tale turrets and towers, its panoramic views of the Mediterranean, and its fabulous Turko-Florentine-style gardens, was the perfect setting for what was to be the concert of the year—no, the decade. Tickets would be free—this was his present to Alexandria. Interviewed by the *Egyptian Gazette,* Ozan's black eyes had filled with tears when he quoted the old Arabian proverb: " 'If you have much, give of your wealth, if you have little, give of your heart.' I am giving of both," he'd said, omitting to add that the concert would also be the perfect knockout blow against Ya'qub Halabi, the Cairo impresario with whom he competed fiercely.

Preparations began immediately: Luc Lefevre, a well-known Parisian artist, designed a superb art-nouveau-style poster, with the Pharos lighthouse beaming out again, and the caption: *Dance Alexandria Dance.*

A Cairo tent-maker made an elaborate outdoor stage designed to look like the interior of an exotic Bedouin tent; sewing machines whirred in the souks to fill it with sumptuous embroidered drapes and cushions, and in the Attarine souk, three glassblowers worked around the clock to make over two thousand specially designed glass lights to be filled with candles and hung like fireflies from the trees.

For the party afterward, crates of Haut-Brion 1924 and Fonseca 1912, and raki and cognac were ordered for the guests. Madame Eloise, who was promoted to chief costume designer, hired in five extra seamstresses, and became grandly French again and prone to soliloquies about Patou.

And in the streets, the souks, and the coffee shops of Manshiya and

Karmuz people talked of little else: after three years of being bombed, and often hungry and afraid, Alexandria was ready for a party.

I can do this, Dom thought on the day of the concert: I can go back to the squadron—or to Cairo for the few days' leave still owing. That morning, wandering through the Palace Gardens, he'd watched a team of excitable workmen slotting together the steel struts that formed the frame of the tented stage. Yards of embroidered fabrics were flung to hide the ugly skeleton underneath, then long skeins of colored lights were threaded in and out of the trees, and bit by bit an empty patch of grass was filled by a magical and illusory world, a patch that, he reminded himself, would be empty again when they took it all down.

No self-pity, he thought, walking back to his hotel. *No looking back*. This was her world and he was well out of it, and he thoroughly disliked himself like this—desiring and undesired, indecisive. He wanted his old self back. In the distance he could still hear music playing, and then the boom and retreat of a voice testing a microphone: "*Wahd, athnan, thlathh, rb'h, khmsh* . . ." Thanks to Ibrahim, he could count up to twenty fluently now.

And hearing the music, his mind changed again: he could do this, he could stay . . . but *Why go through it?* another part of him argued. What he most needed now was to get back to the squadron, to fly again, to talk to what friends remained, to bed down again in his own reality. A different kind of longing, but just as fierce in its way.

When he went to the railway station to check on train times to Cairo, a smiling ticket clerk told him not to bother to book. Who in their right mind, his wry expression signaled, would want to leave Alex on a night like this?

When twilight fell, he stood on his own at the edge of a jostling and excited crowd, wanting to die of misery.

At the last possible moment, he'd stepped off the train. He wanted to hear her sing one more time; it felt like a vital necessity. The sensible side of him had tried to fashion this into a rational decision. Why not? The clerk was right, it was a historical event; he could go as a disinterested observer, not speak to her, not make his presence known, be simply one of the anonymous crowd already flowing like a river toward the trams and the gharries that would take them to the Palace Gardens.

He knew where she was staying. Earlier that afternoon, he'd followed her in a taxi from the gardens to the small smart private hotel on the Corniche. She'd come up in the world, he noted wryly, remembering her humorous description of that grim little London bed and breakfast before her first audition.

It would have been fun to share these things with her. Now it felt squalid following her, like a private detective, and he'd disliked himself exceedingly for doing so. With his collar up, and camouflaged by a crowd in a holiday mood, he'd watched her leave the hotel, half an hour later, cross the road and sit down by herself on a bench overlooking the bay. She was wearing a dark crimson coat, a velvet hat. She'd looked small sitting against the vast sweep of the sky. She'd shielded her eyes with her hand and looked out to the sea, which was choppy. *You shouldn't be here on your own. It's still dangerous in Alexandria,* he'd told her. *All of us think we lead charmed lives but we don't.*

And then, in a flood of bitterness: *If you'd really wanted to find me, it would have been so easy: you could have phoned the squadron, left a proper letter, left a message with one of your friends.*

He'd almost crossed the road. He might have tapped her on the shoulder and said lightly: "What a coincidence—fancy meeting you here again." Banter might have followed, shrieks of embarrassed laughter. It would not seem at all extraordinary him being in Alex on a night like tonight. He would tell her he was here with the squadron, tell the heart-wrenching tale of being shot down again and rescued in the desert, show her what dangerous and important things took place in the real world.

He took a deep breath, put his toe over the curb and pulled it back again. He imagined her polite double take, the look of panic in her eyes—*Damn, trapped*—a muddled explanation, insincere concern for him—theatricals were good at that. *Darling sweetie pie, what happened? Gosh, so thin! Poor little pet!* Et cetera, except, of course, she'd never really been like that, and what he'd liked about her at first was how straight she'd seemed, which made the trap all the more cleverly disguised.

This was all going through his head when a new agony presented itself. A youngish man—twenty-five, thirty? Hard to tell from this distance—had approached her from the western end of the Corniche. A blond, long-legged fellow, walking toward her—a civilian arty type by the looks of his pale linen suit and lolloping gait. She turned and looked at him—Dom was almost certain she smiled. He'd sat down on the bench beside her. They talked intently, heads together, a stream of words for what felt like a long, long time. A lovers' quarrel? An insistent fan? A new admirer pressing his suit? Impossible to tell. The only thing he must get into his big fat head now was that there would always be men, and they would want to get close to her.

The man stood up; a small boy, a Corniche hawker, approached them, head winningly on one side, to offering souvenirs. She shook her head. The man bowed at her slightly, and raised his hat. He walked off briskly in the direction he'd come from.

Alone again, she'd stood up and looked toward the sea, and then turned her back to it. He'd winced as he watched her fling herself into the busy traffic to cross the road. He'd hidden in a dark alleyway beside the hotel as she climbed its stairs and closed the big brass doors behind her.

She's gone, he'd told himself trembling. Nothing to do with me now.

One or two of the local newspapers had questioned the wisdom of having an outdoor concert in Alex in the middle of winter, and in truth, before the war, and the blackout, had properly ended, but Ozan's confident prediction that the gods would smile on them was correct (oh, how Ya'qub Halabi would gnash his teeth!) because on the night he'd planned, 17 January, the sun set in a molten lava flow of pinks, golds, and oranges, followed by a calm, cold night and a sky full of stars.

By the time it grew dark, the streets were jammed with people making their way down the Corniche, by tram, donkey, gharry, and taxi to the Palace Gardens.

The stones surrounding the statues of Muhammad Ali Pasha were taken down, garlands of flowers left in their place. By eight o'clock, the air in the Palace Gardens was full of the smells of roasting meat and fried chickpeas. Sleepy black-eyed children were hoisted onto their parents' shoulders and given sweets and dates to eat. Old grandpas in djellabas were propped up by their young. Crowds of English and New Zealanders, Indian soldiers, a Scottish piper with his bagpipes were there, and the ATS girls, nurses bused in from local field and military hospitals. And whatever hard feelings (and there were many) remained between the British, the Egyptians, the Jews, the Greeks, the Arabs who were there, they were put off for this one night. Tonight the whole city was breathing a collective sigh of relief: with luck and a fair wind it looked like they'd come through. Tonight was for singing and dancing.

Ten minutes before the curtain went up, the jugglers who'd wandered through the crowd stopped juggling and the lutists who'd been singing the old Arabic songs put away their instruments, and a rapt silence fell over the crowd.

Ozan, working on the principle of nothing succeeds like excess, had gone magnificently overboard, and when the curtain slowly rose on the stage, it appeared to open a fantastic jewelry box. When dancers rose up from the cushions, and the stage began to pulsate with color and glitter and noise, the crowd gasped and groaned with delight. This was living; this was what they'd come for. An orchestra of twenty-five handpicked musicians playing ouds and lutes and violins burst into a frenzy of notes. The crowd yelled, some of the women made strange wild sounds with their tongues.

At the back of the stage, the spotlight suddenly fell on a large mother-of-pearl Aladdin's chest, and there were drum rolls and the shimmering of tambourines as Ozan stepped out. He was wearing one of the beautiful dinner suits his Parisian tailor had made before the war, and a purple cummerbund. He bounded toward the front of the stage, held his hands up to quell the madly cheering crowd, issued a torrent of Arabic words that made them cheer and clap and wave their flags, and then he roared out into the night:

"Dance, Alexandria, dance, Hitler has no chance."

* * *

Longing to leave, rooted to the spot, Dom waited for her. There was no program, or none that he had been able to understand, and he had stayed away from the groups of European people. He sat through the fireworks, the acrobats, the incomprehensible Arabic comedian who had the audience howling with laughter; Faiza Mushawar, exuding a kind of haughty self-confidence; Arleta, singing and wiggling and making the Tommies hoot and yell.

When Saba came on stage after the first interval, he almost stopped breathing. She was wearing a new red dress, her hair was loose. In spite of all the nonsense that had gone on between them, his guts twisted for her. The crowd seemed enormous and she looked so small. There were only three Europeans in her backing group: a pianist, a guitarist, and a double bassist.

The crowd hushed as they began to tune up. She turned and smiled at the pianist, gave him a nod of her head. He felt the surprise of the crowd around him as she sang what sounded like an Arabic song, but he couldn't be sure. He was so hurt, and helplessly admiring, too. She seemed so foreign, so focused, so sure of herself and the night. Around him the fairy lights shivered in the dark trees that swayed and sighed, and the crowd moved with them, the guitarist threw soft notes at her, the pianist looked quietly ecstatic and so did she. What could I possibly have added to that? he thought.

When the song was done, it took a while for the whooping and clapping to die down, and then the guitarist noodled away on his guitar and the lights around the stage faded to a more intimate glow. She sat down on a stool near the piano, and announced matter-of-factly that her next song would be "Smoke Gets in Your Eyes."

Their song. The song she'd sung for him.

As she held the microphone and told her secrets, he felt a sick fury spread through his body. How could you? A million stupid songs to sing, and you chose this one. She seemed to be breathing the song and yet he could hear every word.

When it was over, she looked up, her face like a holy painting in its sadness. A triumph of training and technique and controlled emotion, no running out of air, no false notes—nothing for him, everything for the cheering crowd.

He took a step back. This night would soon be over, he told himself; by this time next year, they would all have packed up their tents and gone home.

He sat under a tree with his head in his hands. Oh Christ! he thought, clenching his teeth tight. *Don't you dare.*

The moon had risen to its furthest height now over the Palace Gardens. It cast its glow over the trees, and the turreted fairy-tale towers at the back of the stage. When the show was over, the principal characters bounded onto the stage again and took their bows like performers in a pantomime. First the Egyptian band, waving and cheering; the local acrobats doing five handstands and a twist apiece; followed by Boguslaw and Lev; Max Bagley clasping his hands in triumph above his head like a prize fighter; Arleta Samson walking her fabulous walk, touching her crimson nails to her mouth and sending out passionate kisses; three Arab horses in scarlet bridles trotting, the fire-eaters; Faiza Mushawar, regal and with a small but distinct distance separating her from the Europeans; then Saba, now in a silver dress, smiling and waving and having the time of her life, graciously accepting the elaborate salaams of the clowns.

And lastly Ozan, hands held out in modest protest at the roar of love and appreciation that greeted him. After what Dom presumed was the Egyptian national anthem and "God Save the Queen," three dozen white doves of peace were released from the bamboo cages they'd been kept in backstage all day. The flustered birds rose in the darkening air, hovered in lights that tinted them red and green, circled, and flew toward the sea.

Dom glanced toward the man who had released the birds and saw him smiling broadly; he didn't give a damn whether they came back or not. Their point was theatrical effect, their usefulness over; that was the way it was in show business it seemed. One showy gesture and they were gone.

CHAPTER 49

The pavements of the Corniche were crowded after the performance, so she took a gharry, pleading with the driver to go as fast as he could. The horse kept shying, frightened by the commotion, and when they got close to the Cecil Hotel, where Cleeve had requested one last meeting, they were held up by drunken soldiers dancing a conga line.

Cleeve had told her to meet him in the cocktail bar, to the right of the hotel's reception area and lifts. Since everyone would still be leaving the concert, it would be quiet and he had some news for her. No need for disguises now, he said, they would simply appear as a couple having a few drinks together.

It seemed to her, as she walked into the hotel with its subdued gleam of well-polished brass, its marble floors and copious flower arrangements, that Cleeve was back in his natural habitat again. In the candlelit bar, beyond the lobby, an elegant negro in a dinner jacket was noodling away at a piano underneath a potted palm tree. She could hear the clink of glasses, the murmur of well-bred voices, and there was Cleeve himself, partly concealed behind a leather banquette, elegant, long-legged, languid, the kind of well-dressed Englishman who contrived to look as if he didn't give a hoot about his clothes, quietly taking it all in.

But that first impression of ease and sophistication didn't last. When he saw her, he leapt to his feet and switched on a quick bright smile—like a gauche boy on his first date—and she saw, above the faultless linen of his shirt, a dried-up trickle of blood where he had shaved too closely. There'd been no time to change after the concert, so she arrived in the same beautiful silver dress she'd taken the curtain call in, her shoulders covered in a fine floating silk stole.

"Saba," he said. "You look wonderful. Gosh, you've grown up."

The fulsome compliment threw her; his smile, lopsided, sentimental, raised alarm bells. Was he drunk?

"I'm sorry I'm late, and I can't stay long." She slid into the banquette beside him. "Ozan's giving a cast party—he's asked all the local bigwigs and I can't let him down."

"Of course, of course . . . it's just that I was passing through Alexandria, and I couldn't . . . I felt it was my last . . ." He abandoned this and blathered helplessly, "Look, before I say a word, Saba . . . I mean I've got to . . . well, I'll just say it: what an absolutely fantastic night this must have been for you. I've heard you before but this . . . you were extraordinary—I shan't forget it ever, that's all. There, I've said it. Sort of."

"Thank you." It was hard to see him so lit up when she felt so empty.

"Darling, are you all right . . . what's wrong with me . . . a drink?" His hand went up for the waiter. "It must be jolly tiring." He'd never called her darling before; the word hung awkwardly between them.

"Waiter," he said. "Champagne, hors d'oeuvres, a menu for mademoiselle."

"I can't stay to eat," she repeated. "Did you say you had some news for me?"

"I did. But surely time for a small bite—there's a terrific new chef here."

"Dermot, honestly, I can't," she said more firmly. "It's a working night for me."

"So, all right, sorry, crack on," a note of truculence in his voice. "Here's my news."

He looked around him, checking the other drinkers were well out of earshot, his face wavering through the candlelight.

"Jenke is back in London and has been debriefed. I can't be absolutely specific with you for security reasons, but his information, not just from Turkey but from North Africa, too, has been absolutely vital . . . and you"—he gave her his important finger-on-the-pulse look—"I'm here to tell you that your part in the operation has been noted at the very highest levels. How do you feel about that?"

A slight swelling of piano music from behind the palm tree; their waiter appeared flapping a napkin on her lap. She waited until he left.

"How do I feel about what?"

"About being . . . I don't know . . . how should one put it . . . is heroine too much of an exaggeration?"

"Nothing," she said finally, "I feel nothing."

"Really?" He took a sip of his drink, gave her a quizzical look. "Why not?"

"I don't know." Because the price was too high, because I wasn't particularly brave, more a child drawn into adult games I didn't understand, because the whole thing finally felt sleazy; because it cost me Dom—all this flashed through her head.

He shook his head slightly, with the air of a schoolmaster regretting the wasted talents of a bright pupil.

"Well," he said huffily. "I obviously can't tell you what to think, but I would have thought it was an honor."

"Tell me something." She spoke before the thought had formed in her brain. "Was it really worth it? Or is it something people who get caught up in this sort of thing need to feel—particularly when other people die?"

"I don't understand the question."

"You should do, or at least ask it."

He drained his drink.

"Steady, Saba," he warned her, and gave her the most peculiar look—canny and spiteful and affronted. "No, seriously, steady the buffs, because I have some other news to pass on to you, and you might say something you'll regret."

She took a deep breath and stared at her glass. Calm down, Saba, it's not his fault what happened.

"Really?"

He lowered his voice—the pianist had stopped playing.

"Really."

"What news?"

He took a deep breath and called the waiter over.

"Another whiskey for me, please, and for mademoiselle?"

She put her hand over her champagne flute.

"No, Dermot, please—just order for yourself. I have to go soon."

"I think you'll want to stay for this, Saba."

He leaned toward her and licked his lips.

"They've found him," he whispered. "Your man . . . he's in Alex."

"What man?" He looked so serious she thought for one mad moment he meant Severin Mueller. "Who?"

"Your pilot."

"My pilot?" Nothing in his expression suggested good news. "Jenke?"

"No, not Jenke," he said at last. "Dominic Benson. He's staying at the Waterloo. It's a small private hotel near the railway station. He's been there for nearly a fortnight."

"Is this a joke?" She felt a tremendous numbness, as if all the feeling parts of her were closing down. "How do you know?"

"Because I've been looking for him. Ozan asked me to."

"But you said you couldn't or wouldn't."

He pushed the ice around in his whiskey with his finger.

"I was told to say that. We didn't want you derailed before the concert, but for God's sake, Saba, don't tell anyone I told you that."

"Is this true?"

He nodded his head and sighed.

"Saw him in the street yesterday. He saw me talking to you. And so, Saba," he drained his drink and stubbed his cigarette out, "as the good fairy says in the pantomime: my job here is ended. News of honors and boyfriend in one evening. Or perhaps I'm more the Widow Twankey in this enterprise. Anyway, if it goes wrong, you know where to find me. I'm going back to England shortly."

He stood up, still smiling, and when he tried to put his overcoat on missed the arm. He looked in an owlish, deliberate way at his wristwatch.

"Crikey! *Tempus fugit.* I expect you'll want to dash off now. I can't give you a lift, I'm afraid, I'm wanted in another part of town. Here's the address. Tell him from me he's a lucky man."

As he scribbled down words on a piece of paper, the news began to percolate through her brain and into her blood and down her spine to her nerve endings.

"Dermot," she smiled at him radiantly, "is it true?"

He held two fingers up. "Scout's honor."

"Really true?"

"Yep."

She stared at him.

"Thank you, from the bottom of my heart." She would forgive him, had already, for delaying the news until after the concert. It wasn't as if Ozan hadn't warned her what his priorities were.

"And if it all goes wrong," he put some soiled notes on the table for the waiter, and tucked a piece of paper in her hand, "give your old Uncle Dermot a ring." He picked up his hat. "It's my sister's address in England—shouldn't really give it to you, but what the hell. I doubt you'll use it."

Alive! As she stepped out into the street again and looked at the address, she didn't know whether to laugh or scream or cry. Dom was alive! and in Alexandria. All around her the streets pulsated with crowds and street musicians, dancing, singing, shouting. A bonfire burned in one of the city gardens, its sparks flying into the night. No possible chance of a taxi now. She dashed up the street, propelled by a starry elation, and terror, too. What if she'd missed her chance? Or he had another girl now and didn't want to see her.

When she stopped near the statue of Muhammad Ali Pasha, her chest was heaving.

Hotel Waterloo, she read from the note Cleeve had thrust into her hand. *Off Rue Nebi Daniel, near railway station.*

After half an hour of frantic searching, she found the hotel in a dilapidated street, wedged between a barber's shop and a Syrian bakery.

Inside the deserted lobby, the night porter was reading the evening paper.

"Where is he?" she said when she had caught her breath. "Dominic Benson. He's staying here."

The man looked at her in amazement. A goddess in a silver dress, her sandals filled with dirt and litter, and then he recognized her.

"Madame, madame?" His eyes lit up. "Your singing was very good. Write your name, *merci.*" He thrust a piece of paper at her. "Special for me."

She wrote her name wildly.

"Help me," she said. "Please help me. I'm looking for someone."

"Who?" He was confused.

"Dominic Benson. He's a guest here."

He opened a drawer under the desk, and pulling out a dusty ledger, took an agonizing time locating the page, the day.

"No, madame," he shook his head regretfully, "no here. Not now. Tonight . . ." he mimed the carrying of suitcases, "he's gone to Cairo."

"When, when?" She grabbed his wrist, pointed at his watch. "When train?"

He shrugged. "One hour." He shrugged again. "Two hours, maybe. Train special for concert. Sorry."

The city's main railway station, the Misr, was roughly a mile away from her. She took a taxi, abandoned it when it got stuck in traffic, ran flat out toward the station, her feet sinking into rubbish and horse manure, broken pavements, stones.

When she got to the station, a line of carriage horses stood in a row outside it munching grain from hoods that made them look like prisoners about to be executed. Gasping for air, she ran in and out of them, into a station heaving with people. Searching the crowd for European faces, she saw a group of Scottish soldiers standing near the ticket desk.

"Cairo train," she blurted out.

"Don't break a leg, love," a kilted soldier warned her. "The train's gone, it's just left . . . Hang on . . . hang on." He swayed around, looking at her. "Were ye not at the—"

"Where? Where?" she shouted.

"Platform two," they replied in unison.

She ran toward it, past bundles of sleeping beggars, and drunken partygoers, young lovers, soldiers, a peasant farmer carrying his bed on his back, and saw the backside of the train steaming down a long track into a tangle of wires and shattered suburbs, and then on to nowhere.

She stood on the platform in her beautiful wrecked silver dress, her white stole floating wildly in the updraft.

"Stop the bloody train!" she shouted in a Welsh roar designed to carry from valley to valley. "*Stop it! Stop it! Stop it!* Right now!" She tripped and almost fell as she pounded down the platform after it. The train kept going, out of the gloom of the station and into the night, until at the very last minute a porter standing outside the final carriage saw her: a screaming houri in a white robe leaping through smoke.

He shrieked over and over again, dashed inside, pulled the red emergency cord. The train came to a creaking halt.

Under normal circumstances, it might have been a punishable offense, but the mood in the city that night was defiantly playful. People hung from the windows laughing, cheering as she jumped onto a train still wheezing and protesting at its reversal. She ran down cramped corridors calling his name, and through the glass carriage doors peered at strangers: men in tarbooshes and bowler hats and turbans; families tucking down for the night; a group of soldiers who waved and cheered at her.

When she found him, he was sitting by the window in the last carriage but one. She wasn't even sure it was him at first. He looked older, thinner. Before he turned and saw her there, she saw him sigh.

"Dom." She walked up to him and touched his face. She could hear the grumble of the engine about to start again. The guards shouting. "Get off the train."

"Saba." When he looked at her, there was nothing but pain and confusion in his eyes. "What's this? What's going on?"

"For God's sake, Dom, get off the train—it's moving." She felt it throbbing underneath her feet.

"No," he said. "Not like this."

She stood on the seat, stretched above him, tore down his case and threw it through the window onto the platform.

"I can explain, Dom," she shouted, as the platform moved away. "*Get off the train!*"

Three soldiers leaned from their carriages as they stepped from the train, and stared goggle-eyed at the girl on the platform in the sensational dress having a humdinger of a row with her boyfriend.

"There's no point," Dom yelled over the noise of the engine. "Because it's not a stupid game for me."

"Dom, please," she said. "Shut up and walk with me."

It was too noisy to talk in the station. They stomped off down the street and toward his hotel, she still holding his suitcase.

On the corner of the street, he stopped.

"Saba, listen," he said, his eyes very black under the streetlamp. "I've made up my mind, I don't want it like this . . . it's not possible. I waited for you, it nearly killed me. Where for Christ's sake did you go? Honest answer for once."

"Fine." She slammed his suitcase down. "Honest answer. I went to a party."

"A party?"

They looked at each other in hysterical disbelief.

"Oh for pity's sake," he said. "Well, everything's perfectly clear now. Thank you for at least being straight with me."

"Dom." The strap of her sandal had loosened and she had to hobble to keep up with him. "The party was in Turkey."

"Oh fine." He set his jaw and stepped up the pace. "Fantastic. Terrific. The party was in Turkey. I feel much better already."

"Listen, you blasted nitwit," she yelled. They were passing a small back-street bar where some young naval officers were drinking. "Take me back to your room," she shouted, "and I'll tell you what happened."

"*Woo-hoo*," came from the direction of the naval boys, who were spilling onto the pavement, and from one: "I wouldn't turn that one down, mate!"

"Fuck off," Dom shouted.

Back at the Waterloo Hotel, they walked up the dimly lit stairs like sleepwalkers. A new receptionist, half asleep at the desk, gave them a new key, a new room, no questions asked. Upstairs, Dom switched on a tasseled bedside light. There was only one wooden chair, next to a sink, so they sat side by side on the bed.

"Saba, listen to me," he said. He took hold of both her wrists in his hands and looked into her eyes very seriously. "We're here because it's a quiet place to talk, but before you say a word, I saw you with a man earlier—if you're otherwise engaged, don't bother making up a story, because you see, at the risk of sounding dramatic, or a little bit theatrical myself, I don't want to go through this again, and I'm not going to."

"Dom." The simple miracle of him being there was starting to break through.

"Don't." He stood up and walked to the chair, that was as far away from her as possible.

So she told him what she could about Istanbul and Ozan, Cleeve.

He listened with no change of expression, and then:

"Saba, are you serious?" he said. "Did they give you a toupee and false glasses?"

"Deadly serious." She put her hand over his mouth. "There's more."

She told him about the German parties, but not about Severin. She couldn't, not yet, perhaps never.

"I had an accident. A car accident." He sat beside her on the bed now. She drew back her hair and showed him the scar. "They were taking me away from the house."

"Oh God." He touched her for the first time, a light touch on the temple.

"Why didn't you trust me—tell me where you were going? I could have kept it secret."

"I couldn't." Her face looked pinched in the lamplight. "I was told to avoid boyfriends because, if you were arrested, or captured, it might have been dangerous for you."

"What else happened?" He searched her face intently. "Something else did, I feel it."

"A lot . . . I'll tell you later . . . some good things, too. Cleeve told me tonight that Jenke's information had made a difference, but he wouldn't be more specific. Even telling me where you were broke all the rules."

"You'll probably end up with more medals than me."

"Probably."

He saw the flash of her white teeth, her dimples.

"Incredible," he murmured gathering her in his arms. "Unbelievable. Ridiculous. You on the train," he started to laugh, "and before that . . . I went to the concert . . . it was torture listening to you."

He wiped tears from her face with his handkerchief.

"What happened to you?" she asked at last. "You're not well."

"I had a prang," he said. "I'll tell you later. I don't want to talk about it now."

And because the peace was new and precarious, she let him get away with this.

"We thought you were dead," she said. "Barney gave me a letter from you; he found it in your locker. Didn't he tell you?"

"I haven't seen Barney—he's been away. I've hardly seen anyone since I was picked up, but what letter? Oh for heaven's sake, no." It had suddenly dawned on him. "That stupid letter. I was so angry . . . I didn't mean to send it."

"I got this, too." She held up her wrist and showed it to him.

"The bracelet. Do you wear it?"

"All the time."

He leaned down and kissed her then. He touched her face there, and there; he held her hair in his hands. He led her over to the wooden chair near the sink, and washed the dirt off her feet, grumbling at the state they were in.

"Thank you, Nursey," she said. He soaped them and dried them, kissed them gently toe by toe. When he was done, she stood up and he unhooked her dress and they got into the bed together, and she held him close and gave him the sweetest kiss of his life, and then they wept unashamedly. "I thought you were dead," she sobbed. "And I wanted to die with you." And he believed her because she was a truthful person; some part of him had known that from the beginning.

CHAPTER 50

Spring came in a rush of flowers—mallow and poppies, purple and white anemones, coltsfoot, marigolds and celandine. She picked handfuls of them from the back garden of the house Ozan had lent them at Muntazah Beach.

By Ozan's standards the house was no more than a hut, but they were delighted by its long verandas, its sunny whitewashed rooms, and the small garden at the back, where acacia and jasmine were blooming, and oranges, tangerines, and lemons burst from the trees. The house was private, and apart from a honking donkey tethered nearby and some morning birds, it was quiet—a rare luxury after living in camps and communal tents.

In the mornings, Yusuf, one of Ozan's servants, arrived on a bicycle with a basket full of wine and fresh bread, cheeses, and whatever fish had been netted that day. In a sunny kitchen with blue and white tiles, Saba tried, with mixed success, to learn how to cook.

But for the first two days, they lay in their whitewashed bedroom in each other's arms and slept like exhausted animals, laughing when they were awake at what a waste of time this was. Then came the long, lazy days of making love and swimming, of sunbathing and eating barefoot meals by candlelight on their veranda, which overlooked the sea.

"Look," she said one night, gazing up into the night sky. "That's Berenice's Hair." She pointed out a line of stars just above the dark. "No idea who Berenice was," she added. "My dad showed me them. In a book."

"Berenice was the Pharoah's wife," he told her. "When the king went to war, she made a pact with Aphrodite, the goddess of love, that if she cut off her hair he would be protected. She took her hair to the temple, but it disappeared. A court astronomer claimed he'd found it again, as a new constellation, which was tactful otherwise all hell would have broken loose."

"How do you know these things?"

"From flying and general brilliance." He was still peering at the stars, light-years away himself for that moment.

She liked him knowing things. It comforted her.

He'd been reading Cavafy's poems to her. He'd discovered the poet had once lived in the Rue Lepsius, four doors down from them.

There's no ship for you, there's no road.
Now that you've wasted your life here, in this small corner,
You've destroyed it everywhere in the world.

"That was how I felt," Dom told her. "When you left and I couldn't find you. It was the worst feeling in the world."

Sometimes you are happy without knowing it, and sometimes you are happy and completely aware of it—its preciousness, its fleetingness.

And there were times when the almost mystical perfection of these days frightened Saba—everything felt right, nothing was lacking. It was so unlike the rest of life, with its uncertainties, its suffering and boredom, and all the other tragedies, large and small, she had witnessed. She wanted to make it last forever, but was old enough now to know this was impossible. The world was changing and would change again. Dom was waiting to hear about his next posting—the Desert Air Force had mostly packed up its tents and gone home, its pilots flown to other squadrons in Sicily or Burma. Saba was rehearsing for Ozan's next extravaganza in Cairo, and singing for what troops remained in Suez or Cairo. Out in the desert all the bric-a-brac of war—the hangars, temporary runways, fuel depots—disappearing under heaps of sand.

Halfway through their time at Muntazah, Arleta came to stay. She arrived with Saba's mail, two packets of Turkish delight with pistachio nuts in it, a bottle of gin, and a toy camel, found in a souvenir shop, with bulging crimson eyes that glowed horrifyingly when you plugged it in.

She handed Saba a letter written in her mother's round schoolgirl hand.

Saba took it into the bedroom, locked the door behind her. Her hands were shaking as she opened it, thinking it brought news of her father's death—something she dreamed of regularly, always with a shocking feeling of loss.

But here was good news: little sister Lou was back from the valleys, cheeky as ever, doing well in her exams, a proper little grown-up girl. Tan, fit as a flea and with a new friend, another Turkish lady who lived in their street. And in the last paragraph, her mother sounded an unusual note of treason.

Don't you dare not come to Pomeroy Street when you get back to Blighty because this will always be your home, no matter what your father says. He has just signed on for another tour with Fyffes and is away even more than he used to be, so we'll have plenty of time, and to be honest with you, Saba love, I'm glad you've made your decision. You have your own life to lead and I have mine, and I should have left him years ago—he's always wanted things his way and I'm fed up to the back teeth with it.

This was a shock.

Up until now she'd seen her mother in a number of confusing, contradictory guises—good sport, loyal peacemaker, theatrical cheerleader, food maker—but that small snarl of underdog rage in the last sentence made her wonder if she'd ever truly known her at all, and the thought that the war might have changed Mum, too, was upsetting. She talked it over with Arleta during one of their long, lazy morning swims toward a raft, moored a hundred yards or so from the beach.

She told her how Mum, a woman who once wouldn't leave the house unless hair and makeup were band-box fresh, had happily gone off for her daily shifts at Curran's factory in her dreadful overalls and turban, and how she'd told Saba it was a lot more fun than being in the house all day, particularly if your husband was at sea.

"Fair comment." Arleta took this calmly. "It would drive me mad being home all day—and you. *Boring*."

Arleta, who was trying not to get her hair wet, had the look of a startled Afghan hound being forced to swim for the first time.

"I mean, look at all this," she panted. She waved her hand at the wide horizon. "We got it through work, and we'll miss it, won't we?"

Saba looked around her: at the dazzling blue sea, the cloudless sky, the shore with its fine white sand, the house on the cliff where she and Dom had been so happy.

"Do we have to leave?" A pointless question.

"Don't be a prat," said her friend. "England will be horrible, but it's our kind of horrible."

They'd reached the raft. Arleta, trimmer than ever after weeks of dancing, sprang from the water like a glamorous Aphrodite; she shook her hair out and flopped down beside Saba, then lifted each leg in the air, profoundly pleased by what she saw.

They lay for a while, side by side, arms touching, soaking up the sun, and then Arleta asked:

"Have you thought about the India tour yet?" She slid her eyes toward Saba.

Saba sighed—this was tricky. They'd both been offered a three-week ENSA tour in India, but she hadn't yet found the moment to mention it to Dom.

"I honestly can't decide at the moment; it depends on Dom's posting, too, and other things."

"Saba." Arleta sat up and looked at her very seriously. "Can I say something, and don't misunderstand me."

"If you like." Saba sensed a warning she didn't want.

"Well, it's just this . . . not saying that you and Dom don't seem blissfully happy together—you do—and not saying he doesn't adore you and that you're not mad about him, and that it's not all very romantic." Arleta clutched her bosom and swirled her eyes. "Just . . . don't give him everything; keep something for yourself."

"I know that, Arleta," she said, even though she was struggling with it. At this moment, all she wanted was to have his babies, to learn to cook, to carry on feeling this honeyed contentment day after day after day. "One of the best things about being in ENSA has been doing what I was trained to do, and it's been tremendous. I really do know that."

Arleta's eyebrow was still raised. "When you thought he was dead," she persisted, "you stopped singing, or at least you wanted to, and take it from Auntie Arl, no man is worth that."

There was a thread of unhappiness in Arleta's voice. It wasn't the first time Saba had noticed it since she'd arrived.

"Arl, don't say a word if you don't want to, but what happened to Barney? You've hardly mentioned him."

Arleta's voice sounded hazy. "Barney?" she said. "Oh, finished. Completely. I meant to tell you. It's fine, darling, honestly—you don't have to say anything. He's going back to England and I knew it would happen. I didn't want to tell you in front of Dom in case I said bitter and twisted things and Dom felt forced to defend him."

"So good, not upset then?" Saba trod cautiously; Arleta loathed people feeling sorry for her.

"Not at all," Arleta said firmly. "I knew it would happen. It did. End of story, and besides, I need to see my little boy again and to at least try and stop messing around for a few years, but oh God, I shall miss it here, too; it's been heavenly." She sang *heavenly* like an opera singer.

"What will you miss most, Arlie: the scorpions? The dead dog under the stage in Suez? Sand in your knickers? Sharing a canvas sink with Janine?"

"Ha, ha, ha—hard to tell, smarty-pants. Well, all that, too. Let's not get too sentimental."

They were quiet for a while. Arleta sighed deeply.

"I'll miss you," she said, the way she came out with things sometimes, simple and clean.

"You've been a good friend."

They were silent for a moment, and then Arleta stood up and muttered, "Last swim, to hell with it." She flung herself into the air and wildly bicycling her legs, broke the surface of the water with a splash.

With her wet hair plastered around her face, she looked ten years younger.

"Oh God, that's wonderful," she spluttered. "That's the way to have a proper swim," and they headed side by side toward the shore.

Arleta left the next day on the back of Dom's motorbike—he'd offered to drop her at the train station in Alexandria. They were standing on the doorstep when she appeared, a film star today in dark glasses, hair swathed in chiffon. She turned to Saba.

"Give me a hug, you mad little creature." She put her arms around her, and enveloped her in Shalimar. Tears poured down her face. She brushed them away and got on the bike with a chorus girl's high kick. Shortly before she disappeared in a cloud of dust, she kissed her fingers, flung them passionately toward Saba shouting, "*Crepi il lupo,*" a dramatic gesture that almost derailed the motorbike.

And Saba, standing in the dust listening to the fading roar of the motorbike, wondered if she would see her again. Arleta had said it might not be for ages, maybe for never—that was how it was in show business.

When Dom got back at lunchtime he was covered in dust. He was carrying a package in one hand and an envelope in the other.

Saba was in the kitchen inexpertly hacking up some bread, and trying to remember how long Mum had done her hard-boiled eggs for. One of the many pleasures of this time was feeding him—the laying out of cheese and ripe tomatoes, early melons and bread on a plate filled her with a tender protectiveness never felt before.

She stood at the window smiling. She heard the motorbike cut out. He came into the kitchen and kissed the back of her neck.

"My girl." He put his arms around her. "My beautiful girl. Are you sad?"

"A bit." But glad, too, that it was just them again.

He slid his hand around her waist and inhaled her hair.

"Come and have a drink with me. I've got a surprise."

He led her to the veranda. They sat down together on a wicker chair. He handed her the envelope, watching her closely while she opened it.

Two tickets.

She read them, put her hand over her mouth and gasped.

"A cruise up the Nile. Oh Dom! How fantastic!" She squealed and jumped into his lap.

"The timing," he said excitedly, "is perfect. The AOC has given us a fortnight's leave, and who knows when we'll have to leave Egypt now, and I thought, what the hell, I'll go ahead and book it. It's a beautiful old-fashioned boat, the *Philae*, and we can call in on all those old pharaohs in their pyramids, they're all opening again now the war's over. We can go to the Valley of the Kings." His eyes gleamed with excitement.

"Hang on, hang on, Dom." She examined the tickets more closely. She'd stopped listening.

"The first week, that should be fine shouldn't it?"

"No, Dom," she said with a sinking feeling. "No. I absolutely can't. No chance. It leaves on the twenty-third of March—the week of Ozan's Cairo concert."

"Oh *fuck*." He made no attempt to hide his disappointment.

"Didn't you remember that? And do you mind not swearing in front of me like that," even though she didn't mind all that much.

"No," he said flatly, although she had told him. "No, I didn't remember. So, is it always going to be like this?" he said. There was a steely note in his voice she hadn't heard before.

"Like what?"

"Like this."

"Probably," thinking *Blast it, you* should *have remembered—it's important to me.*

She slammed down her glass, stood up, and glared at him.

"Dammit, Saba, don't look at me like that."

"Look at you like what?" she bellowed. "I'm not looking like anything."

And so on until they were shouting so loudly that the donkey in the field next door started honking with alarm.

* * *

He flung open the veranda gate and went down to the beach, and sat down with his head in his hands, childishly crushed. He'd pictured the whole thing on the way home—the boat drifting up the Nile; waking up in her arms; seeing feluccas and little villages, and then the wonderful drama of the Valley of the Kings, with her by his side. He'd waited for so long.

After a few moments of intense self-pity, he stood up and, walking to the edge of the sea, chose a flat stone and hurled it, making it hop four times across the water before it sank.

So would it always be like this? He chucked another stone as hard as he could—the compromises, the confusions, the sense that her plans might be just as important as his. Because if it was, he couldn't stand it. Thank God there was still time to back out—no binding promises had been made.

She watched him from the veranda, skimming stone after stone into the sea, and then she went into the bedroom and lay down.

She wept, furious at first, and then in sorrowful confusion. *I love him, but do I really want this?* The tears, the resentments, the appeasing, the yelling. *I'd simply turn into another version of my mother.*

She was lying facedown on their bed when he walked in. She'd closed the shutters and soaked the pillow.

"I can't do it," she said in a muffled voice, "not like this."

He put his hand on her back.

"I know."

He got into bed, put his face against hers.

"Saba," he said. "It would kill me to lose you now."

"I went through this with my father," she said, "feeling wrong all the time, as if my work was a disgrace."

"I never want you to feel like that."

Oh, the sweetness of feeling his hand on her hair, the relief of knowing he loved her still and that they could talk like this without the world crashing in.

"I'm sorry I ruined your surprise." She kissed his chest. "It was such a lovely idea . . . and I do want to do it. But I can't let the company down."

He was gently unbuttoning her dress; she was smiling at him, but as she lay in his arms afterward, she felt for the first time the rub of trying to jigsaw two lives together. A premonition that it would not be easy, that it could take a lifetime.

That night they ate supper together on the veranda at a moment in the day when the sun was leaving and the moon rising and the two halves of the water in the bay were silver and gold. It was, they agreed politely, beautiful, but she saw it rather than felt it because the row had shaken them both, and Saba felt precariously close to tears as she passed him food and wine and there was a tiptoeing quality to their conversation that was new to them.

At the end of a long silence she said, "Dom, tell me what you're thinking. You look sad."

He took both of her hands in his.

"I was thinking about flying." He looked sheepish.

"Flying! Where to?" She wanted to laugh suddenly. "Away from me?"

"No! No—it's just that, well," he fiddled with his fork, and looked at her, "I was thinking that when you learn to fly, the taking-off part is the easy bit—it's the landing that's tricky." He raised the fork in the air. "It's not like a car, it's more like a one-wheel bicycle—you have to balance the thing longitudinally and latitudinally, and after it's gone up, you have to learn how to gently come down . . ." He looked at her thoughtfully. "I don't want to mess it up."

"I know." She swallowed hard.

In the silence that followed, she heard the rusty cry of the donkey again. He was fed with a bundle of grass every night around eight.

She took a deep breath and held Dom's hand. "Will you solemnly promise me two things?" she said.

"This sounds serious."

"It is." She said it quickly. "I want you to promise that you won't ask me to marry you . . . not yet."

She almost laughed—he looked so surprised, or was it relieved?

He looked at her for a long time. "How strange. I'd sort of worked my way round on the beach this afternoon to going down on one satined knee quite soon."

"I said not yet." She was grinning broadly at him. "I want to feel free for a little while longer—maybe for the first time in my life."

What she'd been thinking that afternoon came out in a rush.

"I want to work. I don't want to feel guilty about it. I've had years of that with my dad, and I've had enough. But I don't want to lose you either."

She could feel him thinking.

"Wedlock," he said at last. "It's such an attractive word, don't you think? It fills one with confidence. The lock bit particularly."

"I'm not joking, Dom." Or was she, now she'd said it out loud? Part of her longed to leap into his arms and forget entirely about being her.

But he was. The old bad habits resurfacing, because this was a new way of thinking for him. It would take some getting used to, and he wasn't sure yet whether he'd been turned down or not.

Around midnight the sea was pitch-black, apart from a strip of gauzy moonlight that ran from the shoreline to the horizon lighting up the raft.

"I think we should stop talking now and go for a swim," he said.

"Are you mad?" She was relieved to see him smile again. "It's probably freezing."

"We're British," he told her, striding toward the waves. "We're bred for it. Take your clothes off, woman, and jump in."

When they'd stripped, he flung her over his shoulder and ran toward the sea, and when he dropped her in, she squealed in fright, both pretended and real, because it wasn't as cold as she thought it would be, and because she liked feeling his arms around her. The comforting maleness of him.

Side by side they swam up the hazy corridor of light, the sea inky black around them, and when they got closer to the raft, they could see in the distance the smudge of the horizon and a boat with one dark sail.

Dom was a strong swimmer and had to slow himself down to stay with her.

She was thinking about the North Sea, and how cold it would feel at night; about her father, who might or might not be sailing there.

Nothing will be the same, she thought; going back to England will be like stepping through a door into the complete unknown.

"I would like to take another run at my proposal," he said. "I stuffed it up last time." They were sitting on the raft together, their feet dangling in the sea. "If I don't, I'll kick myself for the rest of my life. So here goes."

His face looked pearly in the moonlight, and she could see the sharp planes of his cheekbones. You hardly saw his scars at all now except in bright light.

"I had a moment of truth in the desert; I saw it so clearly—my dream version of you and your reality—and I saw that I needed you both. And if having you means the odd bloody great row, or a bit of saucepan-throwing, who cares? At least I'll be with someone I adore and admire, and who can sing in the bath."

"Oh God." She put her hand over his mouth. "Stop it. I shouted so much earlier . . . aren't you terrified?"

"Terrified." He put his hand around her shoulder and pulled her toward him. "You're a brute. And I am going to be a very unhappy, henpecked husband."

"Let's swim," she said. It was too much, too confusing, too wonderful.

"Wait, wait, wait, impatient woman. I haven't finished yet. What I mean is some arrangement that won't involve . . . I don't know, confetti and matching cutlery, but will take in babies, and perhaps an aircraft for me, and you singing. Is that completely impossible?"

"Probably." She kissed him full on the mouth. "It sounds awfully good to me."

The sea was a fraction colder as they dived in—it took their breath away. When they had caught their breath and were swimming side by side, they sang loudly and childishly, "*A Life on the Ocean Wave . . .*" By the time they got to the sandbank, they were planning a new trip up the Nile together, and Dom told her something interesting, something she didn't know before. He told her how Howard Carter, after years of frustration and false hope, had shone his torch inside Tutankhamen's burial chamber and seen the wall of solid gold, the strange animal statues.

Wonderful things. She tasted the words as they swam side by side toward the indistinct shore. To be young, to be alive, to have a future together; the promise of her own life, still hidden. From here she could see a faint straggling light coming from their bedroom window, could feel the water growing warm, then cold, shadowy and clear again, the tug of invisible currents against her skin.

ACKNOWLEDGMENTS

My thanks to all at Simon & Schuster, and especially my editor Heather Lazare; to Clare Alexander my gold standard agent.

I needed lots of expert advice while writing this book and many people gave generously of their time and knowledge. Any mistakes are entirely mine.

I am hugely indebted to John Rodenbeck for his editing skills and fascinating e-mails on Egypt and the Middle East. To Tom Brosnahan and John Dyson for showing me around Turkey and sharing their knowledge of the country.

Sema Moritz and Vanessa Dodd, Leda Glyptis and Virginia Danielson helped me greatly with information about singing. Özgü Ötünç was my guide in Istanbul.

Anthony Rowell for his amusing and invaluable help. Historian Dillip Sarkar, for his vast knowledge of aircraft, squadrons, and Battle of Britain pilots.

For lending a precious family diary my thanks to Sheila Must.

Grateful thanks to: Cordelia Slater, Brian Shakespeare, Jerome Kass, Pam Enderby, Owen Sheers, Michael Haag, Peter Sommer, Ibrahim Abd Elmedguid, Phyllis Chappell for her knowledge of the bay area in Cardiff during the war and her book *A Tiger Bay Childhood*; Tara Maginnis for makeup in the forties.

For reading early drafts and general hand-holding, thanks to my sister Caroline, Delia, Sadie, Annie Powell, and all the shedettes, the entire Gregson clan.

If I've forgotten to thank anyone who helped in the early days, my apologies.

Finally, there aren't words enough to thank Richard, who has been my champion through thick and thin and my dearest traveling companion.